SERIOUS
POTENTIAL

By the Author

Totally Worth It

Serious Potential

Visit us at www.boldstrokesbooks.com

SERIOUS POTENTIAL

by

Maggie Cummings

2016

SERIOUS POTENTIAL

© 2016 By Maggie Cummings. All Rights Reserved.

ISBN 13: 978-1-62639-633-3

This Trade Paperback Original Is Published By
Bold Strokes Books, Inc.
P.O. Box 249
Valley Falls, NY 12185

First Edition: October 2016

CREDITS
EDITOR: RUTH STERNGLANTZ
PRODUCTION DESIGN: STACIA SEAMAN
COVER DESIGN BY JEANING HENNING

Acknowledgments

Sincerest thanks to Rad and Sandy for affording me this incredible opportunity. Thank you also to Ruth for guiding me steadily along the way, and to the entire team at Bold Strokes Books for making this book possible.

I want to thank my parents and my sister for their endless love and support. I'd also like to acknowledge my friends, for their encouragement, enthusiasm, and boundless energy in trying to figure out who's who in my fake universe. There are no direct matches, but all are present in the spirit and energy of these women, in their triumphs, their camaraderie, and their love. Without our history of shared memories to reflect on, I would have an empty fantasy world. Finally, the biggest thank you goes to Kat, who keeps me grounded in this life, makes me smile, laughs at my jokes, and inspires me every single day.

For CPC

CHAPTER ONE

Meg McTiernan tucked her feet underneath the wooden bench, allowing two girls in summer skirts to pass with ease on the outdoor deck of the Staten Island Ferry. Rubbing her short, thick brown hair she laced her fingers behind her head, stretching out again and smiling to herself as she watched them walk the length of the boat. It was crowded today even at three o'clock in the afternoon. It was Friday and the beginning of a holiday weekend, and she obviously wasn't the only one who cut out of work early. Her phone buzzed with a text, stealing her attention from the Statue of Liberty in the distance.

Three weeks from today, bro. Can't wait.

Tracy. Meg smiled at the text from her West Coast bestie and typed back quickly. She was looking forward to her oldest buddy's visit to New York in a few weeks and she breathed out a wistful sigh that Tracy wasn't in town this weekend. It was wishful thinking, but Meg was in need of a wingman for tomorrow night's Fourth of July bash at the Commons in her condo development, and Tracy would fit that role perfectly.

She was totally bummed that her closest friends at the development, Lexi and Jesse, wouldn't be around for tomorrow's open house. They had a command appearance at Jesse's dad's birthday party on the Cape. Meg knew Lexi was sad about it too. As much as her best friend loved going to the Cape with her girlfriend, over the last twelve months Lexi had confided to Meg that she never felt entirely comfortable around Jesse's family and this past week she had vented about it nonstop. Meg knew it was all stress, so she'd listened dutifully and even tried to put a positive spin on the weekend, play-telling Lexi to relax and enjoy the perks that came with having a rich girlfriend. But even as she'd smiled at her own joke, Meg could read the angst on Lexi's face. Come to think of it, Jesse had looked uncharacteristically tense over the last week or so too.

Selfishly, Meg wanted them with her this weekend so they could all go to the party together. Sure, Meg would know people at the open house—other neighbors and acquaintances—but even after two years living in the all-lesbian community of Bay West, she was still shy about walking into the condo-sponsored events alone. Betsy was a possibility, and Meg planned on coercing her friend tonight at dinner, but so far she had been noncommittal, citing her duties as the on-call obstetrician for the holiday weekend as the priority.

Meg continued to scroll through her mental index of friends and breathed a sigh of relief that at least her two exes, Becca and Mia, who'd coupled up sometime back, wouldn't be around. Since they didn't live at Bay West, they needed an invite to an open house, and with the absence of Jesse and Lexi, Meg figured they didn't have one. Of course *she* could put them on the guest list herself; it would be a nice gesture since they were all friendly enough to each other. Then she would at least have some company at the party. But truthfully, even though Meg knew it was a little shallow, she would rather not orchestrate a scenario where it was just the three of them without any of the rest of her crew around to buffer.

She glanced back down at her text from Tracy. Damn if their timing wasn't just a little off. She could sit here for the rest of the ride and sulk about it, or she could move on. Pursing her lips at her thinning options, she thumbed through her phone and texted Taylor Higgins.

They had an unusual track record, she and Taylor. Friends at first, their relationship blossomed on a hot summer night a year ago when Meg had been strong-armed into a setup with a neighbor's cousin, which of course didn't pan out. But the night hadn't been a total loss. When there was no click during the pre-arranged meeting, Meg turned her attention to Taylor, at the time a new resident of Bay West living in the rental section. They were inseparable for a few weeks, but their spark burned hot and fast, fizzling completely by Labor Day.

It was no big deal, really. Despite their physical attraction, they just didn't have that much in common and regardless of their conscious uncoupling months ago, they still went home together fairly often, most recently after a late night at the Kitchen a few weeks back. These episodes only occurred when the circumstances lined up—nights they were both on the prowl where no other prospects had emerged. Meg wasn't proud of it, but these little one-nighters had kept her going all year. She credited them with keeping her from making other, more questionable choices motivated by her libido—take, for example, last Thursday's escapade in the freight elevator when she'd ended up going to third base with Lisette, the building's sole female maintenance worker. Meg was still in shock over that one.

With Taylor, she knew what she was getting. A basic hookup with a nice girl, uncomplicated by day-after drama. Looking ahead to the open house, Meg couldn't help but wonder if tomorrow night would fall into that category as well.

She smiled to herself as she walked to the front of the boat while the ferry docked, not entirely disappointed at the prospect.

"Sorry to be a pain, but I could get called back any minute. We should really get our order in." Betsy scanned the restaurant floor, unsuccessfully searching for their waiter. She tossed her long blond hair lightly behind each shoulder to smooth it down, even though there wasn't a single strand out of place. Perfectly orderly, just like the rest of her, Meg thought as she casually assessed her friend. Betsy had a classic, timeless look—tall and fair, naturally blond with delicate highlights, and eyes that were blue some days, green others—and she always looked just so. Even now, on her meal break from the hospital, her subtle makeup and cap-sleeved chiffon shirt with skinny jeans completely contrasted with Meg's tomboy style anchored tonight by an aged tee and worn-out sneaks.

"First off, is there any chance I'm convincing you to come to the open house with me tomorrow?" Meg started.

"No."

Betsy's sweet but firm tone told Meg there was no wiggle room in the response, so Meg moved on. "So catch me up. What's going on with the nurse and the anesthesiologist?"

Meg loved getting a running commentary of the inner workings at the hospital. She could not care less about the surgeries and scientific breakthroughs, though. She wanted to know who was sleeping with whom, how often, and what the fallout was. It was a universe so completely foreign to her own unbelievably PC workplace that she absorbed all of the details like they were storylines in a soap opera of which she was the sole viewer.

Over the top of her glass, Betsy gave Meg a knowing look. "The anesthesiologist went back to her wife. Like we knew she would," she added, taking another sip of her Diet Coke.

"And what about the nurse?"

Betsy covered her heart with her hand in mock despair and dropped her voice dramatically. "Left with a broken heart, I suppose." She giggled a little at her silly joke. "I'm just kidding. She'll move on. She's kind of known for that actually," she said with a shift of her eyebrows.

"Perfect. Does that mean you're next?"

Betsy opened her eyes widely, not even attempting to hide her disbelief at Meg's suggestion.

"I'm just saying…you should get back out there."

Betsy was a private person who didn't talk much about her past relationship or its demise, even with her closest friends. What Meg knew she'd gleaned in tidbits Betsy had dropped here and there and from Jesse, Betsy's closest confidante, and even when that info was put together the details were sparse. But Meg knew there had been a girlfriend, a guitar player named CJ, whom Betsy had been on and off with for the last decade before things ended for good months ago. Meg thought their breakup inevitable—and long overdue. Honestly, in two years of friendship, Meg had never even laid eyes on the woman.

For years Jesse had been urging Betsy to move on, always suggesting someone new. Meg had even fallen into that category once upon a time. Looking back, Meg was glad she didn't go for it—Betsy either, for that matter—because they fit perfectly as friends. It was simply gravy that their respective besties—Lexi and Jesse—were a couple, making it easy for all of them to hang out.

"So *no* to Nurse whatshername?" Meg asked.

"Alecia. Correct. That is a no to Nurse Alecia."

"Poor Alecia. Can't get no love at this hospital," Meg joked, shaking her head.

"Oh, she gets plenty of love. Trust me," Betsy countered with a smile.

"Okay, see, that's kind of my point." Meg put her hand up to stop Betsy from speaking. "Just hear me out on this." Since Betsy's breakup a few months back, Meg had spent a lot of time listening to her friend and she couldn't help but notice Betsy didn't really seem heartbroken or devastated or scrambling to pick up the pieces of her shattered life. She seemed one hundred percent fine, except she hadn't expressed any interest in revitalizing her love life. After coming out of a long-term relationship that, by all accounts, had been over way before it officially ended, Meg was pretty sure Betsy was a nervous wreck at the prospect of dating again.

Not wanting to overstep, Meg chose her words carefully. "You just came out of a really long relationship. I just wonder if, I don't know, something fun and carefree might not be the worst thing in the world." Meg pulled her paper napkin from underneath the silverware and wiped her hands with it. "You've been out of the dating pool for like, ten years. It's okay to ease back in."

"I understand what you're saying, Meg." Betsy hesitated. "But I don't know." She looked down at her sheer nail polish. "Everyone is like, oh, you should go out, have fun"—she pushed around a crumb on the tabletop with her index finger—"and I know they have my best interests in mind." She reached for her soda and ran her hand along the side of the glass. "I know this may sound ridiculous to you, but I'm thirty-two. I want to get married. Have kids." She made eye contact across the table. "I'm not going to waste my time on something that isn't serious." She raised her shoulders as though she were giving in to something. "Maybe it's just because I'm too square, but the idea of going out and hooking up randomly, it doesn't sound like fun to me." She fidgeted in her chair. "It never did."

Meg let out a deep breath. "For starters, I don't think you sound ridiculous." She reached for a tortilla chip from the plastic bowl in the center of the table. "Secondly, it doesn't have to be a random hookup. That's why I suggested the nurse. You know her. You know she's not crazy. I'm basically suggesting a fling. With someone known and trusted. Just to get back on track."

Betsy gave a halfhearted smile. "Honestly, Meg, I'm not cut out for it." Her elbow rested on the table and she leaned into it, tilting her cheek against her open palm. "I think that's why I stayed with CJ for so long, even with her crazy road schedule. I knew what I had. Despite our differences and the time apart, she's a good person. If we could have made it work, it might have been okay."

Betsy was clearly opening up, something she rarely did, and Meg felt terrible that her cell phone had suddenly lit up with a barrage of texts. She thumbed through them quickly, trying not to be rude.

"Is that Lexi?" Betsy asked, nodding her chin at the phone.

"Sorry," Meg apologized, taking the phone in her hand and studying it as she spoke. "It's actually my friend Tracy in California. She's freaking out because she's going to some charity thing and she's conflicted about what to wear. She sent me a bunch of pictures in different outfits," Meg said as she nodded offhandedly at the latest message.

"Let me see." Betsy motioned for the phone.

Meg scrolled up. "I think this is the winner." She handed the phone to Betsy.

Betsy took a minute to assess the photo of the tanned dark-haired woman decked in all black.

"She looks good, right?"

"I'll say." Betsy looked at the image closely. She nodded, biting her lower lip subconsciously. "She is…very attractive, Meg," she said, handing the phone back.

Meg jumped all over it. "Yeah? She's coming to visit next month. Just saying."

"Let me see your phone again."

"Atta girl."

Betsy ignored Meg's taunt and enlarged the pic with two fingers. "She looks familiar to me."

"You watch golf?"

Betsy furrowed her eyebrows in response to the strange question.

Meg explained. "She's a golfer. Like, professionally. I thought maybe you had seen her on TV or something."

"I've never watched golf, that's for sure," Betsy said, returning the phone for the second time. "She probably looks like one of my patients. That happens to me sometimes."

"Well, she'll be here in a few weeks. Maybe you can see if she needs an exam, if you know what I mean." Meg winked salaciously.

"Gross," Betsy said, but she was unable to conceal her smile at Meg's quick wit.

"I'm going to tell her you think she's hot."

"You are not."

"I don't know," Meg teased. "I think I probably am."

"You're an idiot."

Meg slapped the table with her palm. "Oh my God. This is it." She pointed to her phone. "Tracy should be your carefree hookup." Meg was on a roll and wasn't stopping. "It's so perfect. She comes to visit. You guys hang out. You're awesome. She's awesome. You get it out of your system. She goes back home. You are refreshed, rejuvenated, and ready to meet Miss Right."

"Is she even single?" Betsy asked through light laughter.

She sounded marginally intrigued even though she was pretending to play it off and Meg was so caught off guard at the possibility of Betsy's interest that she couldn't hide the fact she wasn't sure of the answer to her question. She looked off to the right and contemplated Tracy's romantic status.

"See, you don't even know if she's single."

"She's single," Meg answered in spite of her uncertainty. "I'm pretty sure she's single," she repeated more emphatically, remembering as she said it that Tracy had made a vague reference to someone a while back, but nothing at all lately. Meg nodded at Betsy with conviction and was ready to bring the conversation to the next level. But Betsy cut her off.

"Anyway, what's new with you? How's Sullivan?" Betsy asked, referring to Meg's company by its abbreviated name.

"Fine. Things are good." She nodded. "Actually I just remembered this girl is starting next week. I can't believe I almost forgot," she muttered into her soda.

Betsy leaned in and narrowed her eyes waiting for more of an explanation.

Meg brushed her off. "Sorry, it's nothing. Just this chick, *Sasha*." Meg stretched her name out dramatically emphasizing both syllables. "She was supposed to transfer to New York from London last January and it's just happening now."

"Is that a big deal?"

"I guess not really," Meg responded, undercutting her own

statement. "I just don't get the greatest vibe from her." She shrugged. "I mean I've never met her, but I had to cover all her projects like a year ago," she added with a shake of her head. "And now it even takes her six months to get her act in gear, so she conveniently shows up right in the middle of the slow season. I mean, give me a break."

"Hold on, I'm listening," Betsy said while she read a message coming through on her phone. "Damn, Meg." She started typing as she spoke. "I'm so sorry." She pursed her lips tightly, still thumbing her keypad. "I have to go back to the hospital." She met Meg's eyes before quickly scanning the floor again for the waiter.

"Go ahead, Bets." Meg waved her hand back and forth between their drinks. "I got this."

Betsy grabbed her big leather bag and thin cardigan draped over the spare chair. "I hope you're not mad."

Meg shook her head. "Of course I'm not mad." She sipped her soda. "Go bring a life into the world. Show-off," she finished with a friendly laugh.

Meg paid their small tab and headed in the direction of her sister's house across the island in search of free food and good company. On the way she called Lexi, prepared to spend the fifteen-minute drive continuing the pep talk she'd been giving on loop over the last few days. She hung up smiling when she got voice mail, confident Lexi's choice not to talk could only be a good sign.

Chapter Two

Things were definitely looking up, Lexi thought, as she reached for two cold bottles of water from the top shelf of the fridge.

Coming up to the Cape a day early had been a fantastic idea. She made a mental note to thank her amazing girlfriend for suggesting it. Even though Lexi didn't have too many vacation days accumulated at her law gig at the Department of Education, alone time with Jesse was well worth burning a day. With the rest of the Ducane clan arriving on Saturday for the party, they had the whole place to themselves for a full twenty-four hours.

Lexi knew her anxiety over this particular weekend didn't have to do with the party or even the extended group of relatives and friends that would be there. She'd met a lot of them before, anyway. She wasn't even overly bothered that Jesse's former girlfriend Lauren Carlisle, a lifelong friend of the Ducanes, would be on hand. Lexi could get past that particular annoyance. Nope. Her angst over the weekend could be solely attributed to one person—Jesse's mother. Liddy Ducane was classist and mean and completely clichéd in her efforts to make Lexi feel inferior. Every time their paths had crossed in the past year, she had spoken to Lexi with a predictable air of arrogance. And just in case her attitude wasn't enough to show where her favor lay, Jesse's mother made sure to repeatedly ask her daughter how Lauren was doing—in front of Lexi—making it no secret she still held out hope Jesse might rekindle with her ex.

Lexi had braced herself, knowing this weekend would be more of the same. She knew it shouldn't matter. Jesse never acted any differently toward her. But actually, now that she stopped to think about it, that was what had been needling at her. All week Lexi had sensed something different in Jesse. Even through her girlfriend's stoic veneer, Lexi had felt an uncharacteristic edginess looming beneath the surface and she was sure it was because of goddamn Liddy Ducane.

All the more reason Jesse had been a genius to get them up here a day early. When it was just the two of them here together, all stress seemed to dissipate. They focused on each other, relaxed, and connected. The result was evident in the last sixteen hours. Starting right from sleeping soundly in each other's arms the previous evening and carrying over into today when they hit the beach before noon, their moods were light and easy. Even now, hours later, they were calm and comfortable as they lounged in the late-day sun, enjoying a pre-dinner dip in the pool.

From the kitchen Lexi caught a glimpse of Jesse out the back window as she adjusted her black two-piece bathing suit. She watched gratuitously as Jesse reached her long, toned arms over her head, stretching out her entire body before diving into the water. Lexi eyed the plastic bottles of water on the counter and quickly turned back to the fridge to trade them for two beers, grinning to herself over what she was about to do.

Lexi sauntered into the backyard making her way alongside the pool up to the four-foot marker where Jesse was settled with her elbows resting on the pool's tiled edge, her head tilted back in the sun. Lexi crouched down and handed her a beer.

"Cheers, babe." Lexi clinked their bottles together and took a long drink.

Jesse smiled and took a sip. "What are we toasting?" she asked.

Lexi wet her lips. "How about us." She leaned down and kissed Jesse, surprising her with more tongue than Jesse was expecting. Lexi knew she'd caught Jesse off guard, but she could tell her girlfriend was into it. After a year together Lexi knew what made Jesse tick. She placed her beer on the concrete and walked to the front of the pool. Making an overly grand gesture she pulled her tank top over her head and released her hair from its rubber band, shaking her head as the dark curls fell past her shoulders. She stepped out of her wraparound beach skirt and descended the steps into the water slowly, untying the top of her bikini and tossing it aside as she walked. She dipped under the water up to her shoulders and glided over to Jesse.

Jesse straightened up and the corner of her mouth turned up in a devilish smile. "Alexis Russo, what are you doing?" she asked, unable to keep her eyes or her hands off Lexi's body.

Lexi put her arms around Jesse, kissing the top of her shoulder and biting it gently before moving up to her neck. "Saying thank you," she said, drawing in her lower lip as Jesse smoothed her hands along her body up to her breasts, "for the brilliant idea that we come up early, before everyone else gets here."

"You are very, very welcome."

Lexi brushed her mouth along Jesse's collarbone, losing her breath a little as her nipples hardened against Jesse's wet palms. "I know you've been stressed, but I think I may be able to help you release some of that tension."

"Is that so?" Jesse responded playfully, but it was clear from the huskiness in her voice she was game. She turned them around and pressed Lexi up against the wall of the pool, taking Lexi's legs and wrapping them around her. She lowered her face and kissed Lexi's bare chest.

Lexi moved her hands through Jesse's short, unruly hair. She ran her lips along the side of Jesse's face. "Forget dinner," she breathed in Jesse's ear. "Take me upstairs. I want you inside me."

It was more than she ever said and it got a reaction. Jesse responded with a guttural moan finding Lexi's mouth and kissing her possessively. She felt Jesse's hand moving down her torso and was pretty sure they weren't going to make it to the house. Lexi didn't care. She shut out the world, blocking out the distant hum of the boats in the bay and the planes passing overhead. It was just the two of them.

The sudden piercing shriek got their attention. It was followed closely—simultaneously, almost—by a profane plea for divine intervention. At the exact same time, Lexi and Jesse turned their attention to the end of the swimming pool where Jesse's mother, father, and brother were standing. Jesse nobly tried to shield a half-naked Lexi behind her, but it was too late. Jesse's mother stormed away toward the house, her father a half step behind. Justin stayed right where he was, turning his body as he covered his mouth, his laughter coming through anyway.

❖

The Friday night dinner she was forced to endure with Jesse's mother, father, and brother was beyond awkward and Lexi didn't relax at all until she was finally back at the house having a glass of wine with Jesse and Justin in the downstairs rec room. Right from the very beginning, Lexi had felt completely herself with Justin, and she'd seen right away why he was Jesse's favorite of her three brothers. Just a few years older than she, Justin was down to earth, funny, and kind. True, he teased Lexi relentlessly throughout the night, but he also genuinely tried his best to make her feel better. He told her their mother was uptight, privileged, and narrow-minded, and thought no one worthy of her children. He cited his brothers' wives as examples. Not even attempting to hide his smile, he also pointed out that Lexi had surely made an impression on their father. In fact, he told her she had probably already given him the best birthday gift he was going to get this year. Jesse glared at him, but he laughed it off, saying she knew it was true and he was positive the three of them would be joking about it for years to come. Lexi wasn't ready to laugh about it just yet, but something in the way he said it made her feel like part of their family.

When Jesse excused herself to use the bathroom, Justin lowered his voice and got serious. "Honestly, Lex, who cares about my mother." He checked a look back to the bathroom door. "My sister is crazy about you. You realize she's only ever brought one other girl out here to meet the whole family?"

Lexi sighed. "Believe me, I know all about Lauren. Your mother never stops talking about her."

Justin laughed. "Not Lauren. Lauren's a sycophant who is only around because her mother is an integral part of Mom's high society coffee klatch." He rubbed his thick hipster beard. "And because of her relentless efforts to win my sister back." He widened his eyes, making it no secret what he thought of those odds. He scratched his dark curly hair. "No, the woman's name was Mary, I think. And it was like forever ago." He'd meant to be reassuring, Lexi was sure of it. There was no way he could know that in naming Jesse's former girlfriend, he was also referencing Lexi's godmother, her mothers' best friend and the co-owner of Bay West. No doubt about it, Mary Brown was the biggest sore spot in their relationship.

❖

"Jess?" Lexi could hear the heightened pitch in her own voice and was immediately annoyed at herself for pursuing this topic. "When did you bring Mary Brown here?" She rubbed one finger repeatedly over the textured fabric of her seersucker shorts lying on top of the dresser, unsure if she even wanted to know the answer. Glancing at the mirror in front of her, she made eye contact as Jesse poked her head around the bathroom door frame, her brow crinkling at the question.

Jesse grabbed a hand towel and patted her face dry. "A long, long time ago," she answered, killing the lights in the bathroom. "Where is this coming from?"

"Nothing," Lexi said quietly. "It's just your brother mentioned you introduced her to your family, and, honestly, it caught me off guard."

Jesse took a few steps until she was behind Lexi. She dropped a sweet kiss on Lexi's shoulder next to the thin strap of her cami. "I know that face." Their eyes met in the mirror once more and Lexi felt Jesse's arms loop around her midsection, bringing her in close. "Don't, Lex." Jesse shook her head slowly, brushing her lips gently along Lexi's neck. "Mary was a million years ago. You're who I want to be with. Not Mary or Lauren, or anybody. You. I'm in love with you."

Lexi turned around and smiled, the faith in her relationship easily restored. "You better be," she said playfully. "Cause I'm not going down without a major catfight." She touched her finger to Jesse's lips, grazing over them slowly as she spoke. "And I'm not sure your mother would ever recover from that particular social faux pas."

Jesse kissed the tip of Lexi's finger. "Mmm, enough about my mother. She's already sabotaged me once tonight, if I'm not mistaken." She kissed Lexi's palm, then her wrist, working all the way up her arm until their lips met. She reached down and hooked Lexi's legs, lifting her onto the dresser. "Where were we before?" Jesse's smile was impish and sexy and so full of desire that Lexi felt herself blush.

The connection they had was nothing new, certainly not after a year together, but it was that single exchange that gave Lexi the confidence to hold her head high at the party. As promised, Lauren was there, and as expected, Jesse's mother fawned over her. Lexi had seen Lauren in pictures but of course she was prettier in person. Tall, tan, and blond, she was everything you didn't want your girlfriend's ex to be. And she was obviously still into Jesse even if Jesse politely pretended not to notice. Instead Jesse spent the entire day doting on Lexi, introducing her around and making sure she was never alone.

Sometime after the catered barbecue had been served and cleared, Lexi managed to slip away by herself, escaping through a line of trees along the perimeter down to the boat slip at the edge of the property. She could hear the steel drum band quieting as she made her way down to the dock. Leaning against the wooden post she allowed herself a minute to decompress as she took in the absolute beauty before her. Somewhere the sun was setting, turning the sky a deep orangey pink, the dark water below her barely rippling in the still night.

Her heart sank a little when she heard footsteps behind her but then lifted again when she saw it was Jesse.

"Planning a water escape?" Jesse asked playfully. She slipped her arms around Lexi's waist and stood behind her enjoying the view. "Oddly enough, I suppose, we're not boat people." She dropped a kiss on Lexi's neck, pulling her in close. "But I'm pretty sure there's a blow-up raft in the garage. I can go get it," she whispered, "but you have to promise to take me with you."

Lexi smiled and leaned back into Jesse. She slid her hands over Jesse's and caressed the tops of her toned forearms.

"Is the bourgeois madness getting to you?" she asked, kissing Lexi again.

"It's fine. I just needed a little break." She squeezed Jesse's arms around her belly. "This is perfect."

"I love you."

"I love you too." Lexi only had to tilt her head back a little and Jesse's lips were there. "Jess?"

"Yeah, babe?"

"I am so, so sorry about yesterday."

Jesse laughed her deep sexy laugh. "It's okay. If you take a step back it is actually hilarious."

"No, it's not." Lexi's voice was serious. "It's not okay either." She turned around to face Jesse. "I know you're stressed about me and your mom. I just…" She looked down shaking her head at the ground. "I still can't believe that happened."

Jesse held Lexi's waist and bent down a little so they were eye to eye. "I'm not stressed about my mother."

"I know you are. I know that's why you've been acting so weird lately. And I just thought…" She trailed off. "God, I don't know what I was thinking."

Jesse found Lexi's hands with her own and laced their fingers together. "Babe, it's not my mother. Yes, I hate the way she treats you because it's ridiculous and pretentious. I have told her to back off. Numerous times." She shook her head, indicating it was a lost cause. "But I don't care what *she* thinks. Truthfully, I don't."

"But—" Lexi stopped herself, her face twisted with confusion.

Jesse shoved her hands in the pockets of her linen shorts. "I know I've been a little off the last week or so." She dropped her chin, averting her eyes and chewing on a smile. "There is something I'm a little nervous about." She looked back toward the house and then out along the open water. "I wanted everything to be perfect. I thought if we came out here Thursday night, well, you know this is our place." She rolled her neck back and looked up at the pink, fiery sky. "I had it all planned. Relax together Thursday night. Hang out at the beach Friday. Follow that with a romantic dinner." She bit her bottom lip hiding her smile. "It was all lining up too. But then my parents had to show up and put a damper on everything." She shook her head and swallowed a chuckle at the recent memory. "Suffice it to say, last night—not perfect." She laughed, looking around them again before she spoke.

"The thing is, Lex, I think right now may be as perfect as it's going to get this weekend." She shuffled a little, looking around again as she fidgeted in her pocket. "And honestly, with this sky, plus the water, and music in the background…" Her sexy grin was virtually irresistible. "It's almost like this was the plan."

By now, Lexi knew it was coming, but she was still shocked to her very core. Her mouth hung open a little and she covered it with both of her hands blinking slowly as she savored the moment. She opened her eyes again and Jesse was on one knee holding the diamond ring. She didn't even attempt to hide her enormous smile as she listened to Jesse ask the question.

CHAPTER THREE

*C*oming over right now.

Meg barely had a chance to read the text, much less answer it, before she heard a succession of repeated taps on her screen door. She opened the latch and ushered Lexi and Jesse in, quickly closing the door behind them to keep the air conditioning from escaping.

"What's up, gaylords?" Meg greeted them jovially. "How was the weekend?" she asked as she trailed them into the kitchen. "Anyone want a drink?"

"No thanks, Meg," Jesse said, clapping Meg on the shoulders and squeezing them a little as she breezed by Meg and took a seat at the kitchen table. It was an unusual gesture and Meg turned around to see Jesse had a bizarre smirk on her face as well.

"What's going on? Everything okay?"

Lexi danced over to Meg, her left arm bent at the elbow, fingers spread wide, as she showcased the diamond solitaire on her ring finger. "We're getting married!" she exclaimed, beaming ear to ear, practically hopping up and down as she spoke.

Meg was momentarily stunned and looked back and forth between her two closest friends. Lexi's smile was wide, her dimples taking turns popping out in each cheek. Jesse smiled too, slyly, a little shy even, but also brimming with happiness.

"Oh my God, you guys." Meg gave Lexi a long hug, holding out one arm so Jesse could join them. "I can't believe it," she said, as the three of them broke apart. "Actually, I can. But still, I'm surprised." She threw a mock punch at Jesse, adding, "You jerk, I can't believe you didn't say anything."

"Sorry, kid." But Jesse's smile showed she wasn't sorry at all, and Meg didn't expect her to be. As close as they were, Meg knew in some ways Jesse would always be a lone wolf.

Meg turned her attention to Lexi. "Did you tell your parents yet?"

"Yep," Lexi answered.

"How'd it go?"

Lexi blew out a deep breath. "It was okay." She sounded more than uncertain and she flashed her eyes up at Jesse. "Right, babe? You think it went okay?"

"It was fine." Jesse rubbed Lexi's back reassuringly. "It's going to be good," she added, but Meg couldn't help but notice she didn't sound convinced either.

As good as Chris and Marnie had been to Meg since she'd moved to Bay West—welcoming her into their home, feeding her constantly— Lexi's mothers had been equally lukewarm regarding their daughter's relationship with Jesse. When it came to Lexi and Jesse, Meg knew they got it wrong. Sure there was an age gap, and yes, Jesse had a colorful past, but Meg honestly believed if Chris and Marnie could let all of that go for just a second and see Lexi without all of their preconceived disapproval, they would recognize how happy their daughter was, and Jesse too, for that matter. But it seemed Marnie barely tried. And while Chris had accepted them together at first, her support had waned as the relationship intensified.

"Let me guess, Chris was okay, Marnie didn't do any cartwheels?" Meg tried for light, but the irritation in her tone came through.

Lexi looked down. "Actually even Chris looked kind of shocked. She didn't say anything. At all."

"Lex, give them some time to digest it. They'll come around. You know they will." Meg rubbed Lexi's forearm as Jesse leaned over and kissed her temple.

"I told you Meg was the voice of reason." Jesse looked over at Meg and gave her a small smile of thanks.

"Anyway, I'm psyched for you guys. I think it's awesome." Meg nodded affirmatively. "I want to know everything. When? Where? How big is the wedding going to be?" She grabbed Lexi's hand and brought it closer to her. "Let me see this rock."

"How was the open house?" Lexi asked over Meg's obligatory ring inspection.

Meg looked down giving a small shrug. "Fine. Good. Uneventful."

"Completely uneventful?" Lexi challenged with a smile, obviously picking up on Meg's subtle body language.

"Perhaps not *completely*," Meg answered, playing along. "I hung out with Taylor Higgins a bit."

"Taylor, huh?" Jesse was less than enthusiastic. "I still don't understand why you never gave it a chance with Reina. She's a great girl." There it was—Jesse's continued critique of Meg's decision to not pursue Reina Ramirez. Reina, who, by the way, hadn't been into Meg either. The night Meg and Reina had been introduced over a year ago, neither of them had been interested in the other. Forced into meeting, they'd been cordial, conversing for a good while to appease Teddy, their mutual contact who'd orchestrated the setup. But truthfully, both she and Reina had other pursuits they were following that evening and they'd both recognized those signs immediately. In Meg's estimation, it had all worked out, as neither of them had been interested and nobody's feelings had been hurt. Meg saw no reason to revisit it, but Jesse brought it up a lot.

"I'm not going over this again," Meg said matter-of-factly.

Jesse stood and crossed into the kitchen, helping herself to some cold water from Meg's refrigerator. "But Taylor, again?" She huffed. "I don't know, Meg. She doesn't really seem stable."

Meg laughed, because it was kind of true. Taylor was sort of all over the place. "She is kind of crazy. Sometimes in a good way," she added with a naughty smile.

Lexi opened her mouth wide. "So you are hooking up with her again?"

"I am. I'm not." Meg shrugged playfully. "Who knows?"

Jesse shook her head in the corner. "And what's with this chick from your office building, the elevator operator? What's that about?"

Meg tilted her head toward Lexi and raised her eyebrows in faux disbelief at the obvious source of information. "Nothing," Meg answered in a droll voice as she clenched her jaw and widened her eyes in a playful grimace at Lexi.

"Don't look at her," Jesse teased. "She's going to be my wife. No secrets." She smiled into her drink. "This is stuff you should be telling me anyway."

"I would, but you get mad at me," Meg responded, matching her tone.

Jesse looked right at her, getting a little more serious. "I never get mad at you, Meg. I worry about you. There's a difference." Then she lightened her voice again. "So who was it this weekend? Elevator girl? Taylor? Someone else we don't know about…"

Meg chewed the inside of her cheek, fighting off a grin. "Taylor. Kind of."

"What's that mean?"

Meg looked back and forth between her two best friends, knowing it was useless to keep secrets from either of them. What's more, she didn't want to. "Well, I went home with Taylor, but, if you must know, she was pushing to have a threesome with one of her friends. I'm not into that, so I left."

"Good girl." Jesse nodded her approval.

Meg shot Jesse a look from under her eyebrows and was about to call her out. Jesse had about a decade on both her and Lexi, and she had been single, but rarely alone, for a long time before settling down. Meg was willing to bet at least some of Jesse's past exploits had included something outside the scope of routine, so she was a little miffed that Jesse was being so openly judgmental of her love life. Normally, she wouldn't hesitate to make that remark right to Jesse because they had that kind of relationship. But tonight, in front of Lexi, who'd just become her fiancée, Meg held her tongue. She reminded herself it was her friends' special night. She didn't want to ruin it by dredging up Jesse's extensive sexual history, so she kept her comments to herself.

"Wait. Was the other girl hot?" Lexi asked, filling the silence.

Meg thought about it for a second. "Yeah, she was cute."

"And you're really not into that, at all?" Lexi sounded surprised.

Meg scrunched up her nose. "Not my thing. I don't know, maybe I'm just too self-conscious." She thumbed toward herself as she continued. "Plus, not a good sharer. Even as a kid."

Lexi laughed at Meg's explanation, but Jesse rolled her eyes before adding, "Just promise me you are at least being careful with these girls."

Meg went right back at her. "What does that mean?"

"You know what it means."

Meg stretched her neck back in disbelief. "You're not giving me a lecture on safe sex right now, are you?" She curled her eyebrows. "You're kidding, right?"

"I'm not kidding at all."

This time she couldn't hold it in. She held both of her hands up, effectively halting the conversation. "Wait, you're gonna tell me that before you became Mrs. Monogamous here, you like, busted out the dental dams?" Meg challenged through her laughter.

Jesse smiled mischievously. "We're not talking about me."

"Of course we're not," Meg countered, with more than a little sarcasm.

"I did use my head," Jesse responded assertively. "All I'm saying is"—she exhaled heavily—"just make good choices. Okay?" She barked out the order in her typical husky voice, and because it was paired with a shake of her head that acknowledged the lack of control she had over anything, it managed to come out full of concern rather than condescension.

"Yes, Dad." Meg mocked her, but the message was received loud and clear.

The three of them switched back to talking about the engagement and the weekend past. A red-faced Lexi filled Meg in on how she had inadvertently flashed Jesse's family, and they all laughed about it together.

When her friends had gone, Meg loaded the dishwasher and thought about Jesse's comments. Wiping the countertops clean, she took mental inventory over the last year. There had been a couple of different girls, that was true, but it wasn't because she necessarily wanted it that way. She just hadn't met anybody with potential, not serious potential, anyway.

CHAPTER FOUR

The management consulting firm of Sullivan & Son, Inc. was an interesting place to work. Corporate but relaxed, in both its philosophy and its design, Sullivan believed heartily in core values, hard work, and team building. The company practiced what it preached, expecting long hours rewarded with fair compensation, encouraging all employees to work together. This last bit was done with a bit of a forced hand, making all of the lower-level associates share office space.

Being a junior associate, Meg cohabitated one of these offices. Most days she wished for her own cubicle rather than share the ten-by-ten room. Not that she didn't like Carrie Buckthorn. Her roommate was friendly enough, even if they had absolutely nothing in common outside of their shared employment. But Carrie was kind of loud—on the phone, on the computer, even just sitting at her desk.

Meg had gotten used to drowning her out. Sometimes she listened to music through earbuds if she was doing numbers work or something else she could half focus on. Other times, like right now, when she had to think hard, she simply mentally blocked out everything around her. Which is precisely why she didn't notice Anne standing in her doorway until her boss's shouted attempt at getting her attention.

"Megan!"

Meg heard her name at the exact moment that her officemate rolled back her chair and hit Meg's arm to alert her.

"Sorry, sorry, sorry." Meg snapped her head up from her computer. She only remembered at that moment, when she saw Sasha Michaels standing alongside Anne, that today was Sasha's first day in New York.

Anne cleared her throat. "Sasha, this is Megan McTiernan. Megan, Sasha Michaels."

Meg looked over at Carrie, waiting for Anne to continue the introductions. Carrie returned her glance with a subtle shake of her head. "We just met. You missed it," she said, not at all surprised at how zoned out Meg could get.

Meg stood up and took the few steps to the door. "Sorry. Hi." She smiled warmly as she shook Sasha's hand.

"Nice to meet you, Megan." Sasha's smile was shy but it went all the way up to her eyes and as the boss delved into Sullivan rhetoric, Meg took a second to assess her new colleague. Sasha was wearing a black skirt with a matching one-button jacket, a cream shell visible just beneath it. Her heels were professional, not too high, and she stood exactly even with Meg. She was dressed way too formally for Sullivan—both the New York and London offices had a relaxed dress code and smart casual was completely accepted. Meg immediately pegged Sasha as trying too hard and cattily wondered if this over-the-top tactic had been her success strategy in London. Meg knew firsthand Sasha's stellar reputation was not the result of her work product. She had spent enough time revamping Sasha's half-finished projects to know Sasha's consulting skills were completely average.

Meg squinted her eyes, boring in to search for signs of the scammer she suspected lay just beneath the expensive suit. What she noticed instead threw her. Sasha was a wreck. She was holding it together, but just barely. Shuffling back and forth on her feet, fiddling with the edge of her blazer, chewing her lower lip over and over. And she was hanging on Anne's every word. Meg couldn't help herself. As much as she wanted to dislike Sasha, in this moment her heart went out to her. It wasn't that long ago she'd been the new girl and she remembered the nerves. She almost wanted to go over to Sasha and put her hands on her shoulders, give them a little squeeze, assure her it would all be okay. Maybe give her a hug. Maybe more. God, where was her head? With a long blink she snapped out of her split-second fantasy. Eh, who could blame her, she thought, letting herself off the hook. With her creamy skin and long dark hair that fell in waves at her shoulders, Sasha was beyond beautiful.

Meg tuned back in to the conversation just in time. "Meg, you should take Sasha out to lunch one of these days. Show her the good places to eat. And more importantly the ones to avoid," Anne added with a forced chuckle. "All righty then, introduction complete. Back to work, you two," the boss finished, ushering Sasha out of the office and down the hall.

❖

It wasn't until late Thursday afternoon that Meg saw Sasha again. Out of nowhere it seemed, Sasha appeared in her doorway.

"Hi, Megan."

"Hey. How's it going?" Meg asked, sliding her chair back in search of the flip-flops hidden under her desk. Meg had the tendency to push Sullivan's casual dress policy to the very edge. It was understood if you were working in the office and there were no client meetings scheduled, you could wear whatever you wanted as long as it looked neat. Unfortunately for Meg, flip-flops were one of the few absolute no-nos. She kept them secreted under her desk and broke them out anytime she thought she could get away with it. Two p.m. on a Thursday seemed like a safe bet.

"Did you lose something?" Sasha asked, watching Meg's legs scramble.

"Got it." Meg reached for the errant flip-flop and slid it on. "I know, I know." She cast a glance up at her new colleague. "Don't rat me out, okay?"

"I won't," Sasha answered very seriously.

Meg inched back toward the desk. "So how are you adjusting?"

"Um...fine. Thank you for asking." Sasha looked down at her own strappy sandals before continuing. "I was just on my way out and I was wondering if you wanted to maybe grab something to eat or get coffee or something?" She was probably trying for breezy but a nervous laugh escaped and gave her away. She bit one half of her lower lip and raised her eyebrows looking hopeful. It was positively adorable. Immediately Meg shook off the thought and reminded herself to stay on track. In addition to being her coworker, Sasha was obviously straight. That didn't mean they couldn't break bread together.

Meg glanced at the clock on the wall even though she knew what time it was. "Actually, I am kind of hungry. I didn't eat lunch."

Sasha smiled sweetly. "Good. Well, not good. I just meant I didn't eat either."

"Awesome. Let's go." Meg kicked back her chair and led them both to the elevator. After a little back and forth, they decided to pick up sushi and eat it at Meg's favorite outdoor atrium. The city was loaded with them, tiny sanctuaries where office dwellers could escape for an hour or so. This particular one on Fifty-First Street was a true gem. Tucked between two buildings and set back from the street, it was full of cement planter greenery and even had a water feature along the rear wall. It was usually mobbed, but at this off-peak hour, they had no trouble securing a spot.

Meg snapped her chopsticks apart and systematically rubbed them together. "How's Scott treating you?"

"Fine."

Meg had a truly strange relationship with Scott Ford, Sasha's assigned roommate. Having worked together for years, they were friends by default. Scott had been a first-year associate when Meg had been hired as Sullivan's office manager six years ago. In the last two years, since Meg had been promoted to consultant, Scott had adjusted to the fact that they were equals, but he loved to remind Meg where she came from. It was always done in jest, but it still irritated Meg. Scott also loved to brag to Meg about his success with women. Meg knew he wasn't lying, she'd witnessed enough clients and colleagues throw themselves at him. He was very good looking, which Meg hated to admit, and he loved to tell Meg about his conquests—his word— and then expected her to share stories in return. Meg never told him anything, even though in a weird way she appreciated that he at least asked. Still, she was totally suspect of his motives, and his unspoken competition annoyed the shit out of her.

"He's behaving himself?" Meg asked through a wry smile.

"Mostly." Sasha giggled and rolled her eyes, indicating she'd understood Meg's meaning exactly.

"What about everyone else?"

"Everyone is very nice."

"How about your clients?" Meg's question was purposely vague. Sasha wasn't new to the field, but she'd taken so much time off to look after her mother that Meg felt oddly senior to her. Maybe it was because during Sasha's absences, Meg had been the one to carry her workload. It made it sort of awkward, Meg guessed for the both of them.

"Pretty good, so far. I haven't been assigned much yet. Still getting settled in."

Meg nodded, dipping a bit of her yellowtail into the soy-wasabi mixture she'd concocted. "Well, you'll see this office runs basically the same as London. Anne is more laid back about some things than Mitch, but uptight about others. It's basically an even trade." Meg spoke from experience because in covering for Sasha, she had spent ample time working for the senior partners of both offices.

"About that, Megan." Sasha's voice was so serious it made Meg stop midchew and stare right at her as she continued. Sasha brushed a strand of her long dark hair away from her face. "I don't really know that I'll ever be able to set things right between us. You know, after everything you did for me last year." She lowered her eyes and used her chopsticks to pinch the last cucumber roll on her tray.

"Yeah. No sweat," Meg responded.

Sasha looked at Meg, her dark eyes slightly challenging Meg's cavalier response. "I know it couldn't have been easy. Nigel told me how much you were there. Everything you did. For what it's worth, I just want to say thank you, in person." She blinked once and wet her lips. "Thank you and I'm sorry. For any trouble it may have caused you."

"It's okay. Really." Meg equaled Sasha's solemn tone. "Actually, I learned a lot, to be honest. Sort of helped me in a way." She shrugged one shoulder and redirected the conversation. "How is your mother doing?"

"She's okay." Sasha smiled out of one side of her mouth. She looked relieved to have cleared the air, and unbelievably gorgeous as a stream of sunlight lit one half of her face revealing that her eyes were deep blue under long dark lashes. "I'm going home to see her this weekend."

It hadn't occurred to Meg until that very second, but something suddenly dawned on her. "Hey, how come you don't have a British accent, by the way?" Meg definitely hadn't heard it the other day, but then Sasha had said so little during their first interaction, Meg thought it possible she'd just missed it. After this much conversation, Meg was sure it wasn't there at all. She took a swig from her water bottle and waited for an explanation.

Sasha chewed her food through a huge grin, covering her mouth with the back of her hand as she swallowed. She nodded, keeping her mouth closed as she ran her tongue along the sides of her teeth. "I'm from Maryland," she said with an enormous smile. "Most of us there have American accents. Although"—her voice took on a teasing quality—"we say orange, not *ah-runje*, like you New Yawkers."

"Ha-ha," Meg responded dryly, but her smile was genuine even through her sarcasm.

"You thought I was from England?" Sasha crinkled her forehead in disbelief.

Meg leaned back in her chair and defended her assumption. "It's not that much of a leap. You worked in the London office. You went to Oxford. Makes sense to me."

"You're right, it does." She wiped her mouth delicately. "I'm just teasing you. I'm surprised no one told you, though. Just because"— she tilted her head to the side and twisted a long wavy lock of hair between her thumb and index finger—"really, that's the reason I needed so much time off. I kept coming back home, to the States. My parents are divorced. My little brother is still in college. I felt like I should be with my mom for her surgeries, some of her treatments. That's why I asked for the transfer to New York."

"How come you worked in London in the first place?" Meg was genuinely curious.

Sasha dropped the strand of hair and smoothed down a few wisps that had gone astray in the light breeze. "When I was at Oxford, Sullivan London recruited me." She leaned back in her chair, crossed one leg over the other, and folded her hands over her bare knee. "When I was in high school my dad's company transferred him to London, and I thought it would be cool and exciting to go to school in England. And it was," she added emphatically, "but by the time I graduated I was ready to come home. My dad had already been transferred back to his office in DC. I missed my family. So when I interviewed with Sullivan I asked about the New York office. I was pretty homesick by then." She looked embarrassed and avoided eye contact as she toyed with the hem of her summery cotton dress. "But they were already hiring someone, so it was London or nothing." Meg knew they were talking about her and suspected Sasha did too. As though she was reading Meg's mind Sasha added, "It all worked out anyway. Here we both are."

"Where do you live?" Meg asked, changing the subject.

"Here. In the city. On the West Side."

"Roommates? Boyfriend?"

"No and no."

Sasha didn't seem bothered by the questions, so Meg continued her good-natured third degree.

"Pets?"

"Under consideration."

"Dog or cat?"

"Ooh, that's a tough one." She scrunched her nose as though she was deciding on the spot. "I would say dog, but being in the city, I don't know. Maybe cat." She twisted her lips to the side.

"Why not dog? People have dogs in the city. I see them all the time."

"I know they do. But you'd be surprised at how many people get a dog without realizing the commitment involved." She shook her head. "Gah, sorry. This is a subject I'm a little intense about. I volunteer at the West Side Rescue Mission on the weekends. I see dogs being returned all the time. Even the little ones." She made direct eye contact. "I have to practice my resistance every Saturday and not adopt them all myself."

Meg smiled. "That's sweet." It was out before she could stop herself. "You work there every weekend?" she asked, hoping the question would overshadow her comment.

"Well, most. But not this weekend."

"How come?"

"I'm heading home to see my mom—"

"Right, you said that."

Sasha put the lid on her empty tray and placed it in the plastic bag. "Usually I volunteer on Saturday mornings and then hang out with my friend Jane-Anne and her friends. She lives here too, but I know her from home. We went to high school together. Her twin sister is my best friend." She crumpled down the handles of the bag and pushed it to the side of the table. "What about you? What are you doing this weekend?"

Meg had to think about it for a second. "I think my friends are going to the Kitchen tomorrow night." She said it offhandedly, almost thinking out loud.

"The lesbian bar?" Sasha interrupted her train of thought. "I was there a few weeks ago."

That caught Meg's attention. "Really?"

"Yeah, I went there during Pride. Jane-Anne's cousin is gay. She came in from Philly with her girlfriend, so we all went out with them. I liked that place a lot. Really good music."

Meg nodded, both pleased and disappointed at the same time, and wanting desperately to conceal both emotions.

"Do you have a girlfriend?" Sasha asked.

"No."

"Why not?"

It was a question Meg always hated, no matter who asked it. The annoying thing about it, in her opinion, was there was no good answer. She wasn't going to say she'd spent most of the last year screwing around, that made her sound kind of whorish, even by her standards. On the flip side, admitting no one found her interesting enough to date on a long-term basis was a confession she didn't want to make, and hoped wasn't true. She held her head high. "Just haven't found the right girl, I guess."

Sasha seemed to find her response acceptable and they moved on to other topics as they packed up their garbage and made their way back to the office on Third Avenue.

Meg had to admit despite her long-term reservations and her deep-seated desire to despise the girl, she'd had a really nice time.

As the elevator opened onto the seventh floor, Meg reached for her swipe card with one hand and held Sullivan's main door open for Sasha with the other in an oddly chivalrous manner. She kicked herself inside, biting her cheek and reminding herself this wasn't a date. But when she walked Sasha to her office she couldn't resist.

"Sasha, this was fun. What do you say? Same time next week?" she asked, backing toward her own office.

Sasha grinned. "It's a date."

If only, Meg thought, whipping around to keep her dorky smile from giving her up as she bounced down the hall.

CHAPTER FIVE

Tracy had gotten Meg's voice mail all three times that she tried calling from the sole pay phone she'd found at Newark Airport. Now, as she was meandering through the streets of Bay West, she regretted her decision not to leave a message. Not that it would really matter—her phone was dead anyway, she still wouldn't know where she was going—but at least Meg wouldn't be completely surprised when Tracy showed up on her doorstep. But she had split in such a hurry that the damn thing barely had a half charge to begin with.

For the life of her she could not remember Meg's address. Something inside kept coming back to the one forties, but without a specific number that instinct was pretty much useless. One more time she walked down a street where all the attached houses looked exactly the same, peering at each façade, studying them for clues of her old friend in window dressings and lawn décor. She pulled her wheeled luggage behind her and adjusted the golf bag over her shoulder. A few beads of sweat formed on her forehead and she wiped them with her palm, running her hand all the way back through her short hair knowing after so many hours of travel, the product holding her carefully crafted style in place would be nearly devoid of potency. She frowned on the spot, suddenly less than confident in her spur-of-the-moment decision to leave California.

She needed an out, an escape. She'd packed up her suitcase quickly, grabbed her golf clubs, and made her calls on the way to the airport—first to her father letting him know she was going to New York for a few weeks; then to her sports agent and her coach to inform them she needed a break from the pro tour. They fought her on it—not her dad, but the other two. Tracy didn't waver. She told them both this was what she needed mentally, right now. She assured them all she was not having a breakdown. If anything, her head was clearer than it had been in months.

She just needed some time off. From golf, from LA, from her two-timing, back-stabbing ex-girlfriend.

The trip to New York had been planned anyway. She'd just moved up the timetable by a few weeks. Only, in her rush to flee she'd forgotten to notify her host of the change. And now she was drawing a blank on Meg's address. And she'd neglected to juice up her phone or her iPad. And now she was a little lost.

She took two steps into the street about to cross to the other side, but turned back again. She stood her golf bag upright and leaned on it, all but giving up.

"You okay?"

She turned toward the voice, more than pleased to come face-to-face with a slim blonde, whose eyes stood out in the distance between them.

Tracy made light of her situation. "I'm looking for one forty-"— she bobbled her head back and forth—"eight?" She held her hands up and puckered her lips, squinting a little in the sun. "Or maybe one forty-five? I'm not really sure. But my gut tells me one forties, for sure."

The woman gave her a quick once-over, a friendly smile forming on her lips as she tucked a long lock of hair behind one ear. "You're Meg's friend."

"Oh, thank God. You know her." Tracy breathed an exaggerated sigh of relief.

The gorgeous blonde's smile widened. "She's across the street. One forty-seven, I think it is. But you were close." She walked toward Tracy. "Here, let me help you."

Tracy hoisted her bag over her shoulder with practiced ease. "I got it. I'll just follow you, they all look the same to me."

They crossed the street together and walked right up to Meg's front door. After several attempts at knocking and ringing the bell, there was still no answer.

"She knows you're coming?" The woman looked at her watch. "I'm surprised she's not here. You know Meg, she's never late for anything," she said with surprise audible in her voice.

"I'm a touch early," Tracy said with a lilt in her voice, even though it was a private joke. "No big." She pushed the handle on her suitcase down and brought her hand to her forehead again, trying in vain to look presentable. "At least I'm waiting at the right house now, so that's a plus."

"You could wait at Lexi and Jesse's across the street. They're her friends. I just came from there." She shook her held quickly. "Sorry, I'm Betsy. I should have said that sooner. I'm a friend of Meg's." She tucked one hand under her arm and held the other out stiffly, looking adorably awkward in her self-introduction.

"Nice to meet you, Betsy." She clasped Betsy's hand and looked directly into her eyes. "Tracy Allen," she said, holding on to Betsy's hand longer than she really needed to.

"So do you want to?" Betsy asked.

"Want to what?" Tracy was confused and also so taken by Betsy's beautiful eyes that she had forgotten the question.

"Wait at Jesse's," Betsy answered, casting a look back over her shoulder, in the direction she had come from. "They have water, a bathroom, probably even keys to Meg's place, if you want."

Tracy forced herself to break eye contact. "Nah, I'm okay. It's beautiful out. I'll just hang here." It was one thing to show up out of the clear blue. There was no need to overstep even more by intruding on Meg's friends too. She politely declined the offer and thanked Betsy for her help.

Betsy stuffed her hands in the pockets of her jeans and rocked forward on her feet.

"Well, I guess I'll see you around."

"I sure hope so," Tracy cooed in response. She knew it was over the top and she saw Betsy blush a little as she backed away. Tracy didn't care. The woman was sexy and sweet, and she was here to forget her problems and have some fun.

She rested her golf bag up against the house and leaned against it, lacing her fingers behind her head and crossing her long, tanned legs at the ankles, thinking this vacation was off to a very promising start.

❖

Meg was more than a little surprised, but completely thrilled to find Tracy sprawled on her one-step stoop when she got home from work.

"What's going on?" Meg asked, turning her key in the door. "Is everything okay?" She put her keys and her mail on the small table in the foyer. "What are you doing here? Don't get me wrong, I love it. But what's up?" Meg asked, dropping her messenger bag and hugging her friend.

Tracy smiled and hugged her back. "Change of plans. My schedule opened up earlier than I thought. I tried to call, but my phone died, it's..." Her voice faded. "It's a long story."

Meg raised her eyebrows at Tracy's tone. They had known each other a long time and she could tell there was something her friend wasn't saying.

Reading her expression perfectly, Tracy answered her. "I'll fill you in on everything, I promise. Just not tonight. Is that okay?"

Meg nodded sincerely. She gave Tracy the tour of her modest home, leaving her in the guest room.

"Take however long you need to clean up, unpack, whatever," Meg said as she backed out of the room. "Just be advised I couldn't care less about your strict health code. I'm ordering us a pizza. With pepperoni. Deal with it," she called out, descending the stairs.

Forty minutes later at Meg's kitchen table, Tracy was finishing up her second slice. "God, I forgot how good Staten Island pizza is." She looked over, eyeing up a third.

"Best in New York."

"I think you're right."

"I know I am," Meg said with absolute certainty. "I meant to tell you before"—Meg nodded with her chin as she changed the subject— "I like the shorter hair. Looks good."

"Ditto," Tracy responded as she ruffled through her short coif. "It's a mess right now, but what can I say, it's been a long day." As she ran her hand through it again, Meg could tell Tracy's haircut was way trendier than her own. She knew from Facebook that Tracy had recently moved from a kind of faux hawk cut to a shorter, more andro look, keeping the sides buzzed and pushing the top completely to one side. Meg thought both looks worked for her friend, even if they were a touch too affected for her own style. But Tracy's whole look was striking, her ethnicity a mix of Korean and Greek. The combination gave her a unique appearance, making her distinctively attractive. There wasn't much she couldn't pull off.

Tracy licked her lips, reading too much into Meg's silence. "Dude, are you mad that I'm here?"

"Am I mad? Are you kidding?"

"It's pretty dicky of me to just show up. Sorry." Her thin upper lip curled and her dark eyes revealed her sincerity.

"Trace, it's awesome you're here. I've been counting the days anyway." Meg reached for her soda. "I get that something's up." She pursed her lips. "Not lost on me. And I see you're not ready to talk about it. It's cool." She tipped her head back finishing the last of her ginger ale. "Look, I know whatever's going on, whoever the girl is who did this to you"—she circled her index finger at Tracy sitting across from her—"which sent you clear across the country," Meg finished meeting Tracy's eyes, "I know you're going to tell me about it. There'll be plenty of time for that." She gave her friend a warm, knowing smile. "For now, though, just relax. Chill out. There's a social this weekend and everything. We'll drink, have a good time. You can meet my friends. They're amazing—"

Tracy interrupted her. "I actually met one of your friends today. I almost forgot to tell you. Betsy something."

"Really?"

"I was sort of lost." Tracy shook her head at herself. "She helped me figure out which house was yours."

"That sounds like Betsy." Meg picked up a crust, broke it in two, and tossed one half back in the pizza box. "Her name is Jennifer actually. Jennifer Betsy. But nobody calls her that. Everybody just calls her Betsy."

Tracy picked up the other half of crust and inspected it before biting off the end. "She lives here, at Bay West?"

"No. She might as well, though, she's here all the time."

"Is that right?" Tracy mused, midchew. She took a sip of her drink and tried for nonchalant adding, "She's got some eyes, huh?"

"Betsy?"

"Mm-hmm," Tracy responded, popping the last bit of crust in her mouth.

Meg shrugged. "I guess. They're what, blue? Green?" she asked, as if momentarily unsure of the answer.

"Kind of both." Tracy tried to play it off. "I thought they were pretty amazing."

"I see that," Meg teased.

"What?" Tracy took a swig of her drink to cover her smirk. "All I said is she has nice eyes."

Meg rolled her eyes blatantly. "Subtlety. Not your strong suit."

"I know," Tracy said through a devilish grin. "I just don't see the point of it."

"For what it's worth, she thinks you're dreamy too," Meg said with a cheesy smile. She slid her empty soda can to the center of the table. "She told me."

"Wait. What?" Tracy shook her head in utter surprise. "When?"

"Down, girl." Meg gestured with her hands. "Not today. I didn't even talk to her today." Meg got up and tossed their paper plates in the trash. "A few weeks back. I showed her a picture of you. The night you kept texting me about your outfits for the thing you were going to. Bets and I were out together having dinner. We approved of your clothing jointly," Meg added with a nod.

"That's how she knew who I was." Tracy put the pieces together out loud. "Wait a second. You guys aren't like, you know." She gestured back and forth with her hands, suddenly concerned she had inadvertently crossed a line.

Meg saved her. "Nope. Not like that. Just friends. But, seriously, she did say she thought you were hot." Meg watched Tracy smile and was happy to make her feel good. Meg had known Tracy a long time, and it was obvious she was off her game.

Meg put some aluminum foil on the table between them. "Come on, killer, help me wrap these slices. They're going to hit the spot when we come home in a drunken stupor tomorrow night."

Chapter Six

It was only nine o'clock and already the Bay West Commons was wall-to-wall girls.

"They haven't said a word about it. It's like it didn't happen," Lexi answered in response to her friends' inquiries about how her parents were adjusting to the engagement. She raised her voice over the music and tried futilely to sound unbothered. "Their loss. I'm not going to beg them, if that's what they want. I'm not doing it."

They were standing in a loose semicircle with Lexi directing her comments mostly to Meg and Tracy, while Jesse and Betsy were deep in their own conversation on the fringe of the group.

No one knew how to make Lexi feel better about her parents' lack of support. It was a crappy thing her mothers were doing, but it was also tricky to bitch out Chris and Marnie, who they all knew and liked, and who Lexi adored in spite of their current disapproval. So they simply listened to her vent.

At a break in the conversation, Tracy leaned toward Meg. "Don't look now, but some chick at the bar is totally checking you out."

Meg whipped around to see for herself. Assessing the curvy brunette across the room, she gave the girl a small nod of recognition before turning back to Tracy.

"Way to not listen to me."

"She's not checking me out," Meg corrected. "I know her."

"Dude, I've been watching for the last ten minutes. She's scoping you."

"She's not." Meg laughed her off. "It's a funny story actually. We're supposed to be perfect for each other. Except we're not."

Tracy crinkled her forehead at Meg's half explanation.

"That's Reina Ramirez." Jesse had heard the back and forth and jumped into the conversation to flesh it out for Tracy. "Her cousin Teddy, the woman with the buzz cut she's standing next to," Jesse explained with a nod of her chin, "she lives here." Jesse flashed her eyes in their direction. "Reina comes around a lot. She's a great girl"— Jesse curled her lip and hung her head in defeat—"but Meg won't give her a chance."

"That's not true. I gave her a chance." Meg shook her head, not liking the way her response had come out. She blinked slowly and tried again. "What Jesse isn't telling you is everybody had this, like, fantasy that me and Reina would meet and realize we're meant to be. So they forced us into a setup and surprise, surprise, we're not soul mates." Meg gave an overly dramatic sigh for comedic effect as she continued. "Nobody can believe it. Except, of course, for me and Reina, who are fine with how things worked out, by the way. But every time we're in the same room, Teddy pushes Reina at me, and this one"—she thumbed at Jesse—"never gets off my case about it."

"Because I know a good thing when I see it." Jesse got the last word in with the spirited confidence of someone who undoubtedly believed she was right.

Tracy watched the lighthearted exchange and scanned the group to see who would weigh in next. She was hoping for Betsy to say something that might give her a natural opening to talk to the gorgeous blonde again. They had been at the social for over an hour, and Tracy had yet to have the opportunity to pick up their conversation from the other day. She was looking for a gateway, but it was Lexi who piped up instead.

She playfully swatted Jesse's arm. "You should give Meg a break." Lexi nodded her chin assertively. "You made your pitch for Reina. They didn't click. Let it go." She broke out into a mischievous smile. "Anyway, Meg's got her hands full trying to convert her straight coworker."

Both Jesse and Tracy turned to Meg for an explanation.

Lexi continued to play it up. "What? She hasn't told you guys about how she's wining and dining the new girl at her office?"

Meg challenged Lexi with her expression, but her mouth turned up into a one-sided smile as she spoke. "We have lunch. It's called being friendly." She rolled her eyes up at the ceiling. She had a great rapport with her friends and loved that they all teased each other openly. "Anyway, I'm getting out of the line of fire." She looked over at the bar. "Anybody need a drink?"

"I'll come with you." Betsy wiggled her empty beer bottle.

Without missing a beat Tracy offered to come too, and the three of them headed to the bar together. After they were served, they decided to hit the balcony for some fresh air, but at the end of the bar Meg bumped into Reina, who was still hovering nearby. She urged Tracy and Betsy to go on without her, assuring them she'd catch up in a minute. But she purposely dawdled, spending a few extra minutes with Reina just to give Tracy the one-on-one time with Betsy that she knew her friend was angling for.

She returned to the group just in time to hear Lexi inviting the gang for a barbecue at Jesse's place the following Sunday. Meg knew all the details already, so she half listened, keeping an eye on Tracy and Betsy outside while she surveyed the room for anyone who might catch her eye.

In the middle of her third scan over faces she had mostly seen before, Meg's eye caught a dark-haired stranger walking directly toward them. The woman looked different than the rest of their group—edgier, with jet-black hair that hung in her face and heavy-duty eyeliner around her eyes. She had on a threadbare T-shirt that hung off her gaunt body and dark jeans that crumpled at the top of her unlaced boots, perfecting her purposely disheveled look. To Meg's surprise she stopped when she reached them, causing Lexi to stop talking midsentence.

The stranger gave a nod to Jesse only, thrusting her hands into her pockets as she spoke. "Jen around?"

Jesse answered her only with a nod of her own, pointing toward the balcony with her beer where Betsy and Tracy could be seen in conversation beyond the tinted glass wall. The girl simply nodded her thanks and headed toward the balcony doors.

Meg was amazed at the lack of words that had passed in the exchange. She looked at Lexi, who appeared to be as confused as she was before turning to Jesse. "Who was that? And who the fuck is Jen?"

Jesse took a sip of her drink before answering. "Jen, as in, Jennifer Betsy." She wiped the corner of her mouth and didn't even try to mask her irritation as she continued, "That's CJ."

Meg turned her head so fast her confused reaction fell into the abyss. She watched as Betsy's ex-girlfriend interrupted Betsy and Tracy with the same cocky air she had employed moments ago. Betsy and CJ exchanged a seemingly genuine hug, followed by what looked like an awkward introduction to Tracy. Then they departed abruptly via the outdoor staircase, leaving Tracy to return to the group with her tail between her legs.

"What just happened?" Lexi asked no one in particular.

Meg's comment was more pointed and was aimed at Jesse. "*That* was Betsy's girlfriend? The one with the sleeve of tattoos and the pierced nose?"

"Ex-girlfriend. Allegedly," Jesse responded. "But yeah, that's her."

Meg was truly shocked, and she knew the reason had everything to do with CJ's appearance. It was shallow, but she was so completely surprised that she couldn't get over it. She peppered Jesse with a million questions throughout the rest of the night. They were mostly to satisfy her own curiosity, but she knew Tracy was following the details too, even if she tried not to look too invested in the answers.

Meg finally broached the subject with Tracy on the short walk home to her condo. "You bummed about the Betsy thing?"

Tracy curled up the corner of her mouth in an odd expression that was half smile, half frown. "It's fine," she answered.

"You heard Jesse, they might be broken up," Meg offered optimistically.

"Yeah, maybe." But Tracy didn't sound convinced. "I had a good time anyway."

"It's awesome you're here. I'm so glad you got to meet my friends."

"You know, I was at one of these parties years ago." Tracy crossed her arms as they walked down the path toward Meg's house. "But being here tonight, seeing it from the inside, almost being part of it…totally different." She shook her head, breaking into a spontaneous smile. "This place is amazing." She looked up at the sky and did a full three hundred sixty degree turn. "You can actually see stars."

"You should stay for a while." Meg caught herself off guard by her spontaneous invitation. But hearing it out loud, it sounded like a good idea, so she continued, "Why rush back to LA? Hang out here for a bit."

She fished her keys out of her pocket. "Then you can make a real run at Jennifer Betsy."

Tracy smirked. "It's not beyond the realm of possibility, my young friend." She clapped Meg's shoulders as they entered the house. "She's pretty awesome." She kicked off her shoes as she crossed the threshold. "I mean beautiful, obviously. Smart, funny…" She trailed off, bending down to pick up her Vans with one hand.

"What did you guys talk about anyway?"

"Don't know, really." Tracy looked up thoughtfully. "Nothing. Everything." She rubbed the back of her neck. "She's just easy, you know?" She stuffed her empty hand in her pocket, leaning on the wall as Meg locked the front door behind them. "I'm telling you there is something there." She smiled easily. "I know she felt it too."

Meg stopped dramatically at the foot of the staircase and looked right at Tracy, who was still perched against the wall clearly replaying portions of the evening in her mind. "Oh my God, who are you? You're here a day and you're in love. WTF, dude."

Tracy twisted Meg around and nudged her up the stairs. "I'm not." She tried unsuccessfully to lighten her tone. "She's just different, you know. Real."

"Oh man, you're screwed." Meg snorted and Tracy laughed with her. "First things first. Let me get the scoop on what's going on with her and Joan Jett there."

At the top of the stairs, Tracy pivoted on one foot, heading for the guest room at the front of the house. "Well, don't be obvious." She called out the friendly order with a huge smile on her face.

"You see where I live," Meg answered wryly, meeting Tracy's eyes down the hall. "Give me a little credit, buddy. This is not my first rodeo."

Chapter Seven

Lexi took a deep breath. She squeezed Jesse's hand and gave her a quick kiss on the lips. "I'll see you in a few minutes."

Jesse held on to her for a second. "Why don't you let me come with you?"

"It's better if I go alone," Lexi answered with shaky confidence. She knew she had to deal with her parents sooner or later. Another week had passed without any mention of her upcoming nuptials.

Early in the week, she'd overheard her mothers confirming plans with Kam Browne and Mary Brown for Friday night. Playing cards at the house was something of a tradition for the four friends. On weekend nights that Bay West didn't have a social, open house, or closed party that required Kam's and Mary's presence and supervision as the power couple who owned and operated Bay West, there were good odds they could be found parked at the Russo-Markowski dining room table with big smiles, full drinks, and piles of gambling chips in front of them.

Tonight there were no events, so it was game on.

"I'll be fine." Lexi nudged Jesse in the direction of her house. "I'll be over soon, I promise." She watched her girlfriend—her fiancée— back away, then turned and faced the front door, taking a deep breath and reminding herself yet again that this was a good idea. Mary and Kam were surely waiting to congratulate her on the engagement and, as strange as it seemed, Lexi thought that might be just what her parents needed to get over the hump. Of course it would be awkward in the beginning. But nothing was more awkward than the way things were right now. She hardly spoke to her parents at all lately, and in the past weeks she had found herself steering clear of Kam and Mary altogether.

She'd used a similar avoidance tactic a year ago, when she and Jesse had first started dating. It was just too weird given her family's closeness with Mary coupled with the history between Mary and Jesse. Somehow over the last twelve months they'd all figured out a way to talk around it, but now with a wedding around the corner, Lexi knew she couldn't play cat and mouse for much longer.

It was a good thing, she told herself. Kam and Mary were probably itching to tackle the elephant in the room and have their requisite congratulatory remarks out of the way. Perhaps making a big show of their support would cover the initial discomfort they'd all felt over the fact that Lexi was going to marry Jesse Ducane, with whom Mary had conducted a very long, very secret, very inappropriate affair. Clearing the air might be just what they all needed to move on.

Pressing the handle of the screen door, Lexi almost balked as she heard their distant laughter from just inside the doorway. It got louder and more distinct as she walked up the stairs to the first floor of the split-level setup. When she reached the top of the stairs, she saw Marnie leaning all the way back in her chair, clutching her chest as she laughed, while Mary was doubled over in her seat, her head resting on her arms across the dining room table. She looked up and saw Lexi before the others did.

"Lexi," Mary yelled, waving her over enthusiastically. "You have to hear this story Chris just told us." She patted the shiny wood surface just in front of the empty chair at the head of the table, encouraging Lexi to sit down.

Lexi checked a look at Marnie, who was busy wiping tears from her eyes, as she polished off her margarita. "You know Mush," her mother said to Lexi, employing the nickname all the kids used for Chris.

It was a good moniker. Chris was an absolute softie. She was also a great storyteller, and when the four of them were together, she loved to reminisce about the good old days.

Chris peeked her head up from where she stood at the counter mixing up a fresh round of drinks. She had on a woozy smile. "Hey, Lex. Want a drink?"

"No, thanks," Lexi answered her mother with a smile. She kind of loved seeing them all like this—getting a little sloshed, having a good time together. Someday, when she was their age, she hoped to be just like them.

Kam cleared her throat, looking right at Lexi as she brushed her gray-brown hair off her forehead with one hand. "So what are you kids up to tonight?" She coughed again and answered her own question. "You girls headed to the Kitchen?" She gave a gruff chuckle, and spoke again, still not giving Lexi a chance to answer. "Chris, do you remember that night at the Kitchen with Marilyn Sanders and the cowbell?" They all broke into simultaneous laughter at an obviously shared memory.

Chris walked over with two drinks, placing them in front of Mary and Marnie. Her eyes were glassy as she approached her daughter and gave Lexi's shoulders a genuine squeeze. "What is on your agenda tonight, honey?"

"Not much, really."

"Ooh, are you going to stay and hang with us?" Mary asked excitedly.

Lexi sat down in the vacant chair. "Sure. For a little bit." Marnie gave her a sweet smile and Lexi saw love in her eyes, even though they were at unspoken odds over her future. She inadvertently checked her watch, a little surprised so many minutes had passed without Mary and Kam fawning over her. She supposed it could be nerves or forgetfulness because they were a little tipsy. Either way, she expected their congratulations were imminent, so she sat tight, giving them time to bring up the marginally touchy subject whenever they were ready.

"So what are you all playing?" Lexi asked good-naturedly.

Mary answered her. "It started off as euchre, but bossy, over here"—she nudged Kam sitting next to her—"made us switch to pinochle, because *she* likes it better." She batted her eyes playfully and leaned into Kam. "And we agreed, because we love her." She tipped her head onto Kam's shoulder.

"Let me guess, you all are winning?" Lexi teased Mary, knowing Kam Browne almost never lost at pinochle.

They all laughed amicably.

"Is it even close?" Lexi asked, reaching for the scorecard in the center of the table.

Mary put her hand on Lexi's forearm, stopping it before she was able to slide the score sheet back to her. "Oh my God." She stared at the diamond on Lexi's finger and then met Lexi's eyes directly. Her expression said it all. Mary was absolutely stunned and she stuttered for a second before she asked in a very serious voice, "Is that an engagement ring?"

The table fell silent, as Lexi locked eyes with Marnie first, then Chris.

She couldn't believe it. Mary and Kam had no idea. Lexi was too upset for words as she dropped her eyes to the table and swallowed her anger using everything she had to hold back the tears. "Yes, it is," she managed, before scraping her chair back across the floor as she continued to glare at her mothers. Without another word, she stood up and walked out of the house, leaving her parents to pick up the pieces.

CHAPTER EIGHT

Y ou ready?"

Meg looked up to see Sasha swaying halfway into her doorway, the exact same way she had for the last two weeks in a row when they met up for their standing Thursday lunch date.

"Yep." She saved her document and bounced out of her chair. "Let's go." Trailing Sasha by a half step through the office, Meg browsed her phone. "So there's this new crepe place a few blocks away. Any interest?"

"Ooh, crepes. That could be fun. Sweet and savory?"

Meg nodded. "Yeah, both. It looks like a nice menu. And not that expensive actually." She handed her phone over so Sasha could check it out herself, continuing to talk while Sasha perused. "The only thing is, it's a few blocks north and it's all the way over on First Avenue. Kind of a hike. That okay?"

Sasha nodded emphatically. "Fine."

Meg was enjoying these lunches more than she wanted to admit. In truth, Meg knew she was enjoying Sasha herself way more than she should. Just the other day she'd had to forcibly redirect her thoughts from a Sasha-filled fantasy during the weekly staff brief. There was no harm in it really, but she reminded herself to be careful just the same. Keep it light, friendly. Nothing good could come from falling for a straight girl.

"Hey, I heard you got the Ardmore project," Meg said, as they walked in the direction of the restaurant.

"Yeah, I did."

"Fun."

Sasha curled her eyebrows challenging Meg's enthusiasm. "Fun?"

"Yeah, fun," Meg repeated. "Big client. Massive restructuring. Long-term overhaul." She nodded affirmatively. "Fun."

A labored laugh escaped Sasha's lips. "If you say so."

"What's the matter? You sound stressed."

"I am actually." Sasha twisted her lips to the side. "I have my first deadline on Monday and I'm a little behind already."

"Do you need help?"

"No, I'm fine. Just a little nervous, I guess."

Meg stopped walking and reached for Sasha's arm, forcing her to stop too. "Sash, I will totally help you. It's no big deal." When she saw Sasha's face relax at her suggestion, she was happy she'd pushed it.

"Would you really help me?"

"Yes, of course." Meg smiled and shook her head at Sasha's surprised expression as she opened the door to the restaurant. "Let's stay and work on it tonight."

"Then I'm buying lunch," Sasha said, some calm returning to her voice.

"No, you're not." Meg chuckled. "I'm starving and I may eat everything on this menu. I can't feel like I have to hold back when I'm ordering."

Sasha shook her head at Meg's playful seriousness. "Ice cream, then. Tonight. When we're done."

"Now you're talking."

❖

On Friday afternoon, when she had finished up her own work, Meg stopped by Sasha's office to check her progress. Even though she could see from the hall that Sasha wasn't there, she stayed in the doorway, looking at Sasha's workspace. There was a photo of her in casual clothes surrounded by a group of dogs, probably taken at the recent adoption event at the dog rescue place where she volunteered. Next to it was a double frame photo with a shot of Sasha and her mom on one side and one of Sasha with a guy on the other. Boyfriend or brother?

"Hey, stalker." Scott came up from the rear and walked into the office he shared with Sasha. "If you're looking for Sasha, she's in the production room." He sat down at his desk. "Or you can continue to look around, sniff her seat. Whatever. Just pretend I'm not here."

Meg rolled her eyes and left without responding at all. She hated that Scott caught her looking at Sasha's stuff, but she was equally peeved at herself for being so curious in the first place. She shook it off and located Sasha in the copy room.

"We working tonight?" she asked over the hum of the scanner.

"You don't mind staying again?" Sasha curled her eyebrows looking hopeful.

"I'm in." Meg knocked on the wall emphatically. "We're going to knock it out," she said as though it was a cheer, getting a real laugh from her colleague.

At eight o'clock, they were mostly finished, with just the final set of numbers to add to the breakdown. Meg raided the Sullivan snack closet while Sasha sat at one of the two tables, her feet up on the opposite chair.

"Fritos or pretzels?" Meg said over her shoulder.

"Are the pretzels sticks? Or the small pretzel-shaped ones?"

Meg brought the package close to examine. "Baby pretzels."

"I'll take those," Sasha answered.

Meg tossed the bag to her and grabbed two Diet Cokes from the fridge.

"Happy to be done?" Meg asked, sitting down and ripping into the Fritos.

"Relieved." She took a sip of her drink. "Thank you so much for your help."

"No big." Meg crunched away. "So what's the rest of the weekend look like?"

Sasha shielded her mouth as she chewed. "My mom and brother are coming tomorrow."

"Nice. What will you guys do?"

"I don't know. Walk around. I'll show them my neighborhood. Go to dinner." She popped a tiny pretzel in her mouth. "Nothing fancy."

"How old is your brother?"

"Devon. He's twenty-one. He's a senior at Georgetown." She swallowed with satisfaction. "He's awesome. I wish I had my phone with me, I would show you a pic."

"Is that him in the frame on your desk?" Meg knew she was revealing her hand a little, but she didn't care.

"Yes." Sasha smiled. Clearly thinking about her family made her happy. "Next time he comes to New York, like without my mom, we'll all have to go out. You'll love him."

Sasha loosened her hair from the bun on top of her head and shook it down her back.

"What about you?" She reached up into a stretch. "Anything going on this weekend?"

Meg thought about it for a second. "I don't know. No real plans yet."

Sasha chewed her lip. "How is it living in your development?"

"Awesome," Meg responded without needing to think about it at all.

"What's it like?" She leaned in, her curiosity apparent.

"It's like…regular. It's all condos, or town houses, whatever you want to call them. Lots of trees. It's pretty. Suburban, but nice."

"Do you and your friends always hang out there, where they throw the parties?"

"Sometimes, yeah." Meg searched Sasha's face, wondering what she was really asking. "But not all the time. We come into the city too. Brooklyn, sometimes."

"Oh, cool. I wasn't sure." She fidgeted a little. "I mean, I know you mentioned going to the Kitchen and everything, but I just…" She shook off a self-conscious smile. "We should meet up, hang out sometime."

"Definitely." Meg kept her voice even, but inside her heart pounded.

❖

At 4:20 Saturday afternoon, Tracy turned Meg's spare key in the lock and pushed the door open. She dropped her overnight bag in the hall and flopped into a kitchen chair.

Fresh from a shower, Meg pulled a T-shirt over her head as she descended the stairs. "You're back." She tore two paper towels off the roll and patted her short hair dry.

"Dude, it's hot as fuck out there."

"Here, have a water." Meg grabbed two bottles from the fridge and tossed one across the kitchen to Tracy, who caught it with ease. Meg pulled the chair opposite Tracy out from the table and sat down. "How was your week? Three days, whatever," she corrected, remembering Tracy had left just Wednesday morning to visit her mother and stepfather on Long Island.

Tracy nodded as she downed half the bottle. "Good."

"Family's good?"

"Yep." She twisted the water bottle in place on the table. "Mom and Don are good. I got to spend a lot of time with Lily, which was awesome."

Meg was well familiar with Tracy's family, having spent countless hours at her house during her junior year of high school. Even though she couldn't picture Tracy's decade-younger half sister as anything but a gawky little kid, she remembered Tracy's mother and stepfather being lovely people, warm and supportive. Meg had been genuinely surprised when Tracy chose to move out to California with her dad after graduation, but she'd gotten a full ride to college, and the West Coast lifestyle clearly suited her.

"How's Lily doing?" Meg asked.

"Great. She's a freshman in college, if you can believe it," Tracy said, grabbing her phone and pulling up an updated photo of the two of them.

Seeing them side by side in the picture, Meg could see the resemblance between the siblings. They both had beautiful dark almond-shaped eyes that slanted slightly upward at the corners, courtesy of their mother's half-Korean lineage. They had also both lucked out with her tiny nose and elegant smile. It was there the similarities ended, though. Lily was short and pale like Don, with full hips and a heavy chest, while Tracy was tall and angular like her own father. From his Greek roots Tracy had inherited gorgeous olive skin that turned golden brown in the sun. She had no real curves but was a head turner just the same. Her androgynous look worked for her, making her equally beautiful and handsome at the same time. For a second Meg felt a pang of empathy for Lily, having to grow up in the shadow of such a stunner.

"What did you guys do?" Meg asked, looking back at her friend.

"Nothing. Hung out." Tracy leaned into the chair back, stretching her arms over her head. "I know I said I'd be back yesterday, but Lily asked me to stay so I figured why not."

"You didn't miss anything here."

"You didn't go out last night?" Tracy didn't hide her surprise.

"Nah. I ended up working late."

"On a Friday? That's dedication."

"My friend needed help with a project," Meg offered in her own defense.

Tracy smirked. "Oh, right. The straight girl from your office." Her grin widened. "The one whose pants you're trying to get into. How's that working out?" She squinted as she thought. "Sandra, Sarah? What's her name again?"

Meg couldn't hide her smile or keep her face from going hot. "Sasha. And I'm not trying to get into her pants." She turned in her seat and put her feet up on the chair next to her. "I'm helping her with a client. It's totally platonic," Meg added, as much for her own benefit as Tracy's.

Even though she didn't look convinced, Tracy let her off the hook. "Anything shaking for tonight?"

Meg looked out the window, inadvertently checking a glance to Jesse's house. "Not really." She scratched her head. "No social. Not even an open house, I'm afraid." She assessed Tracy's demeanor. "We could go into the city or Brooklyn, if you're feeling it."

Tracy half shrugged and checked her watch. "Let's go hit some golf balls."

Meg crinkled her brow in disbelief. "It's like four hundred degrees out." It was an exaggeration for sure, but it was midnineties for the third straight day in a row.

"Don't be a pussy," Tracy deadpanned.

Meg gave in easily. "Fine, but that counts as exercise. Which means we are totally stuffing our faces afterward."

"Deal."

❖

The driving range was surprisingly crowded considering the intense heat and they were lucky to find two lanes open next to each other. Meg set herself up on the near mat, brushing off some small debris with her sneaker before selecting a driver from Tracy's set of elite clubs. They each hit a few balls before Meg turned around and faced Tracy. She watched her friend's perfect form and waited until she'd finished to talk.

Meg knew this wasn't the right time, but over a week had passed and the ideal moment had yet to present itself. She had no clue what was going on with Tracy other than she had come out east two weeks early and didn't seem to be adjusting her return date at all. That didn't bother her. As a matter of fact, she was loving her buddy being around. But Meg was concerned because when Tracy had initially scheduled her trip months ago, Meg knew she'd timed it meticulously around major tournaments. While her friend could be spontaneous about some things, she never messed around when it came to golf.

"So did you take, like, a hiatus from golf?"

Tracy bit her bottom lip and huffed out a breath before meeting Meg's gaze as she answered. "I sort of took a hiatus from my life." She broke eye contact and put her driver back in the bag. "A much-needed one," she added emphatically.

"Are we ever going to talk about it?" Meg's voice was full of concern.

"Nothing to talk about. I just needed a break."

"Okay." Meg played along, realizing she was going to have to pull it out of Tracy. "So that's what this trip is? A little R and R from your life, chill out for a few weeks, then back on the bandwagon?" She dropped a ball and took a hasty swing at it, bouncing it in a straight line ahead of her.

"Maybe I go back, maybe I don't." Tracy took a swift cut, driving the ball deep into the field ahead.

Meg looked over her shoulder. "I meant golf. Not whatever is going on in California, obviously that's a bigger issue. We'll get to that next."

"Yeah, I meant golf too."

"Wait, you're quitting golf?"

"I don't know." Tracy looked serious but not uncertain. In fact, she looked like her mind was made up.

Meg turned all the way around to face her. "Trace, don't take this the wrong way. You can stay with me as long as you want. Fuck, move in. Mi casa es su casa, you know that. But golf is your life."

Tracy had taken another beautiful swing while Meg was talking. "That's the problem, though. I spend ninety-five percent of my time doing something I'm mediocre at, at best."

"So you're not the best player in the world. So what?" Meg was ready to give her a mini confidence boost but Tracy didn't give her the chance.

"Meg, I've spent the last six years barely making it onto the tour." She smiled her calm, beautiful smile. "Maybe it's time to find something else."

Meg was genuinely curious. "Like what?"

"That's what I'm trying to figure out." She drew an iron from her bag. "I do a lot of volunteering for Every Youth Counts, the charity, you know, out in LA. They're headquartered here in New York. One of my friends put me in touch with someone in the corporate office. I'm going to meet him for lunch next week. So that's something."

Meg nodded, taking it in as Tracy continued to talk.

"I also have something set up with the head of the LGBTQ center about a sports program they are trying to get off the ground." She sent another drive aloft. "Not really sure what that's about, but I'm intrigued." She tightened the glove on her left hand. "And"—she smirked a little—"the other morning I talked to Toby, he's the manager here, about giving some pro lessons. So that's an option."

Meg smiled ear to ear. "Holy shit. You're staying."

"At least until I figure some stuff out."

Meg did a small happy dance around her club. "Sorry. I mean it's obviously because your life is in shambles—which we haven't even talked about yet—but selfishly, this totally rocks."

"It's okay then, if I crash for a bit?" Tracy's eyebrows were raised in hopeful consideration. "I know I literally showed up on your doorstep. Honestly, though, being around you is awesome. I missed you." She looked down, as if a little shy to admit it. "And Bay West, what a vibe. It's so chill, I think it's maybe just what I need right now."

Meg took three steps and hugged her friend. "Of course you can stay." She couldn't stop grinning as she backed up to her lane. "Hey, I have some news for you." She gave a nod with her chin. "I'm pretty sure Betsy and her rocker girlfriend are officially over." She called over her shoulder as she drew into her backswing.

"Is that right?" Tracy responded, but her tone was flat.

Meg was surprised Tracy didn't sound more interested. "That's what my sources tell me." She sliced a drive to the right. "Anyway, you can see for yourself tomorrow at Lexi's barbecue."

Tracy drove a ball deep into the field, well clearing the two-hundred-yard mark. "Shit. About that, Meg. I can't go." She looked up.

"Why not?"

"I have to go back to Long Island tomorrow."

"Really?" Meg turned to face her.

"My mother is having a dinner. Like, for me. My uncles are coming, my grandmother. I'm just going for the day, but there's no way I'm getting out of it." She pushed back the brim of her bright red Angels cap. "Sorry, dude."

"Don't apologize to me." Meg took another hasty swing. "I'm just bummed you won't get to see Betsy."

"You'll have to keep an eye on her for me." She sent another beautiful shot right down the center of the range. "Anyway, we don't know for sure she's available. She seemed pretty excited to see her ex, or whatever she is, last week."

"I did some digging. Turns out she was just in town to pick up some stuff."

"Yeah, but you know how these things go. One night it's over, the next it's not."

Meg stopped in her tracks and turned to face her friend. "Look, even if something happened between them the other night, I can tell you, from knowing Betsy for the last year, it's mainly over."

Tracy didn't even look up as she set her ball up on the makeshift tee. "Mainly over is not over, my friend." She drew her iron back and whipped it forward with force. She watched as the ball sailed into the distance. "I don't feel like competing for someone's affection."

"I'm sorry." Meg's voice dripped sarcasm. "Who are you?"

Tracy had been serious, but seeing Meg's over-the-top expression lightened up her mood as she explained, "Look, I love competition as much as the next person—"

With a raised eyebrow, Meg cut her off. "I'm gonna say more. Like way more, Miss Varsity Everything with the multiple college scholarships to choose from."

Tracy smiled at the backhanded compliment and reached down to set up a new ball. "Okay, okay. But seriously, if she's still with TJ, CJ, whatever her name is, I'm out." She looked over at Meg as she adjusted her grip.

"What about your connection. I thought you guys could both feel it." Meg laid it on thick, even tossing up some air quotes for effect.

"Number one, I was drunk." Tracy laughed at Meg mocking her. "And two, I'm an idiot." She smiled out of one side of her mouth. "And I didn't say I'm not interested. I just don't want to get in the middle if they are still together."

"Such a gentleman." Meg continued to tease.

Tracy couldn't help but smile. "Just find out the deal for me tomorrow, 'kay?"

"You got it."

They were silent for almost a minute, each hitting their last few balls. Meg finished first and turned to watch Tracy. She didn't bother to wait for an opening as she leaned on her club. "Now, about California. What's the story there?"

Tracy grimaced as she topped the ball off. It was a lousy shot for her, but still way better than anyone else around them. She backed up and used the head of her club to tip the plastic bucket over and guide the last ball her way. She looked up at Meg from under the brim of her hat. "There was a girl." She pursed her lips into a thin line. "And now there's not."

"And?"

"And what?" Tracy put away their clubs and bent down to pick up the ball baskets. "What is there to say, really?" She hoisted the bag over her shoulder and started walking. "She fucking decimated me."

"What happened?"

Tracy scratched her head under her hat and readjusted it perfectly. She looked right at Meg. "I don't even know where to start," she said, equally sad and embarrassed.

"How about with something easy, like her name."

Meg thought she was helping break it down to the most basic components. She had no idea that she had asked the most difficult question. Tracy stopped in her tracks and met Meg's concerned face. "I can't, Meg. I'm sorry."

"Look, you have to talk about it sooner or later."

Tracy huffed. "I mean I can't tell you her name."

Meg's eyes widened. "Oh my God, is she famous?"

Tracy turned away but it was too late, her wry smile had given away the answer.

"No way." Meg couldn't help herself. "Is it Sara Davenport?" she asked excitedly, naming Hollywood's hot new A-lister who was widely suspected of being in the closet. Meg hadn't really believed the rumors, expecting they were mostly perpetuated by the lesbian community hoping for a sexy leading lady they could lay claim to.

Tracy laughed. "She's not even gay."

"The Internet says she might be," Meg countered.

"Well, she's not gay with me." Tracy smiled as she reached Meg's car, waiting for her to pop the mini-SUV's hatchback.

Meg squinted her eyes and shook her head as Tracy laid the golf bag across the trunk. "I can't believe you're not going to fucking tell me."

"I'm not." Tracy smiled. "But I have good reasons."

"I'm listening," Meg said with curiosity and concern, but not anger.

Tracy relaxed a little. She tilted the vent toward her face and sat silently while the air conditioning cooled her off. "Look, I realize now she's a total closet case and while I should have seen that sooner"—she shrugged—"I didn't." She looked straight ahead. "She has a successful career that she, at least, believes would be negatively impacted by coming out." She tilted her head on the headrest. "I happen to disagree, but that's how she feels."

Meg looked over and saw raw emotion on Tracy's face as she continued.

"I have to respect that. Or at least not be the one to out her." She rubbed the tops of her knees anxiously. "No matter how much she lied to me." She took off her ball cap and folded the brim of it between her hands. "I don't want to hurt her like that. I cared about her. A lot. I still do in some way." She made eye contact with Meg as they stopped at a red light. "I gave her my word."

Meg simply nodded trying to take it all in. "Wow." She leaned on her door and looked Tracy up and down. "She doesn't deserve you."

Tracy lifted her shoulder up and sort of smiled. "I feel kind of bad for her."

"Why?"

"I think it's sad that in this day and age she's so worried about being who she really is. I truly don't think her fans would care. She's living a fake life and that's sad, if you ask me."

Meg licked her lips, considering. "Is there a chance she's not a lesbian?"

Tracy gave her a look of utter disbelief from under her furrowed brow.

"I mean like, is she bi, or something?"

"She's not bi, trust me. She has, like, a boyfriend for the media. But that's it." She sighed. "Believe me, I'm not the first girl she's been with or the last, for that matter." She pulled at the back of her neck roughly. "For years there's been rumors floating around about her. I, for one, don't think people would be totally shocked."

Meg glanced over her shoulder as she paralleled into a spot outside her favorite burger joint. "So is she, like, worried about getting movie roles if she comes out?"

"I doubt it."

"Maybe, though. Isn't that what all the closeted homos are afraid of?"

Tracy cocked her head to the side to face Meg. "Except she's not an actress."

Meg gave a slow affirmative nod. "Not an actress." She wiggled her eyebrows. "Now we're getting somewhere."

CHAPTER NINE

I'm going to the pool." Lexi stood in the center of the living room addressing both her parents directly for the first time in days.

"Okay." Chris folded down the corner of the *New York Times* real estate section to make eye contact.

Marnie didn't look up from the Book Review. "Dinner's at five. You know the rules, no wet bathing suits at my table."

Lexi dug deep, swallowing her nerves over what she was about to say. "I'm not coming to dinner." She knew she was playing dirty. But they'd started it.

Marnie rested the newspaper on her lap, giving Lexi the attention she wanted, but it was Chris who spoke, her tone full of concern. "Why not?"

Lexi looked back and forth between her mothers. "I know Sunday dinner is like the most important thing in this family." She was being overdramatic, but she didn't care. She was angry and hurt and she wanted them to know it. "I'm not coming." Lexi cleared her throat, maintaining her composure as she continued. "I told you a month ago—I'm getting married—and you haven't even asked me about it. Not once. Not about what kind of dress I want or where it's going to be. Nothing." Her throat stung as her emotions rose to the surface. "You didn't even tell your best friends about it." Her voice hitched in her throat and her eyes watered. "I can't figure out if you think I'm not going to go through with it or if you are ashamed of me for marrying Jesse." She wiped the tears away hastily, her anger returning. "Whatever it is, I don't care." Her voice cracked again. "I know you hate Jesse because of everything that happened with Aunt Mary."

She licked her lips and shrugged her shoulders. "Believe me, I'm not ecstatic about it either. It's not ideal. She's not perfect." She raked a few wayward curls back off her face and jutted her chin out. "Neither am I," she announced, remembering vividly her own recent gaffe at the Cape. "She loves me anyway." She closed her mouth tightly, clenching her teeth a little. "I am going to marry her," she stated resolutely. "I'm sorry if that disappoints you."

She turned and walked to the top of the stairs but picked her head up and glowered at her parents as she gripped the railing. "But you know what disappoints me?" She looked back and forth between her mothers. "Pretty much everything about the way you guys are handling it."

When Marnie and Chris both tried to interrupt at the same time, Lexi held up her hands to stop them. "I'm not fighting about it," she said, licking her full lips. "Not today." She adjusted her pool bag on her shoulder. "I'm going to the pool with my friends and then I'm having a barbecue at Jesse's." She exchanged eye contact with both of them. "Until you take this seriously, don't expect to see me at your precious Sunday dinners."

Lexi descended the stairs and walked out of the house, hearing their combined silence behind her as she headed out into the afternoon heat.

❖

Meg was already set up in their favorite corner at the pool with bits of her belongings spread out over several lounge chairs pulled close together. She'd even managed to secure a spot that included one of the round picnic tables with an umbrella for shade, in case they wanted it as the day wore on. As the pool area began to fill, she could sense her blood pressure climbing over the amount of space she'd managed to single-handedly commandeer. Unless it was a special event, the Bay West pool was only open to residents and their guests. But on an afternoon like this, with the fourth straight day of temperatures hitting the upper nineties, it was a safe bet every dyke in the tristate area would be calling in favors for an invite. She could feel some looks being tossed in her direction, so she breathed a sigh of relief at the sight of Lexi heading her way.

"Thank God you're here." Meg moved her mesh swim bag off the lounge chair next to her. "How'd it go with your moms?"

"It went." Lexi kicked off her flip-flops, ditched her tank and shorts, and settled her shapely body into the cushioned chair. "Where's Tracy?"

"She has some dinner thing with her family today. Asked me to send her regrets." Meg waved across the distance to Jesse, who was still by the entrance chatting with a neighbor whose name Meg didn't know. "Are you all squared away for the party later?"

Lexi smiled and nodded, sliding on her shades and reaching for the mildest sunscreen Meg had ever seen. Like Chris, who was her birth mother, Lexi had beautiful dark brown eyes and medium-toned skin that the sun burnished a deep brown by July 1. Meg couldn't be more different. Fair with freckles, she saw little point in applying anything with an SPF lower than fifty.

"Is Betsy coming?" Meg asked as she flipped through a magazine.

"Not until later." Lexi lifted her body up and leaned on her elbows as she surveyed the pool area which was getting more crowded by the minute. "Jess said she had some stuff to do this afternoon."

Meg didn't look up from her reading. "With her girlfriend?"

"I don't think so. I think she's helping her mother with something at the house." Lexi sat all the way up and put her hair in a loose bun on top of her head. "They're not together, by the way."

"You sure about that? They looked like they might be together the other night."

Lexi applied a light layer of lip balm and rubbed her lips together. "Nope. Definitely over." She crossed one leg over the other and stole a glance at Meg's magazine. "It's like I told you before, CJ's band was playing in the city last week. She stopped by to see Betsy and pick up some things she still had at her place." She drummed her fingers on the arms of her chair. "It's a done deal. You can tell Tracy she's in the clear," she added with a smile. "Although you know Betsy"—Lexi tipped her head to look at Meg over the rims of her sunglasses—"she's not really the type to go for the random hookup with somebody who's in town for a few days." She pushed her glasses up her nose. "Even if she is hot."

"Yeah, well, you never know." Meg made the comment offhandedly, remembering Betsy's reaction the night she had first seen

Tracy's picture on Meg's cell phone and their subsequent conversation. She scanned the pool area, thoroughly enjoying the throngs of scantily dressed women who were piling in. Her eyes stopped when she spotted Becca and Mia at the gate with Jesse. The words were out of her mouth before she had a chance to filter. "Ugh, what are they doing here?"

Lexi turned to her, thoroughly surprised by Meg's reaction. "We invited them."

Meg didn't answer. There was nothing to say. She just stared at them, already with their hands all over each other's bodies, as Jesse signed them in.

Lexi touched Meg's forearm. "Are you mad?" she asked in a very serious voice.

"No," Meg answered, but her tone gave her away.

"Oh my God, you're mad. Shit, Meg," Lexi said, the disappointment in her voice clearly aimed at herself.

"It's fine, Lex."

"But you told me you were fine with them coming to the barbecue. I really thought you were."

Meg tried to blow it off. "I was. I am." She paused. "It's stupid." She shook her head, cutting herself off. "Forget it."

Lexi kept her voice low. "I'm sorry, Meg. I only invited them because it's like a hundred degrees out." She fussed nervously with her hair, taking it out and retying it up again. "I feel so bad right now."

It was obvious Lexi was upset about her own decision, and the last thing Meg wanted to do was make a scene, particularly since everyone was headed their way. "It's no big deal." She pushed her sunglasses up onto her head, so Lexi could see her eyes and know she was sincere. She wasn't mad at Lexi and she understood her actions. She didn't have time to explain to her best friend that even though she'd seen Becca and Mia out together a slew of times over the last year and she'd hung out with them plenty, she just wasn't in the mood for them today. The thought of having to watch her ex-girlfriend and her ex-casual-fling rub suntan lotion all over each other was enough to make her gag. But she was cordial to them anyway as they dropped their gear on the lounger next to her. She asked them how the summer was going and tried not to roll her eyes as they checked with each other for visual reassurance before answering. Then, as they each took off their outer layer of clothing, Meg saw it. Matching tattoos. Mia's right shoulder, the side of Becca's rib cage. It was some kind of ancient writing, undoubtedly professing their love for each other, etched out in Sanskrit or Aramaic or some other dead language. Meg kept herself from commenting, willing her eyes to stay focused on their faces as she continued small talk for another few minutes before excusing herself to cool off in the pool.

She lowered her body into the water off the side ledge and let herself slide all the way under, kicking off the side and gliding the entire length of the pool through the tepid water. Popping her head out, she looked toward her cohort of friends laughing and talking in the corner. She ran her hand through her short hair, fanning out the excess moisture. She couldn't do it. Not today. She was going to have to come up with an exit strategy. Almost immediately a crazy idea occurred to her.

Pulling herself out of the pool, she made her way back to the group just as everyone else was getting ready to go in. It was perfect. She toweled herself off, sat back down, and reopened her magazine across her bended knees. She reached for her phone and typed the message before losing her courage.

Surviving the heat?

The response was immediate. *Barely. You?*

Same. You have AC?

Yes, but the city is so cut back to avoid power outages that it's not much cooler inside my apartment than outside. The message was punctuated with an old-school colon and open parentheses sad face.

Meg's thumbs moved at a rapid pace. She knew if she thought about it for even a second, she would chicken out. *Want to catch a movie? Buy ourselves some cold air for 2 hours?*

There was a several-minute pause before any response came and Meg hoped her suggestion hadn't freaked Sasha out. She waited nervously until the next text appeared.

The Vengeance Seven is playing at Village Gardens Cineplex at 3:35...

The low-budget thriller was probably the last movie on earth Meg wanted to see. She typed back quickly. *I'll meet you there.*

Thankfully, Lexi exited the pool before the rest of the gang. Meg was just putting her stuff together to go. Before Lexi could say a word Meg started talking.

"Don't take this the wrong way."

"You're leaving?" Lexi asked, completely shocked.

"It's not because of them." Meg nodded in the direction of the pool where Mia and Becca were canoodling as they talked to Jesse. "Seriously, it's not," she emphasized. And in truth, it wasn't just Mia and Becca that had her running for the hills. The barbecue had basically turned into a couples party, and the idea of being the lone single person there was depressing. So she lied.

"Honestly, Lex. Sasha just texted. She's kind of bummed out." Meg shrugged her shoulders. "She asked if I'd meet up with her in the city. I feel bad for her, I think she's homesick." She watched Lexi's eyes squint as she analyzed her explanation and knew her BFF didn't quite believe her. She blew past it. "You don't care, right? You have a ton of people to hang out with today. She's got nobody," she added, playing up the martyr routine heavier than was necessary.

"Sure. Fine."

"Okay. I gotta jet. Explain to the others for me."

Meg grabbed her bag and backed away. She avoided direct eye contact, but could see Lexi's expression soften as she answered, "Yeah, of course."

She knew her friend didn't buy her story but could tell that somehow, even through Meg's string of half-truths, Lexi completely understood.

❖

Meg had to hustle to make the two-thirty boat into the city. There was no time to shower, so she put more product in her short messy hair, ran a few swipes of deodorant under her arms, and threw on a clean T-shirt and shorts.

She stood by the open door of her Ford Escape Hybrid, brushing over the outside of her pockets to make sure she had the essentials. Wallet, check. Phone, check. Keys in her hand, good to go. She was just about to sidle into the driver's seat to chauffeur herself to the Staten Island Ferry, when her neighbors Rose and Teddy flagged her down from across the street. Teddy's cousin Reina was with them, a beach towel slung over her shoulder. Meg started out of the driveway slowly, pulling alongside them.

"Girl, where you running off to in this heat?" Teddy asked good-naturedly.

"I have to head into the city. Long story." Meg shook her head, hoping if she breezed over it there wouldn't be any follow-up questions.

"You're coming back for the barbecue later, right?"

Meg scrunched her face dramatically. "Doubtful. I'll do my best, though." She couldn't help but notice Reina looked genuinely dismayed at her response. Hmm, interesting. "I'll see what I can do," she lied. "I'm off. Have fun, guys." She shifted into drive and zipped down the street.

She had a ferry to catch.

❖

The Vengeance Seven was a completely ridiculous gruesome romp but the theater was ice cold, and Sasha and Meg relished the relief. Sasha spent the two hours alternating shrieks and giggles and on three occasions she grabbed onto the short sleeve of Meg's tee, ducking her head into Meg's arm to shield her eyes. Meg derived far too much pleasure from these moments, which she was sure came purely from Sasha's attempt to avoid the gratuitous bloodshed. Each time it happened, Meg laughed out loud, harder than was necessary, attempting to cover her deep enjoyment of Sasha's casual touch.

After the show they walked a few blocks in the thick heat before taking to the High Line to continue their way-too-serious discussion of whether or not the villain truly got his comeuppance, and the likelihood of the lone survivor's chances at a normal life. As they admired the wild grasses and flowers along the converted train trestle, they switched to talking about work, family, friends, and the summer. Roughly at the midpoint of the elevated park, Meg caught sight of a cute little Mexican place on the corner, half a block up. Swallowing her nerves, she faced Sasha.

"Feel like grabbing a drink?"

"Yes." Sasha accompanied her answer with a firm nod almost as though she had been waiting for Meg to ask.

Ten minutes later they were seated in the open air, each armed with a cold beer, debating appetizers. When Sasha excused herself to use the ladies' room, Meg took the opportunity to answer a string of texts from Lexi that included a heartfelt mea culpa over the Mia-Becca invite. Lexi also expressed genuine concern about Meg's whereabouts and emotional state. Meg typed back quickly that she wasn't mad at all and she was having a good day. She decided to prove her point with a photo. She was smiling big, holding the phone at arm's length trying to get the right angle for a good selfie when Sasha returned, eyeing Meg's actions curiously.

"Just trying to convince my friend that I'm not by myself wallowing." Seeing that her explanation didn't entirely make sense, she blinked dramatically and shook her head. "Just trust me."

"I can do better than that." Sasha nodded. "I can help." She took the phone from Meg's outstretched hand, but instead of taking the picture, she waved expectantly at a member of the waitstaff as she said to Meg over her shoulder, "I have a better idea."

When the waiter approached, Sasha sweetly asked him to take their picture. She handed him the phone and stepped around the table behind Meg's chair. Sasha bent down, wrapped her arms across Meg's chest from behind, and leaned next to Meg, their cheeks brushing up against one another. Meg heard the click of the phone's camera several times before the waiter handed it back to her with a coy smile.

"Send her that." Sasha settled back into her chair smiling. "This way she sees you're not alone."

Meg was virtually speechless. This whole afternoon, from the series of touches at the movie theater to Sasha's spontaneous embrace for the photo—coming from anyone else, Meg would be sure this was flirting. She didn't even allow herself to consider it further, selecting the picture she looked the least surprised in and sending it to Lexi with the caption, *Having fun.* She put her phone away and suppressed a smile knowing her minimalist detail was sure to elicit a flurry of new texts from Lexi.

"So why does your friend think you are wallowing?" Sasha asked, punctuating her question with a swig of her beer.

Meg hung her head a little letting out a playful sigh. "It's a long story," she answered with a smile.

Sasha held the mood. "I have a full drink. And food on the way. Lay it on me."

Meg didn't hold back. She started by telling Sasha about all of her friends at the development and how they knew each other. She went into detail about who had dated whom, who wanted to date each other, and who were still friends despite having slept together. She finished with the rundown of her own two-year relationship with Becca, her fling with Mia, and how Mia and Becca had ended up dating each other.

"Look, I don't even care most of the time. They actually seem really happy together." She took a sip of her drink. "I'm just a little jealous, I guess." She shrugged slightly, surprised at her own candor. "I want what they have." She held her hands up. "I mean, not with either one of them," she added for clarification.

Sasha looked right at her. "I'm still floored you're single."

Meg tilted her head at the comment and opened her mouth to speak but didn't get the chance as the waiter arrived with their entrees. Placing their plates down, he bent toward the table. "I'm sorry to interrupt you ladies." He was heavy on the sibilant *S* as he continued. "It seems the two gentlemen at the bar would like to buy you a round of drinks."

Meg looked over and saw them through the wide-open window. She was about to ask Sasha, but Sasha was already answering. "Tell them thanks but no, thanks." Her voice was stern but friendly.

The waiter looked between them and smirked. "I told them they were wasting their time, but they insisted I ask," he explained.

"It's no problem." Sasha smiled her beautiful broad smile. "I actually could use another drink, though." She looked over at Meg. "Meg?"

"Sure," Meg responded, eying her bottle, which was still a quarter full.

Sasha reached for the waiter's arm. "Just make sure it's on our bill."

The waiter winked at her. "Got it, hon." He smiled with satisfaction as he went to retrieve their drinks and deliver the rejection to the men inside, who were still ogling them.

Meg was appreciating the exchange as much as the waiter, but suddenly she felt bad knowing the three of them were in on a joke, only Sasha wasn't really in on it. Even though there was a huge part of her that was enjoying the confusion, her guilt won out. Meg bit her lip but was unable to remain silent. "They think we're together," she blurted.

"What?" Sasha laughed, confused by the outburst.

Meg hunched forward in her chair. "I'm sorry." She rubbed her temples. "The waiter. Probably the guys at the bar too." She met Sasha's eyes. "They think we're a couple."

"Okay."

Meg gritted her teeth, nervous about Sasha's reaction once she fully caught on to what she was saying. "I'm sorry."

"For what?"

Meg looked around her. "You know…that they think you're a lesbian." She looked down at her food and then up again. "You know, because you're here with me. And the drinks, and the whole picture thing before," she added. "I'm just, I'm sorry."

"Stop apologizing. I don't care." Sasha separated the triangles of her cheese quesadilla, allowing it to cool. "Doesn't bother me."

"Really?" Meg asked, clearly surprised.

"Really."

They locked eyes for a split second before Meg forced herself to look away for fear that Sasha could see right through her. Meg was afraid her thoughts were written all over her face and she worried Sasha would realize right then and there that Meg was into her. Like really, really into her. Meg changed the subject immediately, praying her voice came out calm.

"So, no boyfriend, huh?"

It was a loaded question but Sasha didn't really answer it anyway. She simply shook her head and when she finished chewing she flipped the question around on Meg. "What about you? Did you ever date boys?" She shifted her blue eyes up at Meg, obviously curious about the answer.

"Not really." Meg smiled.

"So you've just known you were gay forever?"

Meg wiped the sweat from the fresh beer the waiter had just brought over. "Not forever." She picked up the bottle and peeled off the cocktail napkin stuck to its base. "I don't know, maybe forever." She let out a little laugh at her own waffling. "I made out with boys in high school," she said, taking a long sip of beer. "But my first real relationship was with a girl. With Tracy, actually, my friend who's staying with me now." Meg shrugged her shoulders and smiled mischievously. "All girls ever since."

Sasha sipped her beer. "What about Tracy now? Are you guys—"

Meg laughed out loud. "Oh my God, no." She raised her eyebrows. "That was a long, long time ago." Meg smiled inwardly at the memory before she decided to turn the tables on Sasha in an attempt at light humor. "What about you"—she nodded with her chin—"you ever date girls?"

"Not date. No." Sasha took a second before continuing. She reached for her beer again. "I did, of course, participate in the requisite college experimenting."

Meg almost choked on her chicken taco. She wanted to ask a thousand questions but tried to play it cool. "I'm listening," she said, playfully encouraging Sasha to continue.

Sasha blushed a little as she pushed her hair away from her face. "It was mostly for my boyfriend's benefit." She looked slightly nervous as she explained. "My last year at Oxford, my boyfriend, his best friend, and his best friend's girlfriend. We all hung out together. Mostly drinking." She tilted her head to the side and lifted up one shoulder. "Sometimes we put on a little show for the boys. You know how it goes."

Meg had no idea how it went. She was dying for the details, but she didn't want to seem overeager so she tried for casual. "And what happened to this boyfriend?"

"Nothing. Didn't last." Sasha didn't seem too bothered by the outcome of her relationship as she pulled off another piece of quesadilla and detached the cheese stringing down. "But, you know, no regrets," she added with a smile before biting off the end.

Meg was more than confused by Sasha's admission and cavalier conversation about her experimentation and the fact that she had no regrets. She didn't know if that referred to kissing a girl or breaking up with her boyfriend, or both. She was terrified to ask for clarification so she let it go when their talk switched seamlessly to work and their friends.

After splitting the bill they walked to the corner, side by side, knowing they were headed in opposite directions. Meg told Sasha she'd had a great day. Sasha responded by saying she was glad Meg had called her. They exchanged a weird hug and parted ways. Meg didn't dare turn around.

Chapter Ten

Tracy had been in New York for a month and had yet to spend even a few hours at the Kitchen—famous girl bar, lesbian landmark, and one of her all-time favorite places to pick up girls. On Tuesday she and Meg had made a plan to remedy that oversight during the coming weekend. By Friday, the whole crew was on board as well.

Their original plan involved grabbing an early bite together before heading over to the Greenwich Village hot spot, but Meg had gotten stuck at work and pushed dinner entirely out of the plan. Tracy didn't mind the change. She'd spent the afternoon playing pickup basketball with some rowdy teenagers at an event sponsored by her favorite charity and was happy to put in some extra volunteer hours while she waited. With the bonus time she even snuck in a quick run along the West Side waterfront before hitting the showers at Equinox.

When Meg and Tracy finally met up at the Kitchen it was nine fifteen and the crowd was still sparse, giving them time for a quick drink together before the rest of their friends petered in.

"How'd it go with Sasha this evening?" Tracy was quick with the sarcasm, while making eye contact with the bartender to place their order. "Make any headway?" she added without looking at Meg.

"Very funny."

"I wasn't kidding. Why didn't you ask her to come for a drink?" She handed the cute brunette behind the bar her credit card and gave her a friendly smile as she clinked her vodka soda with Meg's before taking the first sip.

"I almost did actually." Meg grabbed the short glass and squeezed the lime wedge, before poking it to the bottom with the thin black straw.

"But?"

"I thought it was too, I don't know, weird, I guess." She put the straw on the bar and took a sip of her drink, swallowing hard at the liquor that hadn't quite blended yet.

"What's so weird about asking her to come out with your friends?" Tracy goaded. "You already went on a date with her." Tracy had been teasing her all week after hearing about Meg's outing with Sasha.

"It wasn't a date, jackass."

Tracy dropped her chin dramatically. "Movie. Dinner. Drinks." She looked right at Meg. "That's a date."

Meg had a hard time disagreeing with the logic. "Well, tell that to her," she mumbled into her tumbler.

"Oh, believe me, I will." Tracy grinned, revealing her perfectly straight teeth. "If I ever get to meet her."

Before Meg could come up with a clever response, Lexi and Jesse cleared the archway into the back room and beelined for them. Betsy trailed them, half a step behind, monitoring her phone as she waded into the room. Meg couldn't help but notice Tracy straighten up a little at the sight of Betsy. Watching closely, Meg saw her friend reflexively rub the back of her neck and smooth the front of her shirt. They were small, subtle preening gestures and Meg doubted anyone else noticed at all. But she had seen Tracy in action before. She knew the signs. Meg suppressed her smile and sipped her drink while listening to the others chat about their respective workdays. When Betsy excused herself to take a call outside, Meg watched Tracy make her move, waiting a scant few minutes before following her. It was on. Meg mentally crossed her fingers, hoping her two friends would find a connection.

❖

Tracy's timing was right on the money. By the time she made it through the crowd and exited the back door of the bar, Betsy was standing a few feet away finishing up her call.

"Hey." Tracy angled for Betsy's attention the second she hung up.

Betsy pressed the home button on her phone several times and looked up. "Hi," she answered, still looking at her phone as she spoke.

Tracy walked toward her, full of swagger. Betsy was standing near a railing that cordoned off an outdoor section of the bar that no one was taking advantage of at this early hour. She reached Betsy's side, leaned back against the banister, slid her hands in her pockets, and looked up at the sky. "It's gorgeous out here, huh?"

Betsy crossed her arms, challenging Tracy's intention with a look that was frisky but also cut through Tracy's act. "I'm sorry, did you come out here to smoke? Or..." She let the question hang playfully between them.

Not one to be intimidated, Tracy met Betsy's eyes directly. "I came out here to talk to you." She watched Betsy blush and look down at the ground to hide her smile. "That your girlfriend?" Tracy gestured with her chin at the phone Betsy still held in her right hand.

Betsy whipped her head around and looked behind her.

"No, I meant on the phone," Tracy clarified.

Betsy let a little laugh slip out before she answered. "No. That was work." She looked at Tracy. "I don't have a girlfriend."

"Funny, 'cause when I just asked, you turned around as though she might be behind you." Tracy tapped her finger on her lips in mock interrogation.

"Yeah, sorry. That was..." Betsy slipped her hands in her back pockets and rocked her hips forward and back as she drifted off. She bit her lower lip, still holding in a smile. "My ex had this habit of showing up out of the blue." She widened her eyes. "You might remember that from a few weeks ago."

"So that was your *ex*?" Tracy's emphasis on the word was heavy, her intent obvious.

"Yes." Betsy stopped to look at her phone before continuing. "She was in town for a gig. We had a few final things to sort out." She shrugged a little.

"What does she play?" Tracy asked, knowing some of the details already.

"Bass." Betsy answered, squinting her eyes in question as to how Tracy had come into the particulars.

Tracy gave a quick nod with her head toward the bar. "The girls were talking a little." She pushed a lock of hair off her forehead but the humidity made it droop forward again immediately. "I would have pegged her anyway. She's got the look."

"That's right, you're from LA."

Tracy nodded. "Safe to say I know the type. Crazy hours, on the road all the time." She raised her eyebrows. "So you and the ex…you two are done? For sure?"

"Mm-hmm."

Tracy cocked her head from side to side prying even further. "No lingering uncertainty about the future…"

"Nope." Betsy didn't seem the least bit unsettled by Tracy's probing questions. "That is a closed book," she added demonstratively.

"My condolences over your breakup." Tracy grinned from ear to ear. She looked down in mock gravity and nodded sagely. "But it is possible your not having a girlfriend is a good thing—"

The sound of Betsy's phone ringing interrupted her. Betsy put up one finger, signaling that Tracy should hold her thought. She answered the phone and Tracy watched as Betsy listened, then looked at her watch and tilted her gaze up and to the right as she calculated something in her head. She asked some questions about levels and results, and then she stopped whoever she was talking to by telling them she would be there as soon as possible. She turned to Tracy.

"Sorry." She half frowned. "Duty calls." Betsy waved her phone in the air and started backing down the street. "Do me a favor and tell those guys I had to go."

Tracy nodded and smiled to herself as she watched Betsy jog down the street into the distance. With a little bounce in her step she headed back into the dark bar, not at all discouraged by the course their conversation had taken. Tracy found her friends and explained Betsy had been called into work. She got herself a fresh drink and returned to the group with a paper flyer she ripped off the wall, thrusting it into Meg's face and looking serious as hell.

"Tell me we are doing this."

❖

The Bay West Shuffleboard Social was something of legend at the development. An annual event held on the Sunday of Labor Day weekend, it combined a shuffleboard tournament with a day-long party that turned into a social by evening. It was campy and ridiculous and Meg absolutely loved it.

Since the moment Tracy spotted the flyer she hadn't stopped talking about it. Meg should have realized from the get-go that with Tracy around she'd be strong-armed into playing, and while in theory she wasn't against participating, the tournament was a little intense for her liking and she was less than thrilled to ruin such a good day by being bogged down in matches. She'd had a blast the previous year dividing her time between watching some of the games and bopping around the party. There was great music, good food, and tons of girls. What more could a single lesbian ask for?

Sometime after noon, Meg was still in boxer shorts and a T-shirt flipping over her French toast at the stove, when Tracy burst through the front door sweaty from her run.

"You're just getting up?" Tracy asked tersely.

"I've been up for a while," Meg retorted. "Read the paper, had some coffee. Watched a little porn. Not in that order, mind you," she added offhandedly while reaching for some strawberries in the fridge. "But all in all, I'd say I've accomplished quite a bit already this morning," she said, returning to the stove with a playful grin.

"Jesus, I hope you didn't expend all your energy on yourself." Tracy grabbed a cold water from the fridge.

"Me? You went running."

"You should have come with me. Loosened up a little."

"Oh, I'm loose." Meg flashed a devilish grin. Seeing Tracy was less than amused, Meg breathed out melodramatically. "You have to chill." She pointed at her breakfast. "You want some?"

Tracy looked at her in disbelief at her offer.

Meg answered with bewilderment of her own. "What? It has fruit on it."

"And sugar. And syrup, which is just more sugar."

Meg sat down at the breakfast bar with her plate, noisily reaching for silverware. "Trace." She waited for her friend to make eye contact before she continued. "You have to promise you're not going to be a baby all day after we lose."

Tracy looked unbelievably serious sitting across from her as she wiped the sweat from her forehead. "Why do you think we're going to lose?"

"Promise." Meg made the demand with her fork raised in the air, half a strawberry hanging from its tines.

There was a second of tense silence as they locked eyes. Finally Tracy relented, breaking into a full smile. "Okay. I promise." She got up from her stool. "Geez, a little optimism wouldn't kill you." She headed for the stairs. "Now hurry up and get ready. I want to go over early and scout the competition."

Meg shook her head as she chewed. With her mouth still full, she called after Tracy, "You have problems."

She heard Tracy open the linen closet at the top of the stairs as she sing-songed her response. "I am completely aware of that."

❖

At two fifteen, the setup was in full swing. Meg sat on the makeshift bleachers that had been arranged around the painted concrete courts and watched as Tracy sized up various women breaking into teams and sneaking a few practice slides in. Meg recognized most of them from her neighborhood. She couldn't have cared less about their shuffleboard skills.

She turned her attention instead to the DJ arranging his outdoor booth with piles of colorful leis and other giveaways for the spectators who were slowly dribbling in. The development had its own merch stand set up just outside the court area with loads of Bay West swag for sale—sweatshirts, T-shirts, beer mugs, bumper stickers, key chains, and more. Meg had to hand it to Kam Browne, the woman knew how to capitalize on an idea. From a business perspective, there was very little she didn't squeeze a dime from. Meg's eyes drifted over to one of the two outdoor bars—she'd witnessed several people sipping frozen daiquiris as they passed by, and she made the decision right then and there to get one, figuring the alcohol might alleviate some of her edginess over the impending cutthroat competition.

She walked back to the court area armed with a frothy piña colada and addressed Tracy's look of judgment immediately.

"Relax, dude." Meg found the straw with her lips and took a long sip. "If my pool playing skills are anything to go by, you want me half in the bag. Trust me."

Tracy gave a deep sigh of disapproval but Meg was saved a full-on lecture by the arrival of Betsy, who approached them with a gorgeous blonde in tow. Knowing Tracy had yet to meet her, Meg was quick with the introduction.

"Tracy, this is Allison Smith, she works with Jesse. Allison, this is Tracy. She's visiting from California."

Allison looked Tracy up and down, inspecting her for only a fraction of a second before proclaiming, "Hey, you're Tracy Allen. The golfer." She spoke with an air of confidence in her discovery.

The other girls turned to Allison, their faces expressing unified shock at über-girly Allison recognizing an obscure athlete. She met their blank stares with her signature no-holds-barred attitude.

"What?" She raised her eyebrows at the group. "I can't follow sports?" She jutted her jaw out a little, calling them all out. "Because I'm femme?" She flicked her perfectly highlighted blond hair over each shoulder, and opened her eyes wide for continued emphasis. "Stereotype much?" She finished her tongue-in-cheek quip with a big smile and stuck her hand toward Tracy.

Tracy smiled warmly. "Nice to meet you."

A minute later Lexi and her sister Andrea joined the group, excited to play the tournament together as they did every year. Their arrival split the group in two and Allison took the opportunity to speak to Tracy again.

"I watched your round with Michelle Varga at the Classico Challenge two years ago. You almost beat her." She licked her lips. "You had some really beautiful swings that day."

"Thank you," Tracy answered sincerely. "Were you there?"

"No, I watched it on Golf Network."

Tracy couldn't hide her surprise. "Wow, I didn't even know it was televised."

"It was shown in a late-night spot." Allison looked like she felt bad telling Tracy the truth, but she continued anyway. "On delay." She clutched her purse with both hands. "Sometimes I have trouble sleeping," she admitted.

"Well, golf will certainly help with that," Meg joked, eliciting snickers from the girls and an elbow to the ribs from Tracy.

"Are you playing?" Tracy asked Allison.

She scrunched up her nose. "Purely a spectator." Eyeing Meg's drink, she added, "That looks up my alley, though."

Tracy turned her attention to Betsy and made direct eye contact with her for the first time since she'd arrived. "What about you, Betsy? No shuffleboard?"

"No partner." Betsy cocked her head to the side, in the direction of Allison. "You heard the woman."

"Play with me." Tracy held Betsy's gaze.

Betsy was taken aback and gestured toward Meg. "I thought…" She raised her eyebrows in question. "Isn't Meg your partner?"

"She is," Tracy answered. "But I'm practically forcing her." She looked over at Meg. "She's only doing it because she's an awesome friend and she felt bad saying no to me."

Betsy checked Meg's face to assess the truthfulness of Tracy's statement. Meg looked right at her, thrilled at the possibility of being relieved. "Be my guest."

"You sure?" Betsy asked Meg.

"Absolutely."

Tracy clapped her hands together. "Great, it's settled then."

Meg wagged her index finger up in the air in warning. "Betsy, you should know what you're getting into. Tracy does not adjust well to losing."

"Who says we're losing?" Betsy responded, without missing a beat.

Tracy bent her knees and clenched both of her hands in a small cheer. "Oh my God, you are perfect." She looked at Meg. "You have *so* been replaced."

Meg shook her head playfully. "Come on, Al, let's get some drinks before we watch these novices get schooled by a bunch of old ladies."

With that the group splintered again. Tracy and Betsy headed off to find Kam Browne and notify her of the change while Meg and Allison went to the bar before securing good seats.

Armed with ice-cold beverages, they settled down near the center court on the first row of the bleachers, giving them easy access for replenishments and also the opportunity to get up and chat with friends as they saw them coming in throughout the day. Meg spent the afternoon watching and not watching, which was just how she liked it. She got a chance to talk to Jesse, who arrived late in the day, and together they watched as Lexi and her sister were eliminated by Del and Aimee, a couple in their early sixties who lived around the block.

As the sun began to set, Meg leaned against the fence and caught sight of a pale brunette in the distance. She wished it was Sasha even though she knew it wasn't. The distant stranger didn't even really look like her. But Meg couldn't help but wonder who Sasha was with right now and what she might be doing. They had talked about weekend plans over lunch on Thursday, so Meg knew she was somewhere in the city, spending time with Jane-Anne and the gang. As always, Meg had toyed with the idea of inviting her to the social, but didn't. It wasn't because she was afraid Sasha would say no. Actually the opposite was true. She thought she would say yes. And then Sasha would be here at Bay West with Meg. But not *with* Meg. And that was a reality she was not ready to face.

Several drinks in, she reached for her phone, full of rum-infused courage, and almost dialed. She stopped when she heard a familiar voice over the sound system and turned around to see Lexi and her sister in the DJ booth announcing the semifinals were under way. She had to laugh at her friends, who had commandeered the microphone and were presently giving a full-fledged running commentary on the match, which featured their parents— Chris and Marnie—against none other than Tracy and Betsy. Meg put her phone away and rushed to get a better view.

It was a nail-biter. The two teams were shot for shot, point for point, giving up scoring opportunities to knock each other's best discs out of the way. It was definitely tense but also hilarious to watch, as Lexi continued narrating throughout. Because she knew all four competitors so well, she inserted humor at every chance. They played up the age difference between the teams with Lexi telling her moms not to worry about the outcome because they might be able to protest the match due to Tracy's status as a professional athlete. This led to a very funny back and forth between the sisters about the legitimacy of golf as a bona fide athletic event. The crowd was in stitches, and even Tracy laughed when she missed a pivotal scoring opportunity.

Meg studied her two friends playing as a team. They seemed to fit together amazingly well. She saw Tracy place small touches on Betsy's back and arms, more than was really necessary, as they discussed shots and strategy. Betsy didn't seem to mind, and she sought Tracy's input before each turn, finishing with high-fives after every point. Near the end of the match, on a very tricky turn that could have been the game winner for Tracy and Betsy, Betsy called Tracy over. They assessed the shot together with Tracy standing behind Betsy, her hand on Betsy's hip as she utilized a hand-over-hand illustration, presumably to demonstrate the amount of pressure she should use. It was pretty hot looking and Meg was fairly sure she wasn't the only one in the audience who thought they might kiss before they broke apart and Betsy sailed the game-winning disc down the length of the deck. Even Lexi was speechless.

The crowd erupted in cheers. Tracy picked Betsy up and spun her around.

They moved on to the final round where they faced Del and Aimee, the returning champions who had knocked out Lexi and her sister earlier in the day. Betsy and Tracy put up a good fight, but they were no match for the seasoned couple. Tracy was surprisingly good-natured about the loss as they rejoined their friends afterward.

"Way to go, guys." Jesse was the first to congratulate them. "Second place. Nicely done."

Tracy smiled and looked at Meg, who was not surprised at all. She nodded at Tracy's hand, which held a small off-white envelope. "What'd ya get?"

"Gift certificate. To"—she paused, pulling out the slip of paper inside—"Lombardo's." She slid the voucher back into the envelope and handed it to Betsy.

"No way." Betsy waved her off as she took a really long chug of the draft beer Allison had handed to her. "You should take it. You totally carried us at the end."

"I don't even know where it is."

"It's just down the block," Allison offered, sounding more than a little hopeful her two cents might earn an invite from Tracy.

Tracy kept her attention on Betsy. "Let's go together. Celebrate our near victory."

"Okay." Betsy smiled.

As the night cooled off, the party moved inside the Commons where they all drank, danced, and said good-bye to one more summer.

CHAPTER ELEVEN

"I still can't believe you guys almost won the shuffleboard tournament." Lexi wiped her mouth with a napkin as she sat at Meg's kitchen table. She took another bite of the grilled chicken and avocado wrap Tracy had prepared for their dinner. "This is so good, by the way."

Meg was busy wolfing down her food, so she couldn't immediately agree. She was already loving everything about this night. Her two closest buds, some good-natured gossip, and great food. Swallowing quickly she added, "Who knew you were so good in the kitchen?"

"You're letting me stay here, the least I can do is cook," Tracy said with a wink.

"Did you ever go out to dinner with Betsy?" Lexi asked through another mouthful.

"No." Tracy twisted her mouth to the side a little. "We've been texting back and forth for a while now. Scheduling issues," she said with an eyebrow raise. "Obviously not mine," she added. "I've got nothing but free time."

"Here's something I've been wondering about," Lexi said between bites. "Did anything happen with you and Allison that night?"

Meg perked up with interest to see Tracy's answer. Even though she was pretty sure nothing had transpired, despite Allison's clear desire, Meg had been pretty tanked by the end of the social, so it was possible she had missed something.

Tracy shook the question off immediately. "Not at all."

Lexi licked her lips and reached for her fork. "She was macking it to you pretty hard." She made the statement matter-of-factly as she stabbed at her spinach salad, pinning a few baby leaves before she slid the fork into her mouth.

Meg loved that her two closest confidantes had hit it off so easily. She assessed Tracy's body language as she waited for her response to the nonquestion Lexi had laid out.

Tracy just smiled. "Who is she again?" she asked, before rephrasing the question right away. "I mean, how does she fit in with you guys?" She swirled her wrap in a circle to indicate she meant Meg and Lexi and the larger group of friends, as well.

"She's a lawyer at Jesse's firm," Lexi offered.

Meg expounded. "Lexi used to intern for her." Lexi nodded agreement and Meg blurted out an idea that had just come to her. "You know, Trace, that may be the way to go."

Tracy flashed her dark eyes at Meg with a hint of suspicion, but Meg put her hand up to silence her for a second. "I'm just saying. I know you're into Betsy and all, but if you are looking for a quick hookup, something to help get you over your ex, Allison might be the answer. She's obviously into you." Meg put down her sandwich. "And Betsy"—she breathed out audibly—"Betsy can be complicated."

Tracy glanced down at her mostly empty plate. "Thanks for the tip," she said tersely. "By the way, what's up with you and Reina?" she challenged Meg with some zing in her voice. "I saw you talking during shuffleboard. Still convinced there's nothing there?"

Meg picked up on Tracy's curt tone right away. "Don't get mad at me, Trace. I'm not saying you shouldn't go for Betsy." She reached across the table and grabbed Tracy's tanned forearm. "Dude, I support whoever you date. Or fuck. Or whatever." She let go of her arm. "I'm on Team Tracy, okay?"

Tracy's expression softened, reading the sincerity in Meg's eyes. "I know." She pushed her plate to the center of the table. "Seriously though, about Reina. That girl is into you. It's all over her body language. And she's hot. What's the problem?"

Meg let out a small laugh. "You're wrong." She piled her fork and knife on the plate in front of her and leaned back in her chair. "Believe me, she's sweet, and we had a nice time talking the other night, but she's not interested in me like that."

Tracy stood up from the table. "Well, I'd bet money I'm not

wrong." She walked to the sink with her dishes. "And I think you should maybe take your own advice and give some consideration to what's right in front of you." She shrugged playfully as she started to clear the rest of the table.

During a lull in conversation the television in the background blared and the jingle of an entertainment magazine show filled the room.

A sports-music merger tops tonight's lead story, the host announced.

Meg's attention shifted to Tracy when her friend stopped in her tracks and stared at a picture of famous musician Jezebel Stone on the screen. Tracy quickly huffed out a laugh, but Meg was on to her. She exchanged an uncertain glance with Lexi to see if she'd picked up on it too as Tracy breezed past them to the sink, still looking over her shoulder. On the TV, a taped clip aired showing Jezebel hounded by photographers as she walked along the bright California sidewalk. The singer held up her left hand, showcasing a diamond band on her ring finger. She wore dark sunglasses and fake-smiled at the paparazzi as she told them in her world-famous sultry voice, *It's true.*

The story cut back to the anchorman. *That was Jezebel Stone confirming today she has indeed married San Diego Padres third baseman Jasper Lloyd. The two have had an up-and-down relationship over the past year with rumors of infidelity on both sides. Reps for both camps confirmed the couple wed earlier in a private ceremony at Stone's Hollywood Hills estate. The rushed nuptials have everyone speculating there might be a future musician, or athlete, in the not-too-distant future...*

Where Tracy had laughed mockingly at the segment initially, she seemed anything but amused by the full story.

Meg put it together right away. She muted the television and turned to her friend. "Trace, are you okay?"

"I'm fine." Tracy dropped silverware in the sink noisily. "It's fine," she repeated. She picked up the condiments that were still on the table. "Not my problem anymore. That"—she pointed with the pepper mill to the television in the next room—"is someone else's problem. Not mine."

Tracy walked from the sink to the table, seeming uncertain what to do with herself in the face of this startling information. She took a long gulp of water, wiped her mouth, and placed her glass on the table with a thump, cutting the tension.

"Jezebel Stone." Meg nodded, pulling out the chair next to her. "That's big." She looked over at Tracy, who sat still, twisting her water glass in front of her. "I get why you didn't tell me."

Tracy shifted her eyes to Lexi, who had remained silent the entire time. "I used to date her. Jezebel Stone." She tilted her head back and looked up at the ceiling. "We broke up, like, pretty much right before I came out here."

"I'm sorry." Lexi's voice was a mix of genuine concern and complete shock.

"Don't be." Tracy wiped at her eyes, even though there were no tears. "*I'm* sorry. For being so dramatic."

"Shut up, dude," Meg reprimanded.

Tracy leaned forward and put her elbows on the table. "I'm over it. I really am. I don't want you guys to think I'm not." She rubbed the back of her neck. "I'm used to seeing her face all the time—in magazines, the Internet, bullshit shows like this—I just"—she forced out a laugh—"I have to say, I did not expect to hear that."

"You guys were together a long time?" Lexi asked.

"Almost two years."

"What happened, if you don't mind me asking?" Lexi inadvertently glanced in the direction of the television. "Was it the baseball player?"

Tracy frowned. "Not at all. I knew about him. At least I thought I did." She chewed the inside of her mouth. "She told me they were friends. That he was her cover. They had an understanding." She put air quotes around the word.

Meg interrupted. "Wait, is he gay too?"

"I don't know. I doubt it though, now." Her voice grew agitated. "You heard the guy, they might be having a baby."

"They say that crap all the time about famous people," Lexi offered in support.

Tracy looked a little defeated. "Yeah, but she did marry him. So I'm thinking there's probably something going on." She fake-gagged a little, revealing her disgust at the thought. Then she stayed silent for a minute, looking out Meg's kitchen window as she bit her bottom lip over and over, keeping her gaze on the front lawn. "I knew I should have ended it a long time ago." She shook her head slowly. "I almost did, in fact."

"What happened?" Meg asked.

Tracy let out a big sigh and faced her friends. "Pretty much right after we got together, I realized she was not planning on coming out anytime soon. It was hard for me, so I talked to her about it." She looked over at Meg sincerely. "Meg, you know me. I have never pretended to be something I'm not. And God"—she pursed her lips—"I always swore if I was lucky enough to make it in golf, or anything, I wouldn't change. I would be who I am. I would be a role model." She pressed a sesame seed on the tabletop, picking it up with the pad of her middle finger. "It's just so messed up. There's all these kids, teenagers, out there. They need us." She scooted her chair back from the table and walked to the garbage can, flicking the crumb off her finger. "I explained all of this to Jez. How she could make a real difference in the world..." She shook her head as her voice faded out.

Walking back to the kitchen sink, Tracy seemed to regain her confidence as she told her saga while keeping busy with the cleanup chores. "Anyway, I told her I was done. I hated being a secret. I couldn't stand pretending to be her friend and watching her flirt with everyone right in front of me." She huffed. "*Part of the job*, she would say." Tracy looked over at her friends still seated at the table. "Almost a year into it we were both in Scotland at the same time. We had made plans to meet up. Secretly, of course." She let out a little chuckle. "She finally sent me the details for our rendezvous." She widened her eyes, clearly making fun of the drama surrounding the meeting. "The whole thing was so fucking coded, you'd need, like, a legend to figure it out." She grabbed a sponge and loaded on some dish soap. "The hotel, the room number, what entrance to use. She was under a fake name. I was under a different fake name, even though nobody knows who I am anyway. It was bullshit." She shrugged. "I didn't go. I told her to forget it. It was over." Tracy started scrubbing the pan she'd used to grill the chicken.

"And?" Meg asked, dying to know what happened next.

"She came back to LA. Showed up at my apartment, begged for another chance." Tracy laughed again, out loud this time as she turned on the faucet to rinse the pan. "God, it's so clichéd when I think about it now."

Tracy was trying to mask it, and doing a halfway decent job, but Meg's heart ached a little to see her friend so uncharacteristically rattled. She noticed Tracy couldn't quite meet their eyes.

"You know," Tracy continued, "she came over with her guitar and her sorrow. Played me a song she'd just finished. Gave me the line that she'd written it for me." She looked over her shoulder at her friends. "Let me tell you, that rock-star shit—it works." Tracy snapped her fingers. "Just like that, I was back." She cocked her head back and smirked. "She sat on my couch and sang that song to me and I fell fucking hard as hell."

"What song was it?" Meg's curiosity got the best of her.

Tracy turned all the way around and leaned back on the counter grabbing a dish towel to dry her hands. As she looked between Meg and Lexi a small smile escaped her and she looked more than a little nostalgic. "It was 'Real Me,'" she answered, naming Jezebel Stone's power ballad that still dominated airwaves a year later.

Lexi's jaw dropped. "No way."

"Holy shit," Meg added. "There's some fucking great lines in that song."

"Well, it was genius, I'll give her that." Tracy turned back toward the sink and the remaining dishes. "Every time I heard it on the radio, it was like she tightened her grip on me." Her eyes bored into the cabinet in front of her. "A truly sick, sadistic mind-fuck I realize now, since I am fairly certain I was not the only recipient of the story behind it."

"You think she told Lloyd too?" Meg asked in disbelief.

Tracy shrugged. "I doubt it, but who knows."

Meg nodded to herself, still analyzing the statement she was about to make. "You know, I always thought that song was about a woman. Something about the language, the tone…"

Tracy looked at her and raised her eyebrows. "You might be right." She smacked her lips. "Not sure it was me, though."

Meg crinkled her forehead in confusion.

"After that night, nothing changed." Tracy picked through the silverware at the bottom of the sink, rinsing each fork and knife off before loading them into the dishwasher. "I was still in the shadows. She constantly told me she needed more time, that I didn't understand"— she shrugged again—"but it was all lies." She held up a dirty pair of tongs and pointed them at Lexi. "Which brings me to the answer to your question, Lexi." She leaned against the lip of the sink, the tongs hanging from her left hand. "We did not break up over Jasper Lloyd." She spoke with sincerity and a little sadness. "I honestly believed her when she told me she wasn't sleeping with him. Although it totally grosses me out now to realize she probably was." She looked at the floor. "But no, we broke up over a girl."

Meg couldn't hide her surprise. "Another girl?"

"Another girl," Tracy confirmed.

Lexi interrupted. "Wait, you or her?"

Tracy looked right at her. "Not me."

Lexi winced a little. "Sorry. I just wasn't sure. Sorry," she repeated.

"It's fine." Tracy forgave Lexi's uncertainty with a wave of her hand. "No, I was faithful the entire time we were together. But at some point I suspected she might be cheating."

"With a girl?" Meg asked again, her voice a blend of half question, half amazed statement.

Tracy nodded yes, biting and chewing her lower lip. "You guys know the drill. You start seeing all these signs and you want to believe they're not there. I knew the girl. She was part of her makeup team. Trina." She uttered her name sarcastically, but it obviously hurt her to say it. "I confronted Jez about it. She told me I was crazy." She looked at Meg and Lexi and her irritation came through as she spoke. "She gave me this whole drawn-out lecture about how it was hard enough hiding one girlfriend, forget about two.

"Then Fourth of July weekend, I was playing a charity tournament on the coast. I had gone to the reception after and stayed kind of late. I was having a good time. Had no one to rush home to." She frowned. "Jez was tied up the entire weekend doing a small venue outside of Vegas. At least that's what she told me," she added with a lift of her eyebrows.

"Anyway, I had keys to her place in Santa Barbara. It was where we always stayed together. It was basically our place. That's how I thought of it anyway." She took a minute as though she still couldn't believe it had all happened. Then her expression changed completely and her eyes crinkled in the corners as she smiled. "You know, I was there for like forty-five minutes before I even realized she was there."

"*Nooooo.*" Meg held her head as she cringed in disbelief.

"Yep," Tracy confirmed. She couldn't hold back a laugh as she continued. "I let myself in. Shut off the alarm. Got a drink. Watched

SportsCenter for a while." She nodded, continuing. "Finally I went into the bedroom to put my stuff away and get changed." Her expression was stoic. "There they were."

"The makeup girl?" Lexi asked.

"The fucking makeup girl."

"Were they like"—Meg clenched her teeth together and circled her hands around as she searched for the least offensive wording—"actively—"

"No. They were asleep," Tracy answered. "I arrived postcoitus," she added snarkily.

Meg cocked her head to the side. "Well, that's better, right?"

"Is it?" Tracy countered.

"I mean it's not ideal. But at least you didn't have to see her face in someone else's box." Meg shrugged. "Who needs that image?"

"Point taken." They exchanged eye contact, and in the small moment, Tracy saw Meg's support.

"Wow." Lexi shook her head, her jaw still hanging open. "I can't believe it."

"What part?" Tracy asked.

Lexi pushed her long curly hair off her shoulders. "All of it. It's crazy." She flashed her eyes at Tracy. "And sad. I'm sorry it happened to you."

Meg echoed her statements. "It sucks. You deserve way better than that."

"Thanks, guys." Tracy turned around and began to finish washing the remaining utensils.

They were all quiet for a second before Lexi broke the silence. "Am I the only one who's shocked Jezebel Stone is gay?"

Meg took the opportunity to tease her bestie on her favorite Lexi-ism. "You have the worst fucking gaydar." She gave Lexi a huge smile. "Seriously, I don't know how you survived this long. Thank God you live here, because you'd be lost in the real world."

"Shut up." Lexi swatted Meg playfully before redirecting her attention to Tracy. "On the bright side, she wrote an awesome, heart-wrenching love song about you."

Tracy nodded, considering. "True." She paused. "But"—she drew out the one syllable word before going on—"we should maybe consider the source." She grinned over her shoulder and there was a devilish twinkle in her eye. "I like your theory, Lexi, believe me." She had just finished washing the large knife she'd used to slice the chicken and she held it as she continued to talk. "Honestly, it's pretty likely she was screwing at least one other person at the time." She turned around for full effect, emphasizing her point by wagging the knife in the air. "And anyway, how do you trust someone who parades around as a self-assured international celebrity, pretends to be a role model, marries her beard, and cashes in on a song called 'Real Me,' when the real her is a closet case named Judy Rockwell from Sarasota, Florida."

Meg watched Tracy's confidence return as she completed her zinger with a satisfied smile. But her big show of being over it was overshadowed by what happened next. As she finished talking, she dragged the kitchen knife over the dishtowel with a flourish, not accounting for the blade or its sharpness, slicing clear through the fabric and her palm in one swift motion.

CHAPTER TWELVE

"Fuck, Meg. I'm getting blood all over your car." Tracy wrapped her hand tighter in a teal beach towel. "I'm sorry, dude."

"Would you shut up with the apologies already."

Tracy smiled. She was pleased her voice remained smooth and calm despite the circumstances. "I feel bad." She laughed a little, rolling her head against the seat. "I'm such a tool. I can't believe I did this."

"Does it hurt?" Lexi asked from the backseat.

"It's fine," she lied, clenching her teeth to swallow the pain as Meg pulled up to the hospital's emergency entrance.

Tracy breathed a sigh of relief that the ER was virtually empty and she was taken in almost immediately. After a series of nurses, residents, interns, and more unidentified staffers came by to weigh in on her prognosis and treatment, she urged Meg and Lexi to go home. They refused, of course, instead slipping out on a coffee mission and leaving her with her own thoughts.

Tracy stared up at the ceiling, thinking about the events that had led her here, reclining on the uncomfortable bed and consciously reminding herself not to blame Jezebel Stone, even though, considering the circumstances, it was her fault a little.

She was genuinely surprised and secretly elated when she heard Betsy's sweet voice in the doorway.

"How's the patient?"

Tracy inched up a little, using her good hand to sit up more in bed. "Hi," she crooned, unable to resist ogling Betsy in her hospital getup.

Betsy's eyes stood out even more than usual, their color enhanced by her aqua scrubs under a long white coat. "How did you—"

"Jesse texted me." She held out her hand. "Let's see."

Tracy undid the loose wrap the nurse had fixed for her and looked up at Betsy to assess her reaction. Betsy didn't hold back.

"Geez, Trace. That looks pretty serious." She leaned over to get a better angle. "Obviously not my area of expertise but"—she peered closer, putting her hand on Tracy's shoulder for balance—"Jesse made it sound like you *might* need stitches." She rubbed Tracy's shoulder and continued to evaluate the wound. "I think you'll probably need surgery." Her expression was a mix of concern and disappointment as though she knew she was right, but hated being the one to break it to her. "That is a very deep cut."

When the doctor came, he confirmed Betsy's initial diagnosis. The wound was severe and had caused tendon damage that needed to be repaired right away. Tracy was scheduled for surgery later in the evening. She made Meg and Lexi go home anyway, saying she was a big girl and it was only hand surgery. Meg agreed only after talking to Betsy, who promised to check on her throughout the night.

❖

"Hey, killer."

Tracy looked up from the form she was signing to the welcome sight of Betsy at the edge of her bed in Recovery.

"Hi." Her voice was groggy despite her best efforts.

"I talked to your surgeon. He said everything went smoothly. You can go home."

Tracy nodded. "Yeah. He told me."

"Finish up your paperwork." Betsy nodded with her chin. "I just have one more thing to do. Then I'll take you back to Meg's."

Tracy inched up on the bed, balancing awkwardly with her one good hand. "That's not necessary. It's cool. I'll get an Uber or whatever."

She was dead serious and couldn't help but smile when Betsy turned in the doorway, dropped her head, and looked out from under her long lashes. Betsy pointed to her name on her white coat. "See that?" She grinned. "It says *Doctor*." She made a grand gesture of looking around. "In here, we give the orders. There's even an expression…"

She looked around, tapping her chin playfully, before meeting Tracy's eyes again. "Now finish up. I'll be back in twenty minutes."

As they made their way to Bay West, Tracy felt the full effect of the pain meds dulling her senses. "Were you at the hospital all night?" she asked sleepily.

"Yes."

"Did you deliver a baby?"

"No." Betsy looked at the road ahead of her. "I did an emergency hysterectomy."

"That's sad."

Betsy nodded once, possibly in agreement, Tracy wasn't sure, and continued to drive. When they got to Meg's, Tracy let Betsy help her inside even though it made her feel like a child.

"Do you understand when to take your meds?" Betsy asked seriously.

Tracy nodded.

"And you're going to let me take you to your follow-up in two days?"

"Bets, it's—" She stopped herself when she saw the stern look on Betsy's face. "Okay. Yes."

"You should get some rest. Let's get you to bed."

Tracy put her good hand up in protest. "I'm fine. I can put myself to bed." She met Betsy's sleepy eyes, and while she was appreciative of the offer, Betsy looked exhausted herself, and positively irresistible. Tracy wasn't used to taking any kind of drugs. Under their influence, in the presence of the gorgeous doctor, she didn't trust herself not to say something she wouldn't be able to take back or, worse, be unable to act on.

Betsy relented, but only after Tracy promised to call if she needed anything, and when Betsy used her authority to announce she would be back later anyway to see how she was doing, Tracy didn't fight her at all.

❖

Betsy wondered whether Meg suspected her daily trips to check on Tracy weren't *entirely* necessary. Despite that she stopped by once a day.

On Tuesday, when she popped in for her routine visit, she was greeted at Meg's front door by Lexi and Jesse, who'd hoped she was the delivery person with the gang's Chinese order.

"Well, I hope you ordered Triple Jade, because I am starving," she teased. They pulled her inside and Meg hooked her up with a drink, and when the food arrived, they sat around Meg's table like one big gay family, passing the cartons around and chatting with ease.

Betsy sized up her egg roll before biting off the corner. "Hey, Meg," she asked while covering her mouth, "any chance you want to take a ride with me to P-town tomorrow?" It was a long shot, Betsy knew, but Meg had come through for her a few times in the past year, keeping her company as she drove the five-hour trek to the tip of Massachusetts to check on the progress of her home renovation.

"Sorry," Meg responded, "I have major meetings tomorrow and Thursday."

"What's in P-town?" Tracy asked. Before anyone could answer her, she changed the question. "I mean, I know what's in P-town. But why do you need to go there tomorrow?"

Betsy wiped her mouth and explained to Tracy what the others already knew. She owned a house in P-town that she rented out most of the year, and for the last few months, she had been having extensive renovations done. Sometimes she made the trip to pick out a paint color or tile, other times she zipped up on a day off to monitor the progress.

Tracy nodded into her beef with snow peas. "I'll go."

Betsy waved her off. "It's okay, I can go by myself."

Tracy narrowed her eyes. "Um, it's not like I'm doing anything else." She held up her splinted hand for emphasis. "Seriously, I'm in. I can't really share the driving because of this"—she waved her hand again—"but I'm good company. Right, Meg?"

"The best," Meg offered without looking up.

Betsy licked her lips and smiled. "Okay," she said, hoping her heightened pitch didn't reveal the nerves she felt over the prospect of an overnighter with Tracy Allen.

❖

For a split second after waking up in the guest bedroom of Betsy's modest P-town home, Tracy was so disoriented that she had no clue where she was. A fresh seaside breeze coming in through the open window brought her back to reality. She popped up right away, slid into her jeans, and, using her good hand, wrestled herself into a pullover. Shuffling down the stairs, she found Betsy already sitting at the half-finished kitchen island, reading a newspaper, two cups of takeout coffee in front of her.

"Morning," Tracy said, stretching her arms up over her head as she checked out the living room she'd barely glanced at after their very late arrival the previous evening.

"How did you sleep?"

"Great, thanks."

"Coffee?" Betsy asked, inching a cup toward Tracy. "I got yours black but there's milk and sugar here," she said pointing to the packets stacked neatly in the corner. Tracy nodded her appreciation as she dumped two creamers in and listened to Betsy lay out the morning plan.

"So the construction guys should be here around ten. I just want to go over a few things with them." She spun her paper cup on the counter. "After that I have a meeting with my property manager, which you are more than welcome at, but I can drop you off in town if you'd rather."

Tracy sipped her coffee. "I'll just come with you, if that's okay." She met Betsy's ever-changing eyes with a smile. When the workers arrived slightly after ten a.m., she stood to the side and listened as Betsy meticulously went over every detail with the foreman. Then they hopped in Betsy's car and drove the short distance through town to the property manager's office, where they were greeted by a plump woman with a dyed-red pixie cut. She exchanged a long hug with Betsy.

"It's good to see you, Marie." Betsy broke free of the woman's embrace and turned toward Tracy. "This is my friend—"

"Tracy Allen," the woman blurted out, finishing Betsy's sentence. "Wow. What a pleasure." She extended her hand. "I'm a huge fan." Noticing Tracy's bandage, she added, "What happened there?"

Tracy accepted the woman's handshake and dismissed her injury with a wave of her other hand. "Nothing serious. Just a little scratch."

Marie immediately began straightening up her sloppy office. "Sorry, this place is a mess." She moved a stack of magazines off one chair so Betsy and Tracy could both sit. Walking around her desk, she turned back to Betsy. "What do you think of the progress on the house? Everything meeting your standards?"

"It looks great, Marie."

Marie put both hands on her desk. "Good. I'm so glad you like it." She continued to pile papers on her desk as she spoke. "They should finish the kitchen today. You saw the bathroom upgrades?" At Betsy's nod, she continued, "I had them switch out all the hardware in the master bath, like we spoke about on the phone. Now everything matches." She pulled out a calendar. "So here's what we have lined up for the winter." She pointed to a highlighted series of blocked-out weeks and weekends. "Of course I'll email these dates to you, but I just want you to have an idea."

"Great, Marie."

Marie was visibly having a difficult time keeping her focus and kept stealing glances at Tracy. Finally she stopped trying to hide it. "I'm sorry. I just can't believe Tracy Allen is in my office."

Tracy just smiled at the comment, while Marie continued to gush. "I saw you at the Dinah in April."

"You went to the golf tournament?" Tracy asked, genuinely surprised.

Marie blushed a little. "Sorry, no. I saw you at the panel on youth revitalization programs. The one with Jezebel Stone."

"Right, of course." Tracy nodded, trying hard not to clench her teeth at the memory.

"You ladies were all so funny with each other." Marie beamed. "You really made a serious topic fun and entertaining, as well as informative. It was probably my favorite part of the whole weekend."

Tracy smiled warmly, ever the professional.

"Tell me something," Marie went on, "are you all friends in real life—you, Jezebel Stone, Jennie Kent? Because you all really seemed to click. Or is that just part of the whole celebrity thing?" She waved her hands excitedly. "Sorry, I'm going on and on. Ignore me. But I am curious," she finished, clearly waiting for an answer.

Tracy remembered the event like it was yesterday. There'd been four of them on the panel, but most of the banter had been between her and Jezebel. Back then she'd thought of their light flirting at the event as a kind of secret game between them, a cloaked performance they were putting on for everyone. Of course Tracy remembered the rest of the night too. Hanging with Jez and her crew into the wee hours, partying in her suite until everyone else had gone and it was just the two of them alone for a precious few hours until Tracy was forced to slip out before dawn or risk being caught by Jezebel's entourage—most of whom Tracy felt certain knew anyway—or, worse, the paparazzi.

Tracy swallowed hard at the memory and looked up, realizing Marie still expected some kind of explanation.

"We're acquaintances," she offered. "Some of us are friends." Tracy chewed her bottom lip. "We see each other throughout the year at different charity events we are all involved in." She continued her half-truth. "So a lot of that back and forth is pretty natural."

Marie was still fired up. "Well, you guys were great. That Jezebel Stone had everyone in stitches. She seems like a real good person. I mean, what a trouper she is to lend her support to the gay and lesbian community." She looked right at Tracy, clearly waiting for her to agree.

Tracy pursed her lips and managed a smile, unable to speak in support of Jezebel's concession to comingle with the gay community she was secretly a part of. She hoped her put-on facial expression was enough to satisfy the Realtor's final comment. Just in case, Tracy offered to take a picture with Marie, knowing that it would placate her and change the conversation.

As they walked to the car, Tracy caught Betsy studying her.

"What?" she asked the gorgeous blonde.

"You up for a walk on the beach?" Betsy asked as she grabbed her keys out of her purse.

"Definitely."

It was about one o'clock in the afternoon by the time they got to Race Point. The sun was high in the sky and there was a lovely cool breeze coming off the water as they made their way down to the shoreline. "So you really made an impression on Marie." Betsy nudged Tracy with her elbow.

Tracy looked up from under her furrowed brow. "I don't think it was *me* that made the impression."

Picking up right away on her sarcasm, Betsy asked, "So what *is* the deal with you and Jezebel Stone?"

"Nothing," Tracy responded sharply. "There's no deal."

Betsy was quiet and they walked in silence with the sound of the ocean next to them. Tracy watched the small waves crashing against the beach, hoping the sting she felt over the memory of her failed relationship didn't show on her face.

"Look, you don't have to tell me about it. I'm not trying to pry into your life," Betsy said. "I know we don't know each other that well, but"—she paused briefly, turning to make real eye contact, and the corner of her mouth rose slightly—"I did play high-stakes shuffleboard with you against some serious competition *and* I saw you right after you nearly cut your hand off." She raised her eyebrows knowingly. "In neither of those two completely different, but equally intense situations did I see you get even remotely flustered." She bent down to pick up a shell on the sand. "Last night in the car"—Betsy turned the shell over in her hand, seemingly examining its pretty purple hues—"you got fidgety every time one of her songs came on the radio. And just now"—she put her hand on Tracy's forearm, stopping her—"maybe Marie couldn't tell, but I know you and Jezebel Stone are not *friends*. That came through loud and clear." She started walking again. "So you can talk about it or not, but by the way you clenched your jaw during Marie's interrogation, it looks like you've got something in there that wants to come out."

Tracy reached for a rock in the sand and whipped it across the surf. She kept pace with Betsy, skipping two more stones before she spoke.

"She's my ex-girlfriend."

Betsy nodded. "Didn't end well, I guess?"

"You could say that."

Betsy asked for the particulars, and Tracy gave them to her in exacting detail. After she had finished, she assessed Betsy's casual demeanor. "You're not surprised?"

"About what?"

"I don't know, Jezebel Stone being gay." She picked up a lovely shell, handing it to Betsy. "That I was dating one of the most famous people in the world. Any of it?"

"I'm never surprised to find out celebrities are gay. They are just people, after all." Betsy shrugged. "I am curious about how you two got together, though." She eyed the shell Tracy handed her, dusting off a few grains of sand before putting it in her pocket with the others she had collected on the walk. "Did you meet her after a show or something?"

Tracy shook her head. "Nah, nothing like that." She played with a fraying edge of her bandage. "She's very involved with Every Youth Counts, which is a charity I do a lot of work for too."

"Right, you mentioned that."

"I kept running into her at different events." Tracy tipped her head down toward the ground. "You know, a lot of the Richie Rich types attach their names to a charity for, like, good publicity or a tax write-off. Jez was different." She looked up at the clouds in the sky. "She really believed in the program. She would go to the workshops and work one-on-one with the kids." Tracy smiled. "God, the kids would go crazy for her. And she loved it. Loved that it meant something to them." Did that cloud look like a butterfly? Weird. "Anyway, I met her at the annual fund-raiser they do in New York. After that I saw her at a bunch of the small events. Mostly in Los Angeles, but one in Dallas, of all places." She raised her eyebrows. "We started talking. She was very unassuming. Very sweet." Tracy shrugged. "The rest is history. Secret history, of course."

Betsy turned to Tracy. "So, wait. I'm confused. What do you do at the charity?" She crinkled her brow. "You're into music too?"

Tracy let out a small laugh. "No. Not at all." She licked her lips. "Every Youth Counts is a program aimed toward at-risk kids. The foundation focuses on arts and sports, the theory being between those two fields there is something everyone can be good at, find joy in. This gives kids who might not otherwise have the chance the opportunity to learn, have fun, express themselves, exercise, draw, write, dance, run, jump, play."

"Sounds awesome." Betsy smiled, picking up on the obvious enthusiasm in Tracy's voice.

"It is." Tracy looked out at the water. "Being part of it is far and away the most rewarding thing I've ever done in my life."

"Do you teach the kids to play golf?"

"If they want," she answered, looking out of the corner of her eye. "Mostly they're not interested in that. They want to play basketball, soccer, baseball."

"And you do that with them?"

"Sure." Tracy smiled. "I'll play anything." She looked at her bandaged left hand.

"What are your doctors saying about your hand?" Betsy nodded at it with her chin. "Will you be able to play golf again?"

Tracy nodded. "They're optimistic." She bit the inside of her mouth. "With therapy, should be good as new." She paused, looking away. "I'm not sure I want to."

"Why not?" Betsy asked, concern, but not judgment in her voice.

There was a long second before Tracy answered. "I don't know." She shrugged. "It's getting old. I want a real life. One that's not in a different city every ten days." She stuffed her other hand in her pocket. "Also, truthfully, I'm not that good."

"You're on the women's pro circuit. You are good, Tracy."

Tracy met Betsy's eyes and said in a sardonic tone, "Betsy, I'm ranked one hundred and thirty-fourth out of one hundred and thirty-seven players." She smirked. "Not much to brag about there."

"Nonsense." Betsy waved her off. "You've had a rough couple of years." She bumped Tracy's shoulder with her own. "Right out of college you were called the sleeper to look out for, or something like that." She met Tracy's eyes. "Wait." She put a finger up and closed her eyes trying to remember the exact wording. "They also said you had a nearly flawless…power swing, I think was the term." She opened her eyes and Tracy was smiling. "I did some research. Marie is not the only one who is impressed." She wiggled her eyebrows.

"You're sweet."

"Don't give up on yourself just because Jezebel Stone doesn't know a good thing when she sees it."

Tracy thought Betsy had intended the comment to be light and encouraging, but she heard something else too, embedded in her statement. Tracy looked right at her trying to discern Betsy's intent. She stopped in her tracks.

"Can I ask you a question?"

"Sure."

"Why don't you live at Bay West?"

Betsy let out a laugh. "I live with my mom." She brushed away a strand of hair the wind had blown into her eyes. "I'm only two miles from the development," she added with a shrug.

Tracy shook her head. "I don't think I could take being that close and not living there. The place is amazing."

"I know what you mean," Betsy answered with a knowing smile. "But this works for me right now. I went away for college and med school, and then I was stationed overseas. There was never any need to get my own place." She shrugged. "Then a few years ago my dad passed away. I didn't want my mom to be alone. Plus, the price is right," she joked, making a zero with her left hand. "It's how I was able to afford this place out here," she said referring to her house a few miles away. "But I'm thinking in a few years, I will probably make the move. Buy something at Bay West. Bring my mom along with me."

"She would be down with that?"

"Totally."

"How does that work out when you have a girlfriend?" Tracy squinted her eyes in question. "Sorry, that's none of my business." She held her hands up as she attempted to explain her curiosity. "I just mean, it must be hard, living with your mom as an adult in a relationship."

Betsy let out a small laugh. "It's fine actually." She put one finger up. "I should explain—my mother's house is a two family. I live in the downstairs apartment. So there is privacy. Not that it would matter. My mother is awesome. I mean, she absolutely loved CJ." She shook the shells in her pocket.

"Really?" Tracy didn't even try to hide the shock in her voice.

"Why do you say it like that?"

"I'm purely stereotyping." Tracy shrugged her shoulders playfully. "It's just the tattoos, the piercings. That whole rocker look—not usually a mother's dream for her daughter."

"My mother is anything but typical," Betsy responded with a lilt in her voice. "She liked CJ from the very beginning. Tattoos and all."

"Was she upset when you guys broke up? Your mother, I mean."

Betsy curled her lower lip. "She was okay." She looked at Tracy, her voice getting serious. "That relationship, the romantic part of it, has really been over for quite some time now," Betsy admitted sheepishly. "Even my mother knew that."

Tracy kicked aside a piece of seaweed as they walked. She tried to hide her smile as she looked at Betsy. "I'm sorry, but I have to ask. How did you end up with a girl like CJ?" She put her hand up and waved off her own comment, but continued to talk. "Again, it's none of my business, but I just did not peg you for the bad-girl type."

Betsy smiled all the way up to her eyes. "It's all very clichéd," she said, making fun of herself. "I was in my first year of medical school. She was in the band that played at the local bar. I was stressed out, studying all the time. She was nineteen, fun, and completely carefree." She paused for a second, fixing her eyes, more blue than green at the moment, right on Tracy. "She is not a bad girl, by the way."

"Oh no. I saw her. She's badass."

Betsy rolled her eyes. "And you don't see the allure in that?" she challenged. "Even after dating Jezebel Stone?"

Tracy came back quickly. "Jezebel Stone does not have game like that. CJ is the real deal."

Betsy puckered her lips. "Mm-hmm. Of course." She nodded to herself. "That's why you don't get it."

"Get what?"

"*You* are the bad girl."

"Get out of here." Tracy waved her off with her unbandaged hand.

Betsy stopped short and eyed Tracy head to toe. "Uh-huh. You are."

Tracy leaned into Betsy's space, looked right at her, and touched her forearm, keeping it there as she spoke in a smooth, sexy voice. "Trust me, Jennifer, I am a very, very good girl."

She almost kissed her right there on the windswept beach, but Betsy's body language seemed off so she backed away. Just a little more time, Tracy thought. She smiled to herself, certain the right moment was just ahead of them.

Later that evening as they walked home from dinner, Betsy couldn't help but notice that with each step, Tracy's wrist lightly grazed hers as their arms swayed in unison. With every touch Betsy experienced both disappointment and relief that Tracy didn't make a move to reach for her hand.

"Are you tired?" Betsy asked as they entered her house.

"Not really."

"Wine?" She lifted her eyebrows hoping to encourage a yes.

"Yeah, why not?"

"Great." Betsy moved through the kitchen, grabbing a fresh bottle of red and two glasses. "Let's sit by the fireplace. I hardly ever get to enjoy this." She smiled, flipping the switch to the gas fireplace and putting her feet up on the coffee table as she stretched out across from Tracy.

The hours passed and to her surprise Betsy realized they had polished off the bottle. She glanced at her watch, amazed at how quickly the time had slipped by, how effortless being with Tracy felt. This kind of instant connection was new to her. It was honest and warm and lovely and she didn't want the night to end. But she really didn't want to think about what that meant, so instead she urged them off the couch and up the stairs.

"Do you need any help?" she asked, giving a hesitant nod at Tracy's injured hand. "With that?"

Her eyes settled on Tracy's mouth and she watched as Tracy shook her head, sexy and confident.

"No."

They were standing in the hallway just outside her bedroom. Tracy took a small step toward her, fisting the fabric of her shirt and pulling her closer.

Their lips were almost touching when Betsy panicked. "Sorry, Tracy," she said, dropping her gaze.

"What's wrong?" Tracy asked, releasing Betsy's shirt but letting her hand rest on the soft cotton material above her abdomen.

Betsy shook her head, not quite sure what to say, because the truth of the matter was everything about the entire day had been absolutely perfect. She stumbled, searching for the right words. "I just…I think we shouldn't." She flashed her eyes up at Tracy, knowing the desire in them belied her words.

"Why?" There was no pressure in Tracy's question, just plain curiosity over Betsy's objection to a moment they had both seen coming.

"I like you," Betsy said apprehensively.

"I like you too," Tracy said in response.

"But…" Betsy stopped, still unsure what to say. She knew the truth. It was ridiculous that she had fallen for Meg's friend who was in New York *visiting*. Logically, she knew it made no sense to get involved with someone who couldn't be anything more than transient. All evening she had tried to convince herself to just do it, be like everyone else and have a fling, as Meg had encouraged her a few months ago. But that wasn't her. And, truthfully, she found the idea marginally terrifying. Aside from CJ, she had only slept with one other person in her life. But that tryst had occurred when she was on active duty stationed in a war zone overseas, where even her own strict rules went out the window.

She shook her head, knowing there was no way to explain all of this and not sound like a flake. So she didn't.

"We're both just out of relationships," Betsy started. "It's probably not a good idea."

Tracy maintained eye contact for a second before shifting her gaze to the floor. She looked disappointed, hurt even, but not mad. Betsy knew Tracy wasn't convinced of her reasoning. Hell, she barely believed it herself and it had come out of her mouth. But Tracy didn't argue or try to persuade her. She just bit her bottom lip and nodded, looking resolute. She gave a small smile and kissed Betsy on the cheek, then sauntered down the hall to the guest room.

Betsy watched her go, her perfect behind in equally perfect jeans. She leaned back into the wall and pressed the bases of both hands against her forehead, wondering if she was making the wrong decision. Letting out a long slow breath, she walked into her bedroom and headed straight for her newly overhauled master bath, praying the fancy detachable showerhead she'd let herself get talked into would live up to its price tag.

The remainder of the night was spent tossing and turning as she half imagined, half dreamed what might've happened if she'd just given in to what she knew she wanted. But that was it—she did want Tracy, and it was both the truth and the problem. She wasn't looking for a lost weekend, or even some kind of whirlwind romance that lasted for however long Tracy decided to stay in New York. Betsy wanted more. Way more, and it scared the hell out of her.

❖

The next morning Betsy adjusted her grip on the steering wheel, her eyes focused on the road ahead as they cruised along the open highway. She tried for a subtle glance across the front seat, but Tracy caught her right away.

"What's up?" Tracy asked.

Betsy worried her lower lip. "Can we talk about last night?"

"Yeah, of course." Tracy shifted in the leather seat, angling her body just slightly toward Betsy as they made their way back to New York.

Betsy hesitated, but forced herself to go on. "I was hoping I could explain a few things."

"Bets, you don't owe me an explanation. It's okay. We're cool."

Betsy observed what seemed to be a genuine smile spread across Tracy's chiseled face. Her knuckles whitened around the steering wheel. "I know, but I still feel like I should explain a little," she said, hoping she wasn't about to make a fool out of herself.

Tracy nodded but didn't say anything, so Betsy continued. "Tracy, it's not that I'm not ready to be with anyone, or anything like that." She checked her rearview mirror out of habit. "I was with CJ for a really long time and honestly, from very early on, I think I knew our lives were not headed in the same direction." She stared straight ahead. "But I stayed in it anyway because…it was easy and comfortable. And of course, I loved her."

"Sure."

"The thing is, this probably sounds crazy to you," she said, feeling more than a little embarrassed as she continued. "I'm going to be thirty-three in a few months." She cocked her head to the side. "I feel like I've already used up a lot of time on something that wasn't going anywhere. And I don't have regrets, that's not what I'm saying." She paused momentarily, searching for words that sounded less intense than she knew she was coming off. Finally she gave up. "I don't really do the casual hookup thing."

"All right."

"Not because I think there's anything wrong with it, or anything like that." She waved her hand and kept talking. "It's just not me." She kept her eyes on the road, shrugging her shoulders. "The thing is I have a timeline—for myself. I know it sounds completely uptight. And I guess it is. But there are things I want and, well, maybe because I've spent the last few years on something that wasn't really moving forward, I just feel like right now, I have to stay focused. On my career. On my personal life. So I'm just not going to get involved in something that can't possibly go anywhere."

She looked across the console briefly. "And, Tracy, you live in California."

"Okay."

Betsy's voice dropped an octave. "I'm obviously attracted to you," she said, keeping her eyes glued forward. "I just think that's not enough. I hope you can understand that."

Tracy licked her lips and waited for Betsy to make eye contact. "Understood," she said with an unbelievably sexy grin.

"Can we still be friends?"

"Of course," Tracy answered, clearly surprised at the question.

Betsy let out a sigh of relief. "Yeah?"

"Absolutely."

Feeling the weight of a touchy topic off her shoulders, Betsy relaxed into her seat. "So am I still invited to the Yankee game with you next week?" She bit her lip and looked across the car.

"Do you promise to root for the Angels with me?" Tracy asked in mock challenge, lightening the mood.

"At Yankee Stadium? Even I know that's a bad idea." Betsy chuckled. "I'm afraid you're on your own there. I may even buy a Yankees cap."

"So, it's gonna be like that, huh?"

Betsy answered with a huge smile, relieved the conversation had gone so smoothly, even though she knew she'd glossed over their instant and undeniable connection.

CHAPTER THIRTEEN

L et's do a happy hour."

"What?" Meg was puzzled as she shifted her gaze from the computer to Sasha, who was fingering a long, wavy strand of hair as she leaned against the door frame of Meg's office.

"A happy hour," Sasha repeated. "After work, Friday. You know, drinks, appetizers," she explained in jest.

"Where is this coming from?" Meg laced her fingers behind her head and rocked back in her chair.

"I don't know." Sasha grinned. "I think it'd be fun. Everyone here is pretty young. I think people would go." She turned her attention to Meg's office mate. "Hey, Carrie, would you come to happy hour on Friday?"

"Sure," Carrie responded without looking up from her work.

Sasha raised her eyebrows at Meg. "See, Carrie would go. I'm sure Scott will come too," she added.

"Oh, well, in that case," Meg answered with a sarcastic lilt.

"Come on, he's not that bad. I don't know why you give him such a hard time."

Meg shook her head and acted dramatically disappointed. "It's a tragedy, this." She made an overly exaggerated sound of disapproval out of the side of her mouth. "Truly a shame. Bright young woman, with so much promise, falling for the office player." She fake-frowned and turned to her roommate for support in her playful drama. "Sad, don't you think, Carrie?"

Carrie didn't even turn around. She grabbed a file from her desk and stood up. "It's not that sad," she said, sounding a bit like the cat who ate the canary. Meg and Sasha exchanged a blank glance before Carrie grinned at both of them. "He's got a huge cock," she stage-whispered, lifting one eyebrow as she passed through the doorway. Halfway down the hall she called over her shoulder, "Sash, shoot me the details for the happy hour." She strolled away, leaving Meg and Sasha in slack-jawed shock.

"Holy crap," Sasha breathed out, still reeling from Carrie's admission.

"I had no idea." Meg blinked hard. "I hope she's not mad."

"Well, she didn't seem too put out by it," Sasha added with a shrug. "Anyway, more importantly, back to happy hour. I think Anne, Pat, and Doug would even come by for a little bit," she said, referring to the firm's three most senior partners. "We used to do it in London all the time. It was fun. You get to see a whole different side of people." She let go of the strand of hair she was still playing with. "I'm going to send out an email." She started to leave but then stopped abruptly and looked right at Meg. "You're going to come, right?"

Meg smiled. "Why not?"

❖

The Sullivan sponsored happy hour was an instant success, and by the third event, Meg had an established routine. Party with the work crew until nine or so, then head uptown with Sasha to meet up with her friends and continue the debauchery.

Sasha's friends were super nice even if they were the straightest girls ever. Meg felt a little out of place and she worried Sasha's friends suspected she was trying to make a play for Sasha. Scott certainly did. He teased Meg about it all the time. One night after too many beers, he even suggested they have a competition to see who could get Sasha first, commenting that with any luck they'd end up in a tie. He finished his pitch with a gross wink as he ogled Meg from head to toe.

The problem, Meg knew, was Scott was right. She totally had a crush on Sasha. She'd stopped denying it—to herself anyway. The confusion over her feelings wasn't entirely out of left field, or so she told herself. Sasha egged her on whether she realized it or not. Tonight was a perfect example. After the happy hour, she and Scott tagged along with Sasha to meet up with Jane-Anne and the girls. Throughout the night Sasha's friends danced and flirted with guys—including Scott—but Sasha gave all her attention to Meg. It was…awesome, confusing, and fun. But it completely messed with her feelings and her ability to control them. And then finally, when she was gearing up to leave around midnight, Sasha pulled her aside, suggesting it might not be safe for her to go home by herself at such a late hour, inviting her instead to crash at her apartment. Meg was more than tempted to accept the offer, but she knew her own motives were suspect. In truth, she had on several occasions traveled home alone much later, and drunker than she was this evening. She didn't even allow herself to consider it.

As a consolation prize she let herself splurge on a cab in lieu of the much more economical mass transit option. She arrived at her house a half hour later to find Tracy and Betsy chatting away on the couch as though it was the middle of the afternoon. When Meg asked them what they'd been up to all night, they looked at each other like neither one of them realized where the time had gone before explaining they'd planned to watch a movie but had gotten caught up talking. Meg nodded, wondering what the fuck was really going on between them. Since their little sojourn to P-town they hung out nonstop. Tracy swore to Meg they were just friends, but the energy between them was palpable. Even now, Meg could feel it through her half-drunk haze. She shook her head at them, grabbing a quick glass of water before making herself scarce.

Meg was in the middle of brushing her teeth when her phone chimed with a text from Sasha.

Home okay?

Yep. You?

Yes.

Meg let a few seconds pass, rinsing her mouth out before she typed again.

Scott with you? She punctuated the question with a wink emoji, two hearts, and a kissy face. Meg was playing it for laughs, but she was only half kidding, knowing Scott would up his game once she was gone.

Nope. All alone. With her response Sasha added an emoticon of her own—a sad face complete with tears.

Meg smiled to herself. *Too bad*, she typed back.

I invited you, but you turned me down. Three thumbs down in a row followed.

Funny.

Sasha's response was quick. *Who's kidding?*

While they joked around often, this seemed a new level, even for them, and in Meg's mind it was definitely flirting. She wondered if Sasha realized it. Meg thought briefly about running downstairs and showing the text thread to Tracy and Betsy to get their opinion, but she knew it was pointless. She didn't need their input to know how she felt about the exchange and she certainly didn't want to give them the opportunity to deflate her. Meg knew she was probably reading into something that was just silliness on Sasha's part. She didn't care. She liked the idea of going to bed with Sasha on her mind after such spirited banter. She decided right there to end on this high note. *Good night, Sasha*, she typed.

Good night, Megan.

❖

At three forty-five the following Tuesday afternoon, Meg was watching the clock, calculating the minutes before she could leave work and head out for dinner with Jesse and Lexi, hoping she might beat the storm that was clearly on its way in.

"Take a walk with me?" She heard Sasha's voice in her doorway before she looked up. Sasha spoke again before Meg answered. "I need new glasses."

"You wear glasses?"

"Contacts, mostly." Sasha bit her bottom lip. "I hate the way I look in glasses." She hung off the doorjamb, lolling her body halfway in. "But I'm due for a new pair and I would love some help picking out frames."

"Yeah, sure." Meg signed off her computer and grabbed her thin jacket from the back of her chair.

Once at the optician, despite having 20/20 vision, Meg entertained herself trying on several different pairs of glasses while Sasha squared away her script and insurance with the girl at the counter.

"Oh my God, you look adorable." Sasha came up behind her, smiling at a four-eyed Meg in the small mirror.

"Oh, thanks," Meg responded, blushing at the comment. "Ready to shop?" she asked, still not quite able to meet Sasha's eyes.

"Yep." Sasha reached for Meg's hand and hooked her pinky, completely catching her off guard. "Come over here. I want to check these out."

Sasha stopped by a large wall display and giggled, reaching for a pair of fifties-era cat-eye frames. "What do you think?" She turned to Meg with a toothy grin.

Meg played along. "*So* you."

Sasha chuckled, returning them to their rightful spot, and reached for the next pair. She was a touch more serious this time, picking small wireless rims that Meg scrunched her nose up at.

After at least fifteen frames, Sasha had it narrowed down to two. She held one pair in each hand, alternately trying them on, then looking in the mirror and at Meg for her approval.

"They're nice," Meg said when Sasha looked at her.

She swapped them again with the other finalist and turned, clearly waiting for Meg to weigh in.

"Also nice."

Sasha took them off and eyed the specs she held in each hand. She chewed her lip deep in thought. "Meg, do me a favor?" She nodded with her chin at the clunky tortoiseshell model Meg had been playing with earlier. "Grab me those."

Meg reached for them and handed them over, but Sasha shook her head. "I don't want to put these down." She wiggled the frames she was still holding. "Put them on me?"

Meg swallowed, hoping her hands didn't shake. She slid the glasses gently onto Sasha's face, unable to conceal her smile as she admired Sasha's deep blue eyes, light skin, and dark hair against the medium brown frames. She looked gorgeous and smart and a touch geeky in the best way. Meg didn't even try to hide her reaction and Sasha's facial expression signaled she'd read it in an instant.

"These?"

Meg nodded through her grin. "Those. Definitely, those."

Sasha smiled big. "Thanks, Meg." She leaned forward, surprising Meg with a sweet kiss on the cheek. "You're the best."

❖

Meg headed straight for Jesse's after work, fighting through the rain as she sprinted from the bus stop. She didn't even bother to knock, pushing the door open to escape the downpour. Inside Jesse stood shoulder to shoulder with Lexi as they leaned on the counter scrutinizing a piece of paper.

"Hey, guys. Am I late?" Meg asked.

"Not at all." Jesse turned around. "But you're drenched."

"It's a disaster out there," she responded, shucking her jacket and patting her face dry with the dish towel Lexi handed to her.

"No Tracy?" Lexi wondered aloud.

"She has therapy tonight." Meg made two repeated fists in illustration.

"How's that going?" Jesse asked, as she traded Meg's jacket for a glass of red wine.

"So far, so good, I think," Meg offered. She took a healthy sip from her glass before gesturing to the counter with her chin. "What are you guys reading so intently?"

"My parents' additions to the guest list," Lexi said seriously.

"That's a good sign."

Lexi nodded. "It is." She stole a brief glance at Jesse. "I mean, it's not like we really ever talked about anything," she said, jutting her chin out in mild annoyance. "I shouldn't say that. They did apologize." She walked to the counter and picked up the glass of wine Jesse had poured for her.

"So your scare tactic worked, then? From the summer, when you threatened to not come to dinner or whatever?" Meg asked.

Lexi let out a heavy breath. "Yeah, I guess. That's just it, though. I mean, I'm happy they're finally coming around." She took a small sip of her drink, considering her words before she spoke again. "But I basically had to ultimatum them into it." She shrugged. "I mean, is it totally greedy that I want them to actually be happy for me?" She took a seat next to Meg at the kitchen table and rested her chin on her palm as Meg rubbed her back. "But you're right, I guess. It is progress, and I am thankful for that." She looked over at Meg, finding some optimism to share. "I even looked at dresses with Marnie over the weekend."

Lexi's smile was genuine and contagious, and Meg noticed Jesse smile too as she began slicing a loaf of Italian bread as she stood at the counter. "So Jess, how is *your* mother adjusting? Any progress since Lexi flashed the fam?"

Jesse swallowed a laugh. "Not really, I'm afraid." She glanced over her shoulder and added playfully, "Surprising, right?" She ogled Lexi openly before returning her attention to Meg. "She has such a fantastic body. I can't believe it didn't win my mother over."

Lexi mock-glowered at her and Jesse gave her a wink as she finished the prep work. "Alas, my mother is a lost cause," Jesse said, getting a little more serious as she directed her response to Meg, even though it was clearly for Lexi's benefit too. "Honestly, it's not even about Lexi. Nobody's good enough in her eyes."

"Oh, I think Lauren Carlisle would pass muster," Lexi countered, her voice dripping with jealousy as she referenced Jesse's ex.

Jesse placed the bread down in the center of the table and leaned against the edge. She looked right at Lexi. "I know you think that, but she's really not a fan of Lauren's either. All that stuff she says"—Jesse shrugged, pushing off—"it's just to see if it will get to you." Jesse shook her head. "She would be doing the same thing to Lauren if I were marrying her." She met Lexi's look of disbelief and continued to explain. "It's ridiculous and petty and I don't know why she does it. But I've seen this exact thing play out with both my brothers' wives. Trust me, she tortured Zoey and Steph before they married John and Jake."

"Yeah, well, she's not that nice to them now, either, if that's the point you're trying to make."

"She may not be all warm and fuzzy. Don't hold your breath for that." Jesse sneaked a peek at the stove to check if the water was boiling before walking right over to Lexi. "But they're family and she loves them. She's going to love you too. That is the truth, whether you believe me or not." She kissed Lexi's forehead. "And even if she never came around, what difference does it make? I love you." Jesse kissed her again, a sweet peck on the cheek this time, and Lexi reached for her hand and squeezed it as she met her girlfriend's eyes.

"You guys are so cute, it's ridiculous." Meg tipped her head to the side, admiring her friends as she reached for the heel of the bread and dipped it into the olive oil and herb mixture on the table.

Jesse smiled in response, turning to Meg. "How was your day, kid?"

"Weird," Meg said, between chews. Over the next half hour she explained, relaying the entire story of shopping for Sasha's new glasses, sparing her friends no details over their pasta dinner.

Jesse wiped her mouth with a napkin. "Are you sure she's not gay?"

"I'm with Jess. This whole story sounds really gay," Lexi chimed in.

Meg shook them off. "Straight as they come."

"How do you know?" Jesse asked. When Meg didn't answer right away, Jesse pried further. "She has a boyfriend?"

"Not right now."

"That's a plus." Lexi was quick with her two cents.

"When?" Jesse fished for the details. "When did she have a boyfriend?"

Meg shrugged. "I don't know. A while ago."

Jesse continued with leading questions. "You said she's pretty, right?"

Lexi reached for her phone and handed it to Jesse. "Here's a picture of them from the summer."

Jesse nodded approval, continuing to analyze the image from the day Meg and Sasha had gone to the movies. "She looks, I don't know…" She cocked her head to the side as she scrutinized the image. "She looks comfortable with you. That's something." She handed the phone back to Lexi and speared a tube of penne with her fork. "You guys work together? Talk all the time?"

"Yeah," Meg answered, curious where this was going.

Jesse continued to probe. "Did she ever mention having a crush on a girl? Even a celebrity or anything?"

Meg paused. "No. Not really." She took a sip of her drink. "I mean, she did tell me—" She stopped herself midsentence. "But I don't think it means anything anyway."

"What did she tell you?" Lexi asked eagerly.

Meg toyed with her fork. "She mentioned how once she kissed a girl in college."

Lexi and Jesse exchanged a knowing look before fixing their attention directly on Meg. Lexi said, "Go on."

"That's it."

"That is so *not* it." Lexi was animated. "Who was she? How many times? What did she look like? Was the *other* girl gay?" Lexi puckered her lips as she nodded, obviously proud of herself for coming up with the last question.

Meg laughed. "I don't know. I didn't ask."

Jesse hung her head a little in disbelief at Meg's offhanded response. "How could you not ask? These are crucial facts."

"Fucking lawyers," Meg teased them both. "Sorry I didn't cross-examine her." She picked a cucumber from her salad and popped it in her mouth. "I was trying to be cool."

"Missed opportunity." Jesse raised her eyebrows.

"Well, we can't all be super suave, like you." Meg said it with both wry humor and complete jealousy of Jesse's legendary ease in talking to girls.

Meg looked out the window at the front of her own house and at the rain, still coming down in a steady stream. "Hey, can we talk about something else?" Meg wiped her hands on her napkin. "What do you guys think is going on with Betsy and Tracy?"

Jesse looked at her blankly. "We figured you could tell us."

"Tracy says they're just friends."

"You don't believe her?" Jesse was curious.

"I don't know. You should have seen them the other night at my house. They were, like, gazing into each other's eyes. Apparently they spent all night talking about art, politics, crap like that." She looked right at Jesse. "You know, analyzing every last thing to death, because what you really want to do is rip each other's clothes off." She flashed an eyebrow raise at Jesse. "Like you guys used to do. When Lexi was your intern."

Jesse brushed off Meg's comment by reaching back and pretending to throw a punch. "You've known Tracy a long time, huh, Meg?" she asked, abandoning her fake threat.

"Since high school."

"You guys went to high school together?" Lexi was taken aback.

"Not the same high school," Meg clarified. "We played softball against each other. She was my first gay friend. My first girlfriend," Meg added, sounding a little nostalgic.

It was Jesse's turn to be surprised. "You dated her?"

"I know," Meg affirmed with a nod. "It's funny to think about it now."

"What's the story there?" Jesse asked.

Meg shrugged. "Nothing. It was high school. She graduated and moved to California. We transitioned to friends, simple as that."

Lexi cocked her chin at Jesse. "Why do you sound so surprised? Half of your exes are on that list." Lexi shifted her eyes to the wedding guest list, which was still on the counter.

Jesse met Lexi's jab head on. "Babe, do I need to point out you've got an ex on that list also?"

"Oh my God, are you talking about Julie?" She huffed. "Nice try. I'm going to remind you Julie is not actually on the list. Her girlfriend is. And I don't think Sam can come anyway, which I'm devastated about. And while we're on the subject, *babe*, don't pretend Julie, a girl I dated for a few *months*, is even in the same category as Mary Brown or Lauren Carlisle, because she's not. And you know it."

Jesse dipped her chin. "I know." She looked genuinely affected. "I'm sorry." It was a rare moment of humility for Jesse, and while Meg felt awkward being witness to her friends' tiff, it also gave her the full spectrum of how they worked together.

Lexi walked up to the sink with a few dishes, and on her way back to the table, Jesse grabbed her by the waist and pulled her onto her lap. She buried her face in Lexi's neck, placing a kiss there before moving up to her lips. "I love you. You know that."

"I know." She ruffled Jesse's short dark curls and settled farther into her lap, turning toward Meg. "Oh my God, I have the best idea." She looked right at Meg. "You should invite Sasha to the wedding."

Meg tipped her head to the side. "How does that help anything?"

Lexi was full of excitement. "Come on. Lesbian wedding. Love in the air." She looked back and forth between Meg and Jesse. "It would be perfect."

"Except you're getting married in July." Meg furrowed her brow. "It's October. So I'm pretty sure that will just make me look desperate."

A half hour later as she crossed the street to her house, Meg thought about her predicament and felt slightly bad about taking the wind out of Lexi's sails so quickly. But even though her friend's plan was made with good intentions, it actually made Meg feel worse than before.

The thought that eight months down the road she might be in the exact same position she was now—single and lusting after a straight coworker—was enough to make her reassess her priorities for good. Until this evening, she had been grouping herself and Tracy in roughly the same category. Two single girls on the hunt, each with their sights set on a particular prospect. And while that was true, there were some major differences.

For starters, at least Betsy dated women, giving Tracy a more than marginal chance at success with her strategy of playing the long game. From what Meg had seen so far, Betsy was interested, that much was clear. Whether or not she would allow herself to act on that interest was another matter altogether.

Meg, on the other hand, was chasing a fantasy. It was time she moved on.

CHAPTER FOURTEEN

At six o'clock Friday evening Meg sat at her desk contemplating the happy hour email announcement that had landed in her inbox hours ago. This week's event was at JD's, an Irish pub right around the corner on Lexington Avenue. She was dying to go. She loved the Friday night ritual of light drinks with her colleagues followed by partying with Sasha's crew of friends. And truth be told, she didn't have anything else to do anyway. Lexi and Jesse were at the Cape for the weekend, Tracy had flown back to California for her dad's birthday, and there was nothing going on at the development. But she'd made a promise to herself a week and a half ago to forget about Sasha and get on with her life.

It was proving way harder than she'd thought. She spent countless hours with Sasha at work helping her strategize her projects. They did lunch more than once a week. They had a million inside jokes they briefed each other on daily, either in person or by phone or text.

Meg swayed back and forth in her chair, searching for the courage to get up and go home, head to her sister's, or steal Betsy for dinner, when Sasha texted from the bar asking where she was. Meg fired off a quick response stating she was still in the office and added she wasn't sure if she was going to make it to happy hour. Sasha didn't ask if Meg had other plans or was working to a deadline, she simply texted, *Please come*, and just like that Meg's mind was made up. That was precisely the moment she knew she was in serious trouble.

She was already a few drinks in by the time Sasha found her hanging out halfway down the narrow bar. Meg watched her sauntering over, and she used all her resolve to keep her eyes up and avoid checking out Sasha's figure, complemented tonight by a slim black skirt and fitted top that outlined her curves.

"How come you weren't going to come tonight?" Sasha started. "Something going on at your development?"

Meg shook her head into her pint glass. "Not really."

Sasha looked offended. "So you were just going to not come?"

"Why are you taking it personally?" Meg challenged, even though she was aware of the irony in her question.

"Because this is our thing." She looked into Meg's eyes. "I mean, we sort of started it." Sasha clasped her drink with both hands, holding it close to her. "I thought you liked coming."

"I do." Meg sipped her beer. "It's not that."

"Then what is it?"

The place was getting crowded and Sasha was standing a few feet from Meg in the center of the aisle, blocking the way of people trying to pass. Meg took Sasha's wrist and pulled her closer so some Wall Street types could get by.

She looked up at the ceiling, quietly searching for a way to tell Sasha she needed some space, without revealing why. She blew out a long breath. "The thing is…" She stopped herself right away, not at all sure how to say it. She gave up. "Nothing. Forget it," she finished.

"What?" Sasha demanded.

Meg looked past her. "Nothing."

Sasha touched one finger to Meg's cheek, guiding her attention back. "Tell me," she said softly.

Meg's attention was fixed on Sasha's hand, still on her face, and she widened her eyes at the overly familiar gesture, but let it go when Sasha dropped her hand quickly.

"It's nothing, really." Meg leaned her head against the wall behind her. "It's just, I don't know. I love hanging out with you and your friends." She chewed the inside of her mouth. "Sometimes I just feel like—"

Sasha finished for her. "What, like they're judging you or something?"

"No. That's not it at all." Meg barked out her response because it couldn't be further from the truth. Sasha's friends were sweet and totally accepting of Meg's life. She licked her lips. "I just think maybe I should be spending more time with *my* people."

Sasha looked confused. "Your friends, you mean?"

"No." Meg swallowed. "I guess, yes. But that's not what I meant."

"Wait." Sasha held up one hand. "Do you mean…lesbians?"

"Not for, like, solidarity," Meg responded in defense of her statement. "I just think I should be going out to places where I might actually meet someone. You know?"

Sasha took a second to let it sink in. "Oh." She looked into her drink, considering. "We could do that, if you want." Sasha averted her eyes and sounded a little disappointed. "Go to the Kitchen, or wherever, after." She touched the rim of her glass with her forefinger. "I'm sure Jane-Anne and the rest would come."

"That's all right." Meg's tone was more dismissive than she intended.

Sasha looked right at Meg. "Even if they didn't, Meg, I would go with you."

They were talking close and had to lean in to hear each other over the crowd and the jukebox. Over Sasha's shoulder, Meg saw Scott sizing them up. She knew she didn't have much time left. She leaned in to speak, to give Sasha a halfhearted explanation of why that wasn't necessary, but it was too late. Scott was there.

"Watch out, Sasha. You're getting pretty close there. You don't want Meg to get the wrong idea."

Scott was the only one who laughed. Meg and Sasha held eye contact for a beat but left their conversation unfinished.

In a second, Carrie and Sue from HR joined the group and Scott was quick to steal the limelight by taking out his gigantic phone and pulling up a new video that had just gone viral. The group chatted together for a while until they naturally splintered and Meg took the schism as an opportunity to slip out unnoticed. As she reached for her jacket, she did a cursory scan for Sasha until she located her still next to Scott, laughing away at one of his stupid jokes. Meg dashed out the door and began flagging down cab after cab that passed her by, already loaded with passengers.

Meg heard Sasha's accusation before she even realized Sasha was behind her. "You're leaving?"

"Sorry. I'm just not into it tonight."

"So you just sneak out without saying good-bye?" Sasha reached for Meg's arm and pulled it down, clearly expecting an explanation.

"Why are you so mad at me tonight?"

"I'm not mad. I just don't understand why you would leave like that."

Meg looked over at the bar's façade. "You had your hands full with Scott anyway." She wasn't sure why she'd started down this path, but it was too late, so she pressed on. "As usual."

Sasha folded her arms across her chest against the chilly night air. "Come on, Meg, there's nothing going on between me and Scott. You know that."

"Fine. Whatever." Meg frowned. "It's none of my business anyway."

"Then stay. Please?" she asked. "Or let me come with you," she added, reaching over and tugging hopefully at Meg's jacket.

It was yet another gesture Meg found too intimate for the parameters of their friendship. She didn't know what to say, but it didn't matter. At that moment a taxi flew down the street with its overhead light on, indicating it was unoccupied. Meg shot her arm up just in time. Reaching for the door handle she called over her shoulder, "I'm sorry, Sash. I gotta go."

Meg looked at the driver through the partition and gave him the cross streets for the Kitchen. She didn't really know what she was doing, she just knew she didn't want to go home. She spent the short cab ride overanalyzing Sasha's every move of the night—a waste of time, she knew, but she couldn't help herself. Of course her ride would have been better spent contacting any of her friends, even Taylor Higgins, to see if anyone was hanging out somewhere or wanted to meet her at the Kitchen. Instead she arrived at the bar alone and entered it that way, praying she might find a familiar face inside.

She ordered a drink right away and within two minutes spotted her exes Mia and Becca in the back corner, proving once and for all the Lord above had a warped sense of humor. They were the last people on earth she wanted to run into, given her mood and the pathetic truth that she'd come out alone. She could feel their eyes on her and took a hefty swig from her drink, hoping the alcohol would numb their pity. She gave a chin nod in their direction and was thinking about going over just to be social, when she caught sight of Sasha standing inside the front door, looking anxious as she scanned the crowd. Sasha's eyes found hers and locked with them as she made her way over, maneuvering around several women between them. She stood directly in front of Meg and, without saying a word, she leaned in and softly pressed her lips to Meg's.

When Sasha pulled back slowly, she looked right at Meg. "Come with me." It was at once a command and a plea, and Meg didn't protest. She placed her drink at the edge of the bar and let Sasha guide her through the crowd.

They grabbed a taxi in front of the bar. Sasha leaned forward to the driver to give him her address, never letting go of Meg's hand. They sat together with their fingers interlaced, not saying a word the entire twelve-minute cab ride until they were deposited outside Sasha's gray apartment building.

Sasha finally released Meg's grip as she dug the keys out of her purse to open up the vestibule door. Meg followed quietly as they walked up three flights of stairs, still in silence, until they reached Sasha's apartment and she quickly turned two locks and pushed the heavy door open. Meg took only one step inside before Sasha closed the door, locking the locks systematically, while Meg leaned up against the wall and waited for whatever was about to happen.

Sasha stood in front of her, speechless. For a second Meg thought she was going to say something, but then she didn't. She looked from Meg's mouth to her eyes and back to her mouth again. She licked her own lips and leaned forward. Meg kissed her back, softly at first, but their kiss intensified quickly. Meg tried to hold back—she really had no idea how far this would go, and the last thing she wanted to do was move too fast too soon. But she could feel herself throbbing already and she had to make a concerted effort to keep her hands still. She strategically placed them high on the sides of Sasha's neck, cradling her face, but after a few minutes she got caught up in the moment. Without thinking she let them slide down the front of Sasha's body and inside her peacoat, finding her hips and pulling her closer. After a second, Sasha stepped back, and immediately Meg worried she had gone too far.

Sasha looked down sheepishly. "Sorry." Her lips were bright red and her cheeks were flushed. "We can probably take these off." Her laugh was nervous as she hung her coat on the corner rack and removed her boots, placing them below it. Meg didn't dare move.

"You're not going to leave, are you?" Sasha sounded scared she might say yes. Meg found it adorable and vulnerable and sexy as hell, and even though she had no clue what the fuck was happening, she found a calm voice and responded.

"Of course not."

Meg slipped out of her jacket and handed it to Sasha. She visually scanned the studio apartment for a place to sit but found basically one piece of furniture—a bed—in the center of the small room.

"Sash, I—" Meg started to speak, unsure what to say, but she stopped talking when Sasha took her hand again and guided them toward the bed.

"Do you want a drink or anything?" Sasha asked. Without the heel of her boots, Sasha was a full two inches shorter than Meg, and when she looked up, her eyes were as serious as ever.

"No." Meg shook her head. She sat down on the bed and waited for a second, but Sasha didn't join her. Again Meg wondered if it was over, thinking maybe Sasha would get herself a drink and they would talk, or something. But that didn't happen either. Instead, Sasha stood in front of Meg for a long moment before she took her shirt off and dropped it to the floor next to her.

Instinctively, Meg leaned in and kissed the soft, flat belly inches from her face. She let her hands find their way up Sasha's skirt, along Sasha's smooth thighs. Sasha reached behind her back, undid her skirt, and let it fall to the floor, placing one knee on each side of Meg as she straddled her on top of the mattress.

They kissed each other deeply and were so in sync that their movements were virtually seamless as Sasha reached down and pulled Meg's shirt off while Meg unhooked Sasha's bra. Sliding the straps down Sasha's arms, Meg leaned forward and pressed her lips to Sasha's chest first, then moved down over the curve of her breasts until her lips found Sasha's nipple and she brushed across it gently. Sasha leaned back a little, digging her hands into Meg's hair as she pushed herself deeper into Meg's mouth. Reading Sasha's reaction, Meg stayed focused for a good minute before kissing her way to Sasha's other breast, where she remained until Sasha couldn't take it anymore, pulling Meg's face up toward her own and kissing her with wild abandon.

Meg kept her composure, grazing her hands up and down Sasha's back, through her long, soft hair, until one hand rested at Sasha's neck, the other on the curve of her hip. She leaned backward onto the bed and brought Sasha with her, still kissing her as she rolled over on top. Sasha fidgeted with Meg's bra clasp, but gave up right away and pulled it off over her head roughly before she slid her hands into the back of Meg's jeans, inside her underwear, trying unsuccessfully to push them down together. Meg sat up on her knees and reached for her belt but Sasha took over, gently moving Meg's hand away as she undid the buckle and lowered the zipper of Meg's jeans, inching her pants down. Meg leaned in, kissing Sasha back down to the mattress, while she wriggled out of her jeans and kicked them to the floor. Their hands were all over each other, and despite her efforts at restraint, Meg realized she was already grinding pretty hard between Sasha's legs.

She took it a step further, kissing her way down Sasha's body, only stopping when her face was even with Sasha's underwear, the last barrier between them. Meg looked up and made eye contact to ask Sasha the question she'd been afraid to utter since they entered the apartment.

"Sasha, are you sure?"

It was probably strange to ask such a thing at this point. Meg knew Sasha wasn't drunk. They were both fully aware of what they were doing, but Meg also knew they were about to cross a line and she wanted to make it clear, even though Sasha had instigated pretty much everything, there was still no pressure for her to do anything she wasn't ready for.

Her eyes on Meg's, Sasha bit her lower lip and nodded.

It was one of the sexiest things Meg had ever seen and it gave her the assurance she needed. She carefully removed Sasha's black panties and got to work.

They found a rhythm right away and Sasha seemed into it and relaxed as she moved her hips in unison with Meg. But then she stopped Meg abruptly, tugging at her short hair and pulling her upward. Meg was disappointed, but not shocked, figuring Sasha was having second thoughts after all. She moved herself up Sasha's body and began to mentally prepare to talk it out.

Sasha surprised Meg again by kissing her hard and taking Meg's hand as she directed it between her legs. "In," she whispered, guiding Meg's fingers with her own at first. "Is that okay?" Sasha asked, as she wrapped her arms around Meg's shoulders.

Meg felt no need to answer, concentrating instead on getting her body weight behind her as she pushed into Sasha. She felt Sasha's legs tighten around her waist, forcing her in deeper with each movement. Meg heard Sasha's breathing change and she started to moan—louder than Meg expected—until she dug her fingers into Meg's back and breathed out, "Fuck, Megan," as she came.

❖

Meg lay on her back looking up at the ceiling for a good few minutes, the silence hanging heavy between them. Sasha had barely moved since her orgasm and Meg wondered if she was pretending to be asleep. She'd faced this before—one-sided sex with a straight girl—and she certainly understood it might be the case here, as well.

Almost on cue, Sasha turned on her side to face Meg and gently placed her hand on Meg's stomach. She leaned over and kissed Meg sweetly on the lips, then the cheek, until she began working her way down Meg's neck. In a voice that was a bit huskier than usual, Sasha spoke. "So, I don't really know what I'm doing," she began.

"You don't have to do anything," Meg responded, giving her an out.

Sasha's mouth curled up on one side. "I didn't say that." She kissed Meg's collarbone. "I was just hoping for a little learning curve." She moved her lips across Meg's chest and let her hand drift down Meg's body. She gasped audibly and looked down when her fingers slid easily into Meg, who was very ready. "Is that because of me?" she asked.

Meg nodded slightly, a little embarrassed by how wet she knew she was.

"Oh my God, that's hot," Sasha added, not bothering to filter. Once again she bit her lower lip and slowly began to make her way down Meg's body. Meg was already breathing heavily, both excited for what seemed imminent and worried Sasha might balk. She didn't.

Instead, Sasha took her time, kissing Meg's sides and her belly until she finally put her mouth where Meg needed it most. She moved her tongue slowly up and down at first, not appearing uncomfortable in the slightest. When she looked up, possibly for reassurance, Meg wasn't sure, their eyes locked. It was all Meg could do to resist coming from the intensity of the moment. She held out, but not for very long. When Sasha increased the pace, moving the flat of her tongue against her clit,

Meg's hips bucked furiously beyond her control and she climaxed in what was probably record time.

When they had both finished, they settled into each other with Sasha curling into Meg's body, nuzzling her head into the space between Meg's chin and shoulder. She tilted Meg's head toward hers and gave her a nice kiss on the lips. "That was fucking incredible," she said, placing her head back on Meg's bare chest.

Meg couldn't have agreed more.

CHAPTER FIFTEEN

Meg woke up in the center of the bed, a mass of covers crumpled around her. The light streaming in from the windows was bright—brighter than morning sun. She tilted her head to the side but couldn't seem to locate a clock. Sasha wasn't next to her but as Meg rubbed the sleep from her eyes she saw her standing less than five feet away leaning on the kitchen counter. Sasha had on the tortoiseshell glasses they had picked out together and a heather-gray oversized tee that just brushed the tops of her thighs. She was scarfing down Honey Nut Cheerios as though it might be her last meal.

"Hey," Meg said, lifting herself onto her elbows.

Sasha waved with her spoon and Meg thought, she hoped at least, she saw a smile playing at the corners of her mouth as she chewed. With a small movement she pushed off the counter and crossed to Meg, sitting on the edge of the bed with one leg pulled up under her.

"Morning," she said as she swallowed.

Meg moved herself up farther into a sitting position against the pillows. She wasn't sure at all what to say or what to expect. The full weight of the prior evening's events hadn't really hit her yet and she had no idea what Sasha's reaction would be but thought she should say something.

"Are you, um, okay?" Meg moved her hands back and forth between them. "With everything?"

"Mm-hmm." Sasha nodded.

"Sash, you know it's okay if you aren't. We could talk about it."

"I'm fine." Sasha's smile was a little bashful. "I'm just starving."

"Me too," Meg echoed.

"Here." Sasha spooned some cereal into Meg's mouth, wiping a line of milk that dripped down Meg's chin with her thumb.

Meg leaned her head back into the pillow as she chewed. "God, that's good."

"I know, right?" Sasha helped herself to another bite, before hooking Meg up again.

Meg held on to Sasha's hand for a second, forcing eye contact. "Sash."

Sasha raised her eyes, her dark lashes lifting as she waited for Meg to continue.

"You sure you're okay?"

The spoon clanked against the sides of the bowl as Sasha placed it on the nightstand next to the bed. She put a hand on each side of Meg's face and kissed her long and slow. She pulled away deliberately. "I'm okay. I promise." She leaned forward again but stopped herself. "Wait, are *you* okay?"

"Yeah," Meg breathed out. "Of course."

"Okay." Sasha smiled.

"Would you just hand me my shirt?" Meg asked, nodding toward its location on the floor.

Without even looking, Sasha shook her head. "Absolutely not," she answered, removing her specs and lifting off her own shirt as she slipped back under the covers.

❖

Meg re-woke up in the middle of the afternoon, Sasha's naked body still pressed against hers. She kissed her temple softly and Sasha cuddled into her sweetly before opening her eyes.

"I'm starving. Diner?" Sasha asked through a smile and a yawn.

A half block down, over brunch and coffee, they talked about everyday stuff, never once discussing the last twelve hours, which made Meg a little nervous. But she was too busy enjoying being with Sasha, so she pushed it out of her mind. She thought the feeling might be mutual because even after they paid the bill, Sasha volunteered to walk with Meg as she headed toward a southbound subway.

They strolled next to each other for over a mile, passing one train station after another, until they reached Twenty-Third Street, where

Sasha steered them toward Chelsea Piers to pick up the footpath that ran along Manhattan's West Side. It was a chilly, gray day but the sun popped through the clouds every so often to offset the cool breeze coming off the water.

A few moments of silence passed between them before Meg stuffed her hands in the pockets of her North Face shell. "So, we should probably talk about last night."

"Okay," Sasha replied, waiting for Meg to start.

Meg chewed the inside of her mouth, a little nervous. "So, I mean, I know you keep saying you're okay with everything." She gave Sasha a sidelong glance. "But are you really?"

Sasha looked at the ground. "I think so."

"Yeah?"

Looking back up, Sasha nodded with a smile. "I kind of thought my actions this morning proved I was okay." She hooked her arm through Meg's as they continued along the water.

"I know. But—"

"But what?"

"I don't know. I'm confused, I guess."

"About?"

Meg swallowed her smile. "Everything."

"Wait a second." Sasha's voice held some vulnerability. "Do you regret it?"

Meg looked right at the sweet girl walking next to her. "No, Sash," she said with a smile. She paused abruptly, not really knowing what to say next. She wanted to ask what this meant for them and where they went from here. She was dying to know if this was a one-time thing. But she was scared of the answers, so she asked something else entirely.

"Have you ever done that before? With a girl, I mean?"

Sasha looked right into Meg's eyes and shook her head.

"So that was your first time?"

"Yes."

Meg nodded to herself, inwardly surprised at how comfortable and relaxed Sasha had seemed throughout.

Sasha witnessed her thought process and squinted one eye closed. "I was okay, right?"

"Of course. You were good. Really good," she added reassuringly. "I'm just surprised, that's all."

"You're surprised I'm good in bed?" Sasha teased her playfully.

"That's not what I mean." Meg met her sarcasm. "I'm just surprised you were, that you are still, so calm about everything. No morning-after freak-out. That is sort of unusual, considering you've never done it. I'm happy about it, don't get me wrong. Just a little surprised."

Sasha squeezed Meg's biceps through her jacket. "Did you wig out your first time?"

"Yes," Meg answered quickly, laughing a little at the memory.

"Tell me about it."

Meg moved them out of the way of an oncoming Rollerblader. "Now that I think about it, I didn't really," she said, changing her answer. When Sasha looked confused, Meg said, "My first time was with Tracy, remember? She was really cool."

"I forgot you dated her." Sasha looked past Meg, out onto the water. "And you guys are still friends. That's nice."

"It is." Meg craned her neck to check out a boat speeding through the harbor. "Me and Tracy were never meant to be a couple." She shrugged. "We just needed each other, I think. She'd had a girlfriend before me but they broke up when the girl went to college. We sort of found each other, became friends, and did stuff." Meg giggled.

Sasha dropped her chin and raised her eyebrow at Meg's vague reference.

"We were seventeen. Actually I was seventeen, she was eighteen." Meg's smile was a little naughty. "I knew I liked girls. I didn't have a clue what to do. Tracy was gorgeous and confident and a little lonely. It worked for us. She kind of showed me the ropes." Meg looked at the ground as she walked. "I was really self-conscious. Tracy never made me feel stupid. She was nice."

"You were nervous?"

"I guess by the time we did it, I wasn't nervous for the actual act." She bit the inside of her mouth. "We had been messing around a lot. I mean, there wasn't much we hadn't done." Meg gave a small smile. "So I was kind of excited for that part of it. But I was nervous for what it meant. For me," she clarified. "I just felt like, once I did it, being a lesbian was real and not just an idea in my head. Kind of like there was no going back." She twisted her mouth to the side. "That freaked me out."

Sasha nodded, taking it all in.

"Hey." Meg stopped walking and looked right at Sasha, realizing what she had just said. "I'm not saying that means anything about you. You know that, right?" Meg tried to overcompensate. "That was just how I felt at the time."

"I know," Sasha responded quietly. "I know what you mean, Meg." She reached for Meg's hand inside her jacket pocket. "I wasn't entirely honest with you before."

Meg interlaced their fingers and waited for Sasha to continue.

Sasha took a deep breath. "I told you a while ago I had experimented in college."

"Yeah."

"Well, I was maybe not completely forthcoming about the whole story," she started. She looked away toward the traffic on the street. "It was one girl. Sophie, her name was."

"Okay."

"She was my boyfriend's best friend's girlfriend. And initially it was my boyfriend who suggested it. But I had been planting the seed for a while, pointing out girls I thought were hot. And Sophie and I became friends because of Dave and Tom. So we would all hang out together." She widened her eyes as she looked at the ground. "Insert lots of drinking, and bam, it happened. The first few times, we all laughed. Sophie and I would play it up. The guys loved it." She held her free hand out and let it graze the top of a wildflower planted along the pathway's green space. "The thing is, I loved it too. I loved kissing Sophie." She clenched Meg's hand a little. "I spent a lot of time orchestrating situations where it would be just the four of us."

Sensing Sasha's level of discomfort in her disclosure, Meg rubbed the top of her hand with her thumb and waited to see if she would say more.

"So, one night the guys were meeting us later after some rugby match or football game or whatever. Sophie came to my apartment beforehand to help me get dinner ready. We were drinking and I kind of..." She shook her head. "I mean, I tried to..." She bit her lip and looked away from Meg. "It's so embarrassing," she continued. "I tried to kiss her. Without the guys there," she finished, unable to make eye contact.

"What happened?"

"It was bad."

"She flipped out?"

"She didn't scream at me or anything like that, but she certainly didn't let it happen either. That was it. She knew. We never hung out again after that night." Sasha shrugged a little. "I broke up with Dave not long after."

"Did she tell him? Is that why you broke up?"

Sasha shook her head. "I don't think she told anyone. Ever." She huffed out a weird little laugh. "Dave and I were never that serious. I wasn't anyway." A small smile escaped her. "Even after we broke up, it was Sophie I thought about all the time. Not Dave."

"Were you in love with her?"

Sasha cocked her head from side to side. "Love?" She paused to consider. "Not love, I don't think. I did love kissing her though." She licked her lips. "I secretly imagined doing other stuff with her. It was a pretty serious crush, I guess."

"Did you ever see her after that?"

"Around Oxford." Sasha nodded. "She was always nice to me. But it was weird. I freaked her out. I could tell."

Meg stopped and faced Sasha, taking a brief second to assess where they were, just at the north end of Battery Park City. They had been walking for hours. The late October sun was setting behind them, the cold fall air creeping in.

"I can't believe she didn't want to kiss you. Stupid girl."

Sasha drew in her lower lip with her teeth. "Why? You want to kiss me?" she asked coyly.

"All the time," Meg answered as she leaned forward and met Sasha's lips. The kiss was soft and slow at first but grew deeper by degrees as they pressed against the railing at the water's edge, small ripples of the Hudson River lapping against the seawall beneath them.

Meg pulled away first. She kissed Sasha's lips and her forehead. "It's late. I should get moving if I'm going to make the next boat."

"Why are you going home?"

Meg furrowed her brow in question. "Um, for starters I need a shower. I've been wearing the same clothes since yesterday morning. And believe it or not, I'm kind of hungry again."

Sasha laced their fingers together. "So let's grab a cab, head back to my place. I have a shower, you know."

"And food?"

"We'll order Thai, stay in, watch ridiculous, guilty-pleasure movies all night."

Meg smiled at how easily she was being convinced.

Sasha clearly knew it too. "So that's it. Everything's worked out, then."

"What about clothes? There's still that."

"Entirely optional." Sasha smiled, pulling Meg toward West Street and a string of uptown taxis ready for an easy fare.

❖

Back at Sasha's, Meg was only halfway through her shower when Sasha eased back the curtain and stepped in.

"Hi." She spoke with a question in her voice as though she was unsure if it was okay to join Meg.

Meg couldn't help but smile. "Come here," she said with more confidence than ever. Without waiting, Meg curled Sasha into her body, holding her from behind under the hot shower stream. She took the soap and started at Sasha's abdomen, working her way up the soft curve of her breasts as she touched her lips to Sasha's shoulder. Meg bit down gently as she lathered Sasha's nipples, and she felt Sasha shudder at the contact. She smiled into Sasha's wet flesh, not ready to give in yet, continuing to tease her.

"Meg?" Sasha's voice was needy.

"Mm-hmm."

Meg heard a small moan escape Sasha's lips. "Meg," she pleaded, taking Meg's hand and putting it between her legs. Meg turned Sasha around, leaning into her against the bathroom wall as she pushed her fingers inside. Their kiss was wet and slippery and hungry until she finally dropped to her knees and stayed there until she felt Sasha's legs buckle above her.

Sasha sank down and straddled Meg on the floor of the tub, wrapping her limp arms around Meg's neck. "How do you do that to me?"

Meg tilted her head at the question and placed a kiss on her lips. "Do what?"

"That." Sasha's eyes went to where she had stood a second ago.

"That thing where you reduce me to nothing. Make me completely lose control."

"What, like, make you come?"

Sasha looked down, seeming shy for a second, but she spoke anyway. "It's more than that. Nobody's ever made me feel like that." She bit her lip, still avoiding eye contact. "Not like you do."

"Really?"

Sasha nodded slowly and rested her head against Meg's. "This is so sad. I'm not sure I can move yet but the water is getting cold." She put on a mock pout and stood up, taking Meg's hand. "Don't think I'm done with you," she said, handing Meg a towel. "I just need to get the circulation back in my body," she said with an adorable glimmer in her eye.

When they were dry, they ordered takeout and ate it off one plate, wrapped in the blankets from the bed, feeding each other bites every so often. Sasha sat between Meg's legs. They put the television on in the background, and halfway through *Forgetting Sarah Marshall*, Sasha ran her fingers along Meg's calves, then leaned back and kissed the spot next to Meg's ear. "Is it my turn yet?"

Meg smiled. She was ready, and clearly Sasha was too. Meg kissed her deeply, sliding her hand down Sasha's torso, and touching her through her thin pajamas.

"Nuh-uh." Sasha grinned, turning around and leaning Meg back into the pillows. "You're going first this time." She lifted her eyebrows. "I make no promise I won't completely pass out when you're done with me."

Meg smiled. She was dying to touch Sasha again, to watch her orgasm. Especially now, in light of Sasha's confession. But she relented and relaxed into the mattress, pulling Sasha on top of her and kissing her passionately. She let Sasha pull off her borrowed boxer shorts and smiled into her mouth when she heard Sasha's breath catch at their bodies making contact. Sasha wasn't slow this time. She zigzagged her lips down Meg's body, settling between her legs and staying there until Meg's orgasm came in multiples.

Afterward, Meg took her time with Sasha, teasing and playing until Sasha begged for mercy. But she didn't pass out as she'd predicted she might. They stayed awake half the night watching cheesy movies they had both seen before, passing the time in a mix of talking and touching until they fell asleep in each other's arms.

Meg never asked what any of this meant for them or if it would happen again. When the thought rushed into her mind in the early dawn light, she pushed it out, choosing instead to revel in the feel of Sasha's bare stomach against her palm, the smooth skin of her back against her chest, and their legs entwined together.

When she finally left late Sunday afternoon, Meg felt a pang of regret—not for what they had done, but only that she had to leave and she worried it might never happen again. When she kissed Sasha good-bye in the doorway, she thought Sasha felt it too. Her eyes held disappointment and Meg could only hope it was because she was leaving, and not something else.

CHAPTER SIXTEEN

Tracy was just finishing her jog when she strolled out of Bay West's rental section and caught sight of Meg at the corner of the block.

"Hey, buddy, how was your weekend?" Meg asked.

Tracy gave a full-on leer. "Not as exciting as yours." She playfully shook Meg by the shoulders from behind as she followed her into the house. "I want to hear all the dirty details." She threw her arm around Meg's neck and gave a squeeze. "I'm psyched for you." Tracy saw Meg blush as she backed into the kitchen. "How was it seeing Sasha at the office today?" Tracy drained half a glass of water and wiped the edges of her mouth with her thumb and forefinger. "You didn't say much about it in your texts."

"It was fine, I guess." Meg shrugged her shoulders. "I only saw her this morning. She was out at a client all afternoon."

"How was it when you saw her?"

"Normal," Meg answered.

Tracy lifted her eyebrows and challenged Meg with her stare. "And what is normal for you two, exactly?" Even though she expected an answer, her tone was purposely spirited.

"Hmm, good question." Meg matched her friend's sass. She tapped her chin in faux thought. "I guess…picture whatever normal is for you and Betsy." Meg put on a sugary smile. "That."

"Well played." Tracy laughed. "Speaking of which, can I borrow your car tonight?" She refilled her empty glass. "We're going out to dinner. Me and Betsy."

Tracy cleared her throat and started to explain. "We still have that gift certificate and I just figured it might be a nice change if I picked her up for once, you know." She looked over for Meg's response and thought for a second Meg was gearing up to make a joke, so she braced herself for a racy comment, but Meg just smiled. "Have fun," she said with a wink, tossing the keys across the space between them.

❖

Lombardo's Italian Ristorante was a neighborhood staple. It wasn't fancy, but the food was fantastic and the staff always pleasant. It was quiet tonight, even for a Monday, probably due to the unseasonably cold weather—a fact that was killing Tracy. Over the years she'd become accustomed to the California climate, and even though tonight was in the midforties, it felt subzero to her. Fortunately, the maître d' did them a solid, ushering them toward a cozy back corner table a few feet from the wood-burning oven.

"What are you thinking for dinner?" Betsy peered over the menu.

Tracy let out a long breath. "Probably the sea bass."

"Where do you see that?"

"On the specials board behind you."

Betsy shook her head. "Wow. You really are a health nut. You know this place is known for its chicken parm and the homemade ravioli."

"What can I say?" Tracy fanned over her body with one hand. "This doesn't happen by itself." She smiled at her cocky joke. "Pasta is not my friend."

Betsy rolled her eyes good-naturedly as she reached for her wine. "How was LA?"

Tracy blinked slowly considering the question. "It was good." She opted not to disclose that she had spent an inordinate amount of the last seventy-two hours counting the minutes until this dinner reservation. "Did you make it to the Met on Saturday?" she asked, knowing Betsy had expressed interest in a limited-run Early Italian Renaissance display on loan from Europe.

Betsy curled her lips and shook her head. "I checked the website. It's there for another two weeks." She looked right at Tracy. "You said you wanted to go too." She shrugged. "I figured we could catch it together this weekend." While it wasn't phrased as a question, Betsy lifted her eyebrows, clearly hoping for a positive response.

Tracy's smile was warm and appreciative. "That would be awesome."

They talked through their salads and entrees about everything—noteworthy bits in the news, the weather, the weekend past, and the week ahead. Tracy filled a clueless Betsy in on what she knew of Meg's tryst with Sasha, but was hardly able to answer any of Betsy's follow-up questions, explaining she had taken an overnight flight and gotten in to New York this morning after Meg had already left for work, so they'd only seen each other in the few minutes before Tracy got ready for dinner.

Betsy sucked in a whistle. "The red-eye. That's brutal."

"It's not as bad as it could be," Tracy offered. "It's cheaper, and I slept this afternoon." She smiled, adding, "Not like I have a job or anything." She tried to play it off with a shrug, but even she heard the frustration in her tone.

As she listened, Betsy twisted her wineglass between her expertly manicured fingernails. She seemed to hesitate, almost saying something but then changing her mind at the last minute.

"What?" Tracy asked, picking up on Betsy's subtle facial expressions.

Betsy shifted in her seat. "I know it's none of my business, and if I'm over the line, just say so." She tucked a long strand of silky gold hair behind her ear. "Can I ask, what are you doing for money?"

Tracy hung her head and laughed a little to herself. "It's a fair question." She rubbed the back of her neck where the edges of her short dark hair brushed the collar of her shirt. "Well, I'm making a little cash off my sublet," she said with a single shoulder shrug. "And I have some savings, but my dad is helping me out here and there," she added through a sheepish grin. "Meg is awesome, she won't let me give her a dime for anything." She gave Betsy a knowing look. "You know how she is." She lifted her glass and took a sip of her wine. "So I'm getting by. Also over the weekend, I hung out with my friend Kristen, who works for ESPN. She's from Queens, went to UConn on a basketball scholarship. Anyway, she has a lot of good contacts in this area. So she's going to put out some feelers for me." Tracy swirled the last of her wine before draining the glass. "And I have the Gala next month." She cocked her head to the side, doing a quick calculation. "Well, December, so like a month and a half, but still, I'm thinking that will be a good place to get my name circulating."

"What's the Gala?" Betsy asked over her pasta.

"The charity I volunteer at"—she poked an errant green bean at the edge of her plate—"Every Youth Counts," she added biting off the end. "They do an annual fund-raiser in New York. I've only been once before, but I'm going to hit it up again this year, mostly just to try and get my face out there. See if I can make some connections on my own."

Betsy nodded, taking it in. "Who goes to it?"

Tracy looked up and thought about the answer. "All of the board members. A lot of athletes, but mostly ones either from New York or affiliated with local teams, now that I think about it. Some politicians. Rich people," she continued to drone out the list. "Not my cup of tea really, but it will be a good place for me to at least get the word out I'm looking."

"It doesn't sound so bad."

Tracy pushed the remains of her fish around on her plate and nodded as she thought out loud. "It could be fun." She made eye contact with Betsy. "But I know Jezebel is going to be there, and even though I really don't want to see her, I have to suck it up and go anyway."

"How do you know she'll be there?"

Tracy swallowed hard trying to mask her emotion. "I just know. She goes to the big events." She looked away as she continued to explain. "She'll know I'm going. The Gala is where we met two years ago." She focused her attention on the waiter serving the couple a few tables away. "She'll use that, believe me."

"Use it for what?" Betsy asked in confusion.

"The thing is"—Tracy pulled at the back of her neck—"I haven't talked to her since we broke up." Tracy leaned back in her chair, looking defeated. "She knows I'm in New York. She'll find out I'm going and she'll corner me there. I know she will."

Betsy took a minute to consider Tracy's statement. "How did you leave it, when you broke up?"

Tracy looked at her blankly.

"I mean, what were the ground rules after your split?"

Tracy leaned in and looked at Betsy very seriously from under her lashes. "Betsy, I walked in on her with someone else. All the ground rules went out the window at that point."

"I know." Betsy leaned in also, and for a second Tracy thought she was going to reach for her hand. "I meant after." She pushed her dinner plate to the side and rested both her arms on the table. "When you actually had a conversation, or a fight, whatever, how did you leave it?"

Tracy curled her lip and stretched back into her chair, shaking her head. "I never had a conversation with her. I just left."

Betsy's mouth hung open a little. "Wait a second." She waved her hand in the air, halting the conversation. "I thought you were with her for like a year and a half."

"A little more, but yeah."

"And you never talked to her? At all?" She blinked slowly, allowing the shock to settle in. "You just left?"

Tracy could feel her anger coming to the surface. "I didn't want to see her. I didn't want to talk to her. I still don't."

"Hold on, you said she knows you're in New York." Betsy's brow furrowed as she tried to figure it out. "How do you know that?"

Tracy reached for her wine but, seeing it was empty, she opted for her water glass and took a sip. "She calls me. Leaves me messages, texts." In the silence she knew Betsy was waiting for more details, so she obliged, setting her drink down and studying the room as she spoke. "Usually once a week, sometimes more. She wants to see me." Slightly embarrassed, Tracy lowered her gaze to her napkin on her lap. "She said she would come here to New York if I would agree to meet her."

"Didn't she get married recently?"

Tracy let out a small irritated sigh. "Yeah."

Betsy shook her head in disbelief. "What did you say in response to meeting with her?"

"Nothing." At Betsy's look of confusion, Tracy spelled it out. "I don't answer her. Ever."

They paused the conversation as the waiter cleared away their plates and used his nifty tool to sweep the crumbs from the tablecloth. "Are you scared?" Betsy asked, her eyes heavy with concern as they met Tracy's. "To see her?"

The flames danced at the back of the brick oven and Tracy stared at them as she selected her words carefully. "She is very manipulative," she responded, twisting her thin lips into a half smile. "And charming."

She chose to leave out the part that she and Jezebel had fantastic chemistry and she hadn't slept with anyone since their breakup, opting instead to sum up the entire situation with the simple truth. "I guess I don't entirely trust myself around her," she admitted.

Even though they were talking about Jezebel, Tracy couldn't help but stare at Betsy as she analyzed this new information. She watched Betsy's painted fingernails make small circles on the edge of her wineglass and her perfectly pink lips twist this way and that as she considered what to say next. Out of nowhere, without even thinking about it, Tracy shifted forward in her seat. "I have an idea," she said, her confident energy returning.

Betsy sipped her wine and tipped her chin sideways as she waited to be filled in.

"Will you come with me, to the Gala?"

"Are you serious?" Betsy asked from under a raised brow.

"You can be my plus one." She tapped the table with the top of her middle finger and gave a small shrug. "Honestly, I could use the moral support. There will be good food, amazing champagne," she added, using everything she could to sell it.

When Betsy seemed to be considering it, Tracy pounced on the opening, employing her signature sexy grin. "Come on, say yes."

Betsy looked right at her. "As long as we're clear it's not a date."

"Fine. Not a date." Tracy nodded in agreement. "It'll be exactly like tonight." She waved between them with two fingers and a huge grin. "Just two great-looking single lesbians sharing a meal. Definitely not a date." She smiled again, knowing she had probably gone a little too far. But even though Betsy rolled her eyes, she couldn't keep her smile from stretching ear to ear.

❖

"Hey, Sash, can I ask you something?" Meg jumped right into the question that had been plaguing her more and more in the weeks that had passed since they'd first hooked up. The sex was still great, but something wasn't right.

Sipping her wine, Sasha gave a yes with her eyes, so Meg continued. "How come this"—Meg motioned back and forth between them with one hand—"is a secret?"

Sasha looked surprised by the question, but only for a split second. She took her time responding, focusing her eyes first on the stem of her wineglass then looking around the small restaurant. Finally, she spoke. "I don't know, really," she said softly.

"I'm not mad or anything." Meg subbed in a white lie. "I'm just confused, I guess."

"No, I understand you." Sasha blinked heavily as she nodded agreement. "I'm just…" She let a long breath out. "Honestly I'm not really sure how I feel about everything that's happening, and I guess I'm just taking some time to process."

Meg pulled a piece of bread from the basket between them. "What's hard for me to get, I think, is before we were together you didn't care if people thought we were a couple. You were fine with it." She paused. "But now we are and you seem freaked out." She shrugged. "What gives?"

"Freaked out?" Sasha's voice held a little challenge. "I don't know that I'd say that."

Meg backpedaled. "Maybe that's not the right word." She reached for a packet of butter. "But you don't seem entirely comfortable." She cut her bread open and tried to sound chill. "The thing is, after that first night, you were totally cool about everything. It's like it was no big deal." Her voice stayed even. "But now it's two months later, and we seem to have gone backward."

Sasha nodded, clearly choosing her words carefully. "Let me see if I can explain it." She took a sip of wine. "It's like…you know how you're always talking about sexuality being a spectrum?"

"Yeah."

"I totally agree with you. You know that." Sasha took a healthy sip of wine and wiped at her lips with her napkin. "It's just…I'm not sure, I mean…I don't one hundred percent know where I am on that scale." She worried her bottom lip. "Do you understand what I mean?"

"I guess," Meg lied.

"I feel like if I come out, or whatever, then I'm automatically labeled the gay girl, like, forever. And I'm not sure that's entirely true."

"That's the point of the scale. You don't have to be a hundred percent gay or straight. You do get that, right?" It came out harsher than she wanted.

Sasha flinched. "I know." She looked right at Meg. "And I know *you* get that. Which is why you're amazing. Because I can talk to you about this stuff and I know you get me. But, Meg, the rest of the world is not like you. They judge and label and gossip." She huffed out a little laugh. "I mean can you imagine Jane-Anne trying to deal with this?"

In truth Meg thought Jane-Anne was completely capable of understanding the Kinsey scale and appreciating it, but she thought Sasha would fight her if she said that. So she went a different route. "But Jane is awesome to me. So are the rest of the girls. So…?"

"It's true. They do like you," Sasha said. "They love you, in fact. But they're different with you than they are with me."

"What do you mean?"

"Nothing. Just we talk about different stuff when you're not around. It's a different vibe."

Meg furrowed her brow in confusion.

"It's just, look, you're not one of the girls. I don't mean that in a bad way. But it's different and I can't help feeling like if they find out about me, it won't be the same anymore. They'll put up that wall. Probably not even on purpose. But the boundaries will change. I know it."

Meg nodded, trying to understand.

"Meg." Sasha waited for Meg to look at her before she continued. "I would understand if you didn't want to do this anymore." She chewed her lip and seemed a touch nervous. "I mean, I'd be sad, but I would understand." She twisted her lips to the side. "But, Meg, try to understand where I'm coming from. You've known who you are since you were seventeen. That's like ten years." She looked down at the table. "I'm twenty-five and all of a sudden I'm not sure who I am, where I fit in. I know I'm into you, but I'm not sure I'm done with guys forever. I have no clue how to figure it all out." She raked her hand through her hair and looked Meg right in the eye. "I'm not backing away from this. I just want to go slow and not do anything that doesn't feel one hundred percent honest to me."

Sasha sounded defensive and a little stressed and Meg felt guilty for needing more than she was ready to give. "I'm not trying to pressure you, Sash," Meg said. "I just thought it might be nice to not be in hiding. That's all."

"I'm sorry. I realize it's not entirely fair to you. Can I just have a little more time to try to wrap my head around it?" Sasha asked, just the slightest hint of desperation in her tone.

Meg nodded and gave a small smile, when a thought occurred to her. "What if you talked to your mom about it? She's the voice of reason, right? Ever think about getting her take on things?" she offered optimistically. "She might have some good advice."

"It's funny you should say that," Sasha said seriously. "That was actually my plan this past weekend when I was home for Thanksgiving."

Meg looked up and waited for Sasha to explain, but she was quiet for a long second as she tilted her head up at the ceiling and wiped her eyes. "Meg, my mom is sick." Her voice cracked. "Her cancer is back."

"Is it bad?" It was a stupid question and Meg was immediately annoyed with herself for having asked it, but when Sasha didn't answer, she followed with the equally inane, "It'll be okay," trying for positive but knowing it sounded trite.

Sasha met her eyes. "I don't know, Meg." She sounded lost as she looked off to the side. "I don't know."

CHAPTER SEVENTEEN

Tracy smoothed down the front of her black shirt and adjusted the loose black necktie one more time, making sure it sat perfectly below the open collar button. She turned to the side and checked her profile in the mirror. Dabbing one last spot of hair product between her thumb and index finger, she doled it out sparingly on the longer tips of her short, trendy cut. She slid her arms through the sleeves of her black jacket and jerked it taut in the mirror, confident in her look and feel. Catching herself smiling in the reflection, she shook her head at what a dork she could really be. Finally she grabbed a red silk handkerchief, the only touch of color in her ensemble, and tucked it perfectly in her breast pocket before heading out the front door.

As Meg's car warmed up in the driveway, Tracy surfed the radio for a good song. When her phone rang, she retrieved it from the inside pocket of her suit jacket and, seeing it was Betsy, she started talking without the formality of a greeting.

"Just leaving Meg's now. I'll be there in five minutes. You ready?"

There was a full beat of silence before a woman with a squeaky voice spoke. "Is this Tracy?"

"Yes," she responded to the unfamiliar voice.

"Hi, Tracy. My name is Alecia, I'm one of Dr. Betsy's nurses. Dr. Betsy asked that I call to tell you she's very sorry, but she is still in surgery." The woman paused for a second and Tracy thought she heard empathy in her tone as she continued. "She wanted me to tell you she is going to try to get there as soon as she can."

Tracy leaned her head down on the top of the steering wheel in defeat. "Okay," she breathed out halfheartedly. "Can I talk to her?"

"I'm sorry, but that's just not possible at the moment," the woman replied. "She did want me to tell you she is very, very sorry."

Tracy swallowed her disappointment and shifted into drive, realizing that because she had focused all her energy on Betsy being her date-not-date for the Gala, she had forgotten to be nervous about seeing Jezebel Stone. That is, until this very moment. She breathed out long and hard, willed herself to be both brave and resilient, and continued driving toward the Manhattan skyline.

The first hour of the event passed in a blur. Tracy knew many of the other athletes in attendance from previous events where they had crossed paths. She was also newly acquainted with many of the Every Youth Counts New York board members, now that she had been a presence on the East Coast for the last half of the year. She was doing a bang-up job of making her way around the room, talking to various charity big shots and also making time with some New York politicos in attendance at the request of the foundation chair. These large-scale events were parties, yes, but they were also a major source of revenue for the charity, and artists and athletes alike were expected to schmooze as much as possible.

Even though Tracy wasn't a household name like many of the sports figures, musicians, and actors that supported the nonprofit, she was unmatched in a crowd. People loved to talk to her because she could talk about anything—sports, the arts, politics, current events. Probably her best quality was she listened, exercising a trait many of the Hollywood elite didn't possess. It didn't hurt that she was extremely easy on the eyes, and she worked that to her advantage as well.

The junior senator from New York had just dragged her over to meet a wealthy campaign financier he was attempting to woo for his own political ambitions when she spotted Jezebel staring at her expectantly from near the bar. Ignoring her completely, Tracy focused all her attention on the senator and the old-money retired Army colonel whose support he was trying to garner, but as she exited the dreadfully boring conversation, she turned around to find Jezebel in waiting, less than a foot and a half from her.

"You can't avoid me forever, you know."

Tracy put on a fake smile. "I don't know, I've been pretty successful so far," she snapped, fixing her gaze on her ex for the first time in months. Jezebel Stone was something to look at. Even now in ridiculously high heels, she was several inches shorter than Tracy. What she lacked in stature, she made up for in her larger-than-life persona. Her look was always over the top, crazy hairstyles in an assortment of colors, clothes that constantly pushed the envelope. Tonight was no exception. This evening she was an almost white-blond in a risqué number that revealed as much skin as it covered, highlighting her stick-thin frame and fabulously expensive, perfectly proportioned, store-bought breasts. It was a look only a bona fide rock star could pull off, and she did it with aplomb.

Underneath it all, Tracy knew, Jezebel was a sandy blonde with greenish-brown eyes that were speckled with gold flecks. She had beautiful creamy skin and a layer of soft freckles dotted her nose and cheeks, but she hid all that real beauty under layers and layers of façade. Tracy couldn't help but shake her head at the adaptation standing in front of her.

She didn't even attempt to hide her bitter tone. "The dress is a bit much, don't you think?"

"You seem to be enjoying it," Jezebel countered with a coy smile.

Tracy huffed and turned to walk away but Jezebel caught her arm. "Wait. I want to talk to you."

Tracy glanced at the hand on her forearm. It annoyed her that Jezebel assumed she had a right to touch her, but her irritation was overshadowed by her surprise that the closeted musician dared to make contact with her in public at all.

Seeming suddenly aware of her actions, Jezebel dropped her hand. "Tracy, it's been five months. You made your point." She paused and flashed a look from under lush counterfeit eyelashes. Jezebel was trying for a light tone, employing her signature charm to defuse the situation. It wasn't working, and she must have read the frustration in Tracy's body language because she softened her voice, sounding a little hurt. "So that's it? You're just never going to talk to me again."

"I'm talking to you."

"That's not what I mean."

"What do you want from me, Jez?"

Jezebel smiled and swayed her hips a little as she spoke. "Despite your lack of response, I'm sure you've at least listened to my voice mails, read my messages." She licked her lips. "I think you know what I want."

Tracy raised her eyebrows in disbelief that her ex was still trying to flirt her way out of her duplicitous behavior, but Jezebel was undeterred.

"Come on, Trace." She lowered her voice to just above a whisper. "Don't act like what we had was nothing. That's not true and you know it." She leaned in a hair. "What we had was real. It was special."

The comment stung and although Tracy was keeping her cool, she couldn't hold back her animosity over the situation.

"Who exactly is *we*?" she barked. "I'm curious. Would that be me and you? Or is it me, you, and Trina?" She swallowed hard and tapped her chin for effect as she continued. "Wait, wait, I know." She counted off each finger. "It's me, you, Trina, *and* Jasper, right?"

"I suppose I deserve that," Jezebel said through her clenched jaw.

Tracy was on a roll. "How is your husband, by the way? I didn't see him here." Tracy rose up on her toes, making a grand gesture of looking around the room.

Jezebel was well rehearsed. "Jasper had a previous commitment."

"Oh, I bet he has a lot of those."

Jezebel breezed past Tracy's biting sarcasm. "Tracy, I want to talk about you and me."

"There is no you and me," Tracy said sharply.

Jezebel's voice dropped again. "Can't we just talk? Not here obviously—"

"I don't have anything to say."

"I do."

"Oh, you do?" Tracy's voice was full of sass.

Jezebel focused her hazel eyes on Tracy. "I know our situation was not ideal."

Tracy laughed out loud and lifted a champagne flute from a passing waiter, draining a third of it in one gulp as she tried to cover her nerves while Jezebel spoke.

"Tracy, you know you were always my number one. Always."

A forced chuckle escaped Tracy's grimace. "I'm supposed to be flattered by that, right?" Tracy was trying for flip, but her voice shook and she knew her ex-girlfriend heard her emotion.

Jezebel capitalized on it immediately. "I think given my particular predicament..." She looked at the floor before meeting Tracy's eyes again. "Considering our history, I think I deserve at least a conversation."

"But not a public one, I'm sure."

Jezebel ignored the comment. "Are you going to the Xmas Bash in LA on the twenty-second?"

Tracy didn't bother to dignify the question. It was a foregone conclusion that everyone associated with Every Youth Counts, from the biggest celeb to the D-listers on the foundation's roster, were required to attend the charity's largest fund-raiser of the year.

"I have a new place in Malibu," Jezebel continued. "We could have some privacy there. Afterward."

Of course Tracy knew she should flat-out refuse the invitation. She should be firm and resolute. But she wasn't and they both knew it. If Tracy was being honest with herself, she was more than a little curious as to what Jezebel had to say about their relationship. But agreeing to such an arrangement was as good as forgiving Jezebel, and that was something she wasn't sure she would ever be willing to do.

By the grace of the gods, she was spared a response at all when she spotted a tall, gorgeous blonde in a sleek black dress scanning the crowd from the entranceway. Betsy saw her right away, gave her an enormous smile, and gracefully crossed the room. She took Tracy's hand in her own as she reached her. "Honey, I am so sorry I'm late," she said, placing a kiss on Tracy's cheek. "Did I miss anything?"

They were joined almost simultaneously by the return of the senator, who was obviously using Tracy as a conduit to Jezebel.

"Tracy, introduce the colonel and his wife to these beautiful ladies." He furrowed his brow at Betsy's face, trying to figure out if he should know who she was.

Tracy took over right away. "Of course. Jezebel Stone, you all know." She gave all her attention to Betsy, her smile shy and a little proud. "This is my very good friend, Dr. Jennifer Betsy."

Right away Betsy addressed the colonel by rank, recognizing his military achievements proudly displayed on his left lapel. Then, when the right moment presented itself, she blew them all away, volunteering that she too was a veteran, having served two tours with the Medical Corps in Iraq and Afghanistan. Betsy and the colonel carried the conversation about duty, honor, and country as the others listened.

The senator was seriously impressed. He leaned over. "Tracy, your girlfriend is something else."

"Yeah, she really is," she responded under her breath. She glanced sideways and caught Betsy's eye, taking the opportunity to exchange a wordless thank you. Betsy smiled and squeezed her hand in response. Tracy wondered if she had any clue the effect such a small gesture had on her whole body.

Midway through the evening, when the Gala was at peak capacity, Tracy lost sight of Betsy for more than a few minutes and conducted a small search until she found her outside on the expansive roof deck looking at the breathtaking New York City skyline under a crescent moon.

Betsy smiled over her shoulder as she watched Tracy approach. Fueled by their charade, Tracy decided to take a small risk and walked up directly behind Betsy, placing her hands on Betsy's hips. She kept her hands still only for a second before moving them carefully along each side of Betsy's abdomen until they met at the center. Betsy didn't protest as Tracy thought she might. Instead, she relaxed into Tracy's body. Tracy knew she was enjoying their pretense too much but she didn't care. Betsy seemed not to mind either, placing her hands on top of Tracy's and lightly brushing along each knuckle with her fingertips.

"Are you having an okay time?" Tracy asked.

"Mm-hmm," Betsy responded, without turning around.

Tracy was going to suggest they cut out soon to spare her date any more conversations with the senator and the colonel, but Betsy seemed so content with the view that she didn't want to ruin the moment by speaking. The car horns and sirens from the street were a distant whisper. Likewise, the band and boisterous party crowd were a murmur beyond the glass doors that separated them.

It was a warm night—warmer than it should be in December— and even with the slight breeze they were able to stand on the lavish rooftop forty stories high without overcoats. Tracy was still holding Betsy from behind, gratuitously basking in the feel of her body. Of course Betsy was playing it up for her, fulfilling her role as the dutiful, pretend girlfriend. But then it occurred to her—there was no one outside with them. No one was watching, there was no show to put on. It was just the two of them. This display of affection was for no one's benefit. No one, but their own.

Betsy turned her head slightly and she was inches from Tracy's face. She parted her lips a little to say something—Tracy figured it would be a comment about how beautiful the night was, how perfect the view. But the wind kicked up and sent a strand of her silky blond hair aloft until it caught on her sheer lipstick before she could speak. Betsy smiled at the interruption but before she could remove it, Tracy brushed the hair off her face and brought their lips together in a perfect kiss, slow and deliberate, capturing the moment in a way that surpassed words.

Mere seconds later they were interrupted by a member of the waitstaff announcing the nonprofit's president was about to make the evening address. Following the cue, Tracy and Betsy moved inside, and while the moment had been broken, the mood held up for the rest of the evening.

The second the speech finished, Jezebel crossed the floor with her small entourage trailing her. She walked right up to where Tracy was seated with her arm around the back of Betsy's chair, caressing the top of her bare shoulder with her fingertips.

"Sorry to interrupt," Jezebel announced in an unapologetic voice. "I'm out of here."

Tracy stood to say good-bye and Betsy followed suit. Jezebel looked right at Betsy, gave a lame smirk, and offered a limp handshake. "Nice meeting you, Doc." Then she reached up and put her arms around Tracy's neck, pulling her in and placing a kiss close to her ear. She slid her hands all the way down Tracy's arms and held on to her hands longer than was necessary. As she backed away, she never broke eye contact.

"Seventeen days, Trace," she announced, as though it were a deadline. "See you in LA."

❖

"I cannot believe she did that right in front of me." Betsy turned to Tracy as they walked to the garage. "Can you believe it?"

"Yes, I can," Tracy deadpanned. They were still holding hands as Tracy gave the parking attendant her ticket, but Betsy wasn't finished ranting over Jezebel's behavior. "I mean, the nerve. As far as she knows I'm your girlfriend." She lowered her voice. "She has no idea we're not really together."

"I told you what she's like." Tracy smiled as she held the door open for Betsy and gave the garage attendant a tip at the same time.

"Just who does she think she is, calling me *Doc*. She doesn't even know me." Betsy shook her head in disbelief. "And what happens in seventeen days exactly? What was that even about?" She stared at Tracy, waiting for an explanation.

When she stopped smiling at Betsy's exasperation over Jezebel's antics, Tracy filled her in on the West Coast version of this evening, which was scheduled to take place seventeen days from tonight, providing an edited version of her conversation with Jezebel prior to Betsy's arrival. Tracy then pointedly redirected the conversation to talking about the party itself and Betsy's remarkable impression on the colonel and the senator.

The mood eased as they made their way back to Staten Island and deconstructed everything. Everything, that is, except their behavior toward each other. Tracy watched for signs Betsy hadn't simply been playing it up, that she was finally giving in to what they were both feeling. She was dying to kiss Betsy again and hoped for an opening at every red light along the way. Now, sitting at a full stop outside of Betsy's house, she unbuckled her seat belt and leaned back as Betsy stared straight ahead, seeming in no rush to get out of the car.

"Are you going to go?"

"Where?" Tracy asked.

When Betsy looked over her eyes were serious. "To the Christmas thing in California that Jezebel asked you about."

"Yes." She looked at Betsy and saw an emotion she didn't recognize. "It's a long story, but I sort of have to," she half explained.

Betsy raised her eyebrows in judgment. "You know she's going to try to...to..." She shook her head in frustration. "I don't know what she's going to do exactly, but I'm pretty sure she's going to try to get back with you or, like, seduce you, you know." It sounded adorably awkward coming out, and Tracy bit her cheek to keep from laughing.

"You could come with me." Tracy smiled mischievously. "Keep me from making any mistakes you think I might be prone to." She couldn't keep her mouth from turning up in a devilish grin.

Betsy cocked her head to the side as though that was the most ridiculous thing she had ever heard. She huffed out a breath. "I'm not even sure that would matter. She'd probably just slip you her hotel room key right in front of my face this time."

Tracy tipped her head down and let out a small snicker.

"Why are you laughing?"

"I'm not," she said. She continued to grin as she met Betsy's eyes. "You're jealous. It's hot."

Betsy dropped her jaw. "I'm not jealous."

"I don't know." Tracy raised her eyebrows in confident challenge. "You sound a little bit jealous," she said, pinching her thumb and forefinger together for added emphasis.

Betsy leaned over the console and swatted Tracy's shoulder playfully with her clutch, but Tracy held on to her wrist and pulled her all the way in, their mouths meeting for the second time in as many hours.

Their kiss was long and passionate as they leaned into one another. Betsy pressed her purse tight against Tracy's chest, while Tracy moved her hand from behind Betsy's neck all the way down her body, pulling them closer, before Betsy broke them apart.

"Tracy," Betsy breathed out.

They were both gasping a little from the intensity of the moment, and Tracy held Betsy's face and pressed their foreheads together gently as she spoke.

"Betsy, I want to be with you." She looked down, a little shy over her words. "Not just tonight," she continued, a small desperate sigh escaping her. "I mean, yeah, tonight." She swallowed hard and looked right into Betsy's gorgeous eyes. "But more than that. I want to be with you, like we were tonight, but for real."

"Tracy, we talked about this."

"I know we did." She licked her lips. "But it's different now. Everything is different. You know it is." She leaned forward to kiss her again, but Betsy pulled away.

Betsy shook her head and reached for the door handle. "It's not going to happen. It can't. I'm sorry."

Without looking at Tracy again, she darted out of the car and was gone.

CHAPTER EIGHTEEN

For the first time in her life, Meg understood the desire to wear sunglasses indoors. At ten forty in the morning, Sullivan's fluorescent lights blared through Meg's squinted gaze as she skulked through the reception area. As if her head wasn't already throbbing, Anne came up behind her and boomed into her ear. "Good morning, Megan," she said, before breaking for the kitchen with a hearty chuckle. Her boss had obviously read between the lines of Meg's late-night email stating she would be late this morning and knew she was extremely hungover.

She had barely reached her desk, flopping into her chair to rest her head on the cool wooden desktop as she waited for the room to slow its spin, before Sasha was inside her office.

"Are you okay?" Sasha eased herself onto the corner of Meg's desk.

"I think I might still be drunk," Meg answered from under her covered eyes.

"Did you go out last night?" Sasha's tone had a little kick, like she was annoyed Meg might have ventured out without her approval or knowledge.

Meg could have called her on the hypocrisy of her tone—Sasha often went out for drinks with Jane-Anne without her—but that wasn't her speed, and truthfully she kind of enjoyed hearing Sasha's mild jealousy. Still, Meg didn't want her to think she had stepped out. They were being afforded a rare moment alone in her office, and because Sasha was sitting on the edge of Meg's desk blocking the view from the doorway, Meg was certain no one could see in. She took advantage of the privacy, gently rubbing the top of Sasha's leg over her skirt for reassurance. "No," she answered sweetly.

Meg cocked her head to the side, still using one hand to support it as she rested her elbow on the desktop. She watched Sasha's expression relax completely as she filled her in on the events of Tracy's night, which had stretched into the early morning hours as she and Meg polished off half a bottle of Jameson at Meg's kitchen table lamenting Tracy's spurned advances and decrying women in general. Even though Meg omitted that much of the discussion had focused on her own confusing courtship, Sasha must've read it on her face because she lifted up Meg's hand—an unusually overt gesture for her—and smiled as she played along. "As a member of the offending class, which, by the way, you are actually part of," she said with a huge grin, "how about a peace offering? I'll get you a cup of coffee and we call it even."

"You are a goddess. I take back everything I said about you last night."

Sasha lifted her eyebrows in playful challenge.

"I'm just kidding."

Their fingers were still interlaced when Anne popped her head in the doorway. "Meg, I need to see you when you have a second." Sasha dropped her hand immediately, but Meg was pretty sure it wasn't in time.

Meg tried not to react to Sasha's obvious discomfort as she met her boss's face. "Okay."

"No rush. When you're through, come on in," Anne called out as she headed down the hall to her corner digs.

"Well that sucked," Sasha said.

"Christ, who cares?" It wasn't sensitive or reassuring, but Meg was barely functioning. She didn't have any spare energy, certainly not enough to deal with Sasha's relationship neuroses.

Sasha huffed. "I know you don't get it. But I really don't need the boss to think I'm flirting with anyone at work."

"Whatever, Sash. I gotta go see Anne."

Before making it to her boss's office, Meg stopped by the kitchen and filled a plastic cup with ice-cold water from the cooler, sipping it slowly as she pushed down her frustration over Sasha's knee-jerk reaction over Anne having seen them and what it implied about the fate of their relationship. Logically, she knew she couldn't be completely angry with Sasha for not being totally down with everything yet. Tracy had pointed out that very fact last night, reminding her everyone had different timelines and boundaries and cautioning Meg to cut her a little slack. After all, Meg had known pretty much her whole life she was gay. Sasha had been adjusting for a whopping few months. It would be fine, she told herself. She just needed to give Sasha some time without judgment.

When she shuffled back into her office with her new assignment after her meeting with Anne, she couldn't keep a smile from spreading as she saw Sasha's handiwork in effect. On her desk was a steaming cup of coffee, perfectly doctored, and her favorite—a toasted sesame bagel. Meg lifted the coffee to her lips as she read the note Sasha had written on a napkin in her small, orderly handwriting. "Feel better, baby." She had signed it with a series of *x*'s and *o*'s, and just the first initial of her name.

It was a small but intimate gesture, entirely unexpected, and more than enough to make Meg forget she was annoyed at all.

❖

Three days later, at 7:10 Thursday night, Meg clicked away at her computer reading old budget reports from her new client's case file. Her desk phone rang and she grinned, seeing it was Sasha calling from her own office.

"Yes," she answered.

"Are you almost done?"

"I can go whenever. I'm mostly just doing research." Meg glanced at the clock. "You ready to eat?"

"If you want."

Silently Meg tried to figure out the purpose of Sasha's call, but she didn't have to wait long before Sasha spoke again.

"Will you stay over tonight? At my apartment?"

It was an unusual request for a weeknight, but Meg jumped on it. "Sure." She scanned her office and spotted the spare clothes she kept there. She crinkled her nose at the beat-up jeans and ratty sweater, but tomorrow was Friday, so she figured it could pass. "What's up, everything okay?"

"Mm-hmm," Sasha purred into the phone. "I'm just not sure I want to let you leave tonight." Her tone was beyond suggestive. "Is that okay with you?"

"Absolutely."

Sasha hurried off the phone, explaining she needed another five minutes to run off some copies before they headed across town to her place. Meg closed out her search, logged off her laptop, and got her things together. She dropped her satchel outside the office production area, a glassed-in enclosure adjacent to the kitchen, where she saw Sasha making copies.

Meg knew they were alone in the office, and sensing Sasha's mood, she stepped behind her, put her arms around her waist, and kissed her neck. Sasha only had to turn her face slightly and reach back to pull Meg into a long kiss.

"Hi, gorgeous." Meg smiled, wrapping her arms tighter around Sasha.

"Hi, baby," Sasha said sweetly. "Just two minutes, and I'm ready."

Meg slid her hand down the front of Sasha's skirt and rubbed gently over Sasha's underwear. "I think you might be ready now." She was half kidding, half serious, and completely turned on even as Sasha moved her hand away.

"Megan, we are at work." Sasha scolded her playfully as she pressed the green start button on the copy machine. Placing her stack of papers to the side, Sasha turned and put her arms around Meg, kissing her fully as she pressed their bodies together while she let Meg feel her up over her blouse. The hum of the copier stopped and Sasha breathed in Meg's ear. "Come on, let's go," she said, grabbing all her stuff and dropping it on her desk, before grabbing Meg's hand as they headed to the elevators.

Their night was off to a fantastic start until they bumped into Anne Whitmore in the reception area.

Meg couldn't hide the shock in her voice as she stuttered out her words. "Hi, Anne. I didn't know you were here." She felt her pulse race.

Anne pressed the down button repeatedly. "I grabbed dinner nearby. Just needed to get a file from the office before heading uptown." She could barely make eye contact with either of them.

When they reached the lobby Anne held the door open so they could all pass through. Meg and Sasha were headed to the West Side while Anne lived north. Before they parted ways, Anne looked directly at Meg and Sasha, the corners of her mouth turned up a little. "Have a good night, girls." She did a terrible job of hiding her grin as she continued, "Don't work too hard."

Sasha clutched Meg's arm and buried her face in her shoulder. "Gah, Meg. She definitely saw us."

Meg knew Sasha was right. There was no sugarcoating it. "I think she did." A laugh slipped out. "I mean, she couldn't really look us in the eye, and that comment at the end about working too hard." She laughed in earnest. "It's kind of funny. You have to admit it."

Sasha whacked her playfully. "For you, maybe. Not me."

Meg stopped on the sidewalk and turned. "Hey, now. Why is it funny for me, but not you?" Her voice still had humor in it, but she was genuinely curious about the sentiment underneath Sasha's comment.

"I didn't mean it like that." She rubbed the sleeve of Meg's jacket. "It's just I would prefer not to be thought of as the office slut."

Meg put on an exaggerated pout. "Because you're sleeping with me? That makes you a slut?"

Sasha couldn't help but smile. "It's more complicated than that." She shook her head. "You don't get it because you're good at the work we do. Maybe the best. Your reputation is, like, known." She slid her hands in her coat pockets. "But me"—she closed one eye and tilted her head—"eh, mediocre, on a good day." She reached for Meg and tugged her coat. "But you help me. All the time." Her voice got suddenly serious. "I just feel like if Anne or anybody knew...I think it would look like I was doing it for, you know, self-serving reasons." She looked up and met Meg's eyes. "Particularly since I'm not out as gay or bi or whatever."

Meg decided to keep it light. "Wait, you're not in this for selfish reasons?" She faked a snicker. "Well then, tonight, I am going to be a total pillow princess."

Sasha pulled her close. "That's too bad," she teased back. Lowering her voice to a whisper she added, "Because I almost let you fuck me in the office."

Meg's voice was a mix of shock and desire. "Really?"

"Really," Sasha cooed. She pulled Meg in and breathed in her ear. "So you can imagine the possibilities tonight if you actively participate."

"Taxi!" Meg yelled, throwing up her arm and breaking into a huge grin.

Chapter Nineteen

A ll set?" Tracy turned away from staring out the window at the holiday decorations toward Meg descending the stairs.

Meg nodded, grabbing a thick coat as they headed out the door to the Commons and briskly walked the few hundred feet to the building where the Bay West Holiday Extravaganza was already in full swing.

Tracy paid her admission fee, still a guest price even though she had basically been living here for six months, while she checked out the setup. Although she had been to Bay West socials before, Meg had warned her the Christmas party was in a category all its own. The development didn't even really need to advertise it because its reputation was so established in the gay community.

She took the ice-cold beer Meg handed her and nodded her thanks. She scanned the room from her vantage point on the edge of the semicircle of Meg's buddies—girls she now considered to be her friends as well—while she half listened to the gang talk about their holiday plans, smiling a little at how unbelievably PC the decorations were. All the major celebrations were accounted for—Hanukkah, Christmas, Kwanzaa, even Winter Solstice got a nod. Her ears perked up reflexively at the sound of Betsy's voice when she arrived.

She watched as Betsy made her rounds, saying hello to everyone. When she got to Tracy, she gave her the same warm hug she'd given the rest. Only when she pulled back, she held Tracy's gaze for a moment longer, as though she was trying to communicate something. Was it an apology for the other night? Tracy might have asked, but Betsy was drawn into a ridiculous debate some of the girls were having regarding the truth about how herpes was spread. It was a gross conversation and Tracy tuned out completely before walking over to the glass wall and peering outside at the treetops and the stars beyond them.

After a few minutes she returned to the group and pulled Meg aside. "Hey, dude, I'm gonna split."

"You're going home?" Meg asked, obviously confused.

Tracy shook her off. "I'm leaving for California on Sunday to spend Christmas with my dad." She let out a deep breath. "I was planning on going to Long Island tomorrow to see my mom first, but I'm all packed." She shrugged. "I think I may just grab a train tonight."

Meg looked into her half-finished beer and then set it on the table next to them. "Let's go. I'll give you a ride."

"Meg, you don't have to do that. Stay. Hang out with everyone."

"Nah."

She saw Meg scan the room briefly, her eyes stopping for a split second on Reina Ramirez across the floor before she returned her attention to Tracy. "Not really feeling it tonight."

"You sure?"

"Yep."

Twenty minutes later Meg zipped through the toll plaza and headed for the lower level of the bridge. "I'm just going to go ahead and assume things are still weird with you and Betsy?"

Tracy leaned on her elbow and looked out the window. "They're fine," she said halfheartedly. "They're the same," she answered, swallowing her feelings. "I know I'm being over dramatic, but"—she breathed out heavily—"I just couldn't do it tonight."

She drew small shapes in the condensation on the passenger-side window as she spoke. "I just didn't feel like being that close to her, pretending there isn't something between us." She paused for a second. "I know I sound full of myself," she said, dropping her hand to her jeans. "Maybe I am. I just know what I feel."

"You're not full of yourself." Meg shifted lanes. "I'm with you. I think there's something there. What do you think is stopping her?"

"I don't know." Tracy sucked at her cheeks, considering. "I think she's scared." She made another weird noise with her mouth. "We almost hooked up in P-town a while back. At the time she gave me all these reasons why it was a bad idea."

"Like?"

"I don't even remember. I guess the gist was she was looking for something serious, and I live out in California." She looked over at Meg. "That's the thing, though. I don't. I pretty much live here. I'm looking for a job *here*. So…" She held out her hand as if she had proven a point. "Maybe she's just not into me and I'm misreading everything."

Meg flashed a look that suggested she seriously doubted that theory.

"I don't know, dude." Tracy shuffled her phone from hand to hand, still thinking about it. "Tonight was the first time I've seen her since the Gala. I thought it would be fine. But then she walked in…" She shook her head. "It's like I can't go back to being what we were before. The flirting, the pretending. Not after experiencing what it might be like to really be together. I don't want to." She exhaled, stretching her neck against the seat. "Christ, maybe I just need to chill." She smacked her palms against both legs. "Thank God I'm going to California," she added, rubbing her hands on her thighs repeatedly. "I think these next few weeks will be good for me. Put a little space between us. Give me some time to decompress a little. See my dad, my friends. When I come back, I'll be good as new."

Her voice evened out as she spoke, as though her little pep talk was cathartic as much as it was informative.

When she looked over at Meg, her calm carried forth with her. "What's your deal? You heading to Sasha's?"

Meg nodded her head. "I know. I'm whipped," she added lightly.

"Want to grab a drink at the Kitchen before you head uptown to join her and the straights?"

"She's actually at home," Meg confessed.

"Oh." Tracy's surprise was audible. "I figured she'd be out somewhere with her friends," Tracy finished, knowing the routine.

Meg tightened her grip on the steering wheel as they idled at a red light. She chewed her lip, looking over at Tracy before the light changed. "You think I'm pathetic for going there? To her place, I mean?"

"I didn't say that."

"It is lame though, right?"

"Don't look at me," Tracy quipped. "I've been chasing the same girl for months without getting anywhere."

They were silent for a few blocks, the radio playing holiday music quietly in the background. "You know what? Fuck it," Tracy said out of nowhere. "Drop me off at the Kitchen."

"Are you serious?" Meg asked.

"Yeah."

"Trace, you can hang with me and Sash if you want company," Meg offered.

Tracy crinkled her nose. "Thanks, but that's not really the kind of company I'm looking for." Tracy's voice held a level of confidence Meg was instantly jealous of.

"Holy shit, you're gonna hook up." Meg's mouth hung open a little as she looked over at her friend.

"Probably not." Tracy smiled as they pulled up across the street from the bar. "I'm not looking for anything, that is." She leaned her head back into the headrest. "There's a train every hour until after midnight. I'm just going to stop by and have a drink at a place where there's no Betsy, no pressure." She couldn't keep an impish grin from coming out. "But I'm not going to lie. I haven't gotten laid in six months. So, I can't say for sure that if there's something halfway decent in there"—she nodded at the bar with her chin—"I'm not going for it." She curled her lip. "Because to be honest, I think the release might do me a world of good."

Meg nodded and laughed a little at Tracy's naked honesty. "Be careful. And text me when you get to your mom's, no matter what time it is. I will make no judgments and ask no questions." She leaned across the console and gave Tracy a hug. "You're back for New Year's?"

"I'll be in Long Island with Mom and Lily for New Year's Eve. Back by you after that."

"'Kay, dude. Merry Christmas."

"See you next year, Meg."

Meg was still smiling at Tracy's cheesy joke as she shifted into drive and headed to Sasha's apartment.

❖

Meg kicked off her shoes and settled on top of Sasha's Lilly Pulitzer duvet, leaning back into the stack of fluffy pillows to watch the reveal of a home makeover on Sasha's flat screen. Sasha padded in from her galley kitchen and placed a tall glass of water on the night table. She scooched Meg's legs apart and settled herself between them, twisting her body a little to face Meg.

"I'm so glad you came." Sasha gave her a nice kiss and handed her an ornately wrapped envelope. "Here. Merry Christmas."

"What is this?" Meg asked through a smile.

"Open it."

Meg pulled at the red and gold ribbon, opening the envelope, and took out two computer-generated tickets.

Meg's jaw dropped. "You got me tickets to see Cameron Esposito?" She was still wrapping her head around the surprise. "How did you know…?"

"Hello, you talk about her all the time. I even heard you trying to convince Carrie to listen to her podcast with you the other day." Sasha smiled. "She's doing a show in New York in March."

Meg was still beaming as she examined the tickets. "Unbelievable." She looked at Sasha. "Will you come with me?"

"Duh," Sasha said with a smile. "Do you really think I'm going to let you loose in a room full of lesbians by yourself?" Sasha shook her head. "Uh-uh," she added playfully. "You arc far too cute for that." She took Meg's face in both her hands. "I plan on keeping my eye on you the whole time," she said, leaning forward and kissing her quickly. "It's a miracle I made it through tonight," she said, settling her body comfortably with Meg's as she breathed out a sigh in relief. "I was a nervous wreck."

"Really?"

"Yes, really."

"Why?"

"Because, Meg." She squirmed a little, sounding vulnerable. "You're adorable. And sweet." She brushed a piece of lint off the bedspread, keeping her head down as she spoke. "I'm constantly worried someone is going to snatch you up."

Meg lifted her chin with one finger. "I don't want anyone else."

"Now, maybe," she responded in a low voice. "But what happens when you get fed up waiting for me? You've been awesome, and I know it's not fair to you. Honestly, why are you so good to me?" For a rhetorical question, she looked genuinely interested in Meg's answer.

Meg brushed a long wavy strand of hair from Sasha's face. "Baby, I know you're stressed out about your friends, which, I'm not going to lie, I don't really get." She kissed the tip of her nose. "Why don't we just hang out with my friends, then? You totally could've come to the social tonight."

"I know. I should have." She got up off the bed and reached for the remote, muting the television before sitting back down cross-legged in front of Meg. "I spent a lot of time thinking exactly that while I was pacing the floor wondering who was checking you out while I was here watching HGTV."

"Why didn't you come?"

Sasha looked at the window, her brow crinkling with stress. "I don't know." She made eye contact. "I was nervous, I guess."

"Why?" Meg couldn't conceal her surprise.

"*Gah*"—Sasha rolled her eyes—"I can't make any decisions at all lately." She rubbed the tops of her knees nervously. "Between work, where I'm barely treading water, and everything with my mom..." She shook her head. "I'm a basket case."

"Hey, hey, hey." Meg kissed her sweetly. "You have to relax. It's all going to be fine. I promise."

"You think so?"

"Yes." Meg squeezed Sasha's hands for emphasis.

Sasha leaned back and touched her forehead to Meg's. "I was thinking..." She toyed with a button on Meg's shirt. "What are you doing for New Year's?"

The truth was Meg really didn't have any plans. She hated going out in the city on such a crazy and expensive night. Tracy was out of the picture, and Lexi and Jesse were headed to the Cape. She had never even considered the possibility Sasha would be willing to spend such a traditionally public holiday together. Completely at a loss, Meg stared at her blankly.

"Is your development having anything?" Sasha's voice sounded hopeful and Meg hated to deflate her, but she was pretty sure there wasn't anything on Bay West's schedule.

"Not that I know of. Why?"

Sasha drifted her hand from Meg's shirt to her exposed chest, her finger making tiny lines along the freckles there. "I thought it would be nice for us to be together on New Year's Eve." She was blushing as she continued. "I want to kiss you at midnight." She pulled back a little. "Why do you look so surprised?"

Meg resisted the urge to answer truthfully, replacing her instinctive reaction with an entirely new option. "What about going to Cape Cod?" she asked.

Registering Sasha's complete confusion, Meg explained. "Look, I don't really know if anything is going on at the development. There might be an open house. I can check, if that's what you want to do. But most of my friends wouldn't be there anyway." She tried not to sound as completely excited as she was over this new possibility. "Lexi and Jesse are spending New Year's up at Jesse's family's house on the Cape. They invited me. Initially I said no thanks. But if you came with me, that would be fun. It might be really nice to get away for the weekend."

Sasha hesitated for a second. "Would, like, their whole families be there?"

"No." Meg smiled. "It's just Jesse and Lexi going. They have some wedding stuff to finalize still. It would just be the four of us."

Sasha's eyes softened. "Then, yes. I would love to go to Cape Cod with you for New Year's."

CHAPTER TWENTY

Midafternoon on New Year's Day, Tracy trudged along Bay West's icy sidewalks making her way to Meg's unshoveled walkway, already missing LA's milder temperatures. Dropping her bags inside the foyer, she reached for the snow shovel inside the coat closet and made quick work of the fresh six inches that had fallen overnight. The snow was light and powdery, providing a clean surface on top of the previous week's ten inches, piled high on lawns and driveways and in between parked cars and packed into every available inch of free space.

Even though it was hardly a workout, it felt good to move her muscles as she cleaned off Meg's car blanketed in snow. She watched her breath come out in a white puff against the cold as she looked up at Meg's house from the base of the driveway. The time away had done her good but she was happy to be home, which was suddenly how she thought of Bay West. Even though she hadn't gone so far as to officially change her address, there was no denying she lived here. She had even started paying rent, and while Meg was reluctant to take it, Tracy had insisted. It made her feel better to contribute, and to her, it was a sign her life was getting back on track. Sure she didn't have any leads on the job front, but it was a new year and Tracy was thoroughly optimistic.

On her minibreak, Tracy had purposely avoided two phone calls from Betsy, letting them go to voice mail, choosing instead to communicate distantly via text. It wasn't that she didn't want to talk to Betsy; honestly, the exact opposite was true. It had simply happened that on both occasions, Tracy had already had a few drinks and she didn't really trust what she might admit about her feelings over the phone to the gorgeous blonde three thousand miles away. Instead she played it safe, texting in the days that followed, offering vague apologies over their inopportune timing. Where Betsy was concerned, Tracy had made some steadfast resolutions. She knew she still had real feelings, and wholeheartedly believed Betsy had them too, but Tracy was done stopping her life over it. If Betsy couldn't see they were right for each other—or more likely, was too scared to admit it—that was her loss.

Tracy shook the snow from her shoes as she stepped into the house, wiping her feet diligently on the welcome mat. The snow had given her a fantastic idea: she was going to call Betsy right now and convince her to go sledding down the golf course hills together. She suppressed a grin thinking the feel of her arms around Betsy's waist might be just the push the good doctor needed to realize what she was missing out on.

As she reached for her phone, it rang in her hands with Betsy's name and photo appearing on the caller ID.

"I was just going to call you," Tracy said smoothly into the speaker. "Hi."

Betsy's voice was a higher pitch than usual and Tracy was sure it was from surprise that she'd answered on the first ring.

Tracy didn't miss a beat. "Want to go sledding with me?"

"Are you back in New York?"

"Yeah. I just got to Meg's a few minutes ago."

"How was Christmas?

"Good. Yours?"

"It was nice." Betsy hesitated a little, like there was more she wanted to say, but then didn't.

"So did you deliver the Baby New Year?" Tracy asked, peeling a clementine as she held the phone between her cheek and her shoulder.

"No." Betsy laughed sweetly at the comment. "I did work, but it was actually really quiet," she added, sounding a touch nervous as she spoke. "What about you?"

"I was at my mom's in Long Island. Originally we were going to go out to dinner, but with the weather, we just stayed in. Mom cooked, we played cards, I watched a movie with my sister and her boyfriend. Pretty tame stuff. I was in bed by twelve thirty."

"Oh."

She heard unmistakable relief in Betsy's tone and it gave her the encouragement she needed. "So what do you say, feel like hitting the Staten Island slopes?"

"Actually," Betsy started, "I was calling because, well, I was wondering, if you didn't already have plans," she continued, sounding nervous as hell, "I wanted to invite you here, to my house. For dinner."

Tracy chewed her orange slice quickly. "Okay."

"My mom and my brother and his girlfriend will be here too. I should mention that. New Year's Day dinner is kind of a family tradition for us." She was silent for a second. "I would really like it if you were here," she finished.

"Sure," Tracy said, wondering if Betsy could hear her smile through the phone.

Tracy took her time showering and shaved everywhere, even though there was no real reason to think anything would be different today than it had been before. No reason, except Betsy's obvious nerves, and the slight lilt in her voice when she spoke, and the fact she had invited her to a family event. Tracy picked her clothes meticulously, going with dark cords and an antiqued button-down that she left untucked with the three top buttons open, showing off her California color. She selected a bottle of wine from Meg's meager collection and shot her roomie a text briefing her on her plans, adding a smiley face at the mention of borrowing the Ford sitting in the driveway. Meg responded immediately, confirming she was still at the Cape and didn't expect to be home until much later in the evening. Tracy laughed out loud at Meg's lascivious remarks that followed, which were punctuated with several enthusiastic and symbolically graphic emoji.

❖

Tracy rang the front doorbell and was relieved when it was Betsy who answered. In the doorway they exchanged a warm hug that was longer than necessary and Betsy held on to her tightly, breathing slightly in her ear.

"Hi," Betsy whispered, pulling back and allowing their eyes to make contact for the first time in weeks.

Tracy just smiled, feeling her heart bottom out at the immediate realization this was going to be way harder than she'd bargained for.

Betsy guided her into the living room, oddly still holding on to her hand. She introduced Tracy to her mother and to her brother James and Felicia, his fiancée. They were nice people, like Betsy, and Tracy couldn't help but smile every single time they referred to Betsy as Jen or Jennifer, naturally, since that was her name, and of course with the exception of herself and Felicia, they were all Betsys.

Over pasta bolognese and cabernet, they asked about her family, California, her job hunt. James was totally bummed she'd quit golf and made her promise to hit the links with him in the spring anyway. All throughout the evening, Betsy touched on Tracy lightly, casually—a hand on her thigh during dinner, a slight shoulder squeeze when she got up to fetch another bottle of red.

Tracy loved every second of the affections bestowed on her, even if she was completely confused about what it meant. So when James and Felicia got up to leave, Tracy took her cue.

"I should get going too." She stood and pushed the chair in, approaching Betsy's mom to thank her for a lovely dinner.

"Nonsense," Betsy's mom said, swatting her arm lightly. "There's still half a bottle of wine left." She looked between Tracy and her daughter. "You girls take it downstairs and finish it off." She walked into the kitchen with the dessert dishes. "Shame for it to go to waste."

Betsy blushed at her mother's overt meddling, but she raised her eyebrows hopefully just the same. "What do you say, Trace? One more drink?" she asked, biting her lip a little as she waited for an answer.

Tracy nodded her response and followed Betsy downstairs to the modest apartment located there. She was dying to ask Betsy what the heck was going on, but equally she wanted to ask no questions, follow the momentum, and let the night lead them right into Betsy's bedroom. She took a seat on the couch while Betsy poured their drinks, taking in the nuances of Betsy's digs which were entirely different than upstairs. Where her mother's space was somewhat dated with its worn rugs and proudly displayed photos of her children—Betsy in her military uniform, James at his college graduation—Betsy's place was updated, her walls covered in artistic photos, fields and deserts, the beach at sunset. The images were serious and serene and unbelievably breathtaking, like Betsy herself.

Betsy handed over a glass of wine and took a seat facing Tracy at the opposite end of the couch. Tracy was just about to ask what exactly was happening between them, but Betsy spoke first.

"How was the charity ball?" she asked quickly.

"Fine."

"And Jezebel?" Betsy asked sharply, her voice taking on a chilly tone.

Tracy shook her head and frowned. "Didn't see her." She took a sip of her wine. "That's not true. I did see her from afar. I didn't talk to her though." Tracy placed her wine on a coaster. "I made my appearance then skipped out with a few of my friends."

"How come?" Betsy was obviously surprised and she stumbled over her words. "I mean how come you didn't talk to her?"

Tracy leaned back, her arm stretched across the back of the couch, as she looked at Betsy. "I told you. I have no interest in talking to her."

"I called you," Betsy said. "That night. I called you and you didn't answer."

"I know."

"I thought when I didn't hear from you, I thought maybe you were with her." Betsy's voice was adorably desperate, and it made Tracy's heart pound.

Tracy looked her right in the eye. "I wasn't." She took another drink hoping the small action might break the tension. "I texted you back the next day."

"It was two days later," Betsy corrected.

She took another small sip before speaking. "Look, Bets, I was in no condition to talk to you that night." She shifted her body and leaned forward, smoothing the fabric of her pants. "I didn't know what you wanted. I still don't." She shook her head. "I mean, I think I do, but honestly, I don't even know what this is right now." Tracy looked over at Betsy. "Don't misunderstand me." She reached over and touched Betsy's forearm. "Bets, honey"—she shook her head—"I love that you invited me here and you spent half the night with your hand on my leg and obviously your family thinks there's something going on between us." She kept her voice calm, even though her heart was racing. "But if this is just some kind of test to make sure I'm still into you, I'm going to make it easy." She covered Betsy's hand with her own. "I am," she said, removing it just as quickly. "Having said that, I'm not going to wait around forever."

Betsy got up and walked across to the window that looked out onto the street. "You left the Christmas party at Bay West without so much as saying good-bye. Then you went to California. I drove by Meg's every day hoping to bump into you until Jesse broke it to me that you were gone." She turned around and leaned against the frame of the window. "You didn't return my calls. I thought you were still mad at me over the Gala. I thought you went back to Jezebel. I thought a million crazy things." She wiped at a tear forming in the corner of her eye.

Tracy looked down at her boots. "I was never mad at you over the Gala." A slight laugh slipped out. "Frustrated, maybe. Not mad." She stood up and closed the distance between them. She gently but possessively put her hands on Betsy's hips and stared into her eyes. "Betsy, I'm in love with you." She smiled slow and sexy. "I think you're maybe a little bit in love with me too."

"Tracy, I am so scared."

"Don't be." Tracy moved Betsy's hair away and kissed her cheek softly. She looked right into the gorgeous eyes that had hooked her from minute one. "I am going to be so good to you."

She framed Betsy's face with her hands and kissed from her hairline down to her collarbone, slowly, savoring each second. There was no rush, even after the months of anticipation, and Tracy took her time.

She felt Betsy's hands in her hair, down her back, along her bottom pulling her in close. Between Tracy's gentle touches, Betsy asked quietly, "What if it doesn't work?"

"It's going to work," Tracy said covering her face in baby kisses.

"I'm nervous." Betsy held Tracy's face directly in front of her. "Aren't you nervous?"

Tracy's confidence emerged on a smile. "Not even a little."

When Tracy kissed her, finally, in front of the big bay window, Betsy felt it in every part of her being. Tracy's touch was sweet and passionate and so unbelievably genuine, all her fear dissipated. She kissed her back, only stopping when she heard herself moan into Tracy's mouth. She pulled back and touched her forehead to Tracy's, smiling a little as she took her hand and led them to her bedroom.

In the dark Betsy let her guard down and allowed herself to indulge in the moment she had fantasized about for months. She raised her arms as Tracy lifted her shirt over her head, and then rested them on Tracy's shoulders as Tracy slipped off her pants. She could only focus on Tracy's fingertips caressing her abdomen, moving over the tops of her breasts, stroking them gently before she unhooked her bra.

"Betsy," Tracy breathed in her ear, brushing her lips along the side of her face. She didn't say anything else, simply repeating her name again over and over. Her voice was low and soft and filled with desire. Betsy melted.

Tracy continued kissing her neck and her chest, finally teasing her breast into her mouth, and Betsy almost lost it at the touch of Tracy's hot tongue on her nipple. Tracy kept one hand on her breast and traced the other down the front of Betsy's body, inside her underwear. She bit her lip a little and let out a slight moan, enjoying the feel of Tracy's fingers on her, almost in her. She let Tracy stay there for a minute relishing the sensation before she reached down and pulled Tracy's hand upward, holding it at the wrist as she brought it to her mouth. Holding Tracy's eyes with her own, she brushed Tracy's middle finger across her lips, back and forth, letting her tongue slip out and run the length of Tracy's finger. Her teeth got in on the action too, toying with Tracy's fingertip until she brought the whole thing into her mouth, drawing it in and out slowly. Tracy only lasted a few seconds before she withdrew her hand completely, replacing it with her tongue, kissing Betsy possessively as she pressed their bodies together.

"You have way too many clothes on," Betsy said as she began removing them slowly. First her shirt, then her bra, leading with her mouth in a straight line down Tracy's unbelievably toned body. Without stopping, she undid Tracy's pants, holding her hips as she knelt in front of her, grazing open-mouthed over the cotton of Tracy's boyshorts before sliding them down. She looked up once, making brief eye contact, and then moved forward, putting her mouth directly on Tracy.

Betsy stayed there, luxuriating in the feel of Tracy's body pressed up against her face, her hands in her hair. She heard her breath catch one second before Tracy pulled her up and kissed her. Her knees hit the back of the bed, and it was only seconds before Tracy was on top of her, slipping off her panties, sliding two fingers deep inside. It had been a while since Betsy had been with anyone, and she hoped Tracy wasn't put off by how tight she knew she was. She heard Tracy gasp a little and it made her gush. In no time at all they were moving together, the rhythm perfect. Tracy kissed her lips, her neck, her breasts, and all the way down, putting Betsy's legs over her shoulders. Her tongue was warm and soft and gentle at first, until it wasn't, eventually increasing to match the pace of her fingers, bringing her right to the edge and finally over it.

Betsy trailed her fingers along Tracy's forearms as Tracy held her firmly from behind. "I cannot believe I waited so long to do that," she said with a slight chuckle.

"You and me both," Tracy responded with a laugh of her own. "I was beginning to give up hope."

Betsy turned around. She touched Tracy's beautiful face. "I'm sorry I put you off for so long," she said very seriously.

"It's okay." Tracy snuggled in and kissed her sweetly. "I'm glad you waited until you were sure. You feel okay with everything now?"

"I do." Betsy bit her lip and met Tracy's eyes. "There's only one thing." She let the words hang between them for only a split second before breaking into a real smile. "I suppose we're going to have to make up for some serious lost time," she said leaning forward and kissing Tracy seductively.

"I'm in. Can we start right now?" Tracy asked with a satisfied grin as she pulled Betsy on top of her.

Leaning on her forearms, Betsy looked down Tracy's body and then met her eyes, not even trying to cover the need she felt rise to the surface again. "Most definitely."

❖

At six twenty in the morning, a groggy Tracy stretched her arm across the empty space beside her where Betsy had spent the few hours of sleep curled against her. Shifting onto her back, she caught sight of Betsy walking into the bedroom wrapped in a towel, wet from the shower.

"Come back to bed." Tracy's voice was thick with sleep.

"I have to go to work." Betsy sat on the edge of the mattress patting the ends of her hair. "But you can stay as long as you want."

Betsy leaned forward to drop a kiss on her lips, but Tracy,

undeterred, placed a hand behind Betsy's neck and pulled her all the way in. She kissed her deeply and peeled the towel away, using her whole body to coax Betsy back into the bed. As they kissed, Tracy maneuvered Betsy on top of her, their naked bodies touching everywhere.

"A few more minutes?" Tracy breathed in her ear.

"I shouldn't." Betsy started to get up, sliding a leg to each side of Tracy's waist as she righted herself. She stopped for a second and leaned back down to kiss her again, the ends of her wet hair touching both their faces. "I have patients at eight," Betsy whispered, making no further movement to leave.

Tracy smiled, knowing she had her. "Not a problem." She ran her hands along Betsy's legs, settling her hands on her hips, inching Betsy's body up slowly, while she shimmied herself down underneath, pressing her lips gently to the insides of Betsy's thighs when she reached them.

"What are you doing?" Betsy's voice hitched in her throat.

Tracy's self-assured chuckle was quickly drowned out by Betsy's low moans.

Despite her initial halfhearted protest, Betsy relaxed easily, moving with purpose against Tracy's mouth, gripping the headboard and breathing out Tracy's name as she let herself go completely.

CHAPTER TWENTY-ONE

Meg was locking the front door heading out to work when Tracy pulled into the driveway. "Good morning," she called out with a knowing smile.

"It is a good morning," Tracy responded definitively. She opened the car door but only got out halfway. "Hey, do you want me to drive you to the ferry or something?"

"Nah, I'm good. I'll just grab the bus." Meg ticked her head to the side in the direction of the bus stop just outside the development's perimeter. "I'm sure you could use the extra sleep right about now," Meg added, wiggling her eyebrows. "I can't wait to hear all the details, though. Call me when you get up."

"I want to hear about your weekend too," Tracy said. "Everything good with Sasha?"

"Everything is good." Meg smiled big.

"How about I meet you in the city for dinner after work? We can give each other the play-by-play."

"No Betsy tonight?"

"Tomorrow night. She's working late tonight."

Meg nodded. "The only thing is, I wanted to check out this hot yoga class after work." At Tracy's surprised reaction, Meg shrugged her shoulders. "New Year's resolution, don't make fun of me."

"Never, dude. Text me the address, I'll go with you. We'll eat something healthy afterward. My treat."

❖

As with everything even remotely physical, Tracy seemed born to contort her body with ease, the one hundred and five degree room appearing to barely faze her. Meg struggled a good deal more, but she survived the Bikram class without passing out or puking, both major feats in her opinion.

Ninety minutes later, sitting in a sleek wooden booth in Soho, Meg sipped coconut water and listened as Tracy filled her in on what had happened—finally—between her and Betsy.

"So how 'bout your weekend at the Cape with Sasha?" Tracy asked.

Meg smiled. "It was good. So good." She knew she sounded wistful. She didn't care.

"What did you all do for New Year's?"

"We just stayed in. Jesse made this unbelievable dinner for the four of us." Her mouth turned up at the memory. "We played games. Told stories." Meg leaned forward and toyed with the edge of her napkin. "I was nervous Sasha would back off around them. The way she does at work or with her friends." A full smile came out. "I couldn't have been more wrong."

"Yeah?"

"Trace, she was amazing." The pitch in her voice was high, but she couldn't stop smiling, even though she knew she sounded dorky. "She was relaxed. Funny, charming. She told us about her time at Oxford, living in England. But it wasn't even that." Meg licked her lips. "She was herself. The way she is with me, when it's just the two of us. And"—Meg looked down, a touch embarrassed about going on and on, but she didn't stop talking—"she was affectionate. I mean not just when we were alone." She felt herself blush. "In front of Lexi and Jesse. She was constantly touching me, holding my hand, rubbing my back. It was…it was, well you know. It was great."

"Oh my God." Tracy grinned devilishly. "You are so in it."

"I so am."

Tracy raised her glass. "That makes two of us."

❖

"Hurry up, hurry up, hurry up." Meg nuzzled into Sasha for warmth in the freezing vestibule as Sasha searched for her apartment keys. Finally reaching them in the bottom of her purse, she pulled them out slowly, distracted by the buzz of her vibrating phone. Her body stiffened as she read the text.

"What's the matter?" Meg asked.

"Shit, Meg." Sasha stepped away, putting some space between them as she peered down the street. "My friends are on their way here."

"What?" Meg was confused. "Who?"

"Jane-Anne and Sabrina." Sasha nervously tried to force the wrong key in the door. "Sabrina's here. She's been talking about coming up but when I didn't hear from her, I figured it wasn't happening."

"Shouldn't you be happy?" Meg took the keys, finding the correct one and handing them back to Sasha. "Isn't she your best friend?"

Sasha shuffled nervously from foot to foot. "Yes, but"—she opened the door and talked over her shoulder—"you can't be like this in from of them."

Meg stopped. "Like what?"

"You know what I mean."

"Um, I actually don't."

"Look, I just don't want to be all couple-y in front of them." Sasha turned around at the foot of the stairs. "I don't feel like answering questions about us. I'm not even really sure what this is yet."

Meg felt her frustration rising to the surface. "What does that mean?" She shook her head. "Am I the only one who's into this?" She took a deep breath and got her voice under control. "Come on, Sash. I thought we were together. Aren't we?"

Sasha looked nervous and her voice came out shaky. "We are. I don't know." She tipped her head to the side letting a long breath out. "I'm not where you are, Meg." She looked at her shoe. "Not yet, at least."

Meg felt both anger and hurt coming to the surface, but there wasn't a chance to deal with either. Inside the vestibule on the other side of the glass door stood the twins, identically excited at their arrival. Sasha moved past Meg and opened the door for them.

"Hey, guys." She greeted them with warm hugs.

Jane-Anne walked to Meg and gave her a quick hello hug and kiss. "Meg, this is my sister, Sabrina."

"Nice to meet you." Meg forced a smile and pushed off the wall heading to the door. "I was just heading home."

"Meg," Sasha started, but she didn't say anything more.

"I have an early morning meeting tomorrow," she lied.

"Geez, why go all the way back to Staten Island then?" Jane-Anne asked through a laugh.

"Meg, you can stay if you want," Sasha echoed. But the flat tone she put on to convince her friends the offer was made out of convenience rather than shared intimacy pissed her off even more.

"Nope. I'm good." Meg didn't even try to mask her annoyance. "'Night, girls. See you at work, Sash," she added, pushing the door roughly and heading out into the cold January night.

❖

The next day Meg purposely stayed busy with work calls until one thirty. She was dying to talk to Sasha to hear what she had to say, to smooth over their tiff from the previous night. But she was still frustrated and she wanted Sasha to come to her. She lost that battle when she bumped into Sasha in the break room.

"Hey." Meg was already annoyed at herself for speaking first. She reached past Sasha and grabbed a seltzer from the company fridge.

"Hey," Sasha responded, looking up from the tea she was brewing.

Meg leaned into the counter. "So, are we going to talk?"

Sasha looked around nervously.

"Not here obviously," Meg clarified, reading Sasha's body language.

But Sasha spoke anyway. "Meg." She dropped her voice. "I think we should stop."

"Stop what?"

"You know." Sasha gestured between them with her eyes. "*This.*"

Meg put her aluminum can on the counter, her voice full of disbelief as it matched Sasha's quiet volume. "Are you serious?"

"I'm sorry." Sasha's eyes welled up, but she continued anyway, her voice shaking ever so slightly. "I don't know what I want. And with everything going on in my life right now"—she paused, clearly trying to keep it together—"I'm not going to ask you to put your life on hold to wait for me. I'm sorry," she called over her shoulder, leaving her steaming teacup on the counter as she fled the kitchen.

In the days that followed Meg expected Sasha to call, or text, or corner her at work and say she had made an enormous mistake, beg for another chance. But she didn't. A week rolled by, and then another with nothing.

Their day-to-day routine changed very little. They still saw each other in the office and participated in group projects as required. It was what was missing that got to Meg—gone were the after-hours meet-ups, post-happy-hour or otherwise. Thursday lunches disappeared as well, a loss no one else noticed, but one that cut Meg to the core. Meg felt her heart sink when Sasha sat next to Scott during last Monday's all-hands meeting instead of taking her usual chair next to Meg. Even though she was dead sure nothing was going on between them, Meg almost couldn't control her facial expression when he leaned over to whisper in Sasha's ear and Sasha held in a laugh at whatever moronic thing he had said.

Meg confided her sorrow in Tracy and Betsy, who was around more often than not lately. They were awesome listeners and great friends, but Meg tried not to bring it up constantly. They were in their honeymoon period, spending every free moment together, cuter than cute could be. There was no need to bring them down with her drama.

❖

Valentine's Day approached and Meg was downright depressed, even in the face of Bay West's newest brainchild. It was a miracle Meg had allowed herself to get talked into going to the event by her four closest friends, but probably not her best decision considering her emotional state. Still, she couldn't really think of a plausible reason to not attend the Sweethearts and Singles Social that was slated for Saturday night. The premise that all couples—the Sweethearts—in attendance would receive a reduced admission rate, a package price, if they brought one unattached, single friend along was kind of genius.

Both of her coupled pairs of friends—Lexi and Jesse, and Tracy and Betsy—made a game all week of getting Meg to be their single. They were having fun with it, each offering over-the-top incentives to sign her loyalty over. Meg barely played along.

The night of the party was so brutally cold Meg couldn't believe anyone would bother leaving the warmth of their living room. But then she did so herself, shaking her head at the packed crowd inside the Commons as Tracy negotiated their discounted entry fee.

With a slight frown, Meg slipped on the pink rubber wristband handed to her at the door, the color indicating she was unattached. She looked around for a place to drop her stuff, but most of the tables were already claimed. Finally she spotted Jesse in the far back corner and headed that way to secure a seat with her friends. Marnie and Chris were present too, making a rare but welcome appearance at a social.

Meg pounded two drinks, spending her time talking to Lexi and Marnie about the wedding until she excused herself to say hello to some girls she knew from the rental section. She spotted Tracy and Betsy swaying in a corner on the dance floor, looking adorable and happy and completely lost in each other. She was a little drunk by the time she spied Reina across the room and she had to narrow her eyes to focus, but sure enough Reina was sporting a pink band as well. Taking one final sip of her drink, Meg was about to go chat her up but a blondish tomboy beat her to it. For the best, she thought as she quietly grabbed her jacket and slipped out of the Commons.

Meg pulled her winter hat down to her eyes and followed the path that wound behind the pool and the tennis courts and through the auxiliary parking lot until she found herself at the back of the rental section standing on the bluffs at the edge of the development. She was hoping the amazing view on such a clear night might lift her out of her doldrums. But when she stood by the rocky cliff staring ahead at the lights of the city across the water, she thought only of Sasha and what she might be doing.

Walking the path back, she kept her head down until a movement by the front door of the business office of the development caught her attention. Squinting her eyes to get a clear picture, she watched as Taylor Higgins walked out the front door, looking both ways before turning back to launch herself at Kameron Browne, who exited just behind her. They groped each other openly, kissing hard as they fell into the shadows of the doorway. Meg stayed where she was, her eyes frozen open, shielded by the side of the building until she saw them depart separately in opposite directions.

Meg's mind populated with a million thoughts at once. For starters, she was kind of grossed out seeing Taylor, who was twenty-five at best, making out with Kameron Browne, who had to be pushing sixty. On top of that, it appeared Taylor had moved directly from Meg to Kam, which pretty much decimated her already fragile ego. But putting that self-centered thought aside, what dismayed Meg the most was what Kam and Taylor's tryst said about long-term relationships in general, to say nothing of Kam and Mary's relationship specifically. She'd heard the gossip about their past infidelities, but they seemed happy together when she saw them around the neighborhood. Yet here was Kam, sneaking around with a renter young enough to be her daughter, while Mary worked her butt off at the social.

Meg shuffled back home wondering if there was hope at all for any of them.

She brushed her teeth and washed her face quickly, wanting to avoid Tracy and Betsy when they returned from the dance. She checked her texts, and both her work and personal email accounts, but there was no message of any kind from Sasha. Reaching for the remote, she tuned into reruns of the legal drama she used to watch with her mother and fell asleep with the covers over her head to the distinctive drumbeat of the program's signature theme song.

CHAPTER TWENTY-TWO

S asha was a no-show at work on the Monday after Valentine's weekend. Come to think of it, she'd been out the second half of the previous week too. Her absence caught Meg's attention because she knew Sasha had a client proposal scheduled on Wednesday and she was always such a wreck about big meetings that it was unlike her to miss any days leading up to one.

Early Tuesday Meg was still watching the clock in hopes Sasha would come by and say hello, following a routine that had become somewhat regular since they'd split. Deep down Meg knew Sasha missed her, despite her inability to be ready for a real relationship. At nine twenty, Meg got up from her desk and went into the kitchen, just to pass Sasha and Scott's shared office, but there was so sign of her, just Scott banging away on his keyboard. Meg returned to her own room just as an email addressed to the entire agency popped on her screen.

It is with great sadness that I must inform you of the passing of Sasha Michaels's mother, Ellen Michaels. Ms. Michaels lost her battle with cancer early Monday morning. Please keep Sasha and her family in your thoughts during this incredibly sad time...

There was more, only Meg couldn't read it through her watery eyes. She reached for her phone and speed-dialed Sasha. She was barely fighting back tears as she listened to the phone ring until Sasha's voice mail picked up.

Meg was completely unprepared and unbelievably choked up. She ended up leaving a somewhat garbled and totally disjointed message expressing her concern, condolences, and sadness but knew it sounded weird, so she signed off saying she would call again later.

Meg knew she shouldn't be this upset. She didn't even know Sasha's mother. Pretty soon the entire office would be abuzz and she couldn't bear the thought of talking to any of them about this. Nobody knew Sasha like she did, knew how close she was with her mom and how lost she would be without her. She grabbed her things and called a client she was friendly with downtown to arrange a spur-of-the-moment brainstorming session. With a hasty email she informed her boss she'd be at Ferguson and Tyler for the rest of the day.

Meg chugged the subway to the Financial District keeping all her emotions inside. She stopped by the Starbucks on Wall Street and threw some water on her face before spending the next three hours going over pension alternatives. After her meeting she wandered around Downtown somewhat aimlessly, unable to think of anything but Sasha. Without realizing her path, she found herself directly outside of Jesse's building. She shuffled into the lobby to warm up and walked to the elevator, pressing the floor for Jesse's law firm. None of what she was doing made sense—Jesse was probably in court or at a meeting—but she kept moving until she was through the glass doors at Stanton Ducane, standing in front of the receptionist's desk.

"Can I help you?" the mature woman behind the desk asked in a friendly voice.

"I'm looking for, I mean, I was hoping to see if Jesse Ducane is in," Meg said in a questioning tone. "She's not expecting me or anything, so she may not even be here."

Meg knew she was babbling and probably sounded like a loon but the receptionist was kind and pretended not to notice.

"Let me check for you. Your name?"

"Sorry. Megan McTiernan."

"Just have a seat, please."

Meg sat down roughly and waited as the woman whispered into the phone. Seconds later Jesse appeared.

"What's up, kid? Everything okay?"

"Yeah, sorry. I probably shouldn't have come. Are you busy?"

"Never too busy for you." She waved Meg up. "Come on back."

Once they were in Jesse's office, Meg breathed a sigh of relief.

"I'm sorry to barge in unannounced. I was sort of in the area and I just needed a place I could...I don't know, let my guard down, I guess."

"What's going on?" Jesse's eyes were full of concern as she sat facing Meg on the couch.

"Sasha's mother died," Meg said.

"Oh my God."

Meg leaned her head back into the hard leather of the couch and looked up at the ceiling. "I know it shouldn't hit me this hard. It's not my mother. I didn't even know her."

"Stop," Jesse ordered. "How's Sasha?"

"I don't know," Meg answered as she stared vacantly out Jesse's huge office window at the bright cold day outside. "I called and got voice mail. I haven't heard back."

Jesse nodded.

"I found out from my boss. She—Sasha, I mean—has been out for almost a week, now that I think about it. I guess she called Anne at some point to tell her. Anne, sorry, that's my boss, she put it out over email this morning."

"She had cancer, right?"

"Yeah."

"That's terrible."

"She was only like forty-eight or forty-nine, I think."

"Jesus."

"What do I do, Jess?" Meg looked up, hoping Jesse would make the decision for her.

"Are you considering going there?"

Meg breathed out hard. "I want to but...I don't know." She looked down at her feet. "I don't want to stress her out any more than she already is by descending on her like some lesbian stalker in front of her family when I know she's not ready for that, or comfortable, or whatever." Meg bit her lower lip. "But I know, Jess. I know she needs me right now. I know it."

"I hear you." Jesse nodded matter-of-factly. "Let's take a step back. We're going to figure this out." She looked at her watch and Meg did the same, realizing it was almost three thirty. "Did you eat?" Without really giving Meg a chance to answer, Jesse spoke again. "Come on, let's get a bite downstairs."

Inside a cozy but upscale restaurant, Meg and Jesse sat at the oak bar and rehashed the situation. Meg had a drink at Jesse's behest, even though Jesse abstained, mentioning she had a class to teach in a little while. Meg still felt stupid being so taken aback by everything, but Jesse promised her reaction was normal. Even if it wasn't, Jesse's presence and her supportive comments made Meg feel better anyway. She was just about to thank her when Lexi strolled in.

She wrapped her arms around Meg without a word. Only in her release did she meet Meg's eyes. "You okay?"

"How'd you know?"

"I texted her." Jesse gave a small smile. As she spoke, Lexi turned to her fiancée and gave her a quick kiss on the mouth. Lexi ran her hand slowly down the side of Jesse's face in a gesture so sexy and natural it made Meg instantly jealous of their connection.

Meg looked at Jesse, puzzlement in her eyes. "When did you text her? I didn't even notice."

"I'm very stealthy." Jesse smiled. "And I'm very sorry, but I have to get to class." She hopped off the bar stool. "I didn't want to leave you alone." She put her credit card on the bar and signaled to the bartender that all charges should be applied to her. He returned her gesture with a familiar nod. "You girls should stay and have dinner," Jesse instructed before giving each of them a warm hug and heading out into the cold night.

They followed Jesse's suggestion and ordered food, settling into a nice table in the corner. Meg reiterated the details, or what little she knew of them, for Lexi. Lexi listened and provided comfort, but like Jesse she had no real advice to give. She, too, asked if Meg planned on going down to Maryland, adding that she strongly believed Sasha would want her there, but understood Meg's explanation that her presence might put Sasha in an awkward position.

When Meg got home it was almost eight o'clock and she was thankful Tracy was out. She couldn't stomach going over the scenario for the third time of the day. Meg knew once she filled her buddy in, Tracy would completely agree with Lexi anyway. Not that it mattered. She wasn't making a move before talking to Sasha.

❖

Later that night, in the confines of her own bedroom, Meg called Sasha again. This time she answered.

"Hi." Sasha's voice cracked a little, and Meg couldn't help but marvel at the amount of hurt audible in such a small word.

"Sash, I am so sorry." Meg choked up. "Are you okay?"

There was silence for a second and Meg imagined Sasha clenching her teeth, swallowing her pain. She heard a sniffle and then a throat-clearing cough.

"Yeah. I mean no, not really. Of course not. But yeah, I guess so, in a way. You know what I mean?" Sasha let out a weird little laugh.

Meg didn't know what to say. She wanted to offer to get in her car and drive there but couldn't face the thought of Sasha's rejection. "What can I do?"

"There's nothing to do."

"I don't know what to say."

"Nobody does."

Meg found her courage. "I could come there. Now, I mean. If you want."

There was more silence and for a second Meg thought Sasha might say yes.

"No, it's okay. I'm fine. My whole family is here. Aunt Karen just got in from Florida. She'll be here all week with me."

"Okay."

"Meg, there is something you could do for me."

"Sure, what is it?"

"I have a video meeting set up with Ardmore Incorporated next week. Would you just cancel it or postpone it or something for me?"

"Yeah, no problem."

"I spoke to Anne before to give her the details for—" She stopped abruptly, as if unable to finish the sentence. "You know, the wake and everything. I guess some people up there were asking. She said she's going to send it out over email." There was a long pause. "You'll come, right?"

"Of course."

It was getting loud in the background and Meg knew they were almost out of time.

"Sash, I…"

"Yeah?"

There was so much Meg wanted to say but she couldn't find the words. "If you need anything, just call. Okay?"

She could almost hear Sasha nod acknowledgment through the phone. "'Bye, Megan."

❖

The next few days at Sullivan were characterized by a vacant kind of quiet. Meg worked on her projects and finally made the call to Ardmore Incorporated's Chicago office to reschedule Sasha's video conference. Then on Friday, Meg, along with Anne Whitmore, Scott Ford, and a handful of Sullivan colleagues who'd cleared their schedules for the day, boarded an Amtrak train to DC to attend the afternoon visitation rites for Sasha's mother.

Meg waited in line behind the other mourners, nervous for what would happen when she saw Sasha. She half expected Sasha to break down, be unable to let her go once she saw her, but that wasn't the case. Sasha looked sad and thin but she held herself together stoically, embracing Meg and thanking her for coming. She told her she appreciated her support—likely the same sentiment she'd made to everyone else in the room. For a split second Meg thought she saw something more in Sasha's eyes, but she couldn't be sure and her surge of hope felt pathetic in light of the circumstances.

On the train back to New York, she grabbed a window seat in the hopes of shutting her brain off entirely, but she had no such luck when Anne parked squarely next to her. For the next forty-five minutes, her boss rambled on about work projects and timelines while Meg half listened.

"It breaks my heart to think of what she's going through right now." Meg tuned in as her boss turned the conversation personal. "You know how close she was with her mother." Anne's voice dropped as she looked past Meg out the window. "I can't even imagine it." She patted Meg's leg once. "Take care of her, Meg. She's going to need you."

Meg was positive the confusion over Anne's remarks showed on her face, but Anne ignored her expression by looking down and opening her iPad, signaling the conversation was over. Meg closed her eyes and pressed her head up against the cold glass windowpane, wishing she could follow Anne's gentle advice.

She spent the next few days in a fog going through work by rote, her nights filled with the company of Tracy and Betsy, who were obviously trying to keep her busy. Lexi did her share too, stopping by to check in more than was necessary. Meg appreciated her friends and their support but she was happy to have the house to herself Thursday evening after she returned from her Bikram class. She walked naked across her bedroom, downing a glass of water as she waited for the shower water to regulate to the right temperature. She was just about to hop in when her cell phone screen lit up and started vibrating across the bathroom counter. A nanosecond later, Sasha's name appeared on the screen.

"Hey," Meg said, answering right away.

There was only quiet on the other end before Meg heard Sasha's weak voice. "Meg?"

"Yeah."

"Meg, I need you."

"Okay," Meg answered, even though she wasn't at all sure what Sasha meant.

There was another short pause. "Can you come here?"

"Of course," Meg said without even thinking about it. "Where are you?"

"At my house. In Maryland," Sasha answered quietly.

Meg reached into the shower and shut the water off, walking back into her bedroom to jot down the address. She pulled on some clean track pants and a long-sleeve T-shirt, quickly throwing some essentials in a bag before heading through the front door. Only as she hit her empty driveway did she remember: Tracy had her car. She glanced across the street and spotted Lexi's Toyota parked in front of Jesse's house. She dashed across the street and rang the bell. When Jesse opened the door, Meg wasted no time.

"Is Lexi here?" she asked, looking past Jesse into the living room.

"She's over at her mothers'. What's the matter?"

"Shit. I wanted to borrow her car."

"Take mine," Jesse said, not missing a beat. "Where are you going?"

Meg was slightly nervous to tell Jesse the truth, but knew she had little choice. "Um, actually, Sasha called me." She met Jesse's moss green eyes. "She asked me if I would come there. To Maryland. But Tracy has my car." She shuffled uneasily from foot to foot. "I could just call her, I guess, ask her to come back. She's probably just at Betsy's, or out to dinner or something."

Jesse walked into her kitchen and lifted a set of keys from a hook above the countertop. "Here. It's got a full tank of gas."

"But what about you, with work and teaching? I don't know if I'll be back tomorrow or the next day…"

Jesse waved her off. "I'll be fine. Just be careful, Meg."

"I promise," Meg said, taking the keys to Jesse's high-end Range Rover. "I'll pay attention to the speed limit. I won't drive like a maniac," Meg offered sincerely.

"I know," Jesse responded, shaking her head a little at Meg's earnestness. "I'm not talking about the car." She held Meg at arm's length. "Text me when you get there, okay? I worry about you." Jesse pulled her in for a good hug. "Now, go take care of your girl."

The entire ride Meg listened intently to the GPS on her phone, careful not to miss a turn, and despite her promises to Jesse, Meg made it to Silver Spring in what she figured was record time. She actually hadn't realized how nervous she was until she rolled into Sasha's driveway, simultaneously thanking God she hadn't gotten pulled over and greedily asking for more goodwill as she approached the front door. Sasha met her in the doorway, reaching out and clutching Meg's shoulders as she cried into her neck.

When Sasha calmed down, she led Meg over to the couch in the living room and sat with one leg under her as she released her dark hair from the loose bun on top of her head. "I'm sorry," she started, wiping away the tear streaks from her face. "I shouldn't have called you. Or made you come here."

"Shut up," Meg responded with an equal amount of sincerity and sweetness that made Sasha laugh a little. "How are you?"

Sasha took a deep breath. "I was okay until today. You know there were so many people around. My aunt Karen stayed here with me all week. She helped me pack up Mom's stuff." She bit her lip and shook her head a little. "Devon, my little brother," she added, even though Meg knew who he was, "went back to school on Tuesday." She looked around at the quiet room. "Aunt Karen left today." She was stoic when she explained that what was left of her mother and her own childhood fit in a few boxes and she seemed sad but grateful as she explained that her dad's wife, a real estate agent, would take care of putting the house on the market. "I wanted to stay here tonight. This is the house I grew up in." She welled up. "It just felt so lonely."

Meg hugged her again and kissed the top of her soft hair. When she let go, she saw tears slide down Sasha's sunken cheeks.

"You're so skinny." Meg shook her head. "When was the last time you ate?"

"I don't know." Sasha forced out a smile. "But there's a ton of food in the fridge. People keep dropping stuff off. If you want something—"

"I'm okay." Meg took control of the situation. "I'm going to make you something, though. And you're gonna eat it," she added emphatically. "Now, if I know you, there is definitely some bubble bath in this house. If I have to, I'll find it."

Sasha guiltily shifted her eyes to the floor in a vain attempt to hide her true smile.

"Go run yourself a bath," Meg continued. "I'll bring you in some food."

"Meg, you don't have to—"

"Uh-uh." Meg put her hand up. "You called me here. That means I'm in charge," she added playfully. "Those were not suggestions."

Sasha smiled her beautiful smile as she pushed off the cushion to stand. She leaned over and placed one hand on each of Meg's shoulders. Sasha looked right at her and for a second Meg thought they were going to kiss, but Sasha pulled Meg forward and hugged her instead. It got Meg's heart racing anyway.

After Meg brought Sasha some toast and chamomile tea, she made herself useful by locating the five banker's boxes of belongings Sasha had packed up and humped them down the stairs, stacking them neatly by the front door. Finished with her one chore, she sat on the edge of Sasha's bed staring absentmindedly at the lilac walls and thin white drapes. Then Sasha came in wrapped in a towel.

Meg felt incredibly awkward in front of a barely dressed Sasha, so she hurriedly asked if it would be okay if she took a shower also, overexplaining her exercise class and how sweaty she'd been. Under the hot stream of water she centered herself and calmed down, toweling off and throwing on boxers and a T-shirt before she reentered Sasha's room, where Sasha was already under the covers.

"So, should I sleep in Devon's room or maybe the couch?" Meg asked, hoping she sounded as though it didn't matter.

There was a short pause before Sasha answered. "Would you stay here? With me?"

"Sure. Of course." Meg attempted a casual tone, trying to pretend it wasn't a big deal. As she pulled back the covers and slipped in next to Sasha, she was hugely grateful she was not a guy who would have been instantly betrayed by an obvious hard-on. She slid one arm under Sasha's pillow and the other around her waist in a position they had grown accustomed to falling asleep in. As she lay there with her desire undetected, Meg could feel Sasha's body relax into hers. They were both silent for a few minutes until Sasha turned around toward Meg, their faces almost touching. Meg licked her lips out of habit even though she knew it was pointless.

"Meg?"

"Yeah," Meg breathed out.

"Thank you. For coming." Sasha leaned forward and kissed Meg on the lips, slow and soft.

On a different day, under different circumstances, Meg would have brushed it off, dismissing Sasha's heartfelt thanks lightly, probably tell her it was no big deal. She might have even made an off-color joke to break the tension over the awkwardness of their situation right now, lying in each other's arms squished into a twin bed. But she didn't. The seriousness of the moment got the best of her, and instead, she said exactly what she was feeling.

"I love you, Sash."

Meg looked into Sasha's eyes and it was enough that she saw reciprocation there, but Sasha said it anyway.

"I love you too, Meg." Her voice was somehow sweet and sexy, desperate and passionate all at once.

They kissed deep and slow until their hands found each other easily, removing what little clothing they had on. Meg didn't stop to think about the repercussions of their actions or what any of it would mean tomorrow. They were together, and for the moment anyway, it was as if they had never been apart.

❖

The kettle shrieked, interrupting Lexi's scattered thoughts as she sat at her parents' dining room table tapping her lips with a pencil and listening to the wind howl outside the window.

"You want a cup of tea, honey?" Marnie asked from the kitchen. Lexi looked over and watched her mother reach for two mugs from the cupboard without waiting for an answer.

"Sure," Lexi said, tossing her yellow legal pad onto the table with a small thud.

"Is that work?" Marnie asked, sliding a plate of blueberry scones between their steaming cups on the table.

"I wish," Lexi said with a dramatic eyebrow raise. "It's the seating chart for the wedding."

"Ooh, fun." Marnie pulled one leg under her and leaned forward in her chair. "Can I help?"

"Sure." Lexi pushed the pad toward her mother and scooched her chair a little closer as her mother pored over the list and tentative arrangements.

Marnie sipped her tea, holding the cup with both hands. "Looks good so far, but can't you put Aunt Theresa with Jesse's family?"

"Imagine that?" Lexi laughed, breaking a scone in half and reaching for a napkin with her other hand. "They would not know what to do with themselves."

"I love her, but God help me, she does not stop talking." Marnie shook her head. "Sometimes I can't believe she and your mother are sisters."

They laughed together and talked about other details, mostly stuff they had already gone over—the band, the food, the layout of the Ducanes' expansive Cape Cod estate where the outdoor reception would be held. Lexi was having fun. This was always how it was supposed to be, and it was how it had been for the last several months, since the holidays, really. Before that time both of her mothers had technically voiced their support, but since Thanksgiving, Lexi had felt the change as something genuine. Marnie and Chris asked about Jesse; they invited her to Sunday dinner. Lexi often wondered what had been the catalyst for their joint mood swing, but she had never asked. Her curiosity finally won out.

"Hey, Mom?" She clinked the spoon on the side of her mug. "What changed your mind? About me and Jesse?"

Marnie gave her a curious look as she sipped her tea.

"It just all seemed to change." Lexi shrugged, pulling her feet onto the base of the chair under her. "I'm just curious why. Or maybe *what* made the difference. I mean one day you hated her, and the next, it was like she was already part of the family. Not that I'm complaining. I've just kind of been wondering."

Marnie nodded her head as she placed her mug on the table meeting Lexi's eyes. "Honestly," she said, looking a little guilty, "it was Mary Brown."

Lexi tilted her head to the side, confused by her mother's admission.

"She pulled me aside one day. Mary." Marnie fingered the edges of her shoulder-length hair. "She knew I was upset about you and Jesse. God, she saw it on display that night when she and Kam found out you two were engaged. We've known each other a long time," she said with a slight chuckle. "She talked some sense into me."

"About me and Jesse?"

"Yeah."

"What did she say?"

Marnie smiled at her daughter's obvious shock. "Nothing I didn't already know."

Lexi took a minute to digest her mother's brief comment. "But—"

"When Mary talked to me this fall, she pointed out things I already knew. She just…she reminded me how lucky I am to have you." She met Lexi's eyes. "Believe it or not, she threw in a good word for Jesse too." Marnie laughed a little at the memory before she put her hand on top of Lexi's. "Honey, I know Jesse's a good person. Despite what happened with her and Mary." She pursed her lips at the thought and continued. "And truthfully, Lex, it wasn't anything Mary said that changed my mind about you two. But afterward, our conversation made me realize I might lose you. Lose the closeness we have. I love you, Lex, and I want to be involved in your life." Marnie twisted her mug between her hands and looked at the tabletop. "When you and Jesse started dating, I was angry. But after a while I got used to it, and I figured, you know, you're young, you need to have your own experiences." She licked her lips. "And just as I was starting to come around, you told us you were getting married. It was a shock." Her eyes widened. "It had very little to do with Jesse at that point." She met Lexi's eyes. "Except she's older than you and I blamed her a little. For stealing your youth, your innocence."

"Mom, I'm not a little girl," Lexi said defensively.

Marnie's eyes crinkled with amusement. "I know, honey. I didn't think she deflowered you," she added with a smile.

"Gross, Mom." Lexi winced.

"I just have a hard time imagining what it's like for you to be in such a serious relationship that already has so much drama embedded in it. You deserve, I don't know, something better. Something easier."

"But I love her, Mom. I really do."

"I know you do, Lex. I just worry about you." She reached over and rubbed Lexi's forearm, a look of deep concern steeped in her crinkled brow. "You are so young. And marriage is hard."

"But look at you and Mush. You guys have been together forever, and you still love each other."

"We do." Marnie reflexively touched the thin gold band on her ring finger with her thumb. "We are very lucky." She twisted her mouth to the side. "Look at the world around you, though. We are the success story."

Lexi tucked a long brown curl behind her ear, biting her lip as she met her mother's eyes. "You already had two kids by the time you were my age, you know."

"I know. You're right." Marnie nodded. "Honey, I know Jesse loves you and I can't help but love her because of that. And I'm sure before long you'll have children of your own. I can't even tell you how happy that makes me, the idea of being a grandmother." She shook off chills at the thought. "All I can say is when you have kids of your own, you'll see, whether they are five or twenty-five, they are your babies. I'm sure you won't make the same mistakes I did, but maybe someday, when your little girl tells you she's getting married, maybe you'll understand that yes, I made a mistake, but I was nervous to lose my little girl."

"I love you, Mom."

"I love you too, honey."

Chris entered the kitchen just in time to see them hugging each other tightly as tears streaked their faces. "What's going on? Everybody okay?"

Marnie wiped at her cheeks. "It's fine. We were just doing the seating chart for the wedding."

They laughed at Chris's fake horrified expression. "It's my sister, isn't it?"

CHAPTER TWENTY-THREE

Midmorning, as Meg was packing Jesse's trunk with Sasha's boxes, preparing for the journey back to New York, a car slowed in front of the house and Meg saw a familiar face exit. One second before she said hello to Jane-Anne, she realized it was her twin.

"Sabrina," Meg said with a wave.

Sabrina smiled in response. "Hi, Megan," she added nicely, not seeming at all surprised by Meg's presence. "I just wanted to say good-bye to Sash." She motioned toward the house and continued up the walkway with Meg following behind her to grab more stuff for the car.

Sasha called out from upstairs, "Baby, would you grab the tray of vegetable lasagna out of the fridge? I want to take it with us. It's in a clear rectangular dish." She bounded down the stairs to find Sabrina standing there. Sasha was definitely embarrassed, Meg could tell by the color flooding her cheeks, but she played it off. "Hey, Sabrina," she said, greeting her friend with a hug.

On their way out of the upper-middle-class suburb where Sasha had grown up, they stopped by her father's house, where Sasha dropped off four of the five boxes. She introduced Meg to her dad and his wife, stating simply, "Dad, Mel, this is Meg. Meg this is my dad, Andrew, and his wife, Melanie." Meg found it interesting Sasha didn't use any qualifier when making the introduction. She didn't refer to her as her friend or provide any explanation as to why she was here. Meg felt her heart do a little happy dance over the small victory.

They spent the ride north in a mix of quiet and talking, and when they stopped at the southernmost point in New Jersey to gas up, Sasha darted into the rest stop. Meg stared at her as she walked back to the car, a pink knit scarf wound around her neck, her shoulders hunched as she braced herself against the cold, her long hair blowing like crazy in the wind. She was without a doubt the most beautiful girl Meg had ever seen. Sasha caught her looking and smiled, hurrying over and sliding into the passenger seat. Without a word, she leaned over and kissed Meg, slowly and thoroughly, running her hand into Meg's short, thick hair as she finished. It got Meg going more than she wanted to admit.

"God, I missed kissing you," Sasha said.

"Yeah?"

"Yeah," Sasha breathed out. "I missed everything about you."

"What happened with us?" Meg looked right into Sasha's eyes.

Sasha laced her fingers through Meg's but looked down. "I don't know."

"All of a sudden, it was just over. Nothing. We barely even talked about it." Meg was sure this wasn't the right time for this conversation, but it seemed to be happening anyway.

Sasha squeezed her hand and rested her head against the leather seat. She turned and looked right at Meg. "That night, in January, with my friends, when you left my apartment because I asked you to pretend we weren't dating or whatever"—she looked down—"God, I was a mess. Jane-Anne left early but Sabrina stayed. She could tell I was off." She lifted her eyes to Meg's. "I told her everything."

"Everything?"

"Everything."

"How'd that go?"

Sasha puckered her lips, clearly remembering. "Awesome. Sabrina is awesome. She was happy for me that I was seeing someone. She yelled at me for being a jerk. She wanted to get to know you." Sasha loosened the scarf around her neck and toyed nervously with the tassels. "Talking to her made me feel better, but then worse at the same time."

"What do you mean?"

"The thing is, even though she was super supportive, I still had— *have*," she corrected, looking reluctant to admit it, "my own hang-ups." She split the ends of a loose thread. "Deep down I knew I wasn't as okay with everything as I should be. I'm still not, really. I still don't know what I want."

"Sash, we could have talked about it. We should have."

"It wasn't fair to you. *I* wasn't fair to you. What I did to you that night was messed up." She shook her head. "So I backed off. You deserve to be with someone who can give you what you need."

"I wanted to be with you. I still do."

"Meg, I'm a disaster. I want so badly to tell you everything's fine now and I'm totally there. Where you are, I mean. If you even still are." She looked embarrassed and uncertain at her words.

Meg looked right at her. "I am."

"But I'm not." Sasha shrugged. "I don't know why." She looked out the window at the parked cars around them, waiting a second before she spoke again. "I meant what I said last night. I love you, Meg. Being with you feels amazing." She smiled her gorgeous smile. "Not just, you know, physically." She blushed a little. "Although, last night…" She let her jaw hang open a little as she met Meg's eyes again. "Whoa."

Meg laughed sheepishly at the comment, but Sasha wasn't done talking.

"Seriously though, last night was the first time in weeks I've felt…I don't know, like myself, I guess. I swear that's because of you."

"So stay with me, then."

"But I'm just…I'm worried…"

"We'll figure it out."

Sasha looked over, narrowing her eyes as she openly scrutinized Meg's face. "Are you sure?"

"I love you too, Sash."

"You do, don't you?"

"I really do."

Just past exit six on the turnpike Sasha asked if they could spend the night at Meg's. She wasn't ready to go home yet, even with Meg by her side. Meg readily agreed. Sasha talked a lot about her mother on the ride, how sick she'd been the last few weeks, how hard her little brother was taking it. She was sad and she cried off and on, but every so often her tears would mix with laughter as she shared a happy memory. Meg held her hand and hung on every word until she made the turn onto her block and saw her own car in the driveway, blocked in by Betsy's Lexus.

"Shit, Sash." Meg pulled the car to a stop in front of Jesse's house. "My roommate is home. I totally forgot she might be here." She looked over to assess Sasha's reaction. "Her girlfriend is here too," Meg added with a wince. "Give me a second and I can get them to leave."

"It's okay." Sasha smiled. "Don't make them leave. I was actually thinking, you know I brought that vegetable lasagna with us. Aunt Karen made it, and trust me, it's going to be amazing." She lifted her eyebrows. "I was going to see if you wanted to invite Lexi and Jesse over to share it with us." She shrugged. "I mean, I sort of owe them too. Jesse let you borrow her car and everything. Anyway, the thing is huge. There's definitely enough for six people."

Meg crinkled her forehead. "You sure?"

"I am," she answered with an affirmative nod.

Before Meg could question Sasha further, she'd pushed the passenger door open and jumped out. Meg followed her to the house.

"Hello?" Meg called in as she pushed the door open.

"We're in here," Tracy called from the living room a few feet away. "How'd it go?" she asked, before realizing Meg wasn't alone. "Oh, sorry." She moved Betsy's legs off her lap and they both got up.

Meg was quick with the intros. "Sash, these are my friends Tracy and Betsy." They exchanged hellos, both Tracy and Betsy offering condolences.

"We brought dinner. Vegetable lasagna that Sasha's aunt made," Meg said, breaking the mild tension and making eye contact with Tracy, assuring her it was okay to stay. "I texted Lex and Jesse, they'll be over in a bit."

"Cool," Tracy responded in stride. "I'll throw together a quick salad."

Over dinner they kept the conversation light, discussing tomorrow night's open house at the development that they all had plans to attend. Her friends included Sasha in everything, filling her in on silly community gossip and doing their absolute best to keep her smiling. While Lexi and Betsy mused excitedly about the underlying message behind a popular television series, Sasha reached for Meg's hand in her lap.

"Thank you," she mouthed when Meg faced her. Sasha kissed Meg's shoulder and rested her head on it. Meg didn't say anything in return, but she couldn't remember feeling more content.

When Jesse and Lexi got up to leave, Tracy and Betsy followed suit. Tracy pulled Meg aside to explain they were going to stay at Betsy's for the night. Meg told her it wasn't necessary, but Tracy insisted. As ever, Meg was unbelievably appreciative of her friends for everything they had done for her tonight and always, not really sure what she ever did to deserve such amazing people in her everyday life.

The rest of the evening passed with little to do. Meg checked her work email to see what she had missed on her day out of the office. Meg tried to give Sasha her privacy, keeping busy on her iPad in the room she called her office even though she rarely worked from home, while Sasha was in her bedroom fielding condolence calls. She heard Sasha sobbing a few times and peeked in, bringing her a glass of water and rubbing her back for a second while Sasha listened to the caller on the other end of the line, before she left her alone again.

Sometime after ten, Meg heard the shower go on and twenty minutes later Sasha came into the spare room where Meg was still futzing around. She put her iPad aside and swung her legs off the couch to make room.

"Are you doing work?" Sasha asked sleepily. Her eyes were puffy from hours of crying.

"No." Meg let out a small laugh. "I'm playing Bejeweled Blitz."

"What?" Sasha laughed.

"It's a game. Like Candy Crush. But with jewels." She smiled at her explanation. "It relaxes me. And it's fun, if you must know. I just beat my high score," she added with exaggerated pride.

"Oh, well in that case," Sasha teased.

"How are you holding up?" Meg asked seriously.

Sasha nodded and shrugged. "Okay." She looked exhausted. "I'm going to go to bed. I'm beat." She leaned over and kissed Meg. "You don't have to come, if you want to stay up and play your game. I just wanted to say good night."

Meg's heart sank a little. "Do you want to be alone?"

"No." Sasha kissed her again. "I'm really tired and I don't want to be annoying."

"You don't annoy me." Meg stood up and held Sasha's hand as they walked to the bedroom. "Come on. I'm going to cuddle you all night. Even if you are a total pillow hog."

❖

She was awakened by Sasha's voice, whispering loudly in her ear, "Are you awake?" Sasha sounded relaxed and cheerful and it was nice to wake up with her spooned against her back.

"I am now," Meg breathed out while Sasha kissed her cheek.

"I want to come to your party tonight," Sasha blurted out enthusiastically. "What's it called? A social?"

Meg turned onto her back. "Actually it's an open house." She rubbed the sleep from her eyes. "It's different than a social."

"In what way?"

"Well, for one thing if you don't live at Bay West, you have to get put on the guest list. Which means you have to be invited by someone who lives here."

Sasha was leaning on her side, her head propped on one elbow. "So can I come?"

"I told you, you have to be invited," Meg teased.

"Are you gonna invite me?" Sasha swung her leg over Meg, trapping her in place as she straddled her torso, waiting expectantly for an answer.

Meg exhaled dramatically. "I don't know. What's in it for me?"

Sasha raised an eyebrow suggestively as she ran her eyes over Meg's entire body. "Everything."

CHAPTER TWENTY-FOUR

C ome to California with me."
        Tracy felt Betsy's body tense up at the suggestion, so she clarified. "Next week, I mean. I would love for you to meet my dad, my friends…" Her voice trailed off as she continued tracing out lazy circles on Betsy's skin. She looked up at her girlfriend's gorgeous eyes.

"God, I would love to." Betsy's regret was evident in her tone. "If it was just regular patients I would get someone to cover me, but I have two surgeries scheduled for next week," she added with a frown.

Tracy propped up on one elbow. "Did you get nervous that I meant for good?" she asked with a slight laugh.

Betsy turned away from the stream of bright morning sunlight spilling through the shades into Tracy's bedroom. "I hate feeling like you're dropping your whole life to be here with me. It bothers me, I can't help it."

Tracy let her head fall on the pillow inches from Betsy's. "Baby." She brushed one finger along Betsy's cheek. "If I had a great job in LA that I absolutely loved and you were just starting over, wouldn't you do it in California with me?"

"That's not the case, though."

"It is."

"Tracy, you could go back to golf tomorrow. Your hand is fine. I know your coach has been calling you and I know that's at least part of the reason you're going out there next week."

Tracy smiled. "I wasn't going back on the tour anyway. I was staying in New York, whether this happened or not." She leaned forward and kissed the smooth skin on Betsy's chest. "This is just an unbelievably fabulous bonus." She looked up. "And yes, I am going to see my coach, but it's not what you think. We have some business to finalize, and I want to see him. He's been part of my life for years. We're friends."

Betsy turned toward her. "Are you sure about all of this?"

"Yes, very sure." Tracy smoothed her hand the length of Betsy's body. "Aren't you?"

"Yes. But"—she reached for Tracy's hand and gently touched each finger with her own—"it's easier for me. I'm not changing my whole life."

"My life was a mess. It needed to change."

"I don't want you to feel like you're giving up everything to be with me."

"I don't." Tracy leaned over and kissed her. "I'm not, actually." Tracy shifted onto her back and reached for her phone. "You just reminded me," she said, scrolling through her calendar. "My friend Kristen is going to be in New York next month. I told you about her a while ago. She works at ESPN." She checked Betsy's face to see if she remembered. "I was hoping to see her next week, but she'll be out of town. But she told me she's coming here for work next month, with her boyfriend, who is some kind of producer. And she wants to meet for dinner. She thinks he's going to be able to hook me up with a job at the network." Tracy raised her eyebrows. "He's got some solid connections, I guess." She put her phone back on the nightstand and cradled Betsy from behind. "How awesome would that be?"

"It would be awesome." Betsy turned her face slightly to kiss Tracy. She inched herself backward just a touch, pressing her naked body against Tracy's. "I almost can't think of anything more perfect." Her voice had an added huskiness and Tracy picked up on it right away.

"Really? Anything?" Tracy whispered, her lips finding their way along Betsy's neck and shoulder. Her hands took things a step further, one on Betsy's left breast, gently toying with her nipple, while the other moved up inside her thigh and higher as she teased softly.

Betsy was already breathing heavily as Tracy moved inside her. "Maybe a few things," she managed to get out, before she turned, taking Tracy's face in her hands. "I love you, Trace."

"I love you too, baby."

Betsy kissed her, long and slow. She pulled her face away and said in a voice so low it was almost inaudible, "I want it."

Tracy asked no questions—she knew exactly what Betsy meant. She reached down the side of the bed and slid the box out from underneath. Swiftly slipping into her harness she knelt at the side of the bed, reaching over and bringing Betsy toward her, so her legs hung off the mattress. She kissed the insides of her thighs and all the way up, staying there until she knew Betsy was ready. Then she met her on the bed, kissed her way up her belly and breasts, her neck. Their faces brushed against each other and they kissed gently as she eased inside Betsy. She saw Betsy bite her lip a little at first and then felt her relax as Tracy read her body and found the perfect pace, staying the course until Betsy demanded more, harder, faster. She obliged, of course, using all her willpower to hold off her own release until she was sure Betsy was coming. When that happened, and largely inspired by it, Tracy didn't hold back. She moved fast and deep inside, exploding in seconds until she collapsed, sweaty and spent, unbelievably content.

Meg opened the door to the lovely aroma of fresh coffee and bacon filling her kitchen. "Good morning, ladies," she said, greeting Tracy and Betsy in an upbeat tone as she tossed her work bag and her duffel bag on top of each other in the foyer.

"Hey, Meg." Betsy folded her newspaper down and put it to the side of her empty placemat.

"*Meg-an*," Tracy called over her shoulder, matching Meg's enthusiasm and emphasizing both syllables of her name. "What's up?" she asked from in front of the stove where she was whipping up what looked to be a kick-ass breakfast. "I hope you're hungry."

Meg nodded happily. "I could eat," she said taking a seat across from Betsy.

"Don't take this the wrong way," Tracy said with a smile, filling a mug with steaming coffee and placing it in front of Meg, "but to what do we owe this pleasure?"

When Meg curled her eyebrows at the question, Tracy continued. "Correct me if I'm wrong. But you and Sasha always spend Sunday together. You're never home this early. Everything okay?"

Meg stirred in some cream and sugar as she spoke. "Sasha's dad is in town for work. He's got meetings in the city tomorrow." She took a quick sip. "He came in early to spend the day with her."

"Did you meet him?" Betsy asked.

Meg shook her head, as she swallowed. "No. I think they're doing brunch and then a museum or something. I'm not sure. I got up and went to a yoga class, then hit the road."

"You bummed she didn't ask you to come along?" Tracy asked.

Meg shook her head. "Not at all." She turned the newspaper toward her to glance at the headlines. "I have actually met her dad, once before. When I went to pick her up after the funeral." She pushed the paper back. "But today is about them. I get that. She doesn't need me there to have to entertain, or explain, or anything." She moved her mug back and forth by the handle. "It will be a hard enough day without that added stress."

She checked a look at Tracy and registered her concern. "I know you're worried because you get the brunt of my paranoia over Sasha downplaying our relationship. Trust me, it's fine."

Meg said it because it was true even though very little had changed outwardly. Sasha was still mostly closeted—at work, with most of her friends. But between them so much had changed in the last few months. Since the night Meg had driven to Maryland when Sasha called her, their relationship had moved to a new level. Their connection was stronger, the trust deeper. Meg felt the change before she really knew what it was. Sure, she had said the word, but she didn't understand it until it had already taken over every cell of her being. She was in love with Sasha Michaels and Sasha was in love with her, and knowing that made all the difference. Everything would be okay, she was sure of it. She knew Tracy and Betsy would understand what she meant if she took the time to explain it, but she didn't want to. For now, that knowledge was hers alone. So she changed the subject.

Meg looked over at Betsy and winked before she addressed Tracy, her voice full of faux concern. "So, bacon, huh, Trace? Now I know you're a goner."

Tracy rolled her eyes but played along. "What can I say, love makes me do all sorts of insane things." She walked over to Betsy and kissed her forehead. "Anyway, what's on your agenda today? Want to come hiking with us?" she asked.

"I have the dentist today actually."

"On a Sunday?" Betsy was surprised.

"I know. Weird, right?" Meg responded with a shrug. "It's some new place. Well, new to me. A guy at work told me about it. His mother goes there. It's actually only like five minutes from here. Beats trekking into Brooklyn like I've been doing for the last two years. Thanks anyway, though."

Tracy set a plate of egg whites full of brightly colored vegetables in front of Betsy. She nodded at Meg. "What do you want in your omelet?"

"Whatever's going, dude."

"That's my girl."

❖

Meg stared vacantly at the artwork on the wall but barely had time to determine if it was a print or a painting before a girl in lavender scrubs sauntered into the room and opened Meg's chart, whipping her head around immediately. Although surprise was evident on her face, Reina Ramirez collected herself quickly, saying in a smooth voice, "Hi, Meg. How are you?"

"I'm good." Meg knew her own surprise showed as well. "How about you? You work here?" she asked, shaking her head at the obvious question.

"I do," Reina said, coupling her answer with a smile that was a little sultry before she turned back to Meg's chart. For a minute she was all business, asking Meg routine questions and spelling out that she would begin with X-rays. She placed the thick radiation shield across Meg's chest. "I do have to ask, before I start"—she bit one side of her bottom lip—"is there any chance you're pregnant?"

Meg laughed and looked right at Reina. "Yeah…that's gonna be a no."

"I figured." Reina blushed. "Standard question. And hey, you never know."

Meg smiled in response as Reina started the series of X-rays. When she was through, she replaced the heavy apron with a paper bib that she clipped around Meg's neck. While Reina set up, they engaged in pleasantries with Meg asking after Teddy and Rose. Finally, Reina sat on the wheeled stool next to Meg and maneuvered the dental chair all the way back. She put on her latex gloves slowly before reaching for her cleaning utensils. "I'm surprised I haven't seen you here before, Meg," she said, getting ready to start.

"It's my first time," Meg blurted out. It was impossible to miss Reina's smile at Meg's exclamation with its built-in innuendo. "Here, I mean," she corrected. "At this dentist."

"Well, I'll be sure to be very gentle," Reina cooed in response, an unmistakable glimmer in her eye. "I'm going to start," she said, still smiling. "If you have any questions, or if anything hurts, let me know. Okay?"

Meg nodded even though she was slightly mortified at having someone she knew personally, someone she had at least thought about dating—however abstractly—involved in something so oddly intimate. But Reina made it easy.

"You doing okay?" she asked midway though.

Again Meg nodded, trying as hard as she could not to stare at Reina's chocolate-brown eyes, or her long thick lashes. Reina continued to talk her way through what she was doing, not asking questions Meg would be unable to respond to, but rather keeping her abreast of where she was in the procedure. It didn't hurt that she let her thumb linger on the top of Meg's lip, rubbing it softly as she worked.

When she was done, Meg rinsed her mouth while Reina made some notes in her chart. She was leaning on the counter as she wrote, her hip slung out to the side, and Meg was pretty sure she got caught checking out her ass when Reina turned around to talk to her. How embarrassing.

"Dr. Clemente will be here in a minute." Reina looked downright sexy when she bit her lower lip again, the exact same way she had earlier. "You have a gorgeous mouth, Meg. I would love to examine it again, perhaps with my own next time." She reached over and handed Meg a folded slip of paper, before letting her hand graze the length of Meg's arm as she left the room.

The doctor was in the room before Meg could even open the paper and Meg figured he had to have heard at least part of Reina's comment, if not the whole thing. Meg spent the rest of her appointment in a fog, shocked over the course of events and dying to see what Reina had written. It wasn't until she was inside her car that she opened the note.

Underneath Reina's ten-digit phone number she read: *I would really like to go out with you sometime. Call me if you're interested...RR.*

❖

Meg pulled back a kitchen stool and sat down with a thud and a sigh.

"How was the dentist?" Tracy asked from the sink where she was rinsing out a glass.

"Bizarre," Meg answered. She was about to expand on her one-word answer when the sight of a foreign object upright next to the drying rack caught her eye. She squinted her focus. "Is that, like, your strap-on?"

"Huh?" Tracy answered, before she followed Meg's gaze. "Shit. Sorry." She grabbed it quickly, holding it awkwardly in her left hand as she searched unsuccessfully for somewhere to put it.

Meg let out a laugh at Tracy's unsmooth reaction. "Dude, I don't care. It's just not what I expected to see right now." Meg looked around, dropping her voice to a whisper. "Oh my God, is Betsy still here?"

"*Noooo.*" Tracy exaggerated the response, shaking her head. "Trust me, I would never do this now if she was." She glanced down at the object in her hand. "Honestly, I meant to put this away. Completely forgot about it."

"Don't worry about me. I don't care," Meg offered with a shrug. "I want to see it, though." She craned her neck. "Is it big? It looks big."

"Says the girl who sees penises never."

"Ba-dum-bum." Meg pounded the drumbeat on the counter with her fists. "Walked right into that one, I guess."

"Sorry, couldn't resist." Tracy smiled. "It's not that big. Average, I would say. I'm not trying to hurt anyone, you know," she added with a wink.

Meg nodded, mulling some questions.

"Just ask, Meg." Tracy knew her too well.

"So you and Betsy use it?"

Tracy's expression was somewhere between cocky and shy as she answered. "Okay, so here's the deal. It's mine. I use it on her. Not the other way around."

"Okay. Don't get defensive." Meg smiled.

"I'm not. Just want to make sure we're all on the same page."

"Well, I kind of figured. But you never know." Meg nodded, still inwardly assessing. "Honestly, I'm surprised. At Betsy, I mean." When Tracy cocked her head at the comment, Meg explained. "I mean, I obviously don't know her like *that*, but she just seems so…proper. You know, everything's always so orderly with her. I'm surprised, pleasantly surprised," she corrected, "that she's into it."

Tracy licked her lips and nodded. "Look, it's not the only thing we do. But she's definitely into it."

"Nice."

"She would die, by the way, if she knew we were talking about this."

Meg furrowed her forehead in doubt. "Okay, but she knows I'm your best friend. I'm sure she assumes you talk to me."

"Assuming we discuss our relationship is one thing. Specific details regarding our sex life is quite another."

"Got it," Meg said with a nod.

Tracy looked at Meg and nodded with her chin. "You should try it. You'd like it, I think."

"Maybe," Meg said. In truth, she was definitely curious about the experience and had considered what it might be like on more than one occasion. The problem was it seemed such an intimate thing, and Meg felt like she had scarcely been with anyone long enough, or seriously enough, to even broach the subject. But now with Sasha, that wasn't the case. Hmm.

Tracy interrupted her thought. "What happened at the dentist?"

"Wait till you hear this one." Meg set up the story. "So, I go to the dentist and I'm sitting in the chair waiting. Checking out the random artwork on the wall, the weird machines, and who strolls in but Reina Ramirez. She's doing my cleaning."

"Reina is your dental hygienist?"

"Apparently."

"You didn't know that before you made your appointment?"

"I've never been to this dentist before."

"Right," Tracy drawled out, remembering. "Did you even know she was a hygienist?"

"No idea."

"So how was it?" Tracy asked.

Meg shook her head slowly from side to side. "I don't even know what to say."

"Go on."

"It was fine, I guess." Meg blinked long and slow. "It was weird. She was doing my X-rays." She stopped talking altogether, letting the air hang stagnantly between them.

"Meg?"

Meg found her voice. "I don't know. I feel like she kept holding my face while she took those cardboard X-ray thingies out of my mouth. And then when she did my cleaning, she like, I don't know, left her finger in my mouth when she reached for her scraper doodad." She paused again, replaying it in her head. "Then she like, rubbed my lip with her thumb," Meg finished, absentmindedly imitating the action with her own hand.

"Did she have gloves on?"

"Mm-hmm," Meg answered, still thinking about it.

"Dude, you were turned on by your dental exam."

Meg snapped herself out of it. "I wasn't."

"You should hear yourself right now." Tracy raised her eyebrows. "And see your face. Pretty kinky stuff." She wagged her fake cock at Meg. "Don't ever make fun of me for what I like to do after this confessional."

Meg laughed. "I didn't make fun of you at all," she corrected, smiling. She reached in her pocket and slid Reina's folded-up note across the counter. "She gave me this before she left."

Tracy stepped forward and unfolded it, her dark eyes moving quickly over the words. "Holy shit, Meg."

"Right?"

"Are you interested?"

Meg met her friend's eyes. "I have a girlfriend. A secret one," she added, laughing a little. "But still, a girlfriend."

"That's not what I asked." Tracy leaned in close. "I didn't ask if you were going to call her, or cheat on Sasha." She moved her head from side to side. "I asked if you were interested." She paused dramatically. "Are you?"

Meg stayed quiet for a second. She spun the note in a circle with her index finger, not lifting her eyes from it as she spoke. "I love Sasha," she said, picking up the slip of paper and folding it back into a small square. "I'll tell you what, though. Having her flirt with me right out in the open"—she looked up at Tracy—"it was pretty awesome. Not because I'm an exhibitionist or anything," she added in defense of her comment. She turned her mouth up into a slight smile, still thinking about it. "It was just nice to feel, I don't know, validated for a second."

"No progress there, huh? With Sasha?"

"Not really. A few of her friends know, but she's still mostly living the double life. Which, in a weird way, kind of means I am too."

"Nobody at work knows what's going on with you guys? I find that hard to believe."

Meg put Reina's note in the back pocket of her jeans with a sigh. "I think some people are on to us, but who knows." She shrugged off the comment. "Anyway, we're going away in two weeks, did I tell you?"

"On vacation?"

"No, for work actually. My boss, she's one of the people I'm pretty sure knows about us, keeps assigning us to work on stuff together. This one's Sasha's client, but I'm being sent along to assist."

"Sweet. Where are you going?"

"Chicago." Meg added with a knowing smile, "Not bad for you either. You and Betsy have the whole place to yourself for a week."

CHAPTER TWENTY-FIVE

In downtown Chicago, Meg and Sasha were booked in two rooms at a moderately upscale chain hotel, per standard Sullivan procedure. The second they left the hotel registration desk, though, Sasha followed Meg directly into her designated room and made it clear she planned on staying. It warmed Meg's heart.

During the day they worked side by side in Ardmore's conference room, crunching numbers, analyzing data, and running comparisons to come up with the best possible solutions to present to the board on Friday. At the end of the workday, they hurried back to the hotel to change clothes and explore the city's local culture together. Meg could feel how relaxed Sasha was and she attributed it to a number of things—time alone together, a distant city, the excitement of a not-quite-vacation.

On Tuesday night they sat kitty-corner at a small window table waiting for their pizza. Meg was trying to concentrate as she jotted notes, ironing out the remainder of the week's tasks, while Sasha teased her, running her hand the length of Meg's inner thigh, getting closer and closer each time.

Meg smiled, looking right at Sasha as she finished the list. "God, I love Anne Whitmore."

"You love *Anne*?" Sasha teased.

Meg nodded, playing back. "I'm pretty sure it's thanks to her we're here together. I've never heard of the company sending two junior associates into the field alone. So yes, I love Anne." She leaned forward and Sasha kissed her. It was a rare display, but they were far from home and Sasha completely let her guard down. "You're not so bad either," Meg added with a sweet smile.

Sasha pressed their foreheads together, giving her another small peck on the lips. "Meg, I think I may leave Sullivan," she said, turning the conversation in a completely different direction.

"What do you mean?"

Sasha leaned back as the waiter placed their deep-dish pie in the center of the table. "Come on, Meg. You know I don't really like consulting." She shrugged. "I'm not even good at it."

"Sash—"

"Meg, you don't have to say anything. It doesn't bother me. I mean, let's be honest—even now, you're doing most of the work here. Which I completely appreciate, by the way," she added, placing her hand on top of Meg's. "But I want to spend my life doing something I love, or at least like more than this."

Meg could hear the decision in Sasha's voice. "What would you do?"

"I'm thinking of going back to school for education."

"To be a teacher?"

Sasha nodded. "That's what I wanted to do when I was a kid. I had been talking to my mom about it a lot," she paused, "before she died." She let out a long breath.

Meg looked right into Sasha's eyes. "I think you would be an awesome teacher." She reached for a slice, setting it to cool on her plate. "You should talk to Anne. See if you can work out a deal to stay at Sullivan, at least part-time, while you take classes."

"Do you think she would let me do that?"

"I'm not sure, but it's worth asking."

❖

The whole week was this easy. They were a great team, a perfect duo, spending their days buried in work, stealing moments of downtime to research New York City education programs online, and taking full advantage of the nights together.

Meg had made special dinner plans for Thursday night. Throughout the week, they had expensed most of their meals, as was company policy, but tonight she wanted to splurge. She'd reserved a table for them at the swanky Harbor House, a five-star seafood restaurant she knew Sasha would love. She'd kept it a secret until just before lunch when she warned Sasha to eat light. As she expected, Sasha was thrilled.

Cutting through the hotel lobby en route to their shared room, Sasha was uncharacteristically frisky. She pressed the button for the elevator and dragged her middle finger down the front of Meg's oxford.

"I might not be able to wait," she whispered, biting her lip seductively.

Meg's mouth hung open. "What?"

Sasha shook her head slowly. "I'm not going to make it."

"Until after dinner?"

"Oh, I'm definitely not waiting until after dinner." She licked her lips. "I need to work up an appetite." She pulled Meg closer. "I meant"—she let her hand drift along the top of Meg's pants—"I may not make it to our room." She looked right in Meg's eyes. "You might be forced to take care of me in the elevator."

Meg felt herself throb at the suggestion and was about to lean in when a familiar voice caught them both by surprise.

"Aren't you girls cute," Scott teased as he walked over, wheeling his luggage up behind him.

"Scott," Meg said, unable to keep the irritation out of her voice. "What are you doing here?"

He looked between them and Sasha took a step away—more than was necessary, in Meg's opinion. "Didn't you get Anne's email this morning?" At their blank faces, he elaborated. "Artemis Ardmore, the old man who owns Ardmore, Inc., went ballistic when he found out there wouldn't be a partner at the presentation tomorrow." He shrugged. "I'm the compromise." He pressed the elevator button repeatedly. "What rooms are you in?"

"515," Meg responded.

Scott looked at Sasha.

"Oh, 518," Sasha said.

"I'm up on the sixth floor," he volunteered. "You guys want to grab dinner in a little bit?"

"We actually have a reservation at Harbor House," Meg said.

Scott whistled. "Sweet," he added with a nod. "Wait a second." He looked at Meg. "Who's paying for that? Meg, you can't expense that kind of meal without the client being with you."

"I was going to pay for it," Meg said, clearly annoyed at Scott's insinuation that she didn't understand the rules.

"Pulling out all the stops, huh, Meg." He smirked, gesturing at Sasha with his chin as he muffled his slight laugh.

"We were both going to pay for it," Sasha piped up, not meeting Meg's eyes as she lied. "Treat ourselves."

"Fine, whatever. I'm starving. What time are we going?"

"Our reservation is for seven."

"Great, I'll meet you down here at six thirty."

In Meg's room Sasha searched frantically for the keycard to her room across the hall until she found it under a stack of complimentary newspapers piled on the desk.

Meg came up behind her. "Sash, it's okay." She held her tight and kissed her neck sweetly. "You need to calm down. It's going to be fine. I promise."

Sasha was breathing hard and she twisted roughly out of Meg's embrace. "I'm going to put my stuff in my room."

"I think you're overreacting."

Sasha's voice cracked. "Meg, I don't want him to know." She put her hand up. "I just don't." She didn't say anything more.

Meg stepped back and sat on the end of the king-sized bed, feeling her heart break a little as she watched Sasha throw heaps of clothes into her luggage, trying to erase all evidence of herself from Meg's room.

"So, yeah, the old man blew a gasket when he found out neither Pat nor Doug would be there tomorrow," Scott reiterated over drinks as they waited for their table at the restaurant. "But it's complete bullshit. I mean, he's barely involved at all in the redevelopment project, right?" He tossed back the remainder of his gin and tonic. "Anne read between the lines anyway. He's old school, wants a dude involved." Shaking the ice in his glass he added, "Sorry, Meg, you don't count." He barked a hearty laugh at his own joke. "Anyway, as ridiculous as that is, he's still the client, and we aim to please. But everything is status quo. Sasha, you'll still give the presentation tomorrow. I'm just going to sit there, really."

"Actually Meg is doing the presentation," Sasha said, sounding nervous as she revealed the switch she and Meg had worked out earlier in the week.

"Whatever." He signaled the bartender for another round. "I'm just here to placate the old man."

They were seated at a table with a gorgeous view of the city and talked about work, but Meg was barely paying attention. She couldn't focus on anything but the fact that her last night with Sasha had been snaked out from under her. She couldn't care less that Scott had been sent to supervise them. And she believed his explanation. As absurd as it was, it made sense. She'd met Artemis Admore; he was a misogynistic douche. None of that bothered her.

When Sasha ordered her third glass of wine, Meg couldn't resist. She raised her eyebrows in open challenge.

Scott looked back and forth between them. "Whoa, Sash, I think you're in trouble." He laughed and then made eye contact with Meg. "Jesus, Meg, lighten up."

Meg glared at him. "We still have a presentation tomorrow. It would be great if we all weren't drunk at it."

"Well, the good news is you're presenting. And you're clearly the responsible one here." He nodded at Meg's half-full beverage. "Cheers, Sash," he toasted, raising his glass.

On the way back to the hotel, Scott lobbied hard for a final drink at the hotel bar. Meg refused immediately. But Sasha, who was already very tipsy, shrugged her shoulders and agreed amiably. Meg presumed this was Sasha's sad attempt at ensuring Scott didn't suspect anything. Inside Meg was seething. She couldn't even look at Sasha as she stormed through the lobby toward the elevator bank.

Back in her room Meg took a long, hot shower hoping it would calm her down. When Sasha still wasn't back by the time she got out, she threw on sweats and an old T-shirt and thumbed through a magazine, waiting for Sasha to stumble in full of apologies. Maybe it was crazy, but Meg still thoroughly expected Sasha to stay in her room. It never occurred to her she wouldn't. She really believed packing up her stuff and carting it across the hall was all part of an elaborate charade to throw Scott off their scent. But when it finally hit midnight, Meg was over the games. She slid on her sneakers, threw a hoodie over her thin tee, and headed to the lobby.

She was actually almost over her anger. By this point, her feelings had subsided to annoyance and frustration over the situation. She would deal with it all tomorrow, after the presentation, after they were home, she told herself as she stepped out of the elevator. For now she would rescue Sasha from Scott, ply her with water and aspirin, and help her to bed. They all needed to look alive in the morning.

Meg shuffled down the carpeted hotel hallway. Way down the hall, past the lobby, just outside the small hotel bar, her eyes were drawn to them. Sasha leaned up against the wall, Scott pressed into her, his hands all over her body as they kissed heavy and hard in the bright corridor. Meg stood there and watched them, unable to move, until she backed away in slow motion before slipping into the stairwell and sprinting up five flights of stairs, finally collapsing in a heap on the floor of her room.

Meg spent the majority of the next few hours crying, but she must've passed out at some point, because her alarm woke her with a start. She rinsed off quickly in the shower and packed up her stuff, heading for a small coffee shop she'd passed every morning on her way to Ardmore's downtown office. Chugging espresso, she changed her flight from a five o'clock commuter to LaGuardia to a three thirty that landed in Newark. She was running the show today and would make sure she was on that plane. There was absolutely no way she was going to spend any more time with Scott and Sasha than was absolutely necessary.

She had half a mind to bail on the presentation entirely and stick Sasha with it. Ardmore was technically her client anyway. But Meg would never do that. Partly because even though she hated Sasha right now, she still couldn't bring herself to do something she knew would cause her that kind of stress. Plus, Anne Whitmore was relying on her, and Meg refused to let the company down.

At eight thirty, a text from Sasha arrived. It said simply: *hey.* A half hour later, a second, *where are you?* followed. Meg saw through Sasha's thinly veiled efforts to gauge her mood, probably testing to see if she suspected anything. Meg ignored both texts altogether. After the third message, sent in an obvious panic ten minutes before the meeting was to start, Meg responded. She used as few words as possible to convey she was already at the office, set up and ready to go. Her short generic response bordered on rude and she knew Sasha would pick up on it right away. Just in case, she added one more line: *By the way, I saw you last night.* She shut off her phone completely.

Meg waited in the spare office until 9:58, when she strode into the boardroom and launched right into her presentation. Miraculously, she got through it. It wasn't her best performance, but it wasn't bad either, all things considered. She avoided eye contact with Sasha, who looked like hell—pale, pasty, hungover—and Scott, who didn't look much better.

During a break, Sasha tried to corner her in Ardmore's ladies' room. "Meg—"

Meg looked right through her. "Don't fucking talk to me," she said, trying to storm past, but Sasha caught her arm.

"Wait, Meg." Her voice was desperate and pleading, but Meg didn't care.

"I saw you, Sash. Last night. With Scott. I fucking saw you." She wrenched her arm from Sasha's grasp and left the bathroom without looking back.

It was difficult, but Meg managed to stay on point until she left the meeting, shaking hands and smiling at the principals alongside her coworkers. For Sullivan's benefit, she even shared an elevator with Scott and Sasha, parting from them immediately when they reached the street without a word. She grabbed her own taxi, virtually shutting the door in Sasha's face, and raced through the airport, holding in her tears the entire journey home.

❖

When Tracy and Betsy came through the front door a little after seven, Meg was at the kitchen table with her knees pulled up to her chest, her face red and swollen from hours of crying.

They rushed to her side and asked her what was wrong. She told them everything.

"Have you heard from her?" Betsy asked.

"No."

Meg looked between her friends, who had listened to her vent and cry for the last forty-five minutes. "Guys, you don't have to stay here. I'll be fine. Go do whatever you were going to do before you got sucked into my pathetic drama."

"We didn't have any plans," Tracy said. "I am hungry, though. Could you eat?"

"No. But you guys can. Seriously, go."

"No way. It's fine. I'll order something for us."

Meg's phone rang at that precise moment. She picked it up and tossed it back down, seeing Sasha's name on the caller ID. She silenced the call immediately, but it rang again less than a minute later.

"This is classic. I'm sure she's finally free of him, so *now* she wants to talk."

Almost on cue, her phone beeped with a text.

Meg, please answer the phone.

No, she typed back immediately.

I really need to see you. I want to explain.

Meg spoke the words out loud as she typed them. "Fuck you, you fucking whore."

"Don't send that," Tracy said.

"Too late," Meg responded. She glared at Tracy. "Doesn't matter anyway."

Tracy licked her lips, appearing to choose her words carefully. "Meg, just be careful about saying things you can't come back from."

"*I* should be careful?" Meg rushed to her own defense.

"Look, it's just you don't really know what happened. Not yet, anyway."

Betsy put both of her hands on the table. "Tracy has a point, Meg. Is there any chance, and I know this might sound crazy, but is there any chance you're misinterpreting what you saw?"

Meg tucked her chin and answered with an eyebrow raise. "I wasn't drunk. There was a lot of light."

Betsy nodded, considering. "I know, but what if what you saw was the guy—"

"Scott."

"What if what you saw was Scott making a move on Sasha and then you left and she pushed him away, and that was it."

"And then I didn't hear from her the rest of the night?" Meg countered. "And instead of coming to me to explain, she stayed in her own room by herself, where she hasn't slept all week? And she couldn't look at me all morning?" Meg huffed out a breath. "I doubt it." She stared at the tabletop, wishing Betsy's explanation was true, but knowing somewhere deep inside it wasn't. "No, I'm pretty sure what I saw was the beginning, before they went back to his room, before she let him fuck her." Her voice hitched in her throat. "I'm pretty sure that's what I saw."

The three of them sat there, dead quiet, considering Meg's words until a loud knock at the door broke the silence.

"Meg, it's me. Please let me in. I need to talk to you," Sasha's voice pleaded from outside.

Tracy looked at Meg. "We'll go."

"No, stay," she ordered, but when she got up to open the door, they disappeared up the stairs to Tracy's bedroom.

Sasha stood outside Meg's house, still in her suit from the afternoon, her luggage in tow. Meg watched the neon yellow cab speed off down the street, fully aware Sasha had come directly from the airport.

"Please listen to me," Sasha begged.

She opened the door and let Sasha past her but Meg barely moved from the entranceway, saying nothing.

"I don't know what you saw exactly," Sasha started. Her voice shook and Meg could tell she was on the verge of crying. "It's not what you think."

"I saw you and Scott outside the hotel bar." Meg's voice was low but sharp. "His hands were all over you. I didn't see you stopping him."

Sasha nodded at the floor, not denying anything.

"Tell me I'm wrong. Tell me this is all a big misunderstanding." Meg's voice was louder now. "You can't, can you?"

Sasha shook her head, and Meg saw tears sliding down her cheeks. She wiped them away and made eye contact with Meg. "I didn't sleep with him, if that's what you think."

"Oh, well in that case." Meg's voice was bitter. "You went back to his room, though, right?"

Sasha looked off to the side, not quite admitting it. "We didn't have sex, I swear."

"Great. You want a medal, for what? *Only* sucking his cock?" She knew it was mean, but she didn't back off. "Awesome. I'm so proud of your restraint."

Sasha looked hurt, her face was blotchy, and she was unable to keep the tears from coming down in a steady stream. "Meg, I made a mistake. I am so, so sorry."

Despite her anger, Meg was crying too. "I can't even look at you."

"Please, Meg. I'm begging you."

Meg leaned back against the wall and looked up at the ceiling for a long minute, thinking past Sasha's cheating to take stock of their entire time together. She collected herself, swallowing hard, and tried for a calm voice.

"Sash, I'm ready to be in a relationship. A real one." She lifted her shoulders. "I don't want to be a secret or be someone that's good enough until a better offer comes along—"

"Meg, you're not—"

"Let me finish." She put her hand up. "This isn't going to work." She jutted her chin out a little and ignored the sting in her throat. "If I'm going to be with someone, it has to be solid. I need to know where I stand." She blinked back her pain. "And truthfully, you've told me all along. But I just don't see any way to make this be what we both need right now. So let's just stop. Before the stakes get any higher. Before someone gets hurt worse." She was talking about herself, but she saw real sorrow in Sasha's face.

"I just need more time. Another chance."

Meg was fighting the tears, and her voice shook when she spoke. "I can't." She pressed her head into the wall. "I won't," she corrected. "I'm sorry." She wasn't going to be able to hold it together much longer. Her voice was barely audible. "You have to leave."

Sasha didn't protest. She hung her head, crying openly as she wheeled her carry-on behind her. Meg closed the door and laid her head against it, sobbing quietly into the night.

❖

Meg didn't see Sasha again until a full week later, when she spotted her exiting Anne Whitmore's corner office at Sullivan & Son. Again, she was crying. Meg saw her wipe at her cheeks before she hugged Anne. Sasha caught sight of Meg and their eyes locked. Meg's heart sank immediately and she suspected Sasha's did too from the look on her face. They stood frozen for a second, silently acknowledging each other from twenty-five feet away until Sasha's lips turned up in a kind of smile and she looked both incredibly sad, yet relieved at the same time. It was the strangest expression, beautiful and heartbreaking. Meg thought she would remember it forever.

Fifteen minutes later, along with the rest of the company, Meg received an email from Anne stating Sasha Michaels had accepted a consulting position with a rival firm. Today was her last day. Meg sniffled as she read it, blinking back her tears. She grabbed the sweater from the back of her chair and walked out, taking the rest of the afternoon off to wander the city as she mourned her loss in solitude.

Meg was just entering Bay West when Lexi pulled up next to her. Powering down the window, Lexi leaned across and patted the front passenger seat. "Get in."

Meg barely lifted her eyes from the ground. She knew she looked like hell and wasn't in the mood to talk about it. "I should get home." She touched the door with her hand. "Maybe another time."

Lexi shook her off. "Come on, just take a ride with me."

Meg lifted the door handle and reluctantly slid into the front seat. "Where are we going?"

"CVS. We're out of tampons at my house."

"How does that happen?" Meg asked, still avoiding eye contact.

"Four women, same cycle, that's how."

"Your mothers still get their periods?"

"They do." Lexi pulled in to the lot and slid into a diagonal spot along the wall, cutting the engine. She looked right at Meg. "How are you doing with the whole Sasha thing?"

"I'm fine," Meg said as she peered out the window at the traffic light.

"Meg, it's me. Cut the bullshit. How are you really?"

Meg answered with a noncommittal shrug. Lexi pressed on. "How is it at work? Do you talk to each other?"

Meg choked back tears as she answered. "She quit."

"Are you serious?"

Meg nodded. "Just today. She hasn't been in all week. She came in before and resigned."

"Oh my God."

Meg swallowed hard. "It's for the best, I'm sure."

"She texted me," Lexi said.

"What?"

"She texted me. This afternoon." Lexi made eye contact. "She misses you, Meg. I think she loves you."

Meg tried for stoic. "What difference does that make?"

"Come on, Meg. It makes all the difference."

Meg rubbed at her swollen eyes but said nothing for a minute. Finally she looked at Lexi. "How could it possibly work? I mean, forget about everything else." She shook her head dismissively. "How would we ever get past this, even. This thing with Scott? Seriously, Lex, how?"

Lexi reached over and touched her forearm. "Meg, don't get mad at me here. I'm not defending Sasha, I swear." She paused before continuing, seeming to choose her words carefully. "But she was drunk, right? And I'm sure she's still a mess over her mother," she noted. "And she's probably still confused about who she is and now she doesn't even have her mom to talk to about it." Lexi looked out her window at the sea of parked cars around her. "I would be a disaster if I lost either one of my mothers, and I have two of them," she added.

"So that gives her license to do whatever she wants, whenever she wants?"

"I didn't say that." Lexi turned to face Meg. "I just think…I don't know. People make mistakes sometimes, and it takes a really big person to forgive them."

Meg's voice held both sorrow and anger. "You think I should forgive her?"

"Maybe. I don't know." Lexi stared out the windshield. "You love her?" she asked quietly.

Meg waited a second in silence. Finally she nodded. In a small voice she added, "I thought she was it." She swiped at a tear that fell down her cheek and turned to look out her own window. "I never felt anything like it in my whole life," she said, a little embarrassed at the admission.

"I hate seeing you hurt, Meg. You're the best person. Sasha knows it too."

Meg leaned her head back into the headrest, facing forward. "Even if I took her back—assuming that's what she wants, which we don't actually know—"

"I think you do know it."

"But, Lex, think about it. If I forgave her or whatever, isn't that just like telling her it's okay? I mean, what's to stop her the next time?"

Lexi ran her middle finger over the gearshift considering Meg's words. "I don't think it works like that."

"No?"

Lexi shrugged. "Sorry, I don't."

"What if Jesse cheated on you? You would just be fine with it?"

Lexi huffed out a small breath. "God, no. I would die." She didn't meet Meg's eyes as she continued. "But I can't imagine being without her either." She chewed her bottom lip. "I don't know what I'd do. It hurts my heart to even think about it."

Meg knew the feeling. More than once in the last week she'd felt a dull pain in her chest as though she could actually feel her heart breaking apart little by little.

"I can't do it." Meg gritted her teeth, holding back a sob. "I just can't." She pulled an old Starbucks napkin from the door and wiped her nose with it. "But God, it fucking hurts." Meg swallowed hard, but the tears came anyway. "I never want to feel this way again."

"Come here." Lexi pulled her in close and hugged her tight for a long, long time.

Chapter Twenty-six

B etsy knocked on Meg's screen door and opened it at the same time. "Hello?" she called inside.

"Hey, Bets," Meg said from the kitchen table where she was working on her laptop. "Come on in. She's not home yet."

"Are you working?" Betsy said, checking her watch.

"I had a client in Jersey this morning, so I worked from home after that. I'm just finishing up."

"I can wait outside or up in Tracy's room. I don't want to be in your way."

"Shut up." Meg closed her laptop. "It's five o'clock anyway. I'm done." She walked to the fridge and grabbed two Lagunitas, handing one to Betsy. "Happy Friday."

"Cheers," Betsy responded, taking a sip as she looked down at her phone, which had just lit up with a text.

"Is that Trace?"

Betsy nodded. "On her way home from the golf course now."

"I stopped by and saw her there last weekend, Bets." Meg shook her head. "You have to do it. She was giving a lesson to this teenager. I can't even describe it. She's so in her element. You have to see her out there in action. Just trust me on this one."

"I will." Betsy smiled. "I'm so happy she's giving these pro lessons. She loves it," she said, stopping to consider something for a second. "Geez, though, I hope she can keep it up after she gets hired at ESPN."

"What are you talking about?"

"She didn't tell you?" Betsy sounded surprised at first, but then not at all. "Of course she didn't." She twisted her mouth into a sly smile. "In her defense, I guess there's nothing to really tell, just yet." At Meg's confused look, she continued. "We went to dinner a few weeks back with her friend from California. Kristen something or other—"

"Right, I remember."

"Kristen's boyfriend, God, I have no idea what his name was," Betsy added absentmindedly. "Anyway, he's got a big job at the network. They were in New York on business and I'm pretty sure Kristen set up the dinner to introduce Tracy to him and try to get her lined up with a job." Betsy sipped her beer. "Let me tell you, it worked. This guy was completely enamored of Tracy. I would be shocked, I mean completely shocked, if Tracy does not get a job based entirely on that dinner." Betsy smiled proudly. "She has an official interview set up in a few weeks, but I guarantee it's a formality."

"Wow. That's awesome."

"Meg, she was amazing." Betsy bit her lip, obviously remembering the details. "The thing is, she wasn't even trying. She was just being herself. Talking about sports all night. She was completely in her glory too, to finally have someone to go back and forth with on her level."

"I can't wait to grill her about it," Meg said. "What's up with you two tonight?"

"Not sure. No real plans yet." Betsy looked across the table. "Want to hang with us?"

"Thanks, but I'm going out with Lexi actually. We're going to grab dinner, do some shopping, maybe catch a movie." Meg knew her friends were taking turns making sure she wasn't spending all her time alone, wallowing. She appreciated their concern and their coordinated efforts to include her.

"How are you doing with everything?" Betsy asked.

Meg nodded, considering. "I'm okay." She lifted her beer and wiped the ring of moisture it left on the table with her bare hand, before drying her palm on her jeans. "I'm okay," she said again, with more conviction this time because, in truth, she was.

❖

Meg got her life back on track mostly by staying busy. She helped her sister by babysitting her niece often, trying to give Shannon and Matt a chance for a night out here and there before their second baby arrived in July. She also surprised herself by staying with the hot yoga. She never found it relaxing, it was more like an ass-kicking workout, but it was a full ninety minutes where she didn't think about Sasha at all. Mainly because she was too busy using every cell in her body to avoid passing out. The side effect was she had lost ten pounds and three inches off her waist since January. She felt lighter and more agile, and the payoff was showing every Thursday night when she killed it at shortstop in the Bay West softball league.

It was gorgeous and warm for tonight's spring league semifinals. Even factoring in the nice weather, Meg was pleasantly surprised at the size of the crowd watching. Her stomach did a weird flip when she made random eye contact with Reina, who was sitting next to Teddy and Jesse in the bleachers.

Down 4–2 in the top of the fifth, her team was feeling the absence of Tracy, who hadn't yet returned from her big interview this afternoon. Meg dipped into the stands and located Betsy.

"Any word from Trace?" she asked.

"Nothing." Betsy frowned. "I know that's bad news for you guys. But it's probably a good sign for her."

"Yeah, I know. Just being selfish over here," Meg said with a smile. "We could really use her bat right about now." The truth was Tracy was virtually unstoppable and everyone knew it. It almost didn't matter what field Tracy was on—baseball diamond, basketball court, soccer pitch—Tracy Allen was a superior athlete. Hand injury be damned, the girl was good as new, possibly better.

Even after the loss, Meg was still pumped. It was a good game, played on a beautiful night, and tomorrow was Friday. Immediately after shaking hands with her opponents, she found Lexi and Betsy.

"You guys up for drinks and burgers at my place?"

When they agreed readily, Meg grabbed some of the other girls on her team and extended the invite to them as well. She turned around and Reina was in front of her.

"Hey there, Megan McTiernan." Reina eyed her up and down. A nice smile emerged and she raised her eyebrows. "I like your, uh"—she waved her hand up and down to indicate Meg's body—"baseball getup, here." She nodded playfully in agreement with her own statement. "The pants are especially nice."

Meg laughed and looked at her cleats, her cheeks burning from the compliment.

"How have you been, Reina?"

"Good. You?"

"Good, yeah." Meg could see her friends packing up in the distance and she knew she needed to get home to set up for the impromptu barbecue. "Listen, I'm having a thing at my house. Like, now. Would you, I mean, do you want to come by?"

Reina glanced back to where Teddy was standing a few feet away. "Yes. Absolutely." She smiled a little. "Let me just tell Teddy. I'm sure we'll stop by her place first. See if Rose wants to come," she said. "Do you need us to bring anything?"

"Nope. Just yourselves."

❖

Meg couldn't keep the huge smile from spreading as she threw her glove and bat into her bag. The field was almost empty and she needed to hustle home and get ready for company. She shuffled along the dirt field pondering thoughts of Reina's full red lips.

"Meg."

She recognized the voice one second before she looked up to see Sasha Michaels lingering by the third-base line.

"Lexi told me you had a game. I was hoping we could talk."

"I don't think there's anything to talk about."

"Can you just listen to me, then?"

Meg stood still and said nothing, feeling the muscles in her stomach tighten.

"Please. Just hear me out. I've been giving things a lot of thought." Sasha kicked the dirt around with her foot. "You and Tracy and your friends…you guys have all been out, or at least known who you are for a long time. It's still new to me. I know you don't get that." Her voice was pleading and it made Meg's heart hurt. "I can't explain it. It's just how it is," Sasha continued. "I feel like I don't fit anywhere. Maybe because of everything that happened this year—with work, my mom.

You. It all just felt"—she put her hands in the pockets of her jeans and looked up at the darkening sky—"a little overwhelming."

"Look, Sash, you don't owe me—"

"I do, Meg. I do owe you."

Meg lifted her bag higher on her shoulder and waited.

"Meg, I am so sorry." She brushed the hair away from her face. "About Scott." She shook her head. "It was stupid. I was drunk." She folded her arms in front of her. "It didn't mean anything. I was scared." She shrugged in defeat. "Of what, I'm not even sure." When she tilted her head back, her voice hitched. "I can't take it back. But God, I wish I could." Sasha looked right at her and her eyes looked sad as hell. "Meg, please—"

Meg put her hand up. "Don't, Sash." She watched Sasha wipe at her face. "The thing is…I've actually been through this already. I've dated the person who's not sure they want to be with me." She looked off to the side, feeling vulnerable at her admission. "You're right. I am ready to be in a relationship. And you're not. And that's okay. It's totally valid. But this"—she pointed first to Sasha, then at herself— "I'm sorry, but I can't do it." She turned to home plate and swallowed hard, keeping her emotions from coming out. "All the up and down. It's too much."

Deep inside, Meg knew this conversation didn't change anything. It couldn't. Better to keep it short. "I have to go. I have people coming over."

She moved past Sasha, careful not to touch her or make the slightest eye contact because in spite of her brave words, Meg couldn't shake the deep sense of loss she felt as she headed off the field to her house.

❖

Meg's small deck packed with friends and neighbors quickly. She broke out some chips and salsa, fired up the grill, lit the tiki torches. She refused to think at all about her brief interaction with Sasha, instead focusing on the small crowd. She flitted from group to group making sure everyone had a drink. It wasn't long before she realized Allison Smith, who'd tagged along with Jesse and Lexi, might have already had one too many.

She had initially been surprised to see Allison at the game, but back at her house, Meg was part of a three-way conversation with her and Jesse where she got the dirt that Allison was just out of an intense winter-long relationship. She briefed Meg on the details of her breakup, then asked, "So, where is Tracy Allen?" Allison took an unnecessary sip of her wine as she looked around. "I thought she still lived with you."

"She does," Meg answered, looking at her watch. "I thought she'd be home by now, but I'm sure she's on her way."

"Good." Allison wiggled her eyebrows. "I want another turn on that."

Meg furrowed her brow at the statement. Even though she wasn't entirely sure what exactly that comment meant, she felt like she should say something. "You know she's with Betsy now, right?" At Allison's surprised expression, Meg tried for casual. "Yeah, they've been dating since January."

"Oh my God, I had no idea."

"See what happens when you hibernate," Jesse added with a laugh.

Allison shrugged good-naturedly and downed half of her drink. "Good for Betsy." She smirked. "Honestly, I have no idea what she's like as a girlfriend, but I can tell you this. In the bedroom"—she smacked her lips—"completely unmatched."

Meg made sure to control her surprise, averting her eyes as she searched the deck for Betsy, hoping she wasn't in earshot. She made a quick mental note to grab Tracy the second she arrived and give her the heads up that Allison was a) on the prowl and b) chatting freely about whatever had happened between them, an event Meg could only guess Tracy would not be so forthcoming about, considering even she was completely in the dark.

For the next half hour Meg stayed alert, but she got tied up in conversation with Rose and Teddy, who expressed regrets on behalf of Reina, who wasn't able to make it after all. Meg was bummed, but she played it off even though she couldn't imagine what had changed since the softball field. She swallowed her slight hopes, staying upbeat and chatting with her neighbors. A few minutes into the conversation, she saw Allison talking to Betsy at the edge of the deck and panicked a little, realizing she should have been monitoring the possibility of that interaction more closely in light of the dish she'd just been privy to. She raced over to them, but it was too late, Allison was already talking.

"I just heard about you and Tracy," she slurred.

"Yeah." Betsy smiled. She reached out for Allison's arm. "And, Al, sorry about you and the pastry chef," Betsy offered sincerely. "I heard it didn't work out."

"She was a bitch." Allison waved her off. "Truthfully, I think I'm more upset you've snagged Tracy off the market. I wouldn't have minded another go around with her." She was probably too drunk to assess Betsy's flat expression as she continued. "You are one lucky girl, Bets." She finished the last of her wine and held up her empty glass in a weird kind of post drink toast. "Seriously, I don't think I have ever come that hard. Not before, not since," she added with a loud laugh and a slight stumble.

Meg was close enough to see the tears in Betsy's eyes and the muscles tighten as she clenched her jaw. She watched Betsy force a smile and excuse herself, walking right past Tracy who, of course, arrived at that precise moment.

Meg pulled her friend aside and filled her in on what she had missed, offering Tracy her car but not her driving services since she'd already had a couple of drinks. Tracy declined, admitting she was pretty tipsy herself, and told Meg she was just going to walk to Betsy's house, figuring the time it took her to get there might give Betsy a chance to cool down.

Meg returned to her party and her oblivious guests, still reeling from what she had seen unfold.

❖

Three hours later, when she had just finished wiping down the kitchen countertop and was about to head upstairs to bed, Tracy walked in.

"How'd it go?" Meg asked, reaching for a cold beer and holding it out to Tracy.

Tracy scrunched up her nose at the offering. She shifted her eyes to a bottle on the counter, a generous gift from one of the evening's guests. "How about that Johnnie Walker?"

Meg obliged, returning the beer to the refrigerator and reaching for her mother's hand-me-down Waterford crystal tumblers from a high shelf in her cabinet. "Is it bad?"

Tracy shook her head slowly, rubbing her scalp at the base of her head with both hands. "It'll be okay."

"She's pretty angry, huh?" Meg asked placing the bottle between them on the breakfast bar.

"I guess. Mostly I think she's just embarrassed." Tracy filled each of their glasses two fingers high. "I think she thinks it looks like I did her wrong. But, dude, I didn't. I told her that. I mean nicely. Like way nicer than I'm saying it now. But, fuck, I wasn't going to apologize." She downed a swig before letting her glass hit the table harder than she'd meant. "Me and Betsy weren't even together when it happened. Honestly, at the time, Betsy had just finished telling me we were never going to be together. And I didn't even really know they were friends. I spent a lot of time with Betsy and she never once mentioned Allison."

Meg said, "They did go through a period where they hung out a lot."

"I didn't know that." Tracy took a sip of her drink and swallowed it roughly. "I promise you, and you know, I would never deliberately hurt anyone, least of all Betsy."

Meg rolled her drink between her hands. "When was it?" Meg asked, knowing Tracy wouldn't hold back on the details. "You and Allison, I mean."

"December. Right before Christmas," she answered without looking up. "The night you dropped me off at the Kitchen."

"No shit." Meg nodded. Her curiosity won out. "How did it happen?"

Tracy shrugged. "I don't know. We ran into each other at the bar. She was surprised I wasn't at the social. We started talking." She chewed her lip. "Honestly, we were both looking for something with no strings. It just worked out."

"And that was it?"

"That was it. We didn't keep in touch. We never exchanged numbers. Tonight was the first time I've seen her since."

"You think Betsy will get over it?"

"I do." She looked at the front door. "She actually drove me back here. She kissed me when I was getting out of the car. I wanted her to come in. To stay." She blinked slowly adding, "She wanted the night to process." She took another hefty drink. "Dude, I didn't even tell you what happened at my interview."

"Shit," Meg said remembering. "How'd it go?"

Tracy gave a snide laugh out of the side of her mouth. "Crazy. It wasn't really an interview, at all. I met my friend Jeff, that's the guy that set the whole thing up," she explained, "at this really fancy bar in Midtown around the block from the corporate office. I get there and I think he's going to, like, prep me for the other guy I'm supposed to be interviewing with." She frowned. "But then this other guy joins us, another hotshot producer, Ted something. We're talking about baseball mostly, up and comers, who we think has potential this year." Tracy nodded. "Then Bob Balfour comes in. He's the guy behind like a million shows on the network. I can tell by your face you have no idea who he is, but trust me, he is like a big-time sports show producer." She thumbed her own chest. "I only recognized him because I recently looked him up. Jeff was throwing his name out there a lot the last time we were out together, so I did some research. That's when I realized I've seen his name in like thousands of credits." She shook her head, still in some kind of disbelief. "Anyway, at this point, I'm thinking two things. Number one, this place must be some hangout for the ESPN muckety-mucks, and two, I'm going to be fucking late for my interview." She licked her lips. "I'm trying to give Jeff the eye that I should get going, when Bob Balfour says to me, *Tracy Allen, I hear nothing but good things about you.*" Tracy shook her head like she still couldn't believe it.

"That was it. They laid it all out for me. They told me the job in New York wasn't right for me and it had gone to someone else anyway. Instead, he offered me a spot on a new show they're putting together."

"What does that mean, *a spot*?" Meg asked.

"He's starting a new show." Tracy thought for a second. "It's like a panel show with four hosts. They discuss what's trending in the sports world. Big wins, the teams, athletes, scandals, trades, sometimes maybe they bring on an athlete or coach to interview." She snapped her fingers. "Like *The View*. Except without a bunch of ladies yapping about ridiculous nonsense no one cares about."

"Hey, I like *The View*."

Tracy patted Meg's hand. "I know you do, honey."

"So wait, would you be on the show?"

Tracy nodded. "Me and three guys. Two radio dudes you probably never heard of and Jack Duffield, he was the first baseman for the Yankees a few years back."

Meg slapped the counter. "Holy shit, Trace. This is sick." She looked at her friend. "Wait, why aren't you excited."

"There's a catch." She shut one eye, twisting up her face. "The job is in LA. That's where the show tapes, that's where they rehearse, everything."

Meg's jaw dropped. "Did you tell Betsy?"

"No." Her mouth was a thin line. "And you can't either." She took a small sip of her drink and placed it down in front of her. "I just wanted to tell someone. I guess I wanted to imagine it for a second. What it might be like, you know?" She half smiled and cocked her head to the side. "It would have been fun, I think."

"Is there no way it could work?"

"It's a California thing. There's no negotiating that."

"What if Betsy went with you. People do have babies in California."

"I know," Tracy said. "But she loves her job here. She was just telling me the other day, she's set up to take over her practice in a few years. And she does all of this specialty stuff, like these really complicated surgeries other doctors refer to her because she has all this trauma experience from when she was in the military. She's so excited about it. I can't even ask her to give that up for me."

Meg nodded as she listened. "Did you definitely tell them no?"

"Basically. I said I was extremely grateful for their offer and for even being considered, but my life was in New York right now. They told me to take a few days to think about it, and I said I would. I wasn't going to be rude, but my mind's made up."

"Wow." Meg let it soak in. "And you're not going to tell Betsy?"

Tracy tapped her tumbler lightly on the counter. "Not right now. She'll only feel bad about it or try to change my mind." She shrugged and smiled at the same time. "Listen, it would have been cool. No doubt." She rubbed her chin considering. "But who knows, half of those programs don't make it past a few episodes. I'll tell her at some point down the line. I just don't feel like arguing over it with her. I'm sure of my decision." She held her hands up in submission. "She's what I want."

Meg raised her glass. "Women. They make you do the crazy."

"In the best way." Tracy clinked her glass with Meg's.

"Agreed."

❖

Up and dressed for work by seven a.m., Meg heard low voices and light laughter coming from behind Tracy's closed bedroom door. She stopped in the kitchen to wash down two Motrin with a glass of water and smiled when she peeked out the window and saw Betsy's car squeezed into a spot that covered half her driveway. Meg wasn't sure if she'd come in the middle of the night or in the early light of dawn, but it didn't matter, whatever hang-ups she'd had over the Allison situation were clearly on their way to being ancient history.

Walking to the bus stop, Meg thought about Tracy's job offer, shaking her head at the thought of what her friend was passing up. But as she got lost in the beautiful sunrise reflecting off the water below the bridge as she made her morning commute, she knew with absolute conviction that for the right girl, she would do the exact same thing.

Her mind immediately went to Sasha like it always did. But today Reina's face popped into her brain a half second later. The vision was refreshing, and it gave her hope. Meg smiled into the skyline ahead. Her future might have some potential after all.

CHAPTER TWENTY-SEVEN

It was a gorgeous afternoon—warm but not humid, with a clear sky—perfect for Bay West's first ever Pride Music Festival, an outdoor concert-slash-social that showcased various female-fronted bands, all vocal in their support of equal rights. It was the development's effort to kick off Pride week in New York City, and judging by the presale, there was going to be quite a crowd.

The early part of the day focused largely on homegrown talent, but the acts grew bigger and more popular as the day wore on. At three forty-five, Tracy held Betsy's hand lightly as they walked across the development's grounds to the grassy hill where the stage had been set up just outside the Commons. The sound of acoustic guitar greeted them over the trees and through the clusters of women littering the campus as they made their way.

"What time did you say CJ is going on?" Tracy asked good-naturedly.

"I think she said around five or so," Betsy answered, checking her watch.

On the other side of Tracy, Meg pulled out her phone. "I have the schedule. What's her band's name?"

"Spinster City."

"Says here they're on at five fifteen. Plenty of time." Meg slid her phone into her back pocket. "What are you guys drinking?" she asked, breaking for the outdoor bar as Tracy spread their blanket on the edge of the grass. "First round's on me."

"Get me whatever you're having," Tracy said.

"Beer good?"

"Sure."

"What about you, Bets?"

"Nothing for me, thanks."

"Nothing?" Meg answered with surprise.

"Can't." Betsy scrunched up her nose. "I'm on call. Covering the weekend for my friend."

"That sucks," Meg declared.

Betsy frowned ruefully. "It was a good trade actually. My colleague has her sister's bachelorette party this weekend." She smiled optimistically. "And in return she's on call for me when we're all in P-town for the wedding. So it works out." She shrugged a little. "Plus, none of her patients are expected to deliver this weekend anyway, so it should be pretty quiet. And I still get to enjoy some nice music with you guys. I'll just probably be the only one who remembers it," she added with a playful shift of her eyebrows.

"Understood," Meg said backing away. "I'll be right back."

On the return from her second trip up to the bar, Meg slowed her pace as she walked along, trying not to spill the two dark draft beers she'd picked up for herself and Tracy. Across the short distance, she could see Tracy was leaning back on her elbows while Betsy rested her head on Tracy's stomach. They were talking and smiling at each other while Tracy played with Betsy's hair. Meg came to an almost complete stop, wanting to give them just a few more minutes of privacy, when the voice in her ear took her completely off guard.

"They're adorable together, those two."

Meg turned immediately. "Hey, Reina."

"Hi." Reina smiled wide.

Meg tried to greet her with a hug but with two full beers, it wasn't happening. She aborted her lame attempt, cocked her head to the side, and offered up one of the drinks instead. "Buy you a drink?" she added playfully, handing the plastic cup over.

"I don't want to steal your friend's beer."

"Please, she's got her hands full, anyway." Meg nodded in Tracy's direction with her chin. "I'm sure she won't even miss it." Meg gave her full attention to Reina. "How have you been?"

"Good, thanks," Reina said taking a sip of the beer, using her thumb and middle finger to wipe the foam from the corners of her mouth.

"Did you just get here?"

Reina nodded. "Yeah, Rose and Teddy are over there." She gestured to the side. "I saw you up at the bar"—she looked down seeming shy all of a sudden—"and I wanted to say hi."

"I'm glad," Meg responded.

Reina licked her lips. "Hey, Meg, about your barbecue a few weeks back—"

Meg held up one hand stopping her completely. "No worries. You owe me no explanations. It's cool."

Reina spoke again. "I do, though—"

"Reina, it's fine. I get it. Seriously. We're good," Meg rushed out, trying to spare Reina an awkward explanation.

Reina raised her perfectly arched eyebrows. "Meg, stop being a weirdo. I just wanted to tell you—I wanted to come. I really did. But after the softball game my mom called. She's out in Queens. That's where I live." She was rambling a little and she sounded nervous. "See, I was supposed to stay at Teddy's that night, but my mom asked if I would come home." She rolled her eyes. "It's a long story. Anyway, I just wanted to tell you I didn't mean to blow you off." She took a long sip of her drink.

Meg smiled and gestured toward the blanket optimistically. "Feel like hanging with me and the lovebirds?" She lifted her shoulders and added, "Betsy's ex's band is on next. Supposedly they're pretty good."

"Yeah, I do." Reina looked into her half-empty cup. "I owe someone a beer first. Walk with me to the bar?"

"You bet."

As they reached the outdoor bar, Reina turned to Meg. "What is this we're drinking, by the way?" She looked at her cup for effect. "It's actually really good."

Meg smiled. "It's a new IPA from Flagship Brewery, Staten Island's own local craft beer," she said with a proud smile.

"Staten Island has its own beer?"

"Sure does."

"Interesting," Reina said, as the bartender hooked them up with a refill each and a fresh cup for Tracy.

Double fisting, Meg downed the final sip before tossing her old cup in the trash. She decided to go for it. "See that, Staten Island has something you might be interested in after all."

Reina looked right at Meg and tipped her head to the side. "I could have told you that two years ago."

❖

Sharing the blanket on the expansive lawn, Meg and Reina sat close to one another and talked easily. Meg was really having a good time with Betsy and Tracy, who were as cute as ever, and Reina fit seamlessly into the mix. Suddenly, it seemed she and Reina had an endless supply of things to talk about, and as the afternoon wore on Meg almost couldn't believe she had so often insisted they didn't have any click. She caught Tracy's eye more than once, and the look on her friend's face clearly showed she was thinking the same thing.

But that was just it—Meg still wasn't entirely sure what was going on. Was this wishful thinking or was she reading the signs correctly? An hour passed, and then another. Meg and Reina weren't really flirting, but there was definitely a new energy between them. They were chatting nonstop and, yep, there it was again—Reina touching her knee to emphasize a point as she spoke. So weird, the way life worked sometimes. Nearly two years since their initial introduction and she and Reina were finally connecting. Go figure.

It was getting dark and Meg had a good buzz going, giving her the courage to test her theory. She brushed her hand along Reina's lower back, leaning in close to her ear. "Do you want another drink?" she whispered.

"Yeah," Reina breathed out, turning to face Meg as she answered. Their faces were close and the exchange intense as their eyes locked. But Meg's phone vibrated in her back pocket, breaking the moment. Annoyed, she looked down, reached for it, and read the text quickly.

"Holy shit."

"What's the matter?" Reina asked, placing her hand on Meg's forearm lightly as Meg reread the text message.

"My sister." She shook her head. "My sister's going to the hospital."

"What?" Reina was obviously surprised.

"No, it's okay. I mean it's not really okay. But it's okay." She stopped herself, took a breath and explained. "She's pregnant. But she's not due for another few weeks. Shit, my parents aren't even in from Florida yet," she said, thinking out loud. "I have to go there."

Both Tracy and Betsy were listening and Betsy spoke up. "Meg, I'll take you. Find out which hospital." It made sense since she was the only completely sober one.

Tracy looked at them. "I'll take a ride too. Moral support and all." She looked between Reina and Meg. "Reina, if you want to tag along—"

Betsy cut her off. "Hold that thought," she said, checking a message of her own. "Meg, is your sister's doctor Tara Liardi?"

Meg looked at her blankly. "I have no idea."

Betsy's mouth turned up in a funny grin as she began to gather up her stuff. "Ten to one, Liardi's your sister's doctor, and odds are I'll be delivering Shannon's baby tonight." She gave Tracy a quick kiss. "I'll call you in a little bit." Pulling Meg by the elbow, she instructed, "Come on, Meg. Let's move."

Almost an hour after they'd left, Tracy received word from Betsy that her assumption had been correct. The doctor she was covering for was Meg's sister's OB, and Shannon would definitely be giving birth sometime tonight. Betsy informed Tracy she didn't expect to make it back to the music festival at all but would meet her at Meg's when everything was over. Tracy was mildly dismayed, but she was enjoying herself at the festival surrounded by good music and great friends.

The sun had finally set and the crowd was abuzz with wild rumors of a secret headliner not listed on the bill. Tracy laughed a little at her own friends getting in on the guessing as she went to the bar for another drink, which was exactly where she was when the mystery artist began.

All of the lights went black, silencing the crowd as a few bars of acoustic piano pinged out through the darkness. A few short seconds later a single beam of light fell on the stage highlighting the piano player—a petite brunette in jeans and a white tank top—humming the song's melody before her sultry voice started the soft lyrics. It was a performance so quiet and understated it absolutely commanded attention, even though the majority of the crowd couldn't quite place the song. Not Tracy, though. She knew it from the very first chord. She swallowed hard and listened, unable to block out the emotions that accompanied the memory of Jezebel playing this version of this song for her nearly two years ago, right before she told Tracy she loved her, before she promised to find a way to make it work.

In a moment the audience would recognize that the beautiful ballad they were unconsciously swaying to was actually Jezebel Stone's number one dance remix "Dreamcatcher," which had ruled the airwaves for over a year, and that the unassuming person onstage was the musician herself, minus her signature affected look and showstopping theatrics. Almost at the exact time she'd thought it, Jezebel reached the chorus and a few savvy listeners were quick to clap and whistle as they caught on, quickly bringing the others around them up to speed. Hitting the final note, Jezebel Stone stood up from the piano and walked to the center-stage microphone as the lights came up on the full band behind her. "Hello, ladies!" she called out with a smile. The crowd went crazy.

Tracy stood alone at the bar where she had been for the entire song—her song—where she had listened as Jezebel sang it for her, to her. It was an unbelievably intimate gesture, shared among hundreds of women. Stunned into immobility, Tracy remained there for a very long time as Jezebel moved into the next song and the next. She hated that her heart dropped every time Jezebel's smooth voice hit a high note while she crooned out a remarkably personalized set list of Tracy's favorites. She could hardly tear herself away, almost spellbound as she watched Jezebel work the crowd. Finally, she couldn't take it anymore. She forced herself to leave but made it only as far as the adjacent softball field where she sat on the aluminum bleachers looking up at the stars, listening to her ex-girlfriend's gorgeous voice as throngs of women screamed her name.

❖

Tracy waited a full twenty-five minutes after the second encore before she found her way to Jezebel's trailer. The head of the security team, a burly guy aptly named Butch, must have remembered her because he waved her through without any questions.

Tracy knocked lightly on the door but her hand was already turning the lever as Jezebel said, "Come in."

She was sitting in front of a makeshift vanity removing some makeup or possibly applying it, Tracy wasn't really sure. There was a radio on low in the background and Tracy instinctively looked around the trailer.

"It's okay. We're alone," Jezebel said, answering Tracy's unspoken question. She stood up and Tracy noticed she was still wearing the same faded blue jeans but had changed her tank to a smaller strappy black one. She padded over and wrapped an arm around Tracy's neck, reaching up to kiss her on the cheek. "You look good, Tracy."

Tracy hugged her before pulling back and assessing her completely. "So do you, Jez." Jezebel was sporting her true hair color, dirty blond, no extensions, no outlandish highlights. Her makeup was light; Tracy could even see the freckles on her nose. She looked pure and beautiful and innocent. Tracy smiled a little, holding Jezebel at arm's length. "You know, you look like Judy Rockwell," Tracy teased, referring to Jezebel by her real name.

"Stop it." Jezebel swatted Tracy's biceps playfully. "I hate when you call me that," she said, flirting with her eyes. She took a step back. "Come in, please." She dropped her gaze. "I was beginning to think you weren't going to show."

Tracy leaned back against the wall. "I figured if you're willing to come here and play what is for you a ridiculously small venue, just for me, the least I could do is come by and say hello."

"I am a huge supporter of the gay community, you know that."

Tracy nodded at Jezebel's stock answer and withheld the comment she wanted to make in response to her ex's standard and ridiculous response. There was no opportunity to say anything anyway before Jezebel spoke again. "You're not wrong, though, I did come here for you." She looked Tracy in the eye and read her reaction. "I guess you could call it my last-ditch effort," she added with a hopeful smile.

Tracy tried for light, but her voice came out more serious than she expected. "I'm not going to lie. If anything would have gotten me, that rendition of 'Dreamcatcher' you opened with was probably it." She looked down at the floor. "I never did understand why you chose to drown out such a beautiful song in all that bass."

Jezebel waited until Tracy met her eyes again. "Do you remember the night I played it for you just like that?"

"Of course I do." Tracy held her gaze, acknowledging the memory of a night they had felt so completely connected to one another, a perfect night in a time defined by highs and lows, a night, long in the past now, when she had honestly believed they would end up together.

"Just me, you, and the piano," Jezebel said. She waited a beat. "And the bed," she added with an unbelievably needy look in her hazel eyes.

Tracy pulled herself back into the present. "That's not real life, though." She stuffed her hands into the pockets of her jeans. "Jez, the kind of relationship we had, it doesn't work. Not for me, anyway. What you want would never be enough for me."

Jezebel's eyes shot up at her. "But this is?" She looked through Tracy, her eyes boring into her. "Living in Podunk Staten Island? Playing housewife to some doctor? Come on, Trace, I know you better than that." Her tone was completely condescending and a little agitated as she continued, "I heard you even turned down a job at ESPN—"

"I know you don't get it. I'm not surprised," Tracy said in response. "This is what you do in a relationship, Jez. You make sacrifices." Her tone matched Jezebel's. "I don't really expect you to understand that."

"You don't sacrifice who you are."

"This, from someone who's never given up anything—"

"You think I haven't made sacrifices? Are you serious?"

"Jezebel, you fucking cheated on me. So you'll forgive me if your numerous sacrifices don't just rush right into my head."

"Jesus, Trace." Jezebel let out a long sigh, taking a minute to collect herself. "I said I was sorry a hundred times in messages you never even bothered to acknowledge. I told you how I felt. I sent you flowers. I wrote you goddamn love songs. I don't know what more I could have done."

Tracy leaned her head back on the thin trailer wall. "I don't know why we're even bothering to talk about this. You're a married woman now," Tracy said with a bitter smirk.

"And you think I don't understand sacrifice." Jezebel shook her head slowly and looked right at Tracy, her eyes brimming with tears. "I did that for you. For us."

When Tracy's expression revealed both shock and confusion at such a strange statement, Jezebel continued, "I did that so we could be together. You think I wanted to marry Jasper Lloyd? Please." She wiped at her eyes. "He gives me plausible deniability. Gets the press off my back a little. Being married to him gives me the freedom to be with who I really want." She waited for Tracy to meet her eyes. "Which is still you."

Even after she took a second to evaluate the statement, it still didn't make sense to Tracy. "You realize how ridiculous that is, right?" It had come out sharper than she wanted it to, and Tracy instantly regretted her tone because it was obvious Jezebel was being sincere. However warped her decision to get married had been, in this moment Tracy was sure at least part of the choice had involved her. She looked over at Jezebel sitting on the chair in front of the vanity with her head in her hands. She looked small and sad and vulnerable, and Tracy's heart broke for her a little, not because she was in love with her anymore, but because she knew Jezebel's own inhibitions would forever keep her from experiencing anything even remotely similar to what she had with Betsy. Tracy was softer when she spoke again. "Look, Jez, I came here to make peace with you."

Jezebel nodded but didn't meet her eyes.

"Can't we just call a truce?"

"Sure, Trace." Jezebel tilted her head back and dabbed at the edges of her eyes with a fingertip.

"I should go." Tracy took the one step to the door and turned around. "Take care of yourself, Jez."

"Tracy." Jezebel said her name as she got up from her seat and crossed the small space between them. She placed her arms around Tracy's neck and hugged her tightly. Tracy squeezed her back and felt all the emotions expressed between them in the last few minutes and the last few years boil down to this one final embrace.

Tracy left the trailer without looking back, and while she was sentimental, she wasn't sad. She strode through the festival area, making her way past the lingering crowd still finishing their drinks, and found the path that led to Meg's house, where she knew the love of her life was waiting for her.

Chapter Twenty-eight

Packing up?" Meg strolled into Tracy's room and flopped on the bed, watching Tracy load her suitcase.

"I am," Tracy responded with a smile.

As Meg looked around, it occurred to her it had been ages since she'd been in this room. She smiled, realizing what she already knew. This was no longer the guest room—it belonged to Tracy now, and there were signs of her everywhere. Golf clubs in the corner, a poster she'd bought at the Museum of Modern Art framed and hung on the far wall, a picture with her dad in California and one with her mom and sister taken more recently fixed into the corners of the mirror. Directly between those two shots, a five-by-seven of her and Betsy, taken this winter not long after they'd finally gotten together, was propped up in the center of the dresser.

"When are you leaving?" Meg asked.

"Tomorrow morning. Probably around ten or so, I would guess."

"And you're staying until when?"

"A week. We come back next Wednesday."

"Awesome." Meg watched Tracy stack her T-shirts perfectly. "I can't believe Betsy is taking a whole week off from work. She never does that. Good for you guys," she added with a nod. "Anything special planned?"

"Not really. Just the wedding on Saturday." Tracy stood up and walked around the bed to a basket of clean laundry, picking it up and placing it next to Meg as she combed through it. "Other than that, just hanging out. Going to the beach. Out to dinner. Stuff like that."

"Nice."

"You can totally stay with us for the weekend, you know," Tracy said, looking right at Meg. "Betsy said Mia and Becca will probably crash with us Saturday anyway." Reading Meg's flat expression she added, "I just meant it's not like you'd be in the way. It'll be a full house anyway."

Meg smiled. "Thanks, but I'm good where I am," she said in reference to the hotel reservation she'd made months ago when she'd expected to be attending the wedding with Sasha. At the time she'd figured on a romantic weekend, so she had purposely opted not to stay with Betsy. "You guys should have some time to yourselves. It's cool."

"We won't, though. Not on the weekend, that's my point."

"Nah. I'm fine," Meg said, dismissing Tracy's invite with a wave of her hand.

"You sure?" Tracy asked, picking up a few pairs of athletic socks balled on top of the laundry and tossing them underhand into her suitcase across the room.

"Yep," Meg said, not at all dismayed at the thought of having her own hotel room for the weekend in P-town.

Tracy grabbed the last pair of socks with one hand and put the basket on the floor in the corner. With a little flair, she took one step and turned around, launching the socks with a fadeaway jumper. She gave a quiet cheer for herself as her shot landed perfectly in the center of the open suitcase.

Meg laughed at her and shook her head a little. "Nice shot, dude."

Tracy answered with a smile as she grabbed her golf clubs and placed them next to her suitcase.

"Hey, did you hear anything about that job at the college?" Meg asked.

"Not officially."

"You got it, though?"

"I think so. I haven't seen anything in writing yet, but they basically offered it to me at the interview."

"That's awesome. No wonder you're so happy."

Tracy nodded. "I have a lot of good things happening right now," she said, kneeling down next to her suitcase and zipping it closed. "Honestly, though, the thing I am most psyched about is going away with Betsy." She leaned back on her heels. "Meg, do you realize I have not been on vacation with a girlfriend in years." She laced her fingers behind her head. "I mean the whole time I was with Jezebel, everything was a secret. It was all that cloak-and-dagger bullshit." Tracy shook off the memory and replaced it with a real smile. "It's ridiculous how pumped I am just to be able to go out to dinner with my girlfriend. To hold her hand if I feel like it." She rubbed the tops of her knees and shook her head at herself. "I'm like a fucking teenager. I so can't wait."

"I'm happy for you, Trace."

"I'm telling you, Meg, there is something to be said for this wacky idea of dating someone who's willing to be seen with you in public." Her voice was full of levity as she pretended to marvel at the theory. She smiled over her shoulder as she lined up her stuff by the door. "You should give it a try. I highly recommend it."

Meg smiled back at her. "Loud and clear, my friend," she said with playful spunk in her tone. "I'm one step ahead of you."

"Oh, yeah? Are we talking about Reina?"

"Mm-hmm." Meg reached for her phone. "We've been texting back and forth for the last week or so. Unfortunately with my parents in town and with Shannon and Matt's new baby, I haven't had, like, two seconds of free time." She didn't even try to hide her smile. "But next week, I'm taking the plunge. After I get back from the wedding, I'm going to actually call her. And ask her to go out with me. In public and everything."

Tracy clapped. "All right, Meg. That's my girl."

"I'm nervous, though," Meg admitted through her smile. "I mean, what if she's not into me like that? What if this is just friendship and I'm misreading the signs?"

Tracy looked at Meg. "Are you kidding me?" Tracy asked rhetorically. "That girl is into you. I saw that the second I got here." She leaned on the door frame and crossed her arms. "And, Meg, deep down you know it. So stop doubting yourself. You're a fucking catch."

Meg smiled as she slid off the bed. "Thanks, buddy," she said, turning Tracy around by the shoulders. "Come on, let's grab a pizza." Tracy was about to protest, but Meg stopped her. "You're on vacation, that means you can have carbs."

"It does?"

"It sure does."

CHAPTER TWENTY-NINE

Is that the last bag?" Betsy asked over her shoulder as she hung their formal clothes neatly in the closet to keep them from wrinkling before Lexi and Jesse's big day on Saturday.

"Mm-hmm," Tracy said, dropping it in the corner of Betsy's master bedroom as she came up behind her girlfriend and kissed her neck, wasting no time before one hand was under her shirt, the other inside her jeans as she inched them toward the bed.

"Easy, tiger, we have all week."

"Exactly." Tracy's voice was playful and sexy at the same time. "Let's start this vacation off properly."

Betsy felt her body relax into Tracy's and let out a slight laugh even as she did so, unable to disagree with her girlfriend's logic. She absolutely adored Tracy, she loved being with her, loved their connection. These days, when she stopped to think about it, it seemed crazy that for so long she had resisted something that was so natural, so perfect. No doubt about it, what she and Tracy had was beyond anything she had ever experienced before, their affection and respect for one another so deep and honest. Which was exactly why Betsy hadn't been overly concerned a few weeks back when she'd learned Jezebel Stone was the surprise performer at Bay West's music festival. Sure, she'd felt a singular, momentary shiver cut down her spine when she'd heard the news while she was stuck at the hospital delivering Meg's nephew. But it had passed just as quickly. The second she'd walked into Meg's house that very evening, Tracy had told her everything about Jezebel's concert and the details of their conversation, in an instant confirming for her what she already knew—Tracy Allen was one hundred percent completely in love with her.

❖

They woke up to a series of dings coming from one of their phones.

"Yours or mine?" Tracy whispered into Betsy's hair, still curled around her body.

"Yours," Betsy responded. "I can't believe we fell asleep. What time is it?"

Tracy reached to the floor and grabbed her jeans, pulling her phone out of the back pocket. "Five thirty." She leaned back against the pillow and read through her messages. Betsy placed her head on the spot between Tracy's chest and shoulder.

"What is it, baby?" Betsy asked, noticing Tracy's serious expression.

"My contract came through," Tracy said with a smile.

"Oh my God, that's awesome." Betsy reached up and kissed her cheek. "I want to see it. What is your title, exactly?"

"Assistant Athletic Director." Tracy's grin widened.

"Fancy."

"It's not too shabby."

Betsy met her eyes. "I still feel bad about the ESPN job, though."

"Don't." Tracy kissed her forehead. "This is going to be fun. I'm going to get to work directly with all the women's teams at the college. And you know what beats talking about sports?" She didn't wait for Betsy to answer. "Playing them."

"If you say so." Betsy ran her hand along Tracy's abdomen and kissed her lips. "When is Meg coming in?" Betsy changed the subject over her yawn.

"Tomorrow," Tracy answered quickly. "But she's adamant about staying in her hotel." She shook her head a little, still confused over her friend's decision not to stay with them.

"I get that," Betsy said.

"Get what?" Tracy was genuinely puzzled.

"Come on, we're there constantly. She's probably looking forward to some alone time." Betsy absentmindedly pushed the hair off Tracy's forehead as she continued. "God, it's probably going to be a little hard for her this weekend, though. She'd been so excited to come here with Sasha. She was telling me all about her plans in the spring, before they broke up."

"She'll be okay," Tracy responded confidently.

"I know. I just still can't believe they weren't able to work it out."

"Really?"

"I know what you're thinking," Betsy said, brushing her fingertips along Tracy's smooth skin. "Sasha screwed up. I don't disagree with you. It still makes me sad, though. They were both so obviously into each other. That was clear even in the few times I saw them together. And God, Sasha, with her mother and everything. I can't help feeling bad for her. Meg too," she added with a shrug. "I just wish they could have found a way to make it work."

Tracy tipped Betsy's chin up and kissed her lightly. "Meg seems to be bouncing back."

"Yeah?"

"Mm-hmm. She's been talking to Reina a lot lately. Looks like that may pan out after all."

"Still though, she was in love with Sasha. Big time. I can't imagine she's got her out of her system so quickly."

Tracy shrugged off the comment. "She's fine. Trust me." Tracy kissed Betsy again and pulled her in close so their bodies touched everywhere. "Speaking of Meg's exes, are the other two still planning on staying with us this weekend? Mia and Becca, I mean."

Betsy nodded. "They're not coming until Saturday morning though." Betsy kissed her. "And they're leaving early Sunday. Becca has a big work thing on Monday."

Tracy brushed her fingertips down the center of Betsy's back. "So much alone time. Whatever will we do?"

"Lots more of this," Betsy responded, dropping another kiss on her lips. "But for now, let's shower and get dressed. I want to take you to dinner to celebrate your new job."

"Yes, ma'am."

❖

At two thirty Friday afternoon, Meg strolled into P-town's legendary Tabitha's Tavern, looking to stretch her legs after her drive and relax into the wedding weekend with a refreshing beverage. At the bar she ordered her grandmother's favorite—an old-fashioned—and moseyed to the outside deck to kick up her feet on the shaded wooden benches and stare into the harbor. As she was scoping out just the right spot to park herself, she noticed Reina at a table by the railing, flipping though a magazine. Reina saw her at the same time, and met her eyes with a warm, inviting smile.

"Hey," Meg said, approaching as she glanced around to see if there was someone with Reina who might have stepped away for a second.

Reina read Meg's action. "It's just me." She closed her magazine and gestured to the empty chair across from her. "Sit down. Keep me company." She looked past Meg. "Unless…" She shot a look toward the bar and sounded a touch nervous as she continued, "I mean, are you here with someone?"

"Nope," Meg said, planting herself firmly in the chair. Meg took a sip of her drink, not really sure how to start the conversation. It had been almost two weeks since she had left Reina at the Pride Music Festival, and while they had texted a bunch, Reina never mentioned being invited to the wedding. Meg wondered if Reina's presence in P-town was simply a coincidence or if somehow the brides-to-be had forgotten to tell her something so major. Meg was confused, but if it showed, Reina didn't call her on it. Instead she steered the conversation in a completely different direction.

"How's your sister doing?" Reina asked as she touched Meg's forearm.

"She's good. Great, actually." Meg put her drink down and reached for her phone, pulling up a picture of her new nephew. "This is Declan." She swiped to the right, pausing briefly on a few more photos of the newborn. "And that's him with my niece, Deirdre," she said, every bit the proud aunt.

Reina leaned in close to examine the picture, and her silky black hair tickled Meg's arm. "Oh my God, Meg. They're so cute," she added, placing her hand on top of Meg's to tilt the phone for a better angle.

"Thanks."

They were quiet for a second and Reina looked into the harbor, taking a sip of her drink before letting her eyes rest on Meg. "How nice is it here, by the way?"

"It's beautiful," Meg responded checking out the boats along the water's edge. She took a sip of her own drink, hoping the right words would come to her. She had no such luck. "I, um, what are you…I mean, are you here for the wedding?"

"I am." Reina smiled, and her perfect white teeth gleamed in the sun.

"Awesome." Meg nodded. "I had no idea…I mean…I didn't know you were that close with Jesse." She shook her head. "I mean, I didn't know you were coming. You, uh, never mentioned it when we were texting." She picked up her drink, swallowed a long sip, and took a deep breath. She looked right at Reina. "I'm going to start that whole thing over," she said with a grin. Looking right into Reina's eyes she said, "Reina, I had no idea you were going to be here. But it's really, really good to see you."

Reina smiled. "It's good to see you too, Meg." She held the eye contact for a good few seconds. "And you're right. It is totally random that I'm here."

Meg answered with a furrow of her brow.

"I'm here with Teddy. Just yesterday she called me to see if I would come with her." At Meg's confusion, Reina explained further. "Rose's dad has dementia. She helps take care of him with her brother. I guess he took a turn for the worse last week, and at the last minute she was worried about being so far away." Reina pushed her long straight hair behind her shoulders. "Teddy messed up her knee a few years back, so she doesn't like doing the long drives." She shrugged. "She asked me if I would drive her and keep her company at the wedding."

"Nice."

Reina paused, taking a sip of her cosmo. "I figured, free trip to P-town. Lesbian wedding." She bit her lip and smiled. "Not saying no to that."

"Where's Teddy now?" Meg asked, looking around them again.

"Resting." Reina rolled her eyes. "Old people." She chuckled.

Meg laughed with her. "Where are you staying?"

Reina nodded to the left, indicating the East End of town. "The Old Towne Guest House. What about you?"

"I'm up at the Anchor Inn."

"Sweet." Reina nodded. "I took a walk up that way before."

Over their drinks, they fell into an easy rhythm talking about their families, their jobs, their lives. The energy Meg had picked up on a few weeks back was definitely still present between them, and suddenly, Meg wasn't eager to let Reina slip away again. Finishing up her second whiskey cocktail, she found her courage. Without any lead-in, she looked right at Reina. "Want to have dinner with me tonight?"

"Yes," Reina answered right away. But she blinked her eyes closed and added, "I have Teddy, though."

Meg shook the ice in her glass. "It's fine. We'll all go."

They made a plan to meet up at seven thirty and while Meg was showering up in her hotel room she heard from Betsy and Tracy, who were hoping for dinner plans. She invited them along immediately.

The dinner crew was loud and boisterous and lively. Everyone was in a great mood as they ordered drinks and told stories in anticipation of tomorrow's nuptials. It wasn't quite the date Meg had hoped for with Reina, but it was nice in its own right. Reina sat next to her and they read off the same menu, their hands touching surreptitiously under the table. When the evening ended, they all made a firm plan to meet the next afternoon twenty minutes prior to the scheduled departure time of the shuttle bus Jesse and Lexi had graciously provided to make the half-hour journey to Jesse's family's estate where both the wedding and reception would take place.

Leaving the restaurant, Meg was a little bummed out as she said good-bye to Reina and Teddy. All night she had hoped to sneak a minute alone with Reina, but with so many people around it didn't happen. She leaned forward and kissed Reina on the cheek, whispering, "See you tomorrow," as she squeezed her hand before turning to hoof it back to her hotel.

In her room, Meg brushed her teeth and washed her face, trying to convince herself the way things had played out with Reina was fine. They would have all day tomorrow—at a lesbian wedding, no less— and certainly she would find a moment somewhere. She looked at herself in the mirror, the warm water dripping off her face, and it hit her. She didn't want to wait until tomorrow. She didn't want to wait one more minute. Reaching for a hand towel, she dried her face hurriedly and threw her shoes back on. She grabbed her keys and her phone and bounded down the stairs, through the lobby, and onto Commercial Street, walking quickly in the direction of Reina's hotel.

Midway through town, Meg was trying to figure out exactly how she was going to pull this off. She didn't know Reina's room number and she assumed she was sharing with Teddy anyway, so Meg was going to have to text her when she got close. Now, if she could just come up with something cute but not cheesy, that would be perfect. Chewing the inside of her cheek as she thought hard about it, she heard her name from a few feet away. She looked up and saw Reina walking toward her.

They stopped, facing each other on the dimly lit street.

"Reina, what are you—"

"I was coming to find you."

"That is so funny. I was on my way to see y—" She didn't even get the word out before Reina stepped forward and cut her off with a kiss. Meg kissed her back, thoroughly and completely, putting one hand on Reina's hip and the other on the back of her neck as she brought them closer. They stayed together, kissing in the shadow of the streetlight, until a series of wolf whistles clearly intended for them made them both laugh.

Reina wrapped both arms around Meg's neck. "I'm sorry, but I wasn't waiting one more second for that."

"Me either, apparently," Meg responded. She took Reina's hand and they strolled slowly through the town talking quietly about the last two weeks, the last two months, the last two years of their separate journeys that finally brought them together here. Behind Reina's charming inn, they sat cuddled together in a lounge chair on the private beach, kissing under the stars as the surf crashed against the shore.

It was very late when they finally agreed to call it a night. They walked around to the entrance of Reina's hotel and Meg kissed Reina sweetly outside the front door. "I'll come by tomorrow. We can walk to the shuttle together. Okay?"

"Okay," Reina said with an enormous smile. "Good night, Meg."

"'Night, Reina."

❖

"I'm all ears, anytime you're ready," Tracy said to Meg, handing her a cold beer as they stood on the edge of the makeshift dance floor. "I want to know everything. When, how, who made the first move. And remember who you are talking to. I will need precise details."

Meg checked a look over her shoulder at Reina talking with Teddy across the outdoor setup. "I will tell you everything. I promise. At home," Meg responded, sipping her beer as she stuffed her hand into the pocket of her pants.

Tracy nodded. "Fair enough. Admit it though," she added with a grin, "I was right all along."

Meg couldn't help but smile. "Turns out I should never have doubted you."

Their conversation was interrupted as Lexi, stunning in a strapless white gown, sauntered toward them. "What's up, studs?" she said, throwing an arm around each of them.

"Well, if it isn't Mrs. Ducane," Meg said playfully.

Tracy swallowed a sip of her drink. "Is that your name now?"

Lexi nodded and smiled a little. "Technically, yes."

"Alexis Ducane, Alexis Ducane," Meg repeated, trying it out. "I like it."

Using her beer bottle, Tracy pointed at Meg. "Hey, Lex, did you hear about Meg and Reina?" she asked in a low voice.

Lexi looked right at Meg and raised an eyebrow. "I didn't hear, no. But"—her voice dropped dramatically—"I do have eyes. So I am picking up on what's happening." She squeezed her friend's shoulder. "I'm really happy for you, Meg."

"Thanks, Lex."

The three of them made a mini-toast to each other before Lexi said, "Guys, can you believe I'm married?" She blushed a little at her unexpected utterance. "I mean, only a year ago, everything was totally different. Tracy, you didn't even live here." She shook her head and watched Jesse crossing the floor toward them. "I mean, here comes my *wife*. Crazy, right?"

Betsy and Reina joined the group at almost the exact same time, and the six of them paired off slightly as they stood in a semicircle.

As they chatted, Teddy hobbled over to the three couples with her phone out. "Ladies, let me get a picture. This is a really great shot," she said, taking several before joining the group and firing off the best one to Meg. They all quieted down so Lexi could once again tell the story of how Jesse had proposed to her, pointing out the exact location at the property's edge. Meg was listening but she heard her phone sound a second time, and when she looked at it, a new picture came through. This one was a close-up of her and Reina that Teddy must have snapped before they all posed. Neither she nor Reina was looking at the camera. Instead they were looking right at each other, smiling. Talk about capturing a moment.

Meg examined the photo as she listened to Lexi tell the engagement story Meg knew by heart. She thought about Lexi's words minutes ago, recounting how much had transpired in the last twelve months. Come to think of it, it was just about this time last year when she'd met Sasha Michaels for the first time. She swallowed a weird laugh, still finding it hard to believe she'd been so unbelievably wrong—both about the girl she had fought so hard for and the one she had kept at arm's length for such a long time. It was ironic, she supposed.

She looked over at Reina, who was smiling as she listened to Lexi's story wrapping up. As if feeling Meg's eyes on her, Reina found Meg's hand and laced their fingers together, giving a soft squeeze, which was all Meg needed for everything to click. Standing among her closest friends with the sun setting behind them, she pressed Reina's hand with her own and they exchanged the briefest eye contact. It was a small moment, but it was sweet and honest, and it was just enough for Meg to be absolutely certain this was just the beginning.

About the Author

Maggie Cummings lives in Staten Island with her wife and their two children. She has degrees in English, theater, and criminal justice. She works in law enforcement in the NYC metropolitan area. *Serious Potential* is her second novel in the Bay West Social series.

Books Available From Bold Strokes Books

Camp Rewind by Meghan O'Brien. A summer camp for grown-ups becomes the site of an unlikely romance between a shy, introverted divorcee and one of the Internet's most infamous cultural critics—who attends undercover. (978-1-62639-793-4)

Cross Purposes by Gina L. Dartt. In pursuit of a lost Acadian treasure, three women must work out not only the clues, but also the complicated tangle of emotion and attraction developing between them. (978-1-62639-713-2)

Imperfect Truth by C.A. Popovich. Can an imperfect truth stand in the way of love? (978-1-62639-787-3)

Life in Death by M. Ullrich. Sometimes the devastating end is your only chance for a new beginning. (978-1-62639-773-6)

Love on Liberty by MJ Williamz. Hearts collide when politics clash. (978-1-62639-639-5)

Serious Potential by Maggie Cummings. Pro golfer Tracy Allen plans to forget her ex during a visit to Bay West, a lesbian condo community in NYC, but when she meets Dr. Jennifer Betsy, she gets more than she bargained for. (978-1-62639-633-3)

Taste by Kris Bryant. Accomplished chef Taryn has walked away from her promising career in the city's top restaurant to devote her life to her six-year-old daughter and is content until Ki Blake comes along. (978-1-62639-718-7)

The Second Wave by Jean Copeland. Can star-crossed lovers have a second chance after decades apart, or does the love of a lifetime only happen once? (978-1-62639-830-6)

Valley of Fire by Missouri Vaun. Taken captive in a desert outpost after their small aircraft is hijacked, Ava and her captivating passenger discover things about each other and themselves that will change them both forever. (978-1-62639-496-4)

Basic Training of the Heart by Jaycie Morrison. In 1944, socialite Elizabeth Carlton joins the Women's Army Corps to escape family expectations and love's disappointments. Can Sergeant Gale Rains get her through Basic Training with their hearts intact? (978-1-62639-818-4)

Believing in Blue by Maggie Morton. Growing up gay in a small town has been hard, but it can't compare to the next challenge Wren—with her new, sky-blue wings—faces: saving two entire worlds. (978-1-62639-691-3)

Coils by Barbara Ann Wright. A modern young woman follows her aunt into the Greek Underworld and makes a pact with Medusa to win her freedom by killing a hero of legend. (978-1-62639-598-5)

Courting the Countess by Jenny Frame. When relationship-phobic Lady Henrietta Knight starts to care about housekeeper Annie Brannigan and her daughter, can she overcome her fears and promise Annie the forever that she demands? (978-1-62639-785-9)

Dapper by Jenny Frame. Amelia Honey meets the mysterious Byron De Brek and is faced with her darkest fantasies, but will her strict moral upbringing stop her from exploring what she truly wants? (978-1-62639-898-6)

Delayed Gratification: The Honeymoon by Meghan O'Brien. A dream European honeymoon turns into a winter storm nightmare involving a delayed flight, a ditched rental car, and eventually, a surprisingly happy ending. (978-1-62639-766-8)

For Money or Love by Heather Blackmore. Jessica Spaulding must choose between ignoring the truth to keep everything she has, and doing the right thing only to lose it all—including the woman she loves. (978-1-62639-756-9)

Hooked by Jaime Maddox. With the help of sexy Detective Mac Calabrese, Dr. Jessica Benson is working hard to overcome her past, but they may not be enough to stop a murderer. (978-1-62639-689-0)

Lands End by Jackie D. Public relations superstar Amy Kline is dealing with a media nightmare, and the last thing she expects is for restaurateur Lena Michaels to change everything, but she will. (978-1-62639-739-2)